I0642793

Coaching Rayna #2

Bound Hearts

PEBBLES LACASSE

Coaching Rayna #2 – Bound Hearts
Copyright © May 2019 by Pebbles Lacasse

This book is to be sold to ADULT AUDIENCES ONLY. It contains explicit sexually scenes and graphic language which may be offensive by some readers.

All rights reserved. No part of this book may be reproduced or transmitted in any form or by any electronic or mechanical means, including photocopying, recording, or by any information storage and retrieval system, without permission in writing from the publisher, except by reviewers, who may quite brief passages in a review. Illegal copying and distribution of this book is punishable by up to 5 years in prison and a fine of $250,000.

This is a work of fiction. Names, places, characters and events, are the product of the author's imagination. Any resemblance to any persons, living or dead is entirely coincidental. All sexually active characters in this work are 18 years of age or older.

ISBN 978-0-9920069-8-3 print
ISBN 978-0-9920069-7-6 ebook

Cover photos and design © 2019 Pebbles Lacasse
First Edition June 28, 2019
Photographs by Sharon Seguin
Cover Model Chris LaPointe
Edited by Lisa Vincent & Nikki Brackett

Published by Pebbles Lacasse
www.pebbleslacasse.com

ACKNOWLEDGEMENTS

Special thanks to my cover model, Chris LaPointe, my photographer, Sharon Seguin, and all of my beta readers—there are too many to list, but you know who you are and how special you are to me.

I owe an extra big thank you to a special lady, my editor, Lisa Vincent. You are such an amazing woman, and I adore you. The smiles, comforting hugs and kind words you always have for me, mean more than you could ever know. I hold you in my heart, my dear friend.

CHAPTER ONE
Coach

I've been living with Rayna and her two awesome kids for eight months now and I couldn't be happier. I love what we've become; a loving family.

Ken and I are more friends than stepfather and stepson. I still call him my *little man,* but he's growing and will soon catch up to me in height. He's thirteen and has a lot of questions about sex that he's too embarrassed to ask his mom. I do my best to steer the kid in the right direction but it's not easy sometimes.

Kim, Rayna's daughter, is eleven years old. She likes to sit next to me while we're watching television so she can feel the muscles on my arm. She's a sweet girl and the spitting image of her mom. I love that little darling. I don't know how I'll be when she starts dating; an overprotective, threatening, chaperoning stepfather. Yeah, very likely. Nobody is going to hurt her!

I'm in to rough sex; BDSM to be more specific. My whole life before Rayna, the love of my life, I was a wild, vicious, sexual demon. Well, my demon still exists, I just keep him better contained these days. Little by little, she's setting him free, but I have to keep him leashed. I don't want to hurt Rayna.

I've always respected women when we aren't in the bedroom, unless they agree to be my submissive whenever they are with me. I'll admit I was an asshole to all of them. I treated them like shit; degraded them, chained them, fucked them hard and spit in their faces. Strangely, they must have enjoyed my abuse because those women kept coming back for more torture.

It satisfied the viciousness I carry within me, but my heart was frozen, locked inside an impenetrable vault. I kept everyone away from my heart. My friends were just that, friends. I do love them, but my lovers never felt even the slightest of heartfelt emotion from me. If they said they loved me, I forbid them to visit me again. Like I said, I was an asshole.

Until Rayna, that is. She woke up my heart with her eyes. Somehow, that woman looked at me when I was inside of her and it warmed my soul. From then on, she has been mine and I, hers. I will always love this woman.

Rayna was kidnapped, beat up and nearly raped, but I found her before he could hurt her in the worst way. I wanted to kill him. He used to be my friend, someone I used to share my submissive women with. Don't judge. Those women wanted to be with us. Taking two men at the same time can be an ultimate fantasy for some women. They thoroughly enjoyed it, trust me.

That guy, Brett, has always been a scary man. He is a true sadist. If a woman screamed in pain, something in him snapped. He's nearly choked a woman to unconsciousness. He liked to leave them battered and bruised. The women he hurt came back to him again and again, I don't know why. When he was with me, he would never injure a woman, he knew I'd beat the fuck out of him if he did. Sexual play, BDSM, was great but no dangerous play was allowed only visible bruises could be left on parts of their bodies that can easily be hidden from society.

It's been eight months since Rayna was kidnapped and she's doing well. She was quite skittish for a few months but she's a strong woman. She's overcome most of her anxieties and seems to be back to her old self, so to speak.

Rayna is coming out of the bathroom wearing a silky blue chemise that clings to her breasts as she walks. I'm hoping it will soon be on the floor. I never attack her. She lets me know when she's ready and how she wants me. Whether she wants it rough or gentle, she always gets her way and I never leave her unsatisfied.

"Master, would you like to use my body for your own pleasure?" she whispers in her sweet voice as she stands at the edge of the bed.

"I do. How hard would you like me to be?" I whisper back. I'm already getting off the bed and making my way toward her so I can make her my sexual plaything. I just need to know how far she wants to take it tonight.

"You can have my mouth and my pussy but not my ass. Breath control is okay and so is spanking, hair pulling, pinching and very hard fucking."

I walk up behind her and place my hands on her shoulders. She shudders as the heat of my palms radiates through her air-chilled skin. I hear her breath catch. Affecting her this way makes my dick swell.

"Take off your nightie," I whisper with my hot breath caressing her neck. Tiny bumps lift all over her body as if I've electrocuted her. She pulls her chemise slowly, teasingly up, exposing her ass, lower back and finally her shoulders. My dick stiffens even more when her hair falls to her shoulders and the nightie floats to the floor.

My fingers weave into her hair, grasping a wad and pulling her head around so I can kiss her mouth, hard. My tongue invades her while she opens wide. Her tongue, not knowing where to be, rests at the bottom of her mouth, occasionally waving when mine slides along its bumpy exterior.

My groan has her reaching up to cradle my cheek, which she knows she's not allowed to do, not during rough play. There are to be no tender moments after she requests me to Master her. Those loving moments are for making love, which we are not doing.

I take her wrist and pull it behind her back, along with the other. There's always a two-metre rope in the nightstand. I pull open the drawer.

"Get the rope for me," I whisper in her ear.

She doesn't hesitate, leaning in with her face to clutch the rope in her jaws. She stands up, holding the rope tightly in her teeth with her head turned toward me, offering it to me. She's a good girl for not questioning my instructions.

After binding her hands behind her back, I turn her around to face me. "Get on your knees, slut."

She drops, her eyes still locked on mine, awaiting another instruction. I watch her lick her lips, waiting for me to drop my boxers, but she can wait until I'm ready.

On the dresser are a bunch of elastics she uses to tie her hair up. I take one and begin gently gathering her locks until I have a lovely ponytail high at the back of her head.

I drop my boxers and smile as my cock springs forth, solid and thick. Her eyes gaze at my prick. Her focus is to be on my face whenever possible, unless I tell her to look away. That is a rule I don't like her breaking. I don't touch my cock. I wait for her to look up at me, to acknowledge that she faltered.

"I'm sorry, Master," she says after her head tilts back and her eyes meet mine.

"Make it up to me, take my cock down your throat."

She licks her lips again, and with her eyes on mine, my cock slides into her mouth and down her throat with ease. I can't help but moan. It feels so fucking good; hot, wet, snug and deep.

I grasp her ponytail and hold her face against my belly with my prick still buried in her throat. I'm thankful that she's not a gagger. Instead, her body shifts, and her hands start to fidget with the end of rope within their reach, possibly giving her a sense of freedom, should she need it. I pull her head back quickly when I'm sure she's on the edge of panic.

Rayna takes a few quick breaths as her weeping eyes lock onto mine. "Thank you, Sir."

I tilt her head back down and aim my cock, guiding her by her ponytail, making sure she sucks me right.

"I'm going to fuck your throat again. Are you ready? I won't be kind," I warn her.

"I'm ready, Master," she whispers with a quivering voice. I can hear the concern behind her words.

She doesn't care for this, but I would never hurt her, and she knows that. I have asked her many times if she'd rather I don't do this to her, but she always tells me to do it because feeling like she's just an object for me to play with excites her. She enjoys not having any control, but she knows it will stop the second she wants it to.

"Open that beautiful fucking mouth of yours and don't move."

She opens wide. Her focus is on my lascivious grin. I press my hips forward, pushing half of my cock into her mouth and then pull back. She knows I'm getting ready to hump against her face, forcing her to swallow every inch of me.

I fuck her mouth gently for a full minute before gliding all the way in, pulling back until the tip of my cock rests on her lips, and repeating, over and over until she's out of breath and tears are streaming down her face. Since she can't say a safeword, if she wants me to stop while in this position, she's to lift and drop her lower leg on the floor quickly and repeatedly. I will immediately cease.

I grab her under the armpits and lift her to her feet. With the palms of my hands, I smear her tears all over her face and kiss her lips roughly. I suck her bottom lip into my mouth and bite and hold it until she whimpers. This is not a romantic moment.

I look down her body, "You are a beautiful woman."

"Stop it. I'm not," she replies, knowing that pisses me off when she denies her worth.

I pick her up and toss her onto the bed. She squeals as she bounces. I'm on her, straddling her knees, holding her legs together. She lifts her arms over her head, clasping them together, because she knows it's what I require her to do. I slap her right tit and watch the ripple flow. She doesn't yelp. Perhaps that didn't sting enough.

My palm slaps across her breast once again, and then the other hand matches the motion exactly on her opposite breast. They are bouncing, jiggling like gelatine each time my hand cracks down. Now she's whimpering. This pleases me. I stop when they are a lovely shade of pink and her nipples have stiffened up to being slightly larger than pencil erasers.

My mouth envelops her right nipple, sucking hard. I nip now and then just to hear her yip. Her other nipple is just as hard and entertaining to bite.

I slide my finger between her closed thighs, along her womanhood. She's so wet. With my finger drenched in her pussy juice, I lift my hand and shove two of my fingers in her mouth.

"Taste your dirty little pussy. Do you like it?"

"Yes, Sir," she replies even though my fingers are deep in her mouth.

I slide two saliva coated digits between her outer labia and pinch her clitoris between them. I pinch hard, watching her face tense and hear her breath hesitate. I ease off slightly now rubbing either side of it, alternating; one rubs up while the other glides down. I know she enjoys this. Her face says it all. Goddamn, she's fucking sexy!

Now that she's well lubricated, I push further between the clutches of her thighs, slipping those two fingers inside her, just the tips to tease her. Her pelvis tilts upward, giving me a bit more leeway to penetrate her deeper, but I won't, not yet.

As soon as she lets out the slightest moan, I rise up off of her legs just enough to lift and flip her body face down. Her ass is round and firm, not the ass of a thirty-eight-year old woman who's had two children. Most women my age, twenty-eight, don't have asses this perfect.

My finger traces her spine, leading down the crack of her ass. She lifts her pelvis as high as she can manage, which isn't much since I'm straddling her thighs. It's nice of her to offer herself to me. As a reward for her generosity, my palm cracks down on her butt cheek. She drops her hips back to the bed, burying her face in the comforter to muffle a cry. That doesn't stop me from doing it again.

Rayna's yelping into the comforter and trying to cover her ass with her hands, but it's no use. I just lift them using the rope binding her wrists. My hand cracks down three more times on her right cheek. I switch the rope to my right hand and punish her left cheek equally.

I slip two fingers between her ass cheeks and down to her wetness. They slip inside her easily. She's slick with arousal. I bet she tastes great. I sample her flavour, sucking my fingers loud enough for her to hear. She loves it when I do this. After releasing her wrists, I reach beneath her bound arms to grasp her ponytail, lifting her arms while pulling back her head.

"What are you?" I ask her.

"I'm your slut," she replies.

"You're my fucking little whore," I correct her.

"I'm your fucking little whore," she replies.

I slip my fingers back inside her cunt and start waving my strong fingers quickly and powerfully toward her tummy. I pull back on her head, lifting her arms higher in the process. I know it's an uncomfortable position, but she isn't complaining, other than a few grunts.

Her moans are getting louder and starting to fill the room. Our bedroom isn't all that far away from the kids' bedrooms and we fear they might one day hear us playing rough. Rayna always makes sure they are fast asleep before initiating sex. I'd rather be safe than sorry, so I had better muffle her mouth.

I release her hair. I free my hand from between her legs and feed it down between her rope bound wrists, and pull them back with my arm, arching her spine in the process. It pleases me that she is so flexible. I stretch her until I can slip my fingers back into her pussy. This time, I slip my thumb over her clitoris and rub as I wave my fingers. I cover her mouth with my free hand to muffle her erotic sounds and lift her head just slightly, taking some of the strain off her arms.

She's going to cum, I can feel her pussy tightening around my fingers. Should I let her? Hmm, yes, I will. Now all I can hear is her low grunts and the sloshing sounds of my fingers in her sloppy cunt.

Her muscles flex, desperate for her body to straighten. My forearm is holding her bound wrists, but she's still pulling. Her hands are gripped into tight fists and her ass is rock hard. Her whole body holds stiff as the orgasm shreds through her. This is the moment I love the most; when I know she's at the height of the climactic euphoria I allowed her to experience. At this very second, I own her body, her mind, her pleasure. She's mine. At my mercy. I am her whole world.

Her body jerks several times, signifying that she's ridden through her orgasm and is not likely to scream. I free her mouth. She heaves out a long breath. Her groan, as I lower her to the bed and removing my hand from between her legs, is music to my ears.

I untie her hands and roll her onto her back, lying my body between her thighs. My prick is throbbing, aching to be inside her. I slip into her, one inch at a time until she has engulfed me completely. Our eyes meet, gentle smiles lift our lips just before I press mine to her. I wanted to make love to her tonight, as well as satisfy my dominant nature. The demon will stay locked away tonight.

CHAPTER TWO
Rayna

It's early, six-thirty and I'm awake. After only five and a half hours of sleep, I'm exhausted. It's going to be a rough day. Don't get me wrong, I'm not complaining, it's totally worth it!

Last night, Coach took me as he craves; dominant and rough. I would never say that I don't enjoy it. I might not like some things he does, like rhythmically deep-fucking my throat or covering my mouth so I won't scream. For some reason, I cum really hard when he does. Maybe it's the oxygen restriction. Maybe the fearful idea that he could prevent any and all of my future breaths, I don't know. I just know that I don't like it, but my body sure does. And yes, I want him to keep doing it. Besides, by covering my mouth, I can relax knowing that I can't scream which would surely wake the kids. They don't need to wake up from hearing their mother screaming in ecstasy.

I have pancakes puffing up in the pan with a cup of strong coffee in my hand. My eyes feel scratchy and heavy lidded, and I can't stop my excessive yawning.

A pair of warm hands glide around my waist and pull my back against a strong, even warmer body. Tender kisses are placed lovingly just below my ear.

"Good morning love," I say.

"Good morning," he says. "Pancakes? You're up early. Is that because I didn't tire you out enough last night?"

I chuckle, "No, I just woke up and couldn't fall back to sleep. Do you want eggs too or just pancakes?"

"I'd love a few eggs," he says while heading to the fridge with me still in his arms. He releases only one, keeping me pressed firmly against him as he leans in the fridge, collecting two eggs. "Do you want any?"

I'm laughing at how puppet-like I feel. "No, thank you."

He walks me back to the stove, puts the eggs down on the counter and returns to placing delicate kisses on my neck. Fuck! I wonder if he knows that he makes my pussy twitch when he does that? If I tell him, he'll do it more often, which would mean that he would have his lips to my neck almost constantly. The man is so loving, but then sometimes, he's so detached that it doesn't seem like he is even in his body anymore.

"Do you want help?"

"Can you set the table and then wake the kids?" I ask.

"Absolutely!" he releases me, leaving my body feeling chilled, missing the warmth from his absent flesh.

"Orange juice for Ken and me. Apple juice for Kim and you, my love," he says each item as he takes them from the fridge, placing them on the table. "Butter, syrup, strawberries, blueberries, kiwi…"

After he has everything arranged to his satisfaction - *he's such a perfectionist* – he sings his wake-up song loud and way off key.

"Wake-up, wake-up!

Start your day with a smile.

Your tummies are rumbling

So, don't be grumbling.

Get your butts out of bed!"

The kids hate hearing that song because it represents waking up for school. Personally, I find it to be quite entertaining. To see the man I know in the bedroom to be raging with testosterone and dominant as fuck, as a happy-go-lucky, child-friendly comedian, just doesn't match up. But I love his dual personalities and the way he relates so well to my kids. He's a big kid himself, when he's not alone in the bedroom with me.

Ken is last to drag his tired, sagging body to the table. Kim is already starting to eat a strawberry when I plop a pancake onto her dish.

"Thank you, Mom," she mutters while yawning. Her wavy hair has wadded into a big knot that is going to hurt to brush through.

Ken's eyes are half shut but his yawn is wide and lasts a long time. I plop the other pancake onto his plate. He just sits there, hunched over, staring at the puffy slab.

"Hey you! Wake up over there," Coach teases Ken, tossing a slice of kiwi at him. Ken glares at him with an evil leer but Coach smiles at him and chuckles. Ken eventually smirks and picks up the syrup, pouring until he has a mote around his pancake.

They chatter amongst the three of them while I finish cooking. I'm the last to sit, just as the kids are finishing up. So much for having a conversation with them. They wander away, but Coach remains, still picking at the fruit and looking at me with questioning eyes. He seems to be sizing me up for some reason. Does he want to fuck before work? Sometimes, when the kids are in their rooms with their doors closed and getting dressed, we can close our bedroom door and go into the bathroom, close that door and have a quickie without them knowing. I'm up for that today!

"What?" I ask him after a full minute of him ogling me.

He smiles, "I'm going to take you somewhere tomorrow night. Don't worry about a sitter, Renee and Tim agreed to take them for the night. What do you say? Will you go out on a date with me?"

The way he speaks sounds like a teenager asking a girl out for the first time, he even made his voice crack. He's being silly, of course.

"That would depend on where you want to take me," I reply, with a sweet voice, complimenting his teenage roleplay. I even flip my hair and bat my eyelashes.

"Okay, that's hot! Can you do that later?"

"I can do it in our bathroom right now if you're interested," I suggest.

He sucks in a deep breath through flared nostrils, growling as it escapes him. "Fuck! I wish I could, love. I can't do it. Tim is meeting me early so we can work out before the crowd comes. We need our man time to discuss some things. Besides, I'm not a machine you know!"

As he stands to kiss my forehead, I ask, "What things?"

He snickers, "Just things. You know, guy things."

"Why do I think you're up to something no good? Oh, I know, because you usually are."

He places the dishes in the sink and then turns to kiss my forehead again. I stand up and look up into his eyes to judge his expression. I can't read him, and he isn't going to tell me anything. I could keep prying, but the man is like a vault when it comes to secrets. I respect that but wish it wasn't so easy for him to keep things from me. I'm sure it isn't anything I need to be concerned over.

"Fine! Don't tell me. I might have something in mind for later but if I'm left in the dark, I might not go through with my plan. And, that would be a pity," I tease. My hand brushes the front of his pajama pants, rubbing his prick as it does.

He groans, shaking his head with his eyes locked on mine. "If I tell you, it won't be a surprise. Do you trust me?"

I put the juice jugs in the fridge and then turn and look him in the eyes while crossing my arms. "I trust you with every breath I take, literally sometimes. Yes, of course I do. You saved my life once and I'm sure you'd do it again if I ever needed you to."

"Love, I would burn in hell for you," he whispers while sliding his hot hands up my arms until they are wrapped around my shoulders, pulling me in for a hug.

"Honey, you were likely scheduled to go to hell long before you met me." I laugh.

"There might be some truth to that," he replies, and I'm not sure if he believes that to be true or if he's just joking.

"Let me do the dishes and then I'll meet you in the bathroom. Give me ten minutes."

He kisses my forehead. "Sorry, love, I can't this morning. Like I said, I have to meet Tim at the gym."

"Fine! It's okay to say you don't want to fuck me. I get it. You're sick of me already," I say, teasingly.

He just chuckles but quickly, the entertained expression falls, and his eyes harden. "You are a being a little bitch and I'm going to put you in your place later.

My spine tingles and my pussy twitches. How is it that when he looks so vicious, it always arouses me to the point that my mouth suddenly goes dry and my body shudders? Fuck, he's so goddamn sexy!

"Thank you, Master. I will do what I can to piss you off continuously throughout the day, if it pleases you?" It's my turn to make his sex twitch.

His fingers weave in my hair, pulling my head back while he looks down at my face. "Be careful little girl."

"And, what if I whispered, fuck you?" I'm really taunting his demon to break free. I know Coach will keep him caged, the kids are home. I can tease all I want because I know he won't throw me over his knee, not right now anyway. Besides, I know he would never actually injure me, no matter how much I provoke him.

"Careful," he whispers slowly and with a very deep voice that makes my chest vibrate.

He frees my now matted hair, kisses my lips tenderly and then walks down the hall toward our bedroom. I do notice the raging hard-on he's shielding in case he runs into one of the kids in the hallway. I just giggle, loving the effect I have on that man.

CHAPTER THREE
Coach

"Hey Tim! What's up Brother?" Tim grasps my hand, pulling me in for a two-pat-on-the-back man-hug.

"Not much, bro," he replies. "How's things with the fam-jam?"

He's always busting my balls about being an instant father to two young kids. Eventually he wants kids too, but it's his way of teasing me. He's happy for me, really he is, but fucking with your buddy is what guys do.

"Good," I reply. Together, we head to the locker room to dress for our workout.

"So, what's going on? You said you have something important you want to talk about?" he asks.

When I don't speak right away, he stops tying his shoes, realizing that I have something significant on my mind that requires his full attention. He shrugs, his way of telling me to spit it out.

"I'm taking her to Fallen tomorrow night. What do you think? Is it too soon?"

Fallen is a nightclub, of sorts. It's not just your everyday, run of the mill, nightclub. It looks a lot like a large house, but it's so much more. Not just anyone can attend. You must be invited by someone who has been regularly attending for more than a year and can't enter until you've had a thorough background check. The main door is always locked, with two very large men standing in front of it, holding the key, ready to rip you to shreds if you don't have the correct password, which is changed daily.

Tim introduced me to Fallen. He's also a dominant with sadistic tendencies. Renee, Tim's girlfriend and Rayna's sister, seems to love his dominant nature, but isn't so keen on playing the role of submissive, or receiving pain of any kind. Rayna is different. She endures suffering, using it to disappear into herself, thus heightening her orgasmic experiences.

Since Tim started dating Renee, he hasn't been to Fallen. I know he misses it, but he loves Renee. Hopefully he'll be able to return to what he loves, I just hope Rayna and I aren't there when that day comes. The last thing I want to see is Renee's smirking face when I'm playing with someone.

He nods, and I can see a bit of jealousy in his expression. "I hope she likes it there. Renee wouldn't. At least, I'm fairly sure she wouldn't. I don't know, maybe she would."

"Just don't bring her on a night when we're there." He shakes his head as if to say he won't take her anyway. "You can tell her that she wouldn't have to participate. Maybe you could just walk her around and show her what it's all about. It might sway her to give it a shot. Who knows, something might interest her."

"Yeah, I don't know. She's a fucking wild woman but she doesn't like dressing up in leathers or playing the whole dominant/submissive roles. She laughs all the way through it, which really irritates me to no end. We still have rough sex, but it doesn't go any further than that."

"Are you okay with that?" I ask, wondering if their relationship will continue for much longer if they aren't into the same sexual practices.

I'm no one to speak. Rayna was so vanilla when we first met. She wouldn't say the word *cunt*. Now, she's becoming a freak like me and I like it. So does she.

"I'm okay with it for now. I hold hope that she'll fall to her knees in front of me and beg me to punish her for being so fucking vanilla. I hope that day will come sooner than later."

"That day might not ever come. Renee can be a stubborn bitch when she is set on something. Will you stay with her if she refuses?" I ask, unsure if he's happy, or not.

"I love her, man. I really do. If that means I have to curb my sexual perversions, that's what I'll do. She isn't having sex with women anymore, trying to prove to me that she wants to be mine and only mine; her words, not mine. I don't want her to stop being with other chicks. I don't have a pussy and I know she craves it. I've told her to find a hot girl and have fun, but she won't. I suppose, if she's giving that up for me, not whipping her until she's welted simply for my own satisfaction, is the least I can do." He chuckles and shrugs.

He's right, I've also put my demon in a cage for the benefit of Rayna's limited past sexual experiences. The difference is that she's interested in taking things further, learning what it means to be my submissive. She also has masochistic tendencies, but nobody ever told her they were okay, so she hid them away. She thought she wasn't normal because she would become aroused at the thought of a man spanking or choking her during sex. The men she was with were never experimental, nor did they have an urge to bring her to incredible sexual heights. They never thought to show her the ropes, pardon the pun. Now she has me. I'm experienced enough to show her what she's been missing out on all this time. Little by little, I'm introducing her to new and exciting experiences.

Taking her to Fallen is a huge leap, but I want her to see the possibilities before her. If she witnesses other people enjoying the BDSM lifestyle, she might give herself permission to dive head first into these unknown pleasures. I want her to feel comfortable with what I would like her to do. I also want her to discover what kink turns her on. Rayna should be sexually, emotionally and mentally spoiled. I want to be the guy to do just that. I'll do anything to please her.

"You know you won't be happy if, for the rest of your life, you have to pretend to be something you're not. What if she never wants to play your way? Can you live with that?"

He shrugs, turning the question back on me. "What about you? If you take her to Fallen and she runs away screaming, what then? Would you leave her if she only ever wants vanilla sex for the rest of her life?"

"No way, man. She's my bitch and I'm her asshole. Her and I have been through too much to quit now. Will I miss it? Of course. So far, Rayna isn't afraid to let me be me... Well, she pretends she isn't afraid. I can tell she is, but she tries. I'll bury that side of me if I have to."

"You should reconsider taking her to Fallen. It might backfire on you," he warns.

I grumble, placing my gym bag in locker number one, my locker. I do own the place after all. Taking the locker of my choice is one of the benefits.

"Enough of this heartsy-fartsy shit! Are you ready for legs?" I ask with a wicked grin. He hates working his legs.

"Fuck! Let's get this shit-show over with!" He slams his locker with a sneer. "I'd rather do cardio and you know how much I hate cardio!"

CHAPTER FOUR
Rayna

I got off work early today. After zipping through the grocery store to pick up a few things for tonight's dinner, I fill the gas tank and then head home. I'm hosting a dinner with Renee and Tim at our house. It's always at our house. For once, it would be nice if we didn't have to do all the cooking and cleaning.

They are really hitting it off well. She claims the two of them are sexual dynamos so they're perfect for one another. She is always telling me how wild he is with her. I only tell her some things, leaving plenty out. She's on a need to know basis and she doesn't need to know.

She had sex with my ex-husband many years ago while I was still married to him, and I haven't forgotten. I forgave her, but I will never fully trust her again.

Renee made a pass at Coach before we were in an actual relationship, and she knew we had had sex. That's when I scrounged up the courage to ask her about her and my ex; it had been four years since I divorced him. There was always something in the back of my mind that had me wondering if they hooked up at some point. I always hoped I was reading too much into their chilled conversations. Deep down, I knew the truth long before I asked her.

She was drunk after a party at my house. I passed out. He took advantage of the situation. She didn't say no, in fact, she said she didn't protest at all. He was a cheating son-of-a-bitch all throughout our marriage but there's no excuse for fucking my sister.

Needless to say, I don't completely trust her and likely, never will. I love my sister. Don't ever think I don't. I would die for her in a heartbeat, but when it comes to men, she can't help herself. Coach turned her down flat and immediately told me about it. I think that's when I started believing he and I might be able to make a relationship work.

My ex-husband was a cheating, dirty, low-down asshole that still today, hasn't changed. The only difference is that he moved to the other side of the country with some whore of the week. It's unlikely he will ever call to talk to his kids or have anything to do with them. I hope he dies with many regrets about that. But I can't say I'm not happy to know he's gone. Sayonara, Jackass!

Coach has some crazies in his past. The playmate he was with when we started playing, was a real psycho. She served only five, of a six-month sentence she was handed, for attempting to maim Coach when she smashed his truck with her car. His leg was cut and bruised from his door shoving in on him, but otherwise he was unhurt. She had a broken nose from the airbag, a fractured wrist and bruised calves from the engine pushing in on her. They had to cut her out of the car. She got the worst of it, I'd say.

She was obsessed with him and wouldn't let him go. She's on probation now and forbidden to contact either one of us. So far, I haven't seen her around much. I'm happy about that. I don't trust that crazy bitch for a second.

He also had a friend who he used to tag-team with. That guy was something else! He kidnapped me and planned to rape me, but Coach found us, before he did. The guy was handed down a jail sentence and is still in custody, as far as I know. I try not to think about it because it makes me feel weak and vulnerable. I don't like that feeling.

It's strange how I enjoy it when Coach binds me with rope or handcuffs and takes me at his will. When he chokes me as I'm starting to cum, I fucking lose my mind. My orgasm crushes me! How I can enjoy these things with Coach after what his friend did to me, doesn't make any sense. You'd think I'd need to be the dominant one. I've come to realize that I, as his submissive, have more power than he does. Yes, he could hurt me if he so desired and I could do nothing to prevent it, but I trust him completely. If I say one word, it all stops, even if he is just about to orgasm. *That* is power.

The roast has been slow-cooking all day filling the house with a delicious aroma, making my mouth water the second I walked in the house. It only gets stronger as I near the kitchen carrying the bags of groceries.

The house is so quiet when nobody is home. I enjoy this time to myself, just listening to my thoughts about my relationship with Coach, the kids, my sister.

I toss two frozen apple pies into the oven to bake while I chop some potatoes, celery and carrots, tossing them into the slow-cooker, along with extra spices. After the pies are finished, I set them on the stove to cool, with a light towel covering them. I put the dishes in the dishwasher and make my way to the bathroom for a long, relaxing bath while the house is still peaceful and lonely.

Just as I'm getting in the tub, I hear someone walking through my bedroom. My heart thumps and a dizzying fear fills me. Who the fuck is in my house? The bathroom door slowly pushes open, furthering my agony.

Coach's face comes into view and I exhale an exasperated breath. "What the fuck? You scared me! I thought someone was in the house. Don't do that again!"

"I'm sorry, love. That was not my intention. The house smells awesome, by the way. I can't wait for dinner, but I could use a light snack to tie me over and you look delectable."

"I was just about to take a bath," I say as I step into the tub, much to his disappointment.

"You're really turning me down? I left work early because I can't wait until tonight to touch you. Are you going to make me beg?"

"I might." I smile as my body slowly lowers, disappearing beneath the bubbles, leaving just my head visible.

"Yeah, that's not going to happen. Get the fuck out of that tub," he says with a snicker.

I raise my arm, slowly dragging the sponge from my fingertips to my shoulder, along my collarbone and down between my breasts. I don't stop there, I continue to my pussy. My eyes never leave his.

His tongue is stroking his bottom lip before his face lifts, his Adam's apple bobbing, swallowing down his pride.

"Please, get out of the tub. I need you. I want to taste you. I want to make you cum on my face. I'm begging. Do you want me on my knees?"

I'm shocked that I have him under my control, and so easily. Maybe I should deny him more often.

"That might convince me that you're serious about needing to touch me," I tease, while squeezing my tits together. A puff of bubbles pushes between them, gradually gliding along. He's mesmerized, eyes admiring the bubble's journey.

He lowers himself to his knees and tilts his face toward the floor. My mind is whirling with so many questions. Why put his head down? Is that customary? One day I should ask him to explain the proper protocol.

I slowly rise from the tub and step out without drying my body. White puffs are slipping down my chest and legs, pooling at my feet. I walk over to him and take his hair in my hand.

"Come with me," I demand with a calm voice. I don't know who I've become at this very moment, but I think I like her. At any second, he will jump up, grab me and take me at his will. I'm good with that too.

He shuffles on his knees behind me, not standing, which surprised me. I lift my ass onto the counter, spreading my legs and leaning back, resting against the mirror. I wave my finger, ordering him to crawl to me. He does, without questioning. Before he can press his lips to my pussy, I stop him by pressing the palm of my hand to his forehead.

He looks up at my eyes just as I shake my head. His upper lip is twitching. His inner demon likely slapping his soul senseless for submitting his dominance to me. I can see the inner struggle through his eyes.

My fingers explore my pussy, opening my labia for him to admire but not touch. I circle my clitoris with the tip of my finger and make myself moan. He shifts, gritting his teeth and growling. How long can I make him wait? How long will he allow me to make him wait?

His eyes meet mine the instant I push my fingers inside myself. He looks angry, but I know it's only because he wants me and I'm not allowing it. Why he's permitting me to play this role in the first place, has me filled with questions, but this is not the time to ask them.

Has he been submissive at some point? I'm fairly sure he said he's always been dominant, but maybe he lied. I can't picture him as submissive to anyone, even me. What's happening right now has me on the verge of coming. Of course, my fingers have a big role in that.

I'm panting, moaning softly, while I watch his eyes study my hands, as they gently caress my clit. He's just biding his time, patiently waiting to ravish me. His cock must be raging hard, thick as ever and ready to fuck me violently. I can't wait.

My moans are riding each quick breath. I'm going to cum and he still only watches. This is so fucking hot! That's it, I'm coming. My body tenses, my fingers are barely able to continue their massage. My eyelids fall shut as my jaw falls open, no breath escaping my pleasure-filled mind and body. I'm floating in the nothingness that only orgasm can take me to.

It's ending and I'm disappointed. My body jerks. A heavy exhale bursts from my burning lungs along with a high-pitched whimper. My hands grab my breasts and squeeze. I open my eyes to see him still on his knees, his teeth clenched, nostrils flared and looking so fucking dangerous. Not touching me is torture for him, his shaking proves it.

"Fucking take me!" I demand with a quivering voice.

Coach leaps up onto his feet. He yanks my housecoat from the back of the bathroom door and pulls the belt from the loops. He rushes back to me, grabbing my ass to lift me and flip me on his shoulder. He carries me out of the bathroom and into the kitchen while tying one end of the housecoat to my right ankle, which I playfully kick to pretend I don't want to be his victim.

He sits me on the middle of the long island. "Turn and lie back." I do as he says, letting my ankles hang off the end of the counter while my body lies back against the cold countertop.

He pulls my right leg so it hangs at the knee off the side of the countertop. He loops the strap through the drawer's handle, under and around the end, through the handle of the opposite drawer and finally, pulling my free leg to match the other and wrapping it around my left ankle, binding it tightly.

I am left in a very vulnerable position with my legs spread wide and my calves hanging off the side edges of the counter. I lift my upper body so that I'm resting back on my elbows, looking down at myself. When I look up, he's standing at the end of the counter, examining my position with furrowed brows and pursed lips.

"You can still move. I don't like that. Stay there," he hisses and walks away.

"Like I have a choice?" I reply, snickering at my lack of freedom.

Coach returns carrying a blindfold, handcuffs, a dumbbell, and a bottle of something that might be a lubricant. It's not our usual brand, that I'm sure of. Our regular lube has a purple label, this one is yellow. I'm more curious about what he's planning to do with the weight as opposed to the switch in lubricant brands. He won't make me lift that, will he? It looks rather heavy, but he's toting it along like it's nothing.

"Lie back, put your hands over your head." I do as he instructs, anxious to continue what I started in the bathroom.

He sets the weight on the counter above my head and puts the handcuffs on my wrists one at a time. He slides one hand under the dumbbell and the other over, connecting the two together on the opposite side. If I want my hands free, I'll have to lift that heavy weight. I certainly won't be able to do that from this position.

Next, he puts the blindfold on me. Now all I can do is listen to what he's doing. Not being able to see his next move always leaves me a bit skittish, flinching with each of his random touches. I hear the fridge open and close and then hear a plastic bag rustling. What is he doing, having a snack?

I feel the chill from the lubricant, as he dribbles it over my clitoris, and it leaks down between my spread lips. It's cool but seems to heat up the longer it's on me. Oh no! Panic!

"Did you dump hot sauce on my pussy?" I shriek.

He chuckles, "Of course not."

"What the fuck?" I huff. "It's… it's hot!"

"No, it's warm. Calm down," he instructs in an overly calm voice. "What do you feel?"

"Oh… it's, it's tingling," I reply.

"Just enjoy the sensations."

Okay, wow! This is feeling magnificent all of a sudden – warm, tingling, arousing to no end. I think my clit is stiffening by the second.

Something extremely cold presses into me and I cry out. "What the fuck!"

I can't resist, nor escape its frigidity as it slips deeper and deeper into me. Whatever it is, it isn't large, but it isn't tiny either. Is it ever fucking cold! I'm panting and trying to pull my ankles free of the cuffs. My arms pull at the weight, trying to lift it off the counter.

"Hush!" he insists. "Enjoy the sensations."

"You said that already. Whatever you put inside me is ice cold," I complain.

His lips press to mine just as something pinches my left nipple. I gasp, trying to concentrate on his mouth and not anything else. His lips leave mine just as my right nipple receives the exact same pinch. Neither is letting up. It hurts but it's not game ending. He pulls them both simultaneously. The pain shoots down to my tingling clitoris and it's fucking breathtaking.

Whatever he slid inside of me is starting to warm up but it's taking a while to do so.

Something cool strokes and pulls at my clitoris and it's glorious. Wait, it's his fingers but why do they feel so cold? A clamp pinches onto my swelling button and pulls the hood up. It hurts but the urgent need for human contact has me whimpering and tilting my hips up toward the clamp, hoping to find a finger. Suddenly, my nipples are being pulled down toward my clit. He must have the three connected somehow.

Oh, fuck! I want him to lick my clitoris. I'm sure I'll cum almost immediately if he does.

Another cold hard object is slid into my pussy alongside the warmed one. What are they? Yet another is introduced, filling me as much as his cock does, but it isn't a cock, it's harder and colder.

My left outer labia is pinched once, and then again, and yet again. Neither pinch is letting up. Almost immediately, that punishment is subjected to my right outer labia. I'm afraid to move because the slightest flinch is painful. I have to give into it, let it have me.

Each clamp is tugged one by one, causing me to grunt when the pain of it shifting feels like it's digging into my skin, like a needle dragging on me.

Another hard, cold thing is pushed into me, spreading my pussy walls. A moan escapes me slowly as just one more icy object is slowly slid between the others, stretching my opening to its maximum.

Slim leather tassels gently slap my tummy, startling me from my trancelike state. He's going to do this now? Am I not hurting enough? The tassels come down on my thigh with a mediocre crack. The sting is pleasurable, not at all painful. I am starting to enjoy the flogger. When he first started using it on me, I didn't much prefer it, but wow, how that has changed.

He slaps at my thighs until I'm sure they're puffy and pink with small welts left in the wake from the leather tips. When his fingertips caress my hypersensitive skin, my clit twitches, alerting me to the pain the clamp is causing. A cry escapes me in a huff, which causes my breasts to jiggle and the clamps on my nipples to pull, tugging at my clitoris even more. I nearly cum.

He slides another cold thing into me, and I can't stop moaning, loving and hating everything he's doing to me. How defenseless I feel.

Sheer pain on my clit has my head jolting off the countertop, desperately pointing my blindfolded eyes at the source. From past experience, I know the cause is from removing the clamp, allowing the blood to freely flow. It won't last longer than a few seconds. A wail rips from my throat, shrieking the instant his scalding hot mouth presses onto my unbearably painful clit. He immediately sucks and rubs at the hypersensitive, swollen nub. I fucking love this, and hate this!

His mouth pulls and sucks me, driving me to scream through every breath. I can't stop screaming. It feels so fucking good and so fucking bad. My nipples are pulled by the clamps and I'm starting to lose my mind.

My pussy is filled with yet another cold object, stretched open further than I thought possible. I'm lost in the sensations in my body, not able to even moan anymore. All I can do is breathe and let myself fall into the absence of conscious thought; to let go of the earth's gravity and allow myself to float up to the stars.

I cannot feel pain anymore. Everything feels good. Each wiggle of my labia clamps shoots tender waves of pleasure directly at my clitoris He's playing my body like each key on a piano elicits a different sound with each stoke. My essence isn't here anymore. I don't know where I am, and I don't care if I ever return. I am lost. Lost within my body.

My pussy is stretched further, and I love it. Each piano key is pulling away, leaving a very sharp note in its wake. I'm drifting far, far away. I can feel my chest swelling with each breath and my back lifting off the countertop. I can't feel my skin, even though I feel like I'm on fire. It's a strange sensation that I welcome.

I hear someone moaning and I know it's me, but those are not sounds I have ever made. They are foreign and distant, as if from someone next door.

Slowly my mind is becoming clear and my soul is slipping back into my body. Light is easing into my right eye, alerting me to the brightness of earth. Soon it is very bright, too bright. My mask has slid off my one eye. I open that eye and recognize the ceiling light in my kitchen. Then I see Coach's shoulder bobbing up and down. He's fucking me, hard.

He's on top of me, his arms up along mine, his hands are firmly gripping my forearms near to my wrists. His body slams into mine, drilling his cock deep into me with a heavy thud. My vagina tenses as if it has a mind of its own, pulling me into another teeth clenching orgasm.

Coach growls so loud and deep beside my ear that I fear I may never hear right again. His body stiffens, jerking and flinching above me as his breath catches in his throat. His weight increases as if he's quickly deflating. Before it becomes unbearable, he lifts himself on to his elbows.

His heavily lidded eyes meet mine, but he doesn't smile. It's as if he's too tired, which is good because I doubt I could return the gesture, just yet. My body feels numb, tingly, full of life, but utterly exhausted.

Slowly, Coach slides down my spent body until he's standing on the floor. He does his best to quickly untie my ankles and unshackle my wrists. He lifts me, carrying me down the hallway, through the bedroom and into the bathroom. He sets me down on the edge of the tub and pulls the drain. Once the water has disappeared, he plugs the drain and turns on the faucet, filling the tub with hotter water.

He helps me slip in and then adds some lavender essential oil and some Epsom's salts. He kisses my lips and then sinks to his knees on the floor beside the tub, resting his head against his arm that lies on the edge.

"I love you, Rayna. I've never loved anyone as much as I love you. You have me, all of me, at your mercy. Please don't hurt me." I watch his expression turn to one of agony and see his eyes gloss over with wetness.

"Please don't hurt me. I can't take being hurt twice in my lifetime. But you, you could crush me worse than Rick ever could. I thought I'd never recover from him. I love you so very much."

He nods, sniffs and then clears his throat. "I want to take you somewhere tomorrow..." his voice fades away.

"I know, you already told me that. Renee and Tim are going to watch the kids," I remind him.

"Yes, but I didn't tell you where we are going. I want you to promise me that if it's too much for you, that you'll tell me, immediately. You won't crush me if you're too uncomfortable to stay. I just want you to promise that you'll give it a chance. I don't want you to judge too quickly. Can you promise me that?"

"Now you have me curious. I promise not to judge too harshly, too quickly. I'll stay as long as I can tolerate." I frown and add, "This would be a lot easier to promise if I knew what I was promising to."

He smiles and nods, raising his eyebrows. "Just tell me that you won't jump to a quick judgement. That's all I ask."

"Okay, I can promise that," I smile back while still squinting my eyes as if that will help me read his thoughts.

"All right then. You stay here and soak, you've earned it, and I will clean up the kitchen." He turns on his heels and starts out the door.

"Wait!" I shout. He pokes his head back in. "What were you putting inside of me? The cold things?"

He snickers and says, "Carrots," before retreating out the door.

"Throw them out!" I call out after him. I can feel the embarrassment flushing my cheeks to a hot pink. I wasn't freaked out at the time, in fact, I quite enjoyed the carrots. I'll never look at one the same way again.

CHAPTER FIVE
Rayna

Dinner is going really well. The meal is delicious, nothing burned or not cooked enough. Renee and Tim are laughing along with the kids as they talk about something silly that happened at school, this week. I've already heard the stories, but they seem to be slightly embellished on the repeat. That's okay, it adds to the humour.

My wrists and forearms are still a bit red from the cuffs and Coach's vicelike grip, so I decided to hide it with a long-sleeved blouse. I instinctively rub my wrist and then look up at Coach. His eyes meet mine then drop to my wrist. He frowns as he chews. He doesn't like it when he bruises me. His face suddenly lights up with a quirky grin.

"I almost forgot," he announces, standing up to retrieve something from the refrigerator. He returns to the table, setting a glass filled with chopped carrot sticks in front of Tim. "I almost forgot the carrots. Everyone likes carrots, right Rayna?"

He wouldn't! I stare at his face, trying to assess his expression to see if he is being a jerk and teasing me or if those carrots are the actual ones he fucked me with. I cannot read him.

"Go ahead, Tim. You'll like these carrots. I made them special, sort of marinated them." I watch Tim choose one and take a bite. My eyes couldn't get any wider. It takes everything I have to restrain myself and rip them off the table and toss them into the garbage, causing a scene.

Tim stops chewing and looks up at Coach, who is grinning like a fool. He says, "Hmm, yes, they do have a familiar flavour to them, but I just can't quite pin it down."

He hands it to Renee who rams the rest of his piece in her mouth and begins chewing. My arms feel like they're going numb. I can't even speak.

She says, "Yeah, what is that? It is familiar but…" She continues chewing, sampling the taste.

Tim adds, "Do you enjoy carrots, Rayna?" His face is very pointed. He knows what those carrots were used for. I have no doubt. "These carrots are coated in something delicious. Did you make the special coating yourself, Rayna?"

My words fail me. I want to scream at Coach but before I can, Renee very calmly says, "It's just a sweet glaze." She looks at me and says, "Corn syrup, maybe. It's nothing special. They aren't even that good."

I watch her shrug just as the guys crack up laughing. Renee and both kids are looking around the table, wondering what the hell is so fricking funny. I swallow hard, but I'm not laughing, just relieved.

Renee looks at me with a wide smile, oblivious to the joke. She asks, "Why are they laughing?" I simply shrug because I still can't form any words. I'm sure my face is red, proving my embarrassment. A look of horror swoons her expression. She adds, "Eww! Gross! Are you kidding me?"

Coach looks at her and says, "They're carrots I cut up from the bag, honestly!"

I take a deep breath and let it out slowly, glaring at him with eyes that just might melt that expression off his face. He shakes his head to assure me he was only joking. I look at the garbage and see a bunch of carrots tossed away. I simply shake my head.

Renee starts smiling and is soon joining in on the humour of the joke. The kids are looking from one person to the next asking us what's so funny. What am I supposed to tell them? It's not a joke I want to explain, and he will never tell them.

He says, "It's a joke from a long time ago. I dipped some carrots in dog food and fed it to Tim as a joke. Not these carrots though. I just thought I'd refresh the joke in his memory."

The kids are smiling to be polite and accepting the explanation, but not understanding why the others think dog food coated carrots are this hilarious. They shrug and go right back to eating.

Coach is going to pay for this later.

"So, you had a good afternoon, I gather?" Renee whispers.

I smile, feeling my face flush with heat once again. "Coach… he, he… um…"

"Yeah, I know what he *um*. I'm so happy that you're finally having a great sex life. It took a much younger, wilder man to get you to let your hair down. It's about damn time!"

"And, what about you?" I ask her while glancing at the kids to ensure they aren't trying to hone into our conversation.

"Things are great between us. He's a bit of a sexual freak, which is awesome. I wish he'd stop holding back though. There was this one time when he took it too far and I got scared. He was a bit rough with me. He was being very assertive and ordering me to do stuff, calling me a slut, or whatever. He even spanked me, over his knee like a naughty child! I couldn't stop laughing at him. I mean, I was a little high at the time, so it probably wasn't the best time to puff out his chest, if you know what I mean. I told him I didn't want to play rough and ever since that he's being very reserved, like he's afraid to get even the slightest bit wild. I mean, our life outside of the bedroom is absolutely incredible, but our sexual fire has been fizzling out. When we are intimate, he's so tender, but it's like he's acting and not really getting too into it. We used to get freaky, not anymore."

"Have you tried talking to him about it?"

"Yes, but he just tells me he loves me and doesn't want to push me into something I'm not ready for. He avoids that conversation, if he can."

"Maybe you should try again. Corner him. Take him out for dinner, somewhere he can't just get up and walk out without making a scene and casually lead the conversation in that direction."

She grins and whispers, "You just gave me an idea. I can't let him get away. I know exactly what to do and it isn't have dinner with him." I question her by frowning, and she just winks. She must have something naughty planned. "I'll tell you after I do it."

"So, where is Coach taking you tomorrow night?"

I shrug. "I have no idea. He won't tell me."

"Sounds questionable to me." Her eyes light up. "What if he's going to propose to you?"

My stomach drops out, and I suddenly feel very lightheaded and parched. I gulp a mouthful of wine while glancing over at Coach, who's listening to Tim. His eyes shift, catching my stare. We look at one another for several seconds. He smiles at me and then turns his attention back to Tim.

I look at Renee and reply, "No, that's definitely not it. I don't know what he's up to, but it isn't a romantic night out."

"Hmm, I'll dig a little deeper with Tim. I'm sure he must know something. Those two are like peas in a pod."

"I would appreciate a heads-up. He isn't telling me much," I admit.

"Does he usually?" she asks.

"Yes, always," I reply.

"So, to change the subject, how is work going?" she asks.

I roll my eyes, unsure of whether I should get into the topic or not. "I am supposed to go on my yearly convention with Dr. Jessik, but I don't know if I'm going to go this year. That's not true, I am going. I'm just not sure how I'm going to tell Coach about it. You know damn well he's not going to like it. So, I've been putting off the awkward conversation."

"It's been a year already? It feels like you just went." She takes a deep breath and lets it out slowly. "You are going to have to tell him soon. When do you leave?"

"Well, I'm supposed to leave in a week."

"So, when did you think you were going to tell him? You are running out of time, sweetheart!"

She's right, I am running out of time. I'm an adult, for Christ's sake! I need to tell him. This is my job, my career! I go every year, so it's not as if I can just tell my boss that I'm not going to go because I have a jealous, control-freak as a boyfriend.

This is my life, my livelihood. I have worked for years to get to this point in my career where my boss might actually consider sending me back to school to further my education. If he thinks I am no longer taking my job seriously because there is a man in my life, he certainly will not give me the opportunities I have worked so hard for. My dream is to become a dentist and own my own practice one day.

"I will tell him, Renée. I'm just worried he will not accept the fact that I am going to Las Vegas with my boss, even if it is a work convention. What if he insists on coming with me? What do I do then? Do I tell him that he cannot come? I don't think that would go over well with him. It's not as if he doesn't trust me, it's just that his trust has never been tested by me."

"You had better bring it up soon or he's going to think something is planned with you and your boss, if you know what I mean."

"Yes, I will. One day at a time. First, I need to find out where he's taking me tomorrow night and why he feels the need to be so secretive about it."

Renée nods her head, turning it to look at Coach. He and Tim are deep in a conversation, leaning in toward one another to speak in hushed tones.

I say, "Ken, if you're finished, please put your plate in the sink. You've got homework to finish, so please go get to it." He nods, picking up his plate and silverware.

"I'm finished to!" Kim says rather loudly. "Can I be excused?" I nod, much to her delight. She didn't eat much, rarely does. I usually make her eat more, but I'm not in the mood for that battle tonight.

Both kids scurry down the hallway and into their rooms, leaving us adults sitting at the table. The guys have stopped talking and are looking at us.

Coach asks, "So ladies, what's next?"

Renee replies, "Why don't we play a game of cards? That will keep us entertained. Maybe we could get into a game of truth or dare," she says, emphasizing the word truth. She looks at me raising and lowering her eyebrows several times.

Both Tim and Coach are frowning, questioning why Renee is acting so strangely. They look at each other and then at me, as if I'm going to confess.

"We can play a game of cards. What do you like to play, Tim?" I ask.

"I don't know," he replies. "I honestly don't remember any. I used to play Euchre when I was a teenager. I remember something about Trump, but not any of the rules."

Renee and I chuckle because we grew up playing cards with our parents. Every Friday night was game night with family and my parent's friends. Each week, a different house would host. It was fun, but once we became teenagers, we preferred to hang out with our friends. We pouted so much, they eventually begged us not to come. I regret it now. Some of those family members have passed away and the others are simply too old or too busy to continue the tradition. I think it died out with their generation. It's sad.

Coach confesses, "I haven't played a game of cards since I was about ten years old. I have never played Euchre and have no interest in learning it tonight. Why don't we retire to the backyard and have a fire?"

"Sounds great!" I reply. Coach and I cleared the table and stacked the dishes in the sink. After Renee and Tim head outside, Coach stops me from taking more things off the table.

"Hey, what's going on?" he asks

"What do you mean?" I play naïve.

"You were looking at me strangely and I'm just wondering why?"

"What's up?" I ask.

"Rayna, don't be like this. Tell me what's going on."

"Why don't we talk about it, later. Now is not the time, we have guests."

"They aren't guests. Tim is my best friend and Renee is your sister. They do not qualify as being guests. So, what's up?"

"Renée and I were just talking about sex. Her and I are having a bit of an issue and we were trying to work through it. When I looked up at you, you looked back at me. It was a coincidence, plain and simple." I smile, trying to be as convincing as possible. I don't want to discuss my work thing right now. "Why don't we head outside?"

Coach looks at me with squinted eyes, as if to assess whether or not I am being completely honest with him or if I'm holding something back. He leans in and kisses my lips with the utmost tenderness. I love him so much. I wonder why it took me so damn long to let him know how much I wanted him. He lived next door to me for three years while I dreamt about having his body. I could have been having him this whole time.

We spend the night chatting with Tim and Renée over the campfire, and we have a few drinks. We have a great time, likely better than we would have had we decided to play cards. I really like Tim and I think he is perfect for my sister. I just wish they could figure out what each other needs from their sex life and come to a compromise.

Renée has always been a wild child. She will be the first one to tell you that she is not strictly heterosexual. She enjoys penis as much as she does vagina. She loves the tenderness of the female personality, as much as she loves the masculinity of the male persona. With Tim, she cannot get much more masculine than him. He is tall, a bodybuilder and tough as nails, but he has tenderness and emotional softness that you wouldn't think a man with his rugged appearance would have. He looks mean all the time, even if he's smiling. He just has that face. Tim is a deep thinker with a tender heart. Renée can and does benefit greatly, by having this man in her life.

Coach and Tim have been best friends for many years. Coach set Renée up with Tim when I begged him to find her a man, as rough and dominant as he is. She was coming out of a relationship and finally realizing that she needed somebody who was going to be her life-mate, instead of just somebody she was spending time with and enjoying for the moment.

At the time, Coach and I were barely a couple. We had had sex once, but I didn't know that I wanted more than just sex from him. At the time, I also did not know that he wanted more than just physical relationship with me.

"Well, what do you think, Renée?" Tim asks after finishing the last gulp of whiskey from his glass. "I think it's time we take our leave."

"I agree," she says. "Rayna, I love you, woman! I am going to drive this big galoot home and tuck his ass into bed. I think he has had way too much to drink." She looks at Tim.

Tim stands up, wobbling slightly. "I am perfectly fine, thank you. There is nothing wrong with me, other than having a bit too much to drink. But, little woman," he points his finger at her, "you are still getting the fucking of a lifetime, when I get you naked."

I start laughing but she does not look all too impressed. "You know damn well your cock is not going to work, tonight. By the time I get you home and you take off your clothes, if you even make it to the bedroom, you will be passed out long before I get in beside you. Sex, my dear, is going to have to wait until tomorrow. I doubt you will feel much like having sex until at least tomorrow night. You are going to have one hell of a hangover in the morning."

Tim snickers, "Oh, yeah? You wait, little girl. When we get home, I am going to fuck you raw! I am going to hold your body hostage. I am going to pull your hair and spank your ass, until it is hot and you're screaming for me to stop. You are going to call me Master tonight. What do you think about that, Woman?"

The look on her face is disbelief. "So, now that you are drunk, you actually want to have crazy sex with me. How come when you're sober, you only want to make love to me?"

He looks at her and then at Coach. When his eyes return back to Renée, he smiles at her as if to announce that she is everything to him. "Lady, do you have any idea how much I love you?"

36

"Yes baby, I do. Can we talk about this in private, please?"

"I don't want to hurt you," he says. "You did not like it when I dominated you. I was afraid if I did it again, you would leave me."

"I am not going anywhere," she says, "I am so madly in love with you that I think I would die before I could ever walk away."

Tim launches for her, grabbing her around the waist and scooping her up in his arms, as he spins her around, kissing her lips, passionately. I look over at Coach and he is just watching them with a crooked smile. I wrap my arm around his and hold his hand, that's when he turns his attention to me while still carrying the same expression.

"I love him!"

"I know," I reply. "I love her."

"I know that too."

After Tim and Renée leave, Coach and I quickly clean the kitchen before looking in on the kids. They are both passed out, much to our happiness. It has been a long week and I want nothing more than to spend the rest of the evening with my man trying to figure out where he's planning on taking me tomorrow and why he is keeping it such a closely guarded secret.

CHAPTER SIX
Coach

I know Rayna is going to harass me for information on where I plan on taking her tomorrow night. The best thing I can do is to keep her otherwise occupied, so she won't be able to ask me anything. I really enjoy the build-up, the suspense and the anxiety she gets from not knowing something. She's told me she doesn't like it, but I'm sure she does, in some small way.

As she walks into the bedroom, I grab her by her shoulders and spin her around, pressing my lips to hers, while weaving my fingers into her hair, holding her face to mine. My tongue works its way between her hot lips. I want to taste her. I've wanted to taste her all night. Rayna responds by wrapping her arms around my back, holding herself against me.

I wrap my arms around her and pull her into me as tightly as I can, without hurting her. Half carrying and half walking her to the bed. I kneel on it, carrying her along with me, as I slide her to the middle of the bed. My lips never leave hers. My tongue explores the depths of her mouth and the lingering sweetness from the last gulp of wine she swallowed only moments ago.

My hands work her shirt, pulling it up and lifting her bra, allowing her breasts to fall from below it. Goddamn, their warmth and softness in the palms of my hands. I adore the contrast between the creaminess of her warm skin and the stiffness of her nipples. Fuck, this woman is beautiful!

I kiss down her neck in between her breasts, pushing them against my cheeks, burying my face between them. Tiny kisses are placed under her breasts, between them and on her nipples. Rayna weaves her fingers in my hair, holding my head, but not guiding me.

I pop the button on her jeans and slowly lower her zipper, kissing the tender hot skin beneath the denim as it's being exposed to the chill in the air. I pull her pants down over her hips and slide them off her legs, dropping them in a heap on the floor. She spreads her legs, urging me to bury my face between her thick thighs.

I hover my nose over her hotness, feeling the radiating heat on my skin and inhaling her seductive scent. My cock instantly stiffens. The tip of my tongue tenderly strokes between her folds, feeling they're smoothness and sampling her delicious tanginess.

Rayna's gentle moans add to my fire. I want to take her selfishly, but I don't deserve to, not yet. She is my queen and she has earned my restraint. I will not have my release until she is fully satiated.

I watch as her chest rises and falls quickly, anticipating the suction I am about to put upon her clitoris. I place my lips over her pussy and suck, dragging my tongue up and down her slit, hesitating just below her clitoris, not allowing her the pleasure. Rayna shifts her hips, desperate to redirect my attention. Not yet my love.

I wait until she's begging in faint whispers. "Please, please."

That is all I needed to hear. I shift my lips, closing them around her clitoris, sucking it between them and nibbling gently with my teeth. I let my tongue flick wildly, assaulting her stiffening pleasure nub. Rayna's hips lift to meet my mouth. Her legs squeeze my shoulders, trying to hold me to her, so I can't escape.

I slide two fingers inside her wanting pussy, resting my palm against my chin as my fingers wave, pounding against her G spot. She's so aroused, so wet! Her scent fills my nostrils, igniting a primal lust burning deep within me. Tonight however, I will not be rough. I will make love to Rayna. Tomorrow will present many new options for the rough play I yearn for.

She will see things that some would consider to be taboo, perhaps even vile. Maybe Rayna will see something that sparks her interest. She might not be ready just yet, but perhaps in the near future she will. If I continue to slowly introduce her to wilder and more intense pleasures, she will likely be more accepting of the play I seek. Tomorrow, I will enlighten her to the lifestyle that calms me and allows me to feel truly free.

Rayna is moaning, running her fingers through my hair and squeezing me with her legs. She's going to cum soon. I want her to erupt on my face, only then will I fuck her. I will be gentle and loving the way she seems to need me to be tonight. She always sets the mood to our romantic endeavors. How we play is up to her, not me, never me. If she wants to play rough, I am more than happy to oblige her and dominate her the way we both seek. We don't play hard, at least, not what I would consider to be hard.

Her body jerks and spasms, cries of passion hanging in the air, bringing sweet sounds to my ears. She exhales heavily, that's when I know she's finished. I don't even think she realizes how much I adore that. I slide up her body kissing her tender skin, loving how her chest rapidly rises and falls, lifting up, as if craving that touch. My lips find hers and adhere, lovingly kissing my Rayna.

I slide myself into her, burying my prick deep within her spasming pussy. She feels so good.

She cradles more than just my body. I have signed away my heart to her, much like selling my soul to her, in hopes she will not cast it aside. This woman owns me, completely. I will show her how much I love her with my body. If I could only stay in this woman, we would be together forever as one entity, existing for the sole purpose of keeping the other alive, for one without the other will cease to exist.

Her legs wrap around my ass, holding me deep inside her. Her arms stretch down my body and her hands pull at my lower back. Her eyes are closed, keeping her focus on the hurricane building within her, readying itself to explode, shredding her beneath me and ripping open her heart, so I can make love to that too. She taught me how to love, how to adore someone so much that you willingly give them every bit of you and trust them to keep you safe.

Even though her eyes are gazing into mine, she's not looking at me. She's looking at my soul, adoring my deepest core, and I welcome her in. This woman could crush me and take away my will to live, should she so choose.

My inner Demon is pacing while shaking his head, hating every moment of this. Deep down, where the Demon is imprisoned, I hold a shred of doubt. My mind will not allow her everything, not until she knows my truth. All of my truth.

Her lids weigh heavily over her eyes, slowly forcing them closed. Her head rolls to the side, her mouth opening wide, no words escape her. I watch her as long as I can, feeling the tight hold her entire body has on me. Goddamn I love this woman!

I can't do it anymore. I can't hold off. I'm exploding.

As my body twitches over her and my mind comes back into focus, I look down at her beautiful face, admiring her flushed cheeks and puffy lips. Her hair is strewn about the pillow. Fuck me! She's sexy as hell.

I roll to my side and she curls up behind me. We fall asleep, her body pressed against mine, her chest against my back, her arm resting around my chest. Her forehead remains pressed against the nape of my neck. I can feel her breath heating my spine and I can't imagine anything being more perfect than this moment.

She did not ask me about tomorrow, but I didn't give her the chance either. I'm sure she'll be testing my ability to keep my plans to myself, but I will stay strong and not give in to her adorable ways, no matter how much she begs.

CHAPTER SEVEN
Rayna

The kids spent most of the day watching television and playing on their computers. Coach went to the gym because he had some client sessions scheduled. I have spent most of the day doing laundry, sweeping floors, dusting and repeatedly grimacing, while staring into my closet. I don't know what to wear tonight. Do I wear something very sexy like my red dress with the slit riding high up my left thigh? Do I wear something conservative like my pencil skirt, white blouse and blazer? Should I wear a sundress, casual, but still presentable and respectable?

"Gah!" I'm getting frustrated because he won't tell me anything about where we are going. How do I dress for the unknown? Why all the mystery? Is he afraid that if he tells me, I might decide not to go? Does he think I don't trust his judgment? I know he would never take me to a place that would cause me harm or somewhere I would absolutely hate to be.

"Fuck! I really wish you would just tell me, so I can plan my damn outfit! I hate not knowing." He's not home, so yelling at him is pointless, but it makes me feel a tinge better, nonetheless.

I take my phone out of my back pocket and sit on the floor just inside the closet. The season is changing, so my summer clothes are mixed in with my fall and winter clothing. I really need to organize this.

I dial Coach's cell phone and listen to it ring, wondering what I'm going to say to him that I haven't already said. Begging didn't help, it only made his dick harden. It clicks, but it's his voicemail instructing me to leave a message. As soon as it beeps, I simply say, "Would you just tell me what I am supposed to wear tonight!"

I hang up the phone and shake my head, wondering if I should just take a few outfits out and spread them on the bed, telling him to choose which one is proper for the occasion.

My phone rings almost immediately. I bet that's him. More angrily than I intended it to sound, I drill him, "Hi, did you get my message? I have been sitting here all day trying to figure out what the fuck you want me to wear tonight. Why the hell won't you tell me where we're going? Is it someplace I'm not going to want to be? Is it that bad?"

"Love, I would like you to wear something sexy, but you don't have to. You may dress in simply a skirt and bra, if you so choose. Anything goes at this place. I'm taking you to a place you have never been and probably didn't even know existed. Where we're going, you will not be judged by your appearance."

He sounds winded as if he was working out and stopped when I called. Maybe he ran to his phone. I'm not sure why he would, he can always call me back. Is he waiting for somebody else to call him? Why would he? Maybe it has something to do with tonight.

"Why won't you just tell me where we're going? I'm having so much anxiety that my belly is starting to hurt. I don't want to have intestinal issues, if you know what I mean."

"Rayna, okay, I will tell you where you're going when I get home. I should be done here in about an hour and a half. Can you wait that long?"

"And what if I say that I can't? Are you going to come home just so you can tell me? If you do, I promise to be very good to you," I say with a very sexy voice.

"I can't come home right now, love, I have a client coming in twenty minutes. I can't skip out on her."

"What if I were to come to you? I know you have a client and I wouldn't dream of interrupting your session. I could just come and watch you. I do love watching you sweat and grunt through the heavy workouts."

He chuckles and replies, "I'm not the one who's going to be working out. You are always welcome, you know that. I love having you here with me. If I could put you in my pocket and take you everywhere, just to keep you safe and be able to touch you whenever I want, that would be a dream come true. However, that is only in the world of make-believe."

"Well, maybe I'll come, just to see you. I'm only driving myself crazy here anyway."

"You should come then. I can introduce you to Loreen. I've been working with her for a long time and I'm sure she would love to meet you. She is the one that told me to go after my heart. I suppose you should thank her for that, if you are happy having me in your life, that is." he chuckles again.

"Okay, I will see you shortly," I say, hanging up the phone. I take another quick look at my closet and shake my head, deciding to leave the anxiety of choosing my outfit for later today.

"Hey kids!" I yell as I walk from my room and down the stairs towards the basement. Both of my kids are curled up watching TV, with their computers on their laps. Both turn their heads to look at me.

"Ken, are you willing to watch your sister for a while? I will only be gone for about an hour, if that. I'm just going to go to the gym, to see Coach. He has a client he wants to introduce me to."

"I don't mind," he says while shrugging his shoulders.

"Kim, mind your brother," I insist. She rolls her eyes and shakes her head.

It's only a five-minute drive to Coach's gym. I feel awkward coming here because I'm not a member, not that I'd ever want to sign up. Working out at the gym just seems like unnecessary torture. He doesn't ever push me to join, not that I would need to officially join. He does own the place and I could come workout anytime I want. The only physical exertion I hope to be having on a daily basis, is sex, with Coach. That is a workout in itself.

I walk down the main path, trying not to stare at the muscular men, nor the super-sexy, fit women in their spandex pants and crop tops. My arms instinctively cross in front of me, trying to hide my aging physique. I'm not in denial. I really don't compare to these hot young things. Why is Coach with me and not these women? They could run circles around me, literally!

I see him on the lower level, watching a woman work her thigh muscles on one of the machines. She's sweating and puffing her cheeks when she exhales. Yeah, that seems like way too much work to me.

His back is to me, as I approach. The woman lifts her eyes, noticing me as I near. She nods at Coach, letting him know I'm behind him. He spins around and wraps his muscular arm around me, pulling me in for a soft kiss on my forehead.

"Hi love," he whispers.

"Hello to you," I reply. "You're busy, I can wait in your office."

"No, no!" he quickly replies, pulling me over to meet the woman on the machine. She stands to greet me with her hand extended. "Loreen, this is my lovely Rayna."

"I'd hug you but I'm sweaty and gross. It is wonderful to meet you." She smiles as if she's proud of me for some reason. "He talks about you all the time. You must be one hell of a woman to have snagged this handsome hunk of meat. Many have tried, all have failed, except for you."

"Oh," I mutter, not sure of how to respond to that. "He is pretty great."

She looks him up and down with a smug look on her face. "He's a nice guy, but he's one hell of a tough-ass. He kicks my butt into gear three times a week. If he wasn't here to push me, I'd likely be sitting at home on the couch, eating chips and watching animal themed tv shows."

"Don't let her fool you, she's the tough-ass. This woman has six kids and still looks this hot. Can you believe it? Look at that ass!"

This is getting awkward. She turns around to show me her ass. Damn! It's round and firm, not the ass of an aging woman who birthed six kids. I've only had two and don't look that good and likely never will.

"You look fantastic! Six kids, huh?" I'm shaking my head in disbelief.

"Yeah, Coach has been whipping me into shape and I couldn't be more grateful to him. But you missy, you are absolutely gorgeous! He told me you were a stunner, but that didn't do you any justice."

"Thank you so much." I turn to Coach and ask, "So, you talk about me to your clients, do you?"

"Not all of them, just Loreen. She's the one who convinced me that I should grow up and stop being so damn afraid of having a relationship. And no, I didn't start the conversation. Loreen read me like an open book. She's very intuitive."

"I am. It's a curse sometimes. Like right now, you two need to talk about something important. Go on now, I'm fine on my own," she says, shooing us away from her.

"Did I mention how pushy the woman is?" Coach says, sure to speak loud enough for her to hear as we walk away. She simply laughs before sitting back on the machine to continue her leg workout.

"So, you want to ask me something?" he asks while opening the office door and escorting me inside.

I sit on the chair in front of his desk, while he takes a seat behind it. "You know what I want to know."

He takes a deep breath and lets it out slowly, looking somewhat disappointed that he has to reveal his well-planned secret outing.

"Okay, I'll tell you, but I don't want you to pass judgement and refuse to go. I'll explain the place as best I can. When you see if for yourself, it won't seem as bad as what your mind is going to build it up to be. But, then again, it might. It's been a while since I've gone."

"Just tell me," I beg.

He takes a deep breath, looking unsure of how to start. "I'm taking you to an underground place that isn't listed in any directory. It's not somewhere just anyone can get into, you need to be a member or a member's guest."

"Are we guests or members?"

"I am a member, or at least, I was." He's assessing my face for a reaction but my expression hasn't changed. "It's been a few years since I've been. The owner and his submissive are very close friends of mine."

"Where are we going?"

"They call it Fallen, shortened from Fallen Angel. It's a place where like-minded people can get together, find partners, experience new things or just voyeur others as they do what comes natural to them - BDSM."

"So, it's like a bar?" I ask.

"Um, no, not exactly. There's never alcohol served. I'm not sure how to explain it. You'll just have to see it to understand."

"Will people be having sex?"

"Some, yes. Most won't be. There will be Masters with their submissives. Some will be bound, some won't. You'll likely see someone on an iron cross getting worked over. People will be doing whatever makes them happy. It's a place where just about anything goes, safety being the only concern."

I sit back in the chair and put my hand up to my mouth while I process the images of people getting whipped and beaten, fucking and being treated worse than a dog. I can't go in a place like that. What if I'm horrified and start crying?

"Please don't pass judgement until you've been there and talked to some of the people."

I'm terrified! "Talk to them?"

"Yes," he replies. "My friends want to meet you and show you around. Nobody will do anything to you that you don't ask them to. I want you to ask questions and so do they. They're very nice, I promise you."

"You talked to them about me?" I ask. He nods. "Do they know I'm not experienced with this?"

"Yes, and they know I've been slowly introducing you to this lifestyle."

"But, I'm not a submissive, at least, not in the traditional sense. By your own admission, your friend's woman is. How can I relate to her? I will never be a real submissive to you. In the bedroom is one thing but 24/7 is something else. Is she his constant slave?"

"She doesn't like being titled as a slave. She has submitted herself to him almost completely. When they visit her family, they act like a regular couple. They would never understand that it's her choice and that he didn't talk her into it. She came to the club with another couple as his secondary submissive. He made a deal with the other Master to borrow her for a weekend. She never went back to the other man. He treats her very well, you'll see."

"Are there any men submissives at this club or only women?"

"Both genders submit, but female submissives are more common." He stops talking long enough to assess my face. Fearing he may be losing me, he begs, "Please, just come with me and talk to people. Look around and see if something sparks an interest. If you hate it, I'll cancel my membership and we never go back."

"Okay, I'll give it a chance. To be completely honest, I think I'm more curious than afraid. You won't leave me alone, right?"

"Of course not. If you want to separate from me so you and Glitter can go to the ladies' room or wherever, just let me know that you're okay."

"Glitter? That's her name?" I cannot see myself spending time with someone called Glitter. "Isn't that a stripper's name."

"Gear started calling her Glitter because he said her personality shines like glitter. It stuck. She really is a lovely person. I think you'll like her. You two are both strong-minded women."

"Strong-minded? She's a submissive. They aren't strong-minded," I snicker.

"It takes a very strong person to go through the things they do and still come back for more. Submissives are not weak people."

"I suppose I don't know enough about it to pass a fair judgement. All right, I'll go. I'm interested in learning more, talking to people and seeing what they do."

"I'm so pleased," he says, standing up and walking around the desk. He crouches down, taking my hands in his and kissing each of them. "I was afraid you'd refuse to go if you knew where I planned to take you."

"Now who's passing judgement?" I accuse with a smirk. I look down at the floor and shake my head, doing my best to seem distraught. "There's only one huge issue."

He frowns, his eyebrows nearly meeting in the middle. "It's okay, we can figure it out, whatever it is. Just tell me."

I tease, throwing my arms up, "What the fuck do I wear to a BDSM club?"

Coach's concern melts from his face, replaced by laughing eyes and a smile filled with gleaming white teeth. "How about that sexy red dress you have hanging in your closet? You'll look irresistible in that!"

"Are you sure it's enough? I mean, people are probably dressed in leather outfits. Am I wrong? I don't want to stick out and be seen as fresh meat."

He chuckles, "Love, you will be safe and admired. You'll fit in just fine. People wear all different types of clothing. Whatever makes you feel sexy, that's what you wear. You'll see."

"Okay then, I'll meet you at home, soon?" I question.

"Yup, I just have to check in on Loreen and deal with a few small things and I'll be out of here."

He kisses me tenderly, slowly prying his lips from mine. With a mere few inches between us, he whispers, "You are my dream come true. My heart beats for you and only you. You will always be safe with me. I love you."

My lips press to his, kissing him with love and passion, stirring an emptiness within me, an urge to have him fill me and make me feel complete. "Take me!"

Coach quickly wraps his arm around my back, pulling me against his hard body as his mouth works mine and his hand grips my ass, lifting me. My legs wrap around his hips and lock behind him, hanging on like a monkey to its mother.

He spins around setting my ass on the edge of his desk. His fingers work the button of my jeans and then the zipper. Our mouths continue to taste each other. He grabs my shirt and yanks it over my head and then his flies off. We are chest to bra-covered breast. He reaches down, ready to yank off my jeans.

The door flings open, startling us. Just as a rage builds on Coach's face, a sweet voice cuts in. "Hey, everyone is watching the show. Your blinds are open. I can close them if you don't want others to watch this hot scene unfold." Carol starts pulling down the blinds while giggling.

Coach stands up, taking my hand to help me rise up as he's handing me my t-shirt. I'm so embarrassed I want to climb under his desk and never come out. She wasn't lying, people are indeed watching us. I'm so humiliated, my glowing cheeks are proof.

"Thank you, Carol," he says. His face is also flushed a colour I thought I'd never see on his cheeks. Carol walks out, shutting the door behind her. I couldn't even look at her.

"I should go," I say with nervous laughter, while folding my arms over my chest. "Is there a back door I can escape through?"

He chuckles, "There is but you can go out the front. We didn't do anything everyone at this gym hasn't done, we just did it in front of witnesses. It's not a big deal. Half these women are probably jealous, and I know all of the men are. Well, aside from Larry, who's gay. I'm sure he enjoyed it anyway."

"You aren't helping," I comment.

Coach walks me out to my car, kisses me then heads back into the gym. Now for a little me time. A hot bath first, then I'll take an hour to put on my make-up and do my hair, slowly dress, while Coach watches on and then we will go. Somehow, I'll have to figure out a meal plan in there at some point. Maybe he can pick something up on his way home. That'll save me from having to cook anything.

CHAPTER EIGHT
Coach

I very much enjoyed watching Rayna put her make-up on and blow-dry her hair. I had to restrain myself from touching her, even though she wore nothing but a thin nightie. Oh, trust me, it was torture. I wanted to take her and fuck her so hard that I'd ruin her make-up and mess her hair, but she would likely have been pissed at me afterward.

First, she slipped on a pair of sheer black, stay-up stockings. Then she slid a lacy thong up her luscious legs, resting where I wanted to put my tongue; right between her ass cheeks. She continued to dress, slipping on a bra to match the black panties. She stayed like that while she put on her earrings, necklace and perfume. She slowly rubbed lotion on her arms, neck and cleavage. She knew she was driving me insane. Hell, she was doing it on purpose.

The moment she slipped her feet into her three-inch spiked heels, I couldn't resist. I rushed to her and spun her around so we could both look at her in the full-sized mirror. I stood behind her, admiring her while she watched me.

My fingers tickled down her waist, around to the front of her, and just under her bra. I grazed the tender skin all the way along the band below her breasts. She wrapped her hands around my wrists and slowly pushed them away from her. My initial thought was to grab her and take her, not giving a shit that I might ruin hair and make-up, but the look in her eyes had me fighting my instinctual urges.

She's been getting rather bossy with me lately. Any other woman would have been face down on the floor by now, my cock ramming deep into her cunt. But I don't want to do that to Rayna. I like that she's finding her sexual strength. She will learn her place. Either that, or she'll break me. I don't honestly know how this will end.

She continued what I was doing with her own fingertips, gradually cupping her lace covered breasts and pushing them together. Her left-hand slipped down her body and beneath her silky panties. I will remain in control of myself for now. She can be in control, but later, she's all mine. I will own that body before me and make her seize from orgasm after body-shredding orgasm, each taking her higher and higher until her mind floats in a dreamlike ecstasy.

Her fingers work beneath the silky fabric. Her eyes remain locked on mine, even when mine can't resist dropping to watch her masturbate herself. My cock was painfully hard beneath my zipper. I could have fucked her so violently right then, but I think that's what she wanted me to do. The look in her eyes told me that she was trying to get me to act on my urges. I wouldn't give her the satisfaction, not yet.

"Think of this as delayed gratification," I whispered in her ear before kissing her neck, while my eyes stared seductively into the mirror at hers. With every ounce of will-power I could muster, I walked into the bathroom, leaving her to wonder why I didn't take her as I usually do when she teases me.

Instead, I step out from under the steamy water and squirt some shampoo in my hand and grip my throbbing prick in a tight fist. I quickly stroke up and down my shaft. Her image rides through my memory, aiding the fantasy. In my mind, I'm forcing myself on her, ramming my cock in her pussy, so fucking hard that she begs me to ease up, but I don't, I fuck even harder. She'll beg and plead with me, enticing me to cum hard all over her made-up face, ruining her time-staking patience in applying it.

Now that I'm panting with my cum dripping from my fist, I'd better hurry up and get dressed. I don't want us to be late, not that there's any set time to go, I just like to be where I am supposed to be, when I said I would be there. Tardiness rots me, always has.

I can hear voices at the entrance by the front door. It's Rayna, Renee and the kids. Not wanting to be rude, I slip on a pair of grey sweatpants and make my way toward the noise.

"Oh, hey man," Tim says as I come around the corner.

"How's it going?" I ask.

"Good! We're going to take these little brats to the arcade on Tuscan Drive. From there, the theatre to see that new Claymation movie. It looks interesting."

I can't tell if he's just saying that to appease the kids' choice of movie or if he really does want to see it. "Sounds like a fun night. I'm jealous!"

Ken says, "Yeah, we compromised. Kim wanted a movie and I wanted the arcade."

"Then we're going to have ice cream before we go back to Aunt Renee's house."

"Hey, we should get out of here so you two can get going," Tim says with a wink in my direction. "Have fun."

Rayna looks at me as if asking me if he knows where we're going. She must know that I tell Tim almost everything. She tells her sister things she shouldn't tell her. I still don't completely trust Renee not to come onto me at some point. She did once and she always stares at me when she thinks I won't notice. What's to stop her from coming onto me again; the love of her sister? Nope, that didn't matter when she was fucking Rayna's husband. Why would it matter now? Tim keeps her level-headed, or at least he does for now. I just hope she doesn't get bored and crush his heart. He wears his heart on his sleeve, but most people don't know that about him.

They rush out the door, backpacks in hand, Kim skipping in front of Renee, as she mutters on about something cool that happened at school. Renee already looks tired. She's not the mothering type. I get a shot of humour whenever she offers to take them overnight. She always looks so ragged by morning.

The door closes. I look Rayna up and down, admiring the clingy red dress that does nothing to hide the stocking bands wrapping around her thighs. I'm sure Tim noticed. He'll likely tell me how hot she looks, the next time it's just him and I, alone. He would never be inappropriate with Rayna because he respects the boundaries of our friendship, always has.

"Are you ready for tonight, little lady?" I ask her.

She looks at my jogging pants and replies, "Well, at least one of us is."

"I'll be back in a few minutes, don't move."

I pull the locked chest from under the hanging shirts in my closet and dress, as quickly as I can. I put on something first, something I don't want her to see just yet. I finish with a black dress shirt, black leather pants and heavy work boots. I come down the hall and see that Rayna is still leaning against the door where I left her. I was expecting her to be sitting on the steps since her shoes can't be all that comfortable. I must be looking at her oddly because she smiles, shyly.

"You told me not to move, so I didn't. Isn't that what a good submissive is supposed to do; obey?" she asks. There's no hint of sarcasm in her voice and her face tells me that she's awaiting my approval. I step down the stairs slowly, looking her up and down as my prick stiffens at the thought of her giving herself to me completely and without hesitation. That would be a fantasy come true.

"Yes, that would be what a good submissive does. Are you my submissive, Rayna?" I ask, sliding my fingers through her hair until they cradle her head. I look down into her eyes while my cock continues to swell.

"When it's playtime, I can be your submissive. Be patient if I make a mistake, okay?" she begs.

"Of course," I whisper, kissing her bright red lips ever so tenderly. "You look stunning tonight. Everyone is going to want you... but you're *MINE*. You're *MY* submissive, *MY* little cougar. Yes, I like that nickname, Cougar."

"Cougar," she replies, looking a bit annoyed by my nickname. I knew the submissive role wouldn't last long. Oh well, I enjoyed it while I had it.

"What's the matter with cougar?"

"I don't think I like that. It insinuates I'm older than you."

"Well, you are older than I am and that is the nickname for a woman who has sex with younger men, isn't it?" She frowns even further. "Fine, what if I call you Cat?"

"C. A. T.?" She's still obviously, not impressed.

"Is that not how cat is spelled?"

"Yes, but it's still too close to cougar. What if we spell it K. A. T.?"

"I doubt we'll have to write it down, but I suppose K. A. T. will be just fine if it pleases you."

"I'm afraid to ask, but I suppose I should know ahead of time. What are you called? Look, I know you've been there before and people do know you as having a specific nickname, so to prepare myself, I'd like to know it, if you have one, that is."

"Yes, but I'm sure you can guess, if you think about it long enough."

She ponders for a moment while I usher her out the door, locking it behind me. I close her car door, after she's seated and make my way to the driver's seat. She has yet to guess my nickname.

"What are you wearing under your shirt?" she curiously asks as I sit. She reaches for my chest, feeling around.

"It's a harness," I tell her. She feels it through my shirt and bites her bottom lips. "Are you okay with me wearing it? I don't have to. I can take it off and leave it in the car."

"Do you normally wear this stuff when you go there?" she asks, I nod. "Then wear it. I think it's fucking hot! Why haven't I ever seen you in this before?"

"I didn't think you'd be receptive to it just yet. This atmosphere will make it seem more natural to you. If you'd like, I can dress for you one night. Of course, when I do, my caged freak wants to come out with a vengeance, so I'll have to be extra careful to keep him under wraps."

"Yeah, I'm not sure I can handle him quite yet. Little by little, the thought of meeting him doesn't seem so terrifying. Just how bad can it get anyway?"

I can't look at her, as we pull out of the driveway. "You aren't ready. That's all you need to know."

"Will I ever be?" she asks with the innocence that has me wanting to turn the car around and drive her back to the purity of her sheltered life. "I want to be ready."

What stops me is that I sense a tone of disappointment in her voice. Does she want me to free my demon? Should I even be considering it at this point? No, she isn't ready.

"Time will tell, but judging by the way things are progressing, I can't see why it won't happen eventually. You haven't shied away from anything I've proposed to you. You seem to like whatever we've done, which has surprised me, Miss Goodie-Two-Shoes." I snicker.

"I am not a Goodie-Two-Shoes! Well, not since you got your hands on me and corrupted me," she says with a loud laughter and a poke to my arm.

We arrive outside the house and I look to see Rayna's reaction. She's taking in the vast bricks that line the outer walls to the mansion-like building. The first time I was brought here, I'm sure I wore her exact expression.

My tummy is fluttering as I watch her reaction. I can't be sure if her expression is fear, meaning she'll run, or that she's thrilled, eager to expand her horizons. If she runs, that'll put a cap on the level of play we will ever engage in, but if she stays and enjoys it, my demon will very likely rear his ugly head, at some point. I expect that will make her fear me. I don't want her to fear me.

"Hey, Coach!" Rayna says, waving her hand in front of my face. "Hi! Where did your mind go?"

"Sorry, I was just thinking... it's not important. So, are you ready?"

She looks at the house again just as another car pulls in behind ours. The lights shut off and I hear two doors close. High heels are clicking on the cement as a woman walks past the driver's side of our car. She's a mistress, no doubt. She has on leather pants, high-heels and a leather crop top. She crosses in front of our lights and takes the leash of a woman who walked past Rayna's window. Her submissive is dressed in nothing but fashionably wrapped ropes. Her wrists are unrestrained and hanging casually at her sides. She looks beautiful dressed only in rope. My mouth fills with saliva, hoping one day I will have the opportunity to bind Rayna in much the same fashion.

I look over at Rayna to see her staring at the two women. "Can you tie me like that one day?"

I don't think I heard her right, so I ask, "You want me to bind your body in ropes?"

"Yes, I do. She looks pretty. Don't you think?"

"Let's go in," I tell her.

I step out of the car and walk around to her door, opening it for her. She steps out, leading with her stocking-clad leg. I'm becoming aware that I have a cock and it's loving the memory of her getting dressed.

She waits for me to shut the door, but I hold it open and begin unbuttoning my dress shirt. She's watching each button slip free. I want to taste the sweetness of her tongue, as it glides along the red lipstick decorating her top lip. When my shirt falls open, she reaches out, grabbing the straps that rest just under my pecs, with both hands, and pulls me toward her.

"You have to wear this for me later. Please!" she says with her bottom lip quivering. "Fuck! You look dangerous as hell. Fucking scary!"

I tilt my head down and give her my best threatening expression but she's too busy ogling my chest to notice. Her fingers are tracing the edges of the leather. A faint giggle warms my heart, easing my concern about my choice of attire for the evening. I was worried she might not approve.

"If you're finished, we can head in now," I tease. She nods, biting her bottom lip and flashing a shy smile.

I whisper into the ear of one of the very large, dangerous looking men guarding the main entrance. He nods, pulling a key from his shirt pocket and unlocking the huge, hand-carved wooden door behind him. He holds it open while the oversized lion doorknocker seems to size us up, as we walk over the threshold.

There is no music to be heard, not yet. The party is on the lower level. Up here is the social gathering where people remain dressed in proper street attire and abstain from play. People are sitting around chatting amongst themselves, as if they are guests at a fancy hotel and have no interest in the newest check-ins - us.

Rayna's eyes are wide. She looks scared but also intrigued. I think she was expecting to see leather-clad people in various stages of undress while others shriek from pain or moan from pleasurable touches. Not on this floor, that's one level down.

"Love, over here," I whisper in her ear while escorting her toward the elevator.

"I'm nervous," she says after the doors close, capturing us alone inside the small mirrored elevator.

"I am here. I will never leave you," I say after taking her arm in mine, to give her a stronger sense of security. "I will now call you Kat."

"What shall I call you?" she asks.

The doors open and we step out, into a dim corridor lined with candle sconces. I stop and turn her to face me. "People here, call me Demon. You don't have to, but I would prefer you choose something other than my normal titles. Master or Sir would be suitable."

"Demon, really?" she asks. "When you would talk about your demon, I just figured it was a cute name you gave to your badass alter-ego. I didn't know it's the actual nickname that people call you."

"I'm not that person anymore, not with you."

"Would you be if I weren't around?"

"Very likely, yes," I answer her with the heavy dread of honesty.

"If I call you Demon, will you ..."

"There you are!" his voice cuts into our conversation, as his arm slides around my shoulders.

I turn, wrapping my arms around his ribs and picking him up, just until his feet leave the ground, then set him back down.

"Hey, hey, don't bruise the merchandise," he teases. "How the hell are you? It's been too long."

"I'm doing well. How have you been?" I ask.

"Oh, you know, I can't complain," he replies wearing a wicked smirk, as his eyes shift toward the doors I've walked through many times. "Don't be rude, introduce this goddess in the red dress."

"Yes," I reply quickly, taking Rayna's hand in mine. "This is Kat, my..."

"Submissive," she finishes my sentence as she puts her hand out to shake his. Her non-restrained comment takes the man completely off guard. I look at her as if to let her know she spoke out of turn. She realizes her mistake, immediately dropping her hand and casting her eyes downward.

"Have you been a submissive for very long?" he asks her.

"No, Sir," she replies, keeping her eyes down.

"Is she living with you in a regular setting? Is there a mutually respected relationship between you?" he asks Coach.

"Yes, she is my girlfriend. We live together. She is new to the lifestyle and therefore still learning what is and isn't acceptable."

He puts his hand out to Rayna, so she puts hers in his. "My apologies, dear girl, I didn't know you are new. Forgive my reaction. Demon doesn't bring women who aren't trained. I suppose there's always room for fresh meat. Oh, I'm sorry, I should introduce myself. You can call me Gear, for now. This is my submissive, Glitter. She can show you around. I have some catching up to do with Demon."

Rayna looks up at me with fear in her eyes. "Actually, she's going to stick with me for the time being. Can we catch up later?"

He nods, taking her hand in his. "Kat, nobody will touch you here, unless you give them permission to do so. This is one of the safest places you will ever be. Think of this place as a church, only safer." He kisses her hand then walks away with Glitter's hand in his.

"May I speak?" she whispers.

"Of course," I tell her.

"It's just that Glitter didn't speak, so I wasn't sure."

"Our rules will be ours. We can set them up as we go along. If you don't agree with something, bring it to my attention immediately, so we can discuss it. You're here to learn. I would prefer you to remain quiet, unless asked to speak."

"Why Gear? It's an unusual name. And Glitter, what's her story?"

"He earned the name Gear because he can shift gears from playfully calm to sexually raging, quicker than anyone I've ever met. He would never hurt you, unless you gave him permission to do so. He's respectful, unless you tell him not to be. Glitter has a beautiful personality, she will captivate your attention when she's released from her submissive role."

"Freed?" she asks.

"Yes, they live this lifestyle twenty-four hours a day, six days a week. They have been a couple for many years. They share this house. She has her own quarters set away from their joint living quarters so that she can have her one day a week as her own private time, separate from him. I think you'd really like her, if you got to know her. She'd be a great person to talk issues with, other than me, of course."

"Can we get started? I'm anxious and if I don't get moving, I might chicken out," she says. I watch her take a deep breath before leading her through the double doors, and into the lion's den.

CHAPTER NINE
Rayna

The heavy-based music is low enough that I can hear the sounds of people talking, moaning, begging and the occasional scream or moan from both men and women.

It's not as bright in this corridor, as was the last one. The further we walk, the louder the sounds become, and the more people we see. Bodies are clad in everything from designer suits to absolutely nothing. Coach was right, no matter what I had chosen to wear tonight, I'd fit in just fine.

One woman is wearing a leather hood with only eyeholes and nasal slots, to allow for airflow, otherwise she's completely nude. She is quietly sitting on a well-dressed man's lap while he talks to another equally dressed man. He has a woman at his feet, sitting on her heels with her head resting on his thigh as he strokes her hair as if she were his favourite dog.

Both women watch me walk by, with as much curiosity for me as I carry for them. Maybe they don't get many new people in here. The men look up to see Coach and I walking past and both of them nod at him before eyeing me from top to bottom. It's obvious they're talking about us by the way they don't turn their attention away. This happens with most people we pass by.

"Demon? Well, here's a sight for sore eyes! Where the hell have you been lately?" says a larger sized woman with short black hair and heavy make-up. She's dressed in a pair of denim shorts and a leather crop-top. Her black army boots are polished and shined. Behind her tails a very thin woman with scraggly blonde hair. She's wearing a white mini-skirt and red halter-top. She's balancing herself on a pair of red high-heels that would have most women begging to take off. She seems comfortable in them, or she's just putting up a good front.

"Trix, how the hell are you?" Coach replies with his hand out to shake hers.

"You know how it is; one day at a time." She looks me up and down, finally locking eyes with me and furrowing her brow. "And, who might this beauty be?"

I attempt to introduce myself, but hesitate, unsure if I'm supposed to speak or just let him do it. I wish he had told me all the rules of proper conduct for a submissive.

"This is KAT, my new submissive. She's new to the lifestyle."

She looks shocked. "Since when do you train new submissives?"

"She's... different," he replies.

Trix looks at him and nods, "Oh, I see. She's yours."

"Just mine," he says.

"Welcome to our little slice of heaven. You couldn't have found a better Master, unless you had me teaching you the ropes. If you're ever seeking a dominatrix, keep me in mind. I'll treat you right. Besides, my cock is bigger than his," she laughs, and I smirk.

"But my hands are bigger and cover more ass with each swat," Coach jokes. She rolls her eyes. "How are you, Liv?"

The woman nods but doesn't say anything. In fact, her cheeks seem to be a bit puffed out.

"She's not able to speak at the moment. I told her not to wear panties tonight. She thought I wouldn't notice that she defied me, so she's being punished. Open your mouth and show Demon what colour they are."

Liv opens wide to show a pair of red lacy panties wadded up in her mouth. They must have been there for a while because they look very wet.

"I thought about shoving them up her twat, but this punishment suits me for the time being."

"Maybe next time she'll follow instructions better," he says while looking at the offender with steely eyes. She swallows hard but doesn't seem repenting. In fact, she appears to have worn them as a way to defy the woman and earn the attention of a punishment.

"I doubt it," Trix says. "I'll let you get settled; show her around this place. Oh, ah... Ranger's here. I thought I should warn you, so you can prepare yourself."

"Really?" he says with great interest. "I can't believe that fucker came back around."

60

"Well, you haven't been around for quite some time. He likely caught wind of your absence and thought he was safe to return," she says with a shoulder shrug.

"That motherfucker! I can't believe he has the balls to return." Coach turns to glare in the direction Trix's eyes lead him. "Good seeing you, Trix, Liv."

My hand is grabbed rather tightly, as he nearly drags me in the direction his furious eyes lead him. Who is this man she speaks of? What did he do that has Coach this upset?

I haven't seen this look on his face since he found me bound and beaten bloody, while his friend stood before me. I'm worried he's going to do something that will bring back all the memories of that incident to the forefront of my mind. I have been able to bury it and now I'm afraid of what he'll do.

We scurry past a lot of people doing things I really want to stop and watch. I hope we can come back after he deals with whoever he's racing toward. Through another doorway, I catch a glimpse of a man bound to a wooden cross. The only thing I really notice is that he's getting jerked off by another man. I've never actually seen a human on a cross before, nor have I witnessed anything else I saw happening in that room.

Coach stops so suddenly that I smack hard against his back. I can see his chest inflating with every deep breath. I look around his wide back and see three men and a woman sitting at a heavy wooden table. They are all listening to the man in the chest harness talking in a low voice. The woman looks up and smiles.

"Well, look who the cat dragged in." Is she talking about me? How did word spread so quickly that my name is Kat? She's not even looking at me, so the reference is merely the coincidence to the popular saying.

The guy in the harness stands up and walks toward Coach with his hand out. They shake hands and do that quick hug with a single back slap that men seem to always do. My guy isn't smiling.

"What the fuck is he doing here?"

The harnessed man puts his hands up as if to ask Coach to remain calm. "Now, you know nothing was ever proven. The ladies refused to tell their sides. We couldn't ban him without legitimate cause. You know the rules. Unless someone complains, there's nothing to investigate other than hearsay and accusation. As you know, there's always plenty of that going around."

"Get out of my way, Sprat!" Coach says slowly and clearly in a very deep and terrifying tone.

"Demon, you can't start a fight here. You know the rule."

"I don't give a fuck about that rule. Kick me the hell out if you want to, but that fucker is going down. I haven't been here in well over a year and I don't mind getting banned for life, as long as I get to kill that woman beating motherfucker!"

I swallow hard and pull my hand out of Coach's tight grip. My fingers were turning purple. He really hates one of the other two men and I'm not sure which one. The woman stands up and walks over to me, taking me by the hand.

"Come over here," she whispers. I follow her while keeping my eyes on Coach to see what he's going to do to the man, if anything. We stand against the wall a few feet away from the men in case a brawl ensues. "This could get very ugly and you'll be safer over here."

Coach turns to see where I am and that's when it becomes all too clear how he got the name Demon. His eyes have darkened as if they've sunken into his head and he looks bigger, much bigger. How can that be?

One of the seated men stands up and turns his back to Coach. He is wearing black latex pants and a sleeveless shirt. His hair is long and chestnut brown. He is very handsome.

He picks up a half empty bottle of water and turns around. He slowly starts walking towards the two men who are standing. He stops only a few feet in front of them. The man that was trying to calm Coach backs away with his hands up, as if to say he wants no more part of it.

The latex wearing man takes another step forward until he and Coach are face-to-face. "So, we meet again. It's really too bad we can't talk through our issues because I think we would get along, famously. If it weren't for the unproven rumors that were spread around by women who didn't want to face the fact that they falsely accused me of overstepping. I know they were yours. Afterthought has me wondering if I should have told them no, but you know how hot those chicks were. I think we should work at getting past this for the sake of the community. What do you say? Do you want to talk it through?"

"No, I don't. We did all the talking we ever needed to do. You are an abusive motherfucker and you should not be allowed back in this house. You and I both know those two girls were so threatened by you, they didn't want to say anything about what you did. As far as I'm concerned, someone should do exactly the same thing to you that you did to them. I would be more than happy to be that guy."

"So, what you're saying is you want to sexually satisfy me? I mean, I satisfied them and if you say you want to do to me what I did to them, that must mean you want to make me cum hard. Did you hop the fence during your absence? Not that there's anything wrong with it but I don't swing that way."

"You rope bound those women so they couldn't move and then you slowly hung them by their necks until they turned purple. They did not want that, but that's what you did. They told me they used their safeword, but you continued. Why the fuck won't you admit it? Are you ashamed? Just give me five minutes alone in a room with you and a length of rope and you will never fucking walk out of that room."

"Demon, I know damn well you could get the better of me in a physical altercation and I'm not challenging you to one. It's their word against mine. No proof has ever surfaced so I think we should just let this go. Why don't we just agree to disagree. When you're here, I will leave."

"I think you should leave and never come back. I don't ever want to see you again."

The man steps back with his hands raised in surrender. "Okay, I'm leaving. You can't stop me from coming here, but I'll do my damnedest not to be here when you are. That's the best I'm going to do. Do what you will."

The latex wearing man walks past Coach and disappears out the door. Everybody just stands there looking at a seething Coach, wondering if he's going to chase after the man or let him leave on his own, unharmed. He turns his head to seek me out. His eyes lock on mine with a sigh of relief, as if he's happy to see that I am still standing here and haven't run for the hills.

He puts his hand out for me to take it and weave my fingers in his. He kisses the back of my hand and thanks the woman who pulled me away from him.

"Kat, this is Mistress Kristi," he introduces us with anger still present in his voice. She smiles and nods and I do the same, unsure whether I should thank her, myself or leave that up to Coach. I really wish I knew what my role was here. "Thank you, Kristi."

"For you Demon, you know I would walk through the gates of hell and back for you. So, why the fuck have you been gone for over a year? You just dropped off the face of the earth, without a single fucking phone call. I thought you loved me, man!"

He smiles and replies, "You know you're the only Mistress I love with all my heart. If only you were into dicks."

She burst out laughing and then puts her arm around me. "If you ever decide that his needle dick isn't enough for you, give me a call sweetheart and I will let you choose the size you want me to fuck you with."

Coach looks at me and says, "If ever I would allow you to be with a Mistress, Kristi is the one I would trust to keep you safe."

She points from him to me and back to him. "If you allow her to be with a Mistress? Since when have you forbidden you're submissives from choosing another person to entertain them when you're not around?"

"I never forbid it. If they went with another dominant, they didn't come back to me. This one is special to me. This woman is mine."

"No shit?" she says, crossing her arms over her chest and taking a step back. "Kat, I don't know what makes you so unique, but I can't wait to find out. Congratulations!"

I suppose Coach wasn't lying when he said he has never been in a committed relationship before me. I had thought that maybe at least once throughout his life, there will have been somebody who may have come close. I think I was wrong in assuming that.

"I'm going to show Kat around. She's new to our lifestyle, so I'm going to show her the possibilities. If you will excuse us, we will get back to exploring. I'm sure I will see you all soon."

They wave us on, and we leave the room. I'm rather impressed how I have managed to stay quiet for so long. I think this is the longest I have gone without saying anything, especially when I've had so much I wanted to say.

Coach pulls me off to the side and puts his hands on my shoulders. "Are you alright? I'm sorry you had to see that. Do you still want to be here, or should I take you home?"

"If you take me home right now, I will be angry at you. I am not exactly clear about what that guy did to those women and I'm not sure that I want to, but we came here for the purpose of opening my eyes to your lifestyle and dammit, that is what we are going to do. Enlighten me, Demon," I say rather tauntingly.

He smiles wide, showing me his beautiful white teeth. I don't know where the angry demon disappeared to but the guy standing in front of me doesn't look like he has a mean bone in his body. He's so young and cute. His face appears lighter, with a tiny glint of deviousness in his eyes.

"I should also mention how proud I am of you for not speaking when not asked to. It's not a rule I remembered to mention to you and I'm proud of you for playing the role of submissive, so well. You will be rewarded."

"You're not going to do anything to me here in front of people, are you?" Apprehension is swelling up in the pit of my stomach. The thought of being spanked or sexually pleasured while others watch does seem like an arousing idea, but also extremely terrifying. I don't know these people. I don't know anything about this house. Perhaps one day I will feel comfortable enough to let him do something like that, but today is not that day.

"My love, you are here today to learn, not to entertain the other members. Come with me to see what my world consists of."

I follow him as he walks me from room to room, giving me a few moments to watch whatever is happening, before moving on to the next. My pussy is so wet that I can feel my lips slipping against one another as I walk, further heightening my level of arousal.

I want to try a lot of these things, but not all. One of the rooms has me queasy. I cannot fathom why, but a man is sticking hypodermic needles through a woman's labia while she sits bound and shaking, tears streaming down her cheeks. It was horrifying, something nightmares are made from.

CHAPTER TEN
Coach

The scene in this room has Rayna gripping my arm tightly. I can feel her shaking.

"Why is he doing that to her?" she whispers.

"She enjoys it," I reply, knowing she isn't going to understand. Rayna enjoys some pain, but she's never been introduced to anything like this and I doubt she'll ever be interested in taking it to this level.

"That has to hurt like hell," she says while wincing when he slides a needle through the hood of her clitoris. The woman cries out, but takes the pain like a warrior. My dick is throbbing in my pants, not at the needles, but at the woman's reaction to them. If Rayna was any other woman I'd brought here tonight, she'd be on her knees sucking my cock down her throat, until I filled her belly with my jizz.

"Watch her reactions, her facial expressions, her breathing. Trust me, she's not even here anymore. He's taken her to a whole new platform. The man taking her there is very skilled in the placement of needles, allowing her the most pain and heightened pleasure imaginable." I can barely control my breathing, to keep it at a slow and steady rhythm.

Rayna watches for a moment as he begins attaching wires to one of the needles penetrating through her clitoris.

"Have you ever done this to a woman?" she asks the one question I was hoping she wouldn't. I don't want to lie to her, but I don't want her to run away, believing I'm a sadistic fuck.

"Once, but it isn't my thing. Perhaps I'll tell you about it another time," I reply. "Now quiet down."

She looks at me and then down my chest to the swollen lump in my pants. She places her hand on my cock and squeezes. My eyes are burning with desire as I glare into hers. She has to know when I say something here, she's to heed it.

"Why are you touching me?"

"I needed to know if you enjoy watching this woman suffer," her expression is filled with concern.

"I'll never do anything to you that you don't approve of, you know that." The last thing I would ever want is for her to legitimately fear me.

"That's not it, I know you won't. You're very aroused from watching a woman in agony. How can I compete with that? Would you like to hurt me, make me suffer like she is?"

"I just told you, I would not do anything to you that you didn't approve of. Now stop talking."

"That's not what I'm asking," she hisses a bit louder than she should.

Mic looks at Rayna with an angry leer, and then at me as if to tell me to control my submissive. I nod, grasping her bicep and pulling her away from the doorway to rush her down the hall. I push her into the bathroom and shut the door, locking it behind me.

"You must remain quiet when in the open viewing rooms. Nobody is to speak louder than a whisper. If you were anyone else…"

"What? What would you do if I were anyone else?" she questions with a challenging attitude, lifting her eyebrows tauntingly, while pursing her lips.

"Do you really want to know? Should I show you?" Fuck! My dick is so goddamn hard.

She replies, "Do you want to punish me because I caught you in a lie?"

"I did not lie. I said we would talk about it later."

"So, you don't enjoy needles? Well, your cock tells a different story."

"Later, I won't say it again."

"Oh, you won't say it again, huh?"

"I am going to punish you because of the disrespectful attitude you have right now. You seem to have forgotten that you are my submissive. You told me you were when we first arrived. Do you remember? So, tell me Kat, are you my submissive, or not?"

"Yes, I am," she replies, still giving me the same shitty leer, further taunting my level of patience.

As quick as I can manage, I grab her hair and pull her face to mine, kissing her harder than I ever have. My other hand grabs the neckline of her dress and yanks, tearing it to expose her bra. Rayna tries to grab my arm to stop me from ruining her dress but I'm stronger than she is. I grab her bra and jerk it down, forcing her tits to pop out from the top of it.

I squeeze her left breast hard and then pinch her nipple until she screams in my mouth. She knows she can yell the safeword and she will be freed instantly. She won't say it though. I know she won't. She's way too stubborn to let me have that satisfaction. Good!

I slap her tit and then pinch the other nipple equally hard, while she struggles to stop me. Again, she screams against my invading tongue. I grab her neck and apply pressure, not enough to stunt her breathing. My fingers and thumb are pressing against her carotid arteries to slow the flow of blood to her brain. She needs to learn that when we are here, I am in control.

Her lips are going still, and her body is becoming heavier. She's weakening. Good! With my hands still weaved into her hair, I release her throat and push her onto her knees.

"Take out my cock and suck it!" I demand.

Rayna reaches for the waistband of my leather pants, using it to steady her on her knees. She quickly pulls my zipper down. My cock springs forth, hard and thick. She opens her mouth, so I pull her head until her mouth is over the head of my cock and I hold her there. She wraps her lips around the head and sucks, rolling her tongue over my piss hole. She could make me cum in seconds, if I were to let her.

She looks up at me with defiant eyes. Fuck she's sexy! I love that she challenges me, but I'll never tell her that. I pull her face toward my belly, burying my cock down her throat. She wretches, but I don't immediately set her free. Her hands grab my thighs, but I hold her head, sternly. The second time she gags, I yank her head back. Tears are filling her eyes, but are not yet falling.

"I fucking own you!" I hiss.

"No, you don't," she hisses back. She's really pushing her boundaries and I'm so madly in love with her because of it. This woman owns me, not the other way around, and she knows it.

"We'll see," I growl through clenched teeth. My inner Demon is shadowboxing.

I pull her head forward, sliding my prick into her throat again, this time, she doesn't gag, which I find to be disappointing. I hold her in place, humping my prick down her throat, again and again. I won't stop until her tears are running down her cheeks taking her mascara with them. I will mess her make-up and not allow her to make herself presentable before we leave this room. She, along with everyone here, will know she is under my control.

When I pull her face back, the evidence of my punishment is evident with black tears dripping from her chin. She isn't crying, it's just a reaction from gagging. She can make me stop with just one word, Red.

If I keep making her suck my cock, I'll definitely cum. I want to fuck her good and hard. I make her stand using the grip I have in her tangled hair. I spin her, so that my arm is at her waist and she's bent over facing behind me, her waist held tightly against my hip. The grip I have on her waist is vicious. She cannot get away.

With her unable to stand straight up, I yank the hem of her dress up, exposing her lacy thong. I start swinging my arm, spanking her ass until she's crying out and fighting to get away. Her ass is hot and red, swollen with my handprints covering both cheeks.

I grasp the thin material that runs between her ass cheeks and yank, lifting her feet off the ground, but the lace won't give. I pull it to the side, that'll do. My fingers reach between her folds, slipping in her wetness. Fuck, yes!

I shove two of my fingers into her drenched cunt and wave, rubbing her g-spot with a roughness that has her moaning within seconds. She isn't fighting to get away anymore. Now she's squirming and trying to hump my fingers, but my grip on her body is extensive.

Her pussy is tightening around my fingers. She's going to cum. No, she won't! I pull my fingers out just before she reaches orgasm. I resume cracking her ass, alternating from one hot cheek to the other. She's fighting to get away again, panting and wailing, but not saying the word to make it stop.

I jam my fingers into her again, and fuck her hard, not giving her any mercy. It isn't more than ten seconds before she's ready to cum again. Just before she does, I stop again, removing my fingers and continuing with the punishing slaps. She's fighting me and yelling.

"Fuck you! Let me go! Fucking stop!"

"Say the word if you want it to end," I reply in a calm voice.

I ram my fingers back into her and bring her close, again. I repeat this action eight-more times, getting her so near to climax that her body begins to tighten and then stopping, to inflict more pain. She isn't screaming from the pain anymore. Her moans are loud and deep, like a growl.

She's learning what it is to lose herself on that fine line between pleasure and pain, blurring it to the point where you can't tell the difference between the two. This is where I wanted to take her. She needs to experience this for herself, so she can fully understand why that woman would challenge her body in that way.

This time, I don't pull my hand away. My fingers flail wildly inside her as her muscles tighten and cease to ease, holding her in a violent full-body spasm. Her cunt is gripping and pulling and pushing at my hand. A flood of hot cum sprays from her depths, coating my hand and splashing to the marble floor.

I am relentless, not stopping even when the grip she has on my fingers is so tight that I can hardly move them. Her body is quivering, twitching and jerking to get free, but I don't allow it. My fingers don't quit, continuing to invade her body with force until she erupts into a second raging orgasm that has her knees shaking to the point that they give out. I'm holding her up now, keeping the momentum going until she rides completely through her climax.

I stand her up and scoop her into my arms, dropping to one knee and sitting her on the other. Her head rests on my shoulder, her arms hang limply around my neck. She's so weak and I know she's trying to get the fogginess of the euphoria to fade away.

"I'm sorry I had to punish you, but you needed to know your place. I wanted to prove to you that the threshold of pain can be pushed until the person can't decipher between something hurting and something giving them absolute pleasure."

"Yes, I understand," is all she manages to say.

"I love you, Rayna," I whisper, kissing her forehead tenderly.

"I know you do. Thank you," she replies.

"Are you okay now?" She nods, rising to her feet. I hold her elbow knowing her knees are still going to be weak. She wobbles, but quickly regains her control.

"Stand against the wall while I clean the floor." Using paper towels, I clean her cum from the black and white marble.

"I have to pee," she informs me.

"Go ahead," I reply.

"You're going to stay in here when I do?"

"Yes," I tell her. "I don't want you to make yourself look presentable."

"What? Why not? I'm not going out there like this," she tells me.

"Yes, you are. They need to know that you have been punished for your bad behaviour."

"Why? What business is it of theirs?"

I smile at her and tell her, "Just go pee, or don't. You can hold it all night if you choose."

Her eyes are shifty. I can tell she's uncomfortable. Rayna has never used the toilet in front of me. She's way too proper for that.

"So, in your mind, it's okay to gush cum on me, but I can't watch you urinate?"

"It's just..." she shakes her head. "It's a private thing."

"Are you going to go or not?"

"No, I'm not peeing in front of you," she informs me.

"Last chance." She shakes her head. "Okay! This is going to be a fun night," I chuckle, guiding her out of the bathroom while she fusses with her torn neckline to keep her bra covered breasts hidden from inquisitive eyes. It's no use, I purposely tore it wide open. She gives up, leaving herself exposed. The dress is garbage now. I'll gladly buy her a dozen more.

I walk her straight back to that same room. The woman is sitting on a chair wiping her vagina with a cloth. There is blood on it, but not much. I see Mic standing by the chair she was bound to. He's spraying it down and cleaning it with a white rag.

"Mic, my sub has something to say to you," I say as I approach him, putting Rayna between the two of us. He looks down at her, but she doesn't look at his face.

"Sir, I'm sorry for interrupting you. It'll never happen again." Her voice is soft and apologetic.

Mic grins and replies, "Did you not realize that you needed to be quiet?"

"Yes, Sir. I had questions about what you were doing to her."

"What questions? Ask me," he says while putting his finger under her chin, lifting her face so he can admire her smeared make-up.

"I didn't understand why she would let you do that to her. And, Coach, I mean Demon, was very aroused from watching her suffer. I wanted to know if he'd ever done this to a woman."

"Was it explained to you?"

"Demon punished me for interrupting you. He didn't tell me directly, if he's done this before. I do better understand how pain can urge on pleasure. I just can't fathom getting needles stuck through my clit."

"The woman's name is Em. I suggest you talk to her. She can answer your questions better than I can."

"Thank you, Sir," she says. She looks at me and I nod, releasing her arm. I watch Rayna walk over to the woman who is now pulling a black dress over her head.

"So, how the hell have you been Mic?"

"I'm good Brother. What's happening with you?"

I look over at Rayna and smile. "She happened."

He glances at Rayna and then puts his hand out to shake mine. "Congratulations, man. I never thought either one of us would ever let ourselves get shackled."

"Oh, I had no choice in it. I fought it, but she won."

"I had no idea you preferred the chicks with a few years on them."

"It's not her age that caught my attention. It's everything about her." I change the subject before he asks me how we met. "How about you? Anyone special?"

He nods toward the woman talking to Rayna. "That one. She is the one for me. I don't know if I can say I'm shackled, but I sure like her a whole lot. She's fun to play with, but also a great conversationalist. She's university educated, not like my usual prey."

"You're still calling women prey," I chuckle.

"Are you going to tell her everything she wants to know about all of your past subs, and the stories that still haunt you?"

"Yeah, I will. I won't lie to Kat, but I won't elaborate too much either."

"And about the last girl you were here with? Does she know?"

"I'll tell her about Sara, when the time is right."

"It's in the past," he replies, as if that'll soften the painful memories.

"It'll change things," I say with a sigh. "All right Mic, I have to get her home. Hopefully she'll want to come back."

He puts his hand out, so we grip and do the two-pat-hug. "All right man. I'll see you soon, right? You better not stay away so long this time. Oh, by the way, she's fucking hot!"

"You don't have to tell me," I say as I'm walking away to collect Rayna.

Rayna's laughing with the woman, as if they're old friends. Now that I'm closer to them, I can see just how beautiful the woman is. Her skin is smooth and flawless, eyes wide and deer-like, and her lips are full and inviting. Her hair is pulled back in a high ponytail, but the black tresses still hang with a slight wave all the way down to her butt.

"We should go." I don't give her an option to stay.

"If you wish," she replies. "Em, this is Demon."

We shake hands and greet one another with casual pleasantries, ending with my apology for interrupting their conversation and stealing her away. I take Rayna's hand and lead her down the corridor, nodding at the people I used to know and claimed to be good friends with. I no longer know them, unable to even remember their names.

I open the car door and close it once she's settled. After putting my dress shirt back on and buttoning it. I slip in behind the wheel. Rayna looks at me, while I look at her.

"So, what did you think of the place?" I ask her.

She smiles and takes a deep breath, raising her eyebrows and holding them high, as her breath seeps from her lungs. "It was different. I can honestly say you've taken me to a place that I've never been. It's crazy in there. I mean, it was so interesting; wild, but in a non-chaotic manner. Everyone seemed happy, as if all their daily life's stress was left at the door as they came in."

"And, what did you hate about it?"

"I didn't like how angry you were with that man. What did he do to make you hate him so much?"

Here we go! "He was one of my good friends. He was enjoying my submissive behind my back. If I was playing with more than one woman at a time, I always told them about each other. I expected the same respect from my playmates. However, I was to be their only Master. It was a hard rule."

"Surely there's more to it than that."

"Yes, there is." I don't want to tell her any more than that, but I know she won't let it go. "Lisa was her name. She was the ultimate submissive, everyone wanted her. We were together for almost two years. One day, that asshole convinced her to let him Master her. She wouldn't tell me, or anyone, what happened except that he hurt her. She left our community without an explanation to me or anyone else. She was found a month later floating in the river after having been tortured to death. Her killer was never caught. I doubt it was him who killed her, but I blame him for her death. If he hadn't hurt her, she never would have sought a sadist outside of the safety of our community. She tangled with a psychopathic sadist, who fucking used her like a piece of meat."

"Fuck! That's horrible. I'm so sorry. Why didn't she stay with you after he did what he did? If you two were so close, why would she leave you because of him?"

"This is where my guilt lies. I pushed her away for getting involved with him in the first place. She was supposed to be with me or ask permission to be with another. She didn't."

"She betrayed you. It's understandable that you were hurt by that. You obviously cared for her a great deal."

"No, it isn't like that. I didn't love her. I enjoyed her company. She was my friend, just my friend."

"Are you sure?"

"Yes, I'm sure. I know the difference between a physical friendship and love. I didn't forgive her and now she's dead. I blame him. I will always blame him. He shouldn't be allowed in Fallen anymore. I don't know exactly what he did to her, but I have a good idea."

"You said there were two women that he hurt. What happened to the other one?"

"She moved away. People said her job took her to a different city but I'm not so sure. She called me to tell me what he did to her and probably did to Lisa. She hung up before I could tell her to come back. I wanted to tell her that he would be dealt with. She never reached out to anyone from our community again."

"So, why didn't the women go to the police and tell them about the assault?"

"What cop is going to believe a masochist was assaulted by her chosen sadist? They would have laughed them out of the station with a *you got what you asked for* comment to worsen the blow. The chosen house representatives handle the complaints and decide whether someone should be banned, or not. The women wouldn't talk about it, so nothing could be done. He wasn't banned. I threatened to kill him if he returned, but I stopped attending, so he was free to come and go."

"I will be sure to avoid him," she promises.

"I will never put you in a position where you need to defend yourself. I fucked up once and it nearly cost you, dearly. It'll never happen again."

She sighs, recalling that horrible night. "Let's go home."

CHAPTER ELEVEN
Rayna

It's been three days since we went to the house. I've been ravishing Coach, as often as I can. He's been unusually quiet though. I'm giving him his space to work through whatever emotions were brought forth from seeing that guy. I think Lisa meant more to him than he wants to admit.

Some days, being a dental hygienist feels like the worst career choice I could have ever made for myself. I originally wanted to be a dentist, but getting married and having kids, stood in the forefront. I had to settle for a lighter education. Do I regret having my kids – never! Do I regret my ex – absolutely! He's out of the picture now and I couldn't be happier to have watched him leave. The kids haven't heard from him in over a month. He'll never win Father of the Year Award.

I'm between patient cleanings and taking a quick break before my two-o'clock arrives. I drag my weary body to the lunchroom and drink my coffee as quickly as I can, without burning my mouth. I really need the caffeine, after the late-night romp Coach threw into me. We didn't get to sleep until well after one in the morning. Five hours of sleep just isn't enough for me.

I pull my phone out of my locker and text Coach.

Me: How's your day going?

Coach: I'm busy as fuck. How about you?

Me: Good, but I'm tired. Well worth it though ;)

Coach: I agree. I'm with a client.

Me: I just wanted to check in with you.

Coach: Later tonight, I'm going to fuck you hard.

Me: Looking forward to it!

Kelly pokes her head in the lunchroom. "Hey doll, your two o'clock is here."

I drop my head and groan. "Fine, I'll collect him in a minute."

"Okay," she replies. "Why are your eyes lugging around all that purple baggage beneath them? Did your hunky man keep you up late again last night?"

I snicker, "Yes, he did."

"I can't say I wouldn't do the same. If he were my man, I'd never get any sleep. How do you keep your hands off that hot body of his?"

"Who said I can keep my hands off him?" I wink.

"He is so fine! You really have to set me up with one of his strongman friends. I could go for a barbarian-style, beast of a man." She dances a hip-humping cha-cha. "I need a thick-thighed man to give me a good hard fucking with some power behind it!"

I start laughing when Dr. Jessik walks around the corner and stops dead in his tracks. He's watching her hump the air, grunting and groaning, as if she's getting fucked. She spins around and jolts backward like she received an electric zap. Her high-pitched yelp has me in hysterics. Poor Dr. Jessik is so embarrassed that he isn't sure if he should continue forward, or turn around and come back later.

"Sorry, I was joking around with..." she clears her throat while blushing a raging red. "Excuse me," she mutters while walking past him.

"She was just joking about..." I stop talking, not wanting to get into what got her started.

Dr. Jessik once told me that he had been waiting for me to be ready to date, so that he could ask me out. I had no idea he even liked me. It wouldn't have worked out, him and I, we're just too much alike. Two people who are boring, will be extra boring together. I need a bit of fire in my relationships and Coach is exactly the spark I need to keep me from wasting my life away.

"She's a very excitable woman," he replies with an awkward smile. He plugs in the kettle.

"That's an understatement," I say with a smile.

After taking his mug from the cupboard and tossing in a tea bag, he asks, "Would you like me to pick you up so we can travel to the airport in one car? Don't worry, we won't be alone together. I'll be picking up Dr. Myri and Jennifer along the way."

"I'm not worried about being alone with you." I had forgotten about the convention. "I'll have to let you know about that. I haven't made any arrangements yet."

His eyes fill with concern. "You haven't told your boyfriend about the convention, have you?"

"It just kept slipping my mind." I'm not lying, it did. "I'll talk to him tonight. What time is the flight?"

"Kelly has your flight and hotel information in a packet at the front desk. I believe our flight leaves at ten-twenty in the morning. I could be at your house at eight-forty-five, after I've picked up Dr. Myri. Jennifer's apartment is closest to the airport, so we'll collect her last."

"I'll have to let you know later in the week."

"You are coming, right? You go every year."

I nod with a smile, "Of course. I wouldn't miss it."

"How are things going with, ah… what's his name again?"

"Coach."

"Right! Yes, Coach, because he's a bodybuilder; a very large, muscular young man." His jealousy is sadly, obvious, despite his efforts to suppress it.

"We're doing very well together. He really is a good man and he treats me like a queen."

His smile is faulty, not quite reaching his eyes. "As he should be. Seeing you so happy is a consolation. You deserve the very best of everything. Of course, you should insist he allow you to get more sleep. You're looking quite tired these days."

"The kids weren't feeling well last night, so I was up late," I lie because I don't want to hurt him. He's a wonderful man, just not my type.

"Well, I hope they're feeling better this morning." He turns to pour the boiling water into his mug.

"Yes, they are."

As he's walking out of the lunchroom, he pauses, "You don't have to lie to me about your sex life. He's a young man and you're a beautiful woman. I'm sure he's very capable of having a voracious sexual appetite. I wouldn't want to take my hands off you, either."

I don't reply to his confession. First of all, I'm not sure anything I could say would make him feel any better. Second, I'd rather just leave the conversation to die.

It would have been better had he not said anything about his feelings for me. At least we wouldn't be so awkward toward each other. Is he trying to make me feel guilty for not giving him a chance with me? How was I to know he had a thing for me? Besides, he didn't say anything to me until he saw me on Coach's arm. If he liked me so much, he should have told me earlier. He said he didn't think I was up for dating after my divorce, but I hadn't been with my husband for four years, at the time he announced his feelings. How was I to know?

I get up and walk to the sink to reluctantly dump the remainder of my coffee. I rinse my cup and set it in the tray. As I turn to leave, I bump face-first into his chest.

"Oh, I'm sorry," he says as he backs up, waving his hand for me to pass.

"My fault completely," I reply as I shuffle around him.

I'm happy to be away from him. I wish things could go back to before I knew his feelings for me. He was always oddly behaved when alone with me, but at least it wasn't weird, for me anyway.

* * * * *

I finished with my last patient, finally ending my work day. Arriving home at three-twenty, dog tired, I just flop my body face down on my bed, burying my face in the fluffy pillow. I have been dreaming of this moment all day.

The kids are doing their homework quietly, at the kitchen table, while they eat a snack. The house is still and drifting further and further from my thoughts.

"Love, wake up."

"No," I reply, angry that I'm being interrupted from a pleasant dream about Coach, the kids and I having a nice barbeque at the local beach. I don't know why I was dreaming that, but it was wonderful, nonetheless.

"Rayna, it's six-thirty. I made dinner. Come eat something," he replies, as he gently brushes stray locks of hair from my face.

I groan, "Do I have to get up? It's really six-thirty?"

"Yes, love, and you do."

"Fine!" That complaint comes out louder and more vicious than I had intended, but he just laughs.

He jumps on top of me, straddling my ass. His hand weaves in my hair and pulls just enough to let me know he's being his dominant self.

"If you don't get up, I'll punish you, whether the kids are home and awake, or not. But, if you come and eat something, I just might make you scream from pleasure tonight. What do you choose to do, Rayna?"

I giggle, "What if I want both?"

He lifts his left leg off me and then grabs my hips, spinning me onto my back. Damn, he's so fucking fast and strong! His mouth comes down on mine while his hand slides up my shirt, cupping my breast tenderly. Our mouths mesh in a heated contest to see whose tongue will take the lead in the tango they've started.

His fingers tease my nipple, not pinching hard, but just enough to send tiny zaps of lust to my heating pussy. I want him now, not later. A moan escapes me, taunting his manly desire to continue, momentarily forgetting the small humans roaming about the house.

Coach suddenly pulls his face back from mine and removes his hand from under my shirt. He speaks as if he's trying to convince himself to back away from me. "Food, we need nourishment. Children... children are within earshot. Must feed the little people."

I laugh at how hard it is for him to reason with his testosterone riddled mind. He hops off me and onto his feet, holding his hand out for me to accept. With a final groaning complaint, I allow him my hand so he can pull me onto my feet. He doesn't stop there. He flips me onto his shoulder and slaps my ass cheek, hard.

"Let me help you get to the table, lazy woman." He cracks my ass again, this time I yelp. "Do you remember what happened the last time I carried you to the kitchen?"

"Yes, and it has forever changed the way I perceive carrots." I'm not lying, I get wet when I see them. His laughter fills the room.

Coach carries me into the kitchen while I laugh and cackle, slapping his butt. We come around the corner and the kids start laughing. They think him carrying me is hilarious. My face feels like it's going to explode from the blood build-up. He sets me down on the chair I normally sit on and then kisses my lips just once.

I am laughing because the kids are in stitches. Kim snorts, which has us all busting up. Tears are streaming down my face by the time Coach hands me a plate with lemon chicken and asparagus with a side of herbed rice. It smells delicious. My mouth waters. I love that he enjoys cooking and excels at it! He's much more creative in the kitchen than I am.

Halfway through our meal, Coach asks me, "Love, would you like to go on a date with me, this Saturday?"

I look up at him and stop chewing, pushing the food into my cheek. I cover my mouth with my hand and ask, "A date?"

"Yes! You know, when two people go someplace together and have a great time."

"Um, not this weekend."

He furrows his brow, and asks, "Are you tired of me already?"

I smile and shake my head. He knows I can't get enough of him. "No, um… I have to go away to a convention… for work… to Las Vegas… with some of my coworkers."

He sets his fork down on his plate and wipes his beard with his napkin. "You're mentioning this, now?"

I suddenly feel very small and young, like a teenager asking her parents if she can go to a place knowing they won't approve. I simply shrug, unsure of what to say.

"Rayna, I'm not going to stop you from doing something that will benefit your career. I just wish you would have told me sooner, before I made plans for us."

"I'm sorry, and you're right, I should have talked to you about it long before now. I would invite you to come, but you would be so bored. The only fun thing we do is go to the pub on Friday night, for drinks. After that, it's one lecture after another, product sampling, ego stroking… It'll bore you to tears."

Ken announces, "I can babysit Kim so Coach can go!"

I shake my head, and reply, "Not for an entire weekend."

"Your mom's right, little man. Maybe next year," Coach says.

Ken pouts, stabbing an asparagus and watching it flop on the end of his fork. Kim has been sitting quietly, eating her chicken, not caring to participate in the conversation.

He chuckles, "Love, you don't have to invite me to come with you. I want you to go, have fun, party and schmooze with the people who can boost your career. If I'm there, I would only be a distraction to you, anyway."

"It's just… I don't want you to think I don't want you there."

He reaches for my hand, lifting it to his lips and kisses it, as if my skin is as fragile as the wings of a butterfly and if he presses too firmly, he'll tear me.

"I don't think that. Next weekend, you are mine to do with as I please," he replies before taking his glass to the sink to refill it. Before he sits, he leans his mouth just behind my ear and very quietly, whispers, "Every chance I have to take you, I will, so be ready for me. I'm going to fuck you raw and eat you until you scream."

My pussy tightens and my clit twitches. I can feel the heat radiating from between my legs, which are squeezed together. He sits and continues eating dinner while I bite my bottom lip. I want him now. If the kids weren't here, I'd do or say something sassy, just to provoke him to pull me over his knee and spank me. Of course, he would pleasure me afterward. He never leaves me wanting for anything.

"Do you need me to drive you to the airport?" he asks, as if what he just whispered to me isn't affecting him in any way. I admire his self-control. He can be furious about something, or be thrilled, but he has this uncanny ability to prevent his face from revealing what's going on in his thoughts. I can't do that, never could. Everyone knows exactly what I'm thinking.

"Um," I clear my throat, "no. Dr. Jessik offered to pick me up. We're carpooling with two other people from the office. He's coming at eight-forty-five, Friday morning."

"If you change your mind, I'd be happy to drive you," he assures me with a smile.

CHAPTER TWELVE
Rayna

Coach has licked, fucked and dominated me so much this week, my whole body is tired and sore. Not so much that I have to turn him down, of course. I want him, over and over again. Not once has he made love to me, though. It's been hard, rough and I'm usually bound. It's great, but I'd love it if he would be gentle tonight. I leave in the morning and want to hang onto the loving closeness I feel after lovemaking. He likes it rough, I know that. The man is a goddamn machine!

I come out of the bathroom after my shower to find Coach standing in the middle of the room wearing his leather pants, heavy black boots and his harness. This is how he dresses when we go to Fallen. It's so fucking exciting! I know what he's capable of doing while he wears that outfit. Of course, I understand that he doesn't need the leathers to be his dominant self, but they add to the allure.

The way he's looking at me has me swallowing, despite my suddenly dry throat. I stop a few feet from him and stand with my arms hanging down at my sides, eyes on his, as he likes them to be.

"Tonight, I am going to make you mine. You'll remember this night, all weekend." His voice is deep, and his words are spoken slowly.

"Yes Sir." I will be his obedient submissive tonight, as I have all week. He must have something extra special planned for me.

"I need to ask if there's any reason anyone will be seeing you naked. Will you be using the pool and changing room? I will be marking you and I wouldn't want to leave marks on your skin where they could be seen. Too many questions erupt from that. They might think I'm abusing you."

"But you are abusive," I reply as a joke. The look on his face has me wishing I hadn't said that.

"Is that how you feel?"

I shake my head and approach him quickly, placing my hands on his thick and solid biceps. "No! It was a joke. A poorly timed joke, but a joke nonetheless."

"I am going to be marking you tonight."

"What? You want to mark me? Like, how?" Is he planning on cattle prodding me? I hope it's a payback for my poorly timed joke.

"Bruising," he replies as if he's asking to braid my hair.

"You want to leave bruises on me? But you said you don't like to do that."

"I said I don't like to leave marks that can't be covered and that I would never permanently scar a woman. Bruises in places nobody can see, pleases me."

"I don't plan on using a pool or changing in front of anyone." I wonder if I would have been better off not to tell the truth. He is going to mark me, whatever that entails, I'm sure I won't like it.

He nods and says, "You remember your safewords?" I nod, dropping my hands to my sides once again. "And if you can't talk?"

"I am to shake my head, hands or feet to get your attention."

"Very good."

He takes my left forearm in his hand and walks with me to the end of the bed. I am guided to stand with my butt leaning against the footboard. He cuffs both of my wrists and ankles, and binds them to the frame, leaving them spread wide like a starfish. My feet stand far apart and it's already becoming uncomfortable for my legs.

"Open your slutty mouth." His voice rumbles my chest. Dirty talk. I like it.

I do as he says. A rather large ball is shoved between my jaws. The band is fastened behind my head so I can't spit it out. He stands with his body flush against mine. The heat of his chest warms my neck. He pulls my hair until my head tilts back and he can easily lick my lips. His other hand wraps around my throat, applying enough pressure to quickly change the shade of my face to a deeper red. When he releases me, I pull a deep breath in, through my nose.

I watch as he lifts a towel. I hadn't even noticed it when I left the bathroom. I walked right past it. It was spread across the nearby dresser, covering something. He picks up a few of the objects and walks back to me. He squats down, fiddling with my pussy lips. A harsh pain inside of me, fiercely shoots from my clit up to my bellybutton. It's a clamp, a very tight one. My protest is muffled. I'm sure he planned the ball in my mouth to prevent me from screaming, which would alert the kids to our play. They are asleep and our bedroom door is locked, of course.

He applies weight to the clamp and it fucking hurts! It's a pain that will ease into pleasure once my brain can shut out the world around me, but I'm not even close to that point. He will take me there, I'm sure of it. I welcome it. I crave it.

"Open your eyes," he insists.

As I do, the pleasant sting from the tips of the flogger slap at my tits. I jolt and yelp. The leather tassels lick my skin, quickly turn it pink. I love it and hate it, at the same time.

"Lift your chin," he instructs.

I do as he says, tilting my face toward the ceiling. I try to stay focused, but when the tips of the tassels slap at my breasts and nipples, I cry out, the sound escaping through my nostrils. When he thinks I've had enough, he tosses the flogger onto the bed. His fingers grasp my nipples and pull. I love this. I know that I shouldn't, but I do. The pain shoots straight down to my clit, but by that time, it's as stimulating as if he were caressing it with his fingertips.

He squats and rubs some lube on my asshole before working something into my butt. He slides it in and out a few times and then holds it in. I hear a whooshing sound and feel the object growing inside me. It's getting bigger and bigger. Fuck! My clit is burning, begging to be freed from the clamp or for even the slightest touch. As he stands, his fingers glide on either side of my clit, torturing it sweetly. It hurts like hell when the clamp moves but the tenderness of his touch counteracts my hatred of the ache. He stops touching me, all too soon.

Coach walks to the dresser to collect a stick that's about as long as my arm. It's thin, like a switch one would pluck from a tree, but firmer. He cuts it through the air so quickly, it whistles. My eyes open wide when I realize that he might want to hit me with it. I'm rocking my head back and forth, not enough where he'll think I'm tapping out, but it gets his attention. I need him to explain this new stick he's carrying before he touches me with it.

"This is a rattan cane. It can be very painful, but it can also feel very good. This will likely leave bruises on your skin, if I want it to." I'm still protesting. "If after you've tried it, it's too much and you don't want me to use it anymore, wave your right hand. Do you understand?" I try to say *yes* but I merely manage a mumble.

He glides the cane along my right nipple and then lightly taps it. Strangely, I like it. He taps it again, harder this time. Yes, I enjoy that. Once more, the cane contacts my stiff nipple, harder still. No, I didn't like it, but I can bear it. I lift my right hand but don't wave it, letting him know that I've reached my threshold.

He strokes my right nipple with the cane and then *twap, twap, twap*. Three harsh taps in a row. I'm grunting and gasping. Ouch! Fuck! My hands clench into fists and I try to curl my body, so he won't be able to access my nipple, but it's no use. My range of motion is quite limited. I look at him with anger in my eyes. It's not directed toward him, so much as the cane. He enjoys when I protest.

"You don't like that?" he teases. I grunt, knowing I can't form words. I wouldn't tell him I hate it because I don't. It's strangely arousing.

He reaches between my legs and around the clamp, which hurts like hell when he touches it. His fingers stroke between my labia. He retreats, stuffing his glistening fingers in his mouth and sucking them.

"You have a very wet little cunt," he whispers.

I watch as he picks up some more clamps and weights. He stands in front of me and says, "Take a deep breath."

I do as he says. He pinches my nostrils, preventing me from breathing except for the minute amount of air I can suck around the ball.

He reaches down, taking the painful clamp from my clit ever so slowly. The pain rushes through my whole body, desperate to escape me with a scream, but I can't manage more than a muffled wail. He drops the weighted clamp before slapping my clit with three of his fingers. Holy fuck! My knees buckle, putting strain on my shoulders. I fight to regain my legs beneath me, but he slaps it again before I can. This time, the sensation is a mixture of pain with unbelievable, rock my world, roll my eyes back in my head, kind of thrill.

He taps my clit repeatedly and I'm right on the verge of coming, but I need air. I'm not getting enough from around this ball. His fingers release my nostrils and I immediately exhale the full breath that was burning my lungs. I'm quick to take in more and more air, panting feverishly. I'm there, right there, holding on the edge of a mind-blowing orgasm, but it isn't happening.

It's like when you're on the verge of a sneeze but it just won't come. It's the same sense of urgency, the horrendously wonderful tickle, that mind-numbing need. But, there's no relief, no relief at all. Holy fuck, this is awesome!

My legs are locked straight with my hips shoved forward until my wrists are straining against their bindings. I'm holding perfectly still, breathing and waiting for my body to let go. He taps, over and over, never touching my clit for more than a second. Never letting me have my reward.

Suddenly it stops and he's no longer tapping or touching me in any way. My orgasmic urge is subsiding, and I want it back. I need his touch. I'm begging, pleading with him, with the universe, with every cell in my body.

Something cool slides along my clit. I open my eyes and look down, seeing the cane pushed up between my pussy lips. It feels great; firm and smooth - but there's overwhelming fear that he's going to strike it with the that piece of wood. If it hurts as much as it did on my nipples, I will be waving my hand for him to ease off.

He pulls my labia apart with his free hand and lightly taps the side of my swollen button. It doesn't hurt nearly as much as I thought it would, but then again, his goal isn't to cause me pain. He's stimulating me, bringing more blood to the area to heighten my sensitivity, not that I really need more of that. Again, he taps. I watch the concentration in his expression as he aims his rod on either side of my throbbing clit; one side, then the other, back and forth.

I try to say, "Just touch my clit, please," but the words don't form into anything understandable. A long line of saliva oozes from my bottom lip, barely missing his forearm on its descent to the floor.

"Do you want me to touch you... here?" he asks, pressing the cane on top of my clitoris, moving it back and forth slowly. "Like this? Is this what you want?"

I don't know how long I've been staring into his eyes. The green flecks floating in the brown begin to dance. Maybe I'm simply losing my focus. My mind is definitely whirling from my body's heightened state of arousal. Time is irrelevant to me at this point.

He won't let me cum. This is another session of edging; teasing aimed to take me to the edge of climax, but not allowing me to throw myself into the light, airy, pillowy softness of orgasm. There will be no release, not yet. I would be disappointed if he allowed it so soon. I want to enjoy this for a little while longer.

Coach smiles wickedly as he rises to his feet. I'm begging, which is what he likes me to do. He once told me that to hear a woman beg for her orgasm, is the most enticing way to stroke his ego. He loves the ownership that those pleas bring. I didn't understand at the time, but I get it now. He wants to know he owns my orgasm, my pleasure - me. If only for just that moment, he is my everything. It's a moment he can drag on and on, until he gets his fill.

My thoughts are fleeting, and my body is bound and shaking, but I feel free. Freer than I have in a very long time. Nothing matters except his touch and since I have no control over that, I am nothingness. I am simply here, detached from reality, time, even sound has vanished. My screams leave me but never reach my ears. Can he hear them? Am I indeed screaming?

My muscles jerk hard and I'm snapped back to reality. It's overwhelming to have all of my senses and thoughts slam back into focus, so quickly. I'm shaking so violently. I have to allow myself to hang from my wrists and clear my thoughts, giving my body a moment of stillness.

He returns from the dresser with something in his hand, but I couldn't care less what it is. I just want to go back to the nothingness. But I want to cum too, repeatedly. He straps a vibrating wand to my right upper thigh using a leather belt. He spreads my labia, placing the bulbous end against my clitoris.

With this ball in my mouth, my *thank you Sir* sounds more like *ga-goo-er,* but Coach's smile tells me that he was able to understand. The vibration slowly revs up. Oh. Fuck. Yes.

"You may cum whenever you want, as many times as you want. If you become too loud, I'll shut it off and then it's over. Do you understand?" he whispers with his mouth next to my ear. I'm confused; have I not been incredibly loud already? I was screaming with deafening tones, in my head anyway.

I can only nod my head. My deep chested groans sound more like the purrs from a wilderness cat than from a woman. My asshole suddenly feels even more full. He pumps the balloon again. I had actually forgotten it was still in there. One more pump and I'm so goddamn full! Too full! I wave my hand and try to talk. Instant relief when the balloon deflates quite a bit.

I'm hurdled into the most beautiful euphoria. I'm finally coming. Yes, it's happening! I'm floating, lifting off my feet, slipping out of the bindings that imprison me to the bed frame, and rising up, up, up to the ceiling.

This one doesn't ease as quickly as most orgasms do. This one lingers at the high point, holding me in its clutches. I never want it to end.

Twap! What the fuck? *Twap, twap*. No! Why? Why is Coach drawing my attention to my breasts, away from the glory of my climax? *Twap*! It lands directly on my nipple. I want to scream, not because it hurts, but I'm fucking livid that he stole me away from my well-deserved orgasm.

My clit is painfully sensitive to the vibration. I try to tilt forward and back, left and then right, but neither direction shifts it off my hypersensitive little button. Saliva trails from my chin all the way down my belly, as I continue this battle I cannot win. He made sure I couldn't wiggle away from the wand. He knew I would try.

More punishment from the cane, this time his aim is directed to my left inner thigh. Fuck! I think the sharpness of the sting is worse than it was on my breasts. It's not a sting that stops right away, it tends to linger and burn in strips along my tender flesh.

My clit feels hot, swollen and aching but it's fully aroused yet again. He increases the intensity of the vibration and I'm losing myself to it.

CHAPTER THIRTEEN
Coach

Rayna is coming again, so much harder and more intensely than she usually does. The muscles in her abdomen have been flexed for fifteen minutes now, with no sign of letting up. Her legs and arms are shaking vigorously. Tomorrow, she will feel this night. With every little movement, she'll think of me. She'll curse me, and yet want more of me because of it.

The cane stings her skin with every contact. I love canes. Not as much as the close contact from using my hand, but the lingering effect from the cane, is more dramatic. I've caned women until their skin let go. I won't do that to Rayna. It's not that I wouldn't get off on it; I am a sick fucker. I know Rayna well enough to know she wouldn't appreciate it. Never would I do anything to make her angry at me.

I set the cane on the floor, so I can walk my fingertips along the welted stripes that dance on her breasts as her chest rises and falls. Her creamy globes jiggle from her shakiness, and I can't help myself. I lean in and bite her flesh, not hard, just enough to make her yelp.

I squat in front of her to admire my handiwork on her inner thigh. Five perfectly spaced lines trail down to her mid-thigh. Christ, that's a work of art. I can't say I've ever spaced my cane this consistently. My fingers trail from one line to the next, loving the way the pads of my fingers sense their heat.

My cock is thick and craving to be inside her. I don't even care what orifice I slide into, as long as it's wet and hot.

Her body tenses again, jerking in a spastic manner that seems more alien than human. Her cum is spurting onto the floor each time her pussy spasms. Saliva dribbles down her chin, between her breasts and drains in a slick line toward her clit. A moment after her orgasm ebbs, another wave rolls through her. And then another. And another.

To stop her from holding her breath and losing consciousness completely, I unstrap the belt and pull the cord from the wall plug. I untie her ankles, leaving the cuffs on and then do the same for her wrists. She is so weak that I do not trust her legs to hold her weight. I scoop her up and carry her limp body to the bed and lie her on her back.

She's so weak that her legs fall open, inviting me in. I unzip my pants and pull them down just enough to free my cock and balls. I slam into her pussy and hold still, until she opens her eyes. I want her to know she's with me. The thought that she might be imagining another man makes my jaw clench.

She opens her eyes when I start to unfasten the buckle holding the ballgag in place. Her lids are heavy. She seems to be having a tough time regaining her focus, but she soon manages to meet my gaze.

"Just love me," she whispers with tears streaming from the corners of her eyes.

Her words punch at my heart with a tender cruelty that makes it feel like it's bleeding. How was I to know all she really wanted from me was for me to make love to her? What I just did to her was my way of showing her how much she means to me. Does she not see that? I'm with her now, in her bed, between her legs, and my heart beats only for her. Does she not know that I love her more than I've ever loved anything or anyone, in my entire existence?

"I will love you every second, of every minute, of every day, with every heartbeat my body can manage, until I take my very last breath." I whisper, vowing to be hers for the rest of my days and I can't be any surer that it's what I want. She's what I need.

My lips meet hers. I hold her thigh in one hand while I swoop her other leg between my knees. I slowly fuck her, while pulling her thigh up as close to her chest, as possible. Our mouths taste each other as if it's this one thing that will keep this very moment alive, forever.

My hips lift and lower, rhythmically waving between her split legs. I can feel her pussy tighten around my prick and I doubt I can hold off much longer. I pause to regain my control, but my orgasm is already beginning to erupt into a mind-numbing climax. I ram Rayna into the mattress, hardcore. I own her! No, she owns me!

Coming feels like such a relief, but it hasn't satisfied the tightness inside of me. My cock has yet to soften, in fact, it's painfully hard. I reach down, cupping her welted breast, and caress the hot, lifted skin. Another urge builds quickly. I continue my relentless pounding, fucking her, as fast as I can.

A second rush of hot semen releases, and a wail erupts from the deepest reservoirs in my soul, most likely coming from my inner Demon. He's frustrated that I refuse to let him roam freely during playtime. One day, I'll set him free, but if Rayna can't accept him, it's back in his cage he goes. I had never thought I'd see the day that a woman would mean more to me than my Demon ever could.

I whimper and coo, "I love you! I fucking love you! Oh my god, I fucking love you!"

I collapse onto the right side of Rayna, while still holding my painfully sensitive cock inside of her. Soon it will shrivel and slip free from her. It'll be a sad moment for sure. Being inside of her is the best feeling, ever. I wish we never had to be apart.

A few seconds after it slips free, I roll completely off her and fling my arms up onto the pillow above my head. I grab it and slide it under my heavy head. Rayna curls into me. Her slackened movements prove to me just how tired she is.

"I love you, Coach," she whispers.

I kiss her forehead. "I really do love you, Rayna." I kiss her again, placing my hand on her back to help hold her against me. "If you wanted me to make love to you tonight, why didn't you say so when you came out of the bathroom?"

She does her best attempt to shrug. "You were all dressed. You know I can't turn you down when you look so good."

"Next time, just tell me you would rather make love."

"But this was great, too."

"Just promise."

"Okay, I promise." She pauses for a few moments before breaking the silence that fills the dimly lit room. "Coach, why did you use a cane on me?"

"Because I'm a sick son-of-a-bitch," I laugh, trying to make light of my sadistic, inner asshole, and hope she'll be satisfied with that answer.

"No, I mean, why? Is there a reason why you would want to pick up a cane and use it on someone? I guess I'm asking if the cane has a special significance in your life?"

I pause for a moment before replying, trying to decipher if there is a significance or not. "Nobody has ever asked me that. I don't really know. Canes leave straight lines, welts and sometimes bruises. They can also break skin with just the right swing. It's painful and the cries that follow the high-pitched snapping sound, almost mimics it. Maybe it's all of those reasons or just that I love the feel of the cane in my hand. I really couldn't specify."

Rayna yawns, "It's going to be a long day tomorrow."

"Sleep, my love," I kiss her head and sigh, my eyelids weighing heavily.

She slides off me, under my protest. She laughs, "Let me go, I have to pee."

"Let me pour you a hot bath with some Epsom Salts and lavender oil." I begin to pull my back off the bed, but she puts her hand against my chest and pushes me back. "Are you sure?"

"Yes, I'm fine. My butt cheeks don't hurt anymore. My nipples are still stinging, but they'll be fine. Besides, I'm too tired to sit in a tub. I have a very busy day tomorrow, so I'd rather just sleep."

"Well, if you're sure."

"I'm sure. I'll be right back."

"Don't be long or I'll be asleep," I call out as the soft slaps of her bare feet draw distance between us.

"OH MY GOD!" she nearly yells loud enough for the kids to startle awake.

I leap up and run to the bathroom, nearly falling over the stool at the end of the bed. I hop while limping to ease the ache from a scraped shin. I push open the bathroom door. My eyelids slam shut, protecting my eyes from the brightest light I've ever seen – or so it seems, at this very second.

"What? What's wrong?" I ask while fighting to open my watering eyes.

"This!" she says, pointing to her breasts and thighs. "You fucking bruised me! I have welts. Like, a lot of welts! What if someone sees them?"

"You said you weren't going to be changing in front of anyone and you said you wouldn't be putting on a bathing suit, so you'll be all right." I don't see what the problem is.

She turns her whole body to face me. The look on her face carries anger. "Why? Why would you do this to me?"

I lean against the doorframe, feeling the exhaustion wain on me. "I told you I was going to mark you. You are marked, as I said I would do. What's the problem?"

"What's the problem?" she hisses before turning back to look at herself in the mirror. "This! This is a problem! What if the kids see it?"

"How are the kids going to see it? You're leaving in the morning for the entire weekend. By the time you return, they'll be faded, considerably. I don't understand why you're getting so upset. It's not like I locked a collar on your neck and kept the key hidden from you or bruised your arms so everyone would see. I didn't brand you. Your marks are minimal and will disappear; no harm, no foul."

"No harm, no foul…" her words fall away. She stares at herself, shaking her head. She whispers, "Never again."

Her eyes have yet to meet mine. I think I really fucked up. "So, no more cane. Got it! You're going to be okay. If you could have seen yourself coming when I was creating those lovely welts, you would beg me to do it every day."

Now she turns, staring angrily into my eyes, without blinking. So, this is how the kids feel when Rayna is about to punish them. No wonder they don't like it.

Her finger points at me and shakes. "No! No!"

She pushes past me and into bed without another word. I shut off the light after looking down at my calf to see if it's bleeding. It's not. Slipping under the covers, I look over at Rayna. Her back is to me and she's curled into a ball. I roll, attempting to pull her against me, to comfort her, but she swings her hand back, nearly hitting my balls. So, I can't touch her? This won't do. I grab her shoulder and yank her onto her back.

"Don't touch me!" she hisses.

I flip off the covers and hop on top of her legs, pinning her in place. "We need to talk about this."

"No, we don't. Let me work through it."

"Please, talk to me. You're obviously angry. My question is whether you're angry at me for putting those marks on you or for showing you that you enjoyed receiving them? Are you angry that you agreed to be marked and that you were somewhat excited by the thought of it? But now, seeing your body with the physical reminders of your twisted sexual desires, has you unsure of how to express your emotions? Does being angry at me help with all of that?"

"How do you know how I'm feeling?"

"You are not the only one to experience this. Whatever you tell me, whatever you want to talk about with me... you need to know that I've heard it all before. What you're feeling is normal. You cannot shut me out. If we are going to be in a relationship, I need to know how you feel, where your limits and fears lie. Shutting me out when you are hurting or confused, will not help you. Do you trust me?"

"You know I do."

"Then trust me enough to tell me what is going on in here," I say while tapping her head with my finger.

"You pretty much hit everything on the nail. I don't know how I feel. I mean, feeling it – the cane – was painful and awful, but my body used that to create something so wonderful and powerful. To actually see the horror that got me off, is..."

"Is shocking," I whisper.

"Yes, I suppose that's a good word for it."

I flop down behind her and toss the covers back over me. Hugging her to my body would be exactly what she needs, what I need, but I'm afraid to push her. She might bolt to the sofa downstairs. Rayna likes to keep things in her head, mulling them over and over, until she's come to a conclusion as to whether something is good or bad, healthy or destructive.

"Can I hold you?" I whisper.

"Not tonight," she replies.

I roll onto my back and stare up at the ceiling. The painful beating of my breaking heart is more than I can bear. Fuck! Why am I such an asshole? Whatever possessed me to think it would be okay to mark her? She said it was okay. Maybe I took advantage. I don't know. I can't take the damn silence. She'll be leaving tomorrow morning, likely before we have time to talk about this. Fuck! She can't get on the plane while she's angry with me. What if she decides to leave me forever? No! Oh god no!

The covers pull as I slide off the bed. My feet quickly take me around the bed. I drop to my knees and lay my forehead on the comforter inches from her chest. I feel her lift her head, and then her hand touches the top of my head and I grasp it, holding it in my hair.

"Please, please don't leave me. I won't survive. I need you. I love you. I am yours, always." I can't hide the rawness in my voice. "I'm sorry, Rayna. I'm so sorry. Please, don't leave me."

She leans up on one elbow, wrapping her other arm over my head and down my back. Her cheek rests against mine, pinning my other cheek into the mattress. No words leave her mouth but she's speaking volumes. Rayna isn't leaving me for overstepping her limits. She doesn't hate me.

"I'm not leaving you. I will never leave you. The marks startled me. I wasn't expecting them. They barely even hurt anymore. You'll have to give me some time to decide where I want to set the limit on marking me. Give me time, that's all I'm asking."

"Okay, I can give you all the time you need. If you don't hate me, why won't you let me hold you? As a dominant, it's my job to ensure my submissive is physically, mentally and emotionally secure. You refused me that. I thought you hated me."

She shakes her head slightly, "I don't hate you. I could never hate you. Now, get into bed and hold me, so we can sleep. I need to sleep, so I'm not too tired for the flight tomorrow morning."

I nod and stand up, quickly making my way back into bed. My nerves are settling, but my head is all over the place. I shouldn't be questioning my actions, especially since she didn't call out her safeword. She shouldn't be angry at me after the fact, but she is angry, and that worries me. What the fuck is this woman doing to me?

* * * * *

I happen to catch the concerned expression on Rayna's face when I open the bedroom door. She turns away from the mirror, pretending she wasn't just staring at her brownish-purple, cylindrical bruises. The fake smile she wears is aimed to deter me away from what I just saw, it does not reach her eyes.

"Are you almost ready to go?" I ask her.

"Ah, yeah, I think so," she says while scratching her forearm, still sporting the makeshift happy expression.

"Do you want to talk about it?" I ask her.

She shakes her head and turns away from me. I know she wants to get dressed, but that means she would have to remove her nightgown. I'll see her body when she does. Instead of giving her privacy, I wait silently.

"Can I get dressed?" she asks.

"Of course," I reply. "Do you need any assistance?"

"Of course not!" she shrugs. "Maybe the kids need you?"

"Rayna," I whisper, as I slowly approach her. "It's okay to take off your nightgown. I've already seen the marks. Just now, when I opened the door, you were looking at them. Show me, love."

She grimaces, "Well, I suppose since you were the one who marked me, you should be entitled to savour the moment."

Her nightie falls to the floor in a heap. Her eyes are locked on mine, I can feel them. She's waiting to see if I lick my lips or show any sign of arousal. It's important that I don't. My eyes meet hers and I just look at them.

Stoically, I ask, "So, what do you think of them?"

She shrugs, "I don't know. They're bruises that you inflicted upon me, so I'm supposed to be upset about that. But I can admire the skill it takes to apply the cane as uniformly as you did, to create the perfect spacing between the stripes. I also remember how incredibly painful it was and how I used that pain to heighten my senses, bringing forth one of the most powerful orgasmic experiences of my life. So, to be completely honest, I'm not sure how I want to feel. Choosing one emotion over the other, is impossible."

"I can understand that. Are you angry with me?"

"No, because I know how much it would hurt you if I was and how unfair that would be of me. I said you could mark me, I can't deny that. If I told you to never do that again, I know you wouldn't. That's how I know how much you love me. If I asked you to, I believe you would give up all of it, for me."

"I would," my words follow a harsh swallow. I don't have to tell her that I'd be miserable because of it. We both know the truth.

"But you'd be very unhappy, in turn, making me unhappy. I don't want you to stop introducing me to new things. Just promise me that you will never bruise my skin again, not like this anyway. Accidents happen, but this is purposefully done to mark me, and I don't like it."

I take her in my arms and hold her cool skin against me. "I promise to never mark your body on purpose, ever again. I will not cane you or do anything else that might taint your skin. This, I vow to you."

She pulls back and meets my eyes. "I didn't say I didn't enjoy the cane and the pain it produced. I just don't want the bruises. Maybe you shouldn't do it so hard next time."

"Next time? You liked it enough for me to do it again? But you just said…" I step away, scratching my head. "You don't want me to mark you, but you enjoyed the pain you received when being marked. Okay, I think I understand. I will have to think of alternative ways to create the same effect. Challenge accepted."

She smiles shyly before beginning to get dressed, not once looking back into the mirror until she's fully clothed. I have been watching her. I've tried not to, but I'll admit that I'm a sick fuck and I want to touch the marks, lick them and then drop her to the floor and fuck her hard to relieve my deep-rooted ache for release. I won't do all of that, because I don't know how she'd react; badly, I'd bet.

"Did you enjoy looking at them?" she asks.

I reply, "I'd rather you not ask me that question. I'm sure you already know the answer." I watch Rayna's eyes drop to my crotch. I'd be lying to her if I tried to deny my arousal.

"Do you want to hit me again?"

I furrow my brow. "No, I want to lick them, touch them and then fuck you hard. Is that what you want to hear?"

"I just want to know what you're thinking, that's all," she whispers.

"I'm remembering how the cane felt in my hand. The way you flinched from the contact. The pain behind your muffled screams. The way you became quiet as you bravely absorbed the pain. How hard you came and how often. How wet you were. The way your limp body felt heavy in my arms afterward." I look up at her and take a deep breath.

Rayna walks over to me and takes my hand, leading me to the bathroom. She locks the door behind us and pulls down my sweatpants. My prick springs forth, hard and dripping with precum. She rolls the end of her finger over the slit, lubricating the end of my cock with my own slickness.

She pulls down her pants, yanking them off one foot. After sliding her butt onto the counter, she spreads her legs, leaning her back against the mirror. "Fuck me. Admire your handiwork."

Is she serious? I don't care! I want her, she's offering, I'm taking!

I push forward, burying my prick deep into her pussy. It's surprisingly wet. My eyes watch the marks on her inner thighs dance each time I hump into her. I want to cum and it's only been a few seconds.

Rayna lifts her blouse and bra, revealing the bruised stripes on her breasts. I fuck into her three more times, it's all I can do to bear it. My orgasm overwhelms me, forcing my eyes closed while I spill my seed deep inside of her. I'm still jerking when my eyelids slowly open.

She's looking at me with a curious expression. "You really got excited when you saw the bruises, didn't you?"

"Yes, I did." I feel slightly humiliated. Was that her objective; to make me feel like shit? "I'm sorry that I'm such a sick fuck."

"You aren't a sick fuck. You are a bit strange and not what I'm used to, but you can't help being who you are, and you certainly can't prevent what turns you on. We'll work around it, okay?"

I nod and smile. My shrivelling prick slips from her semen drenched pussy, making me shutter. She finds it to be humorous. I snicker and then rinse off using the washcloth I left in the sink earlier. She points her finger toward the door, impatiently waiting for me to leave before she sits on the toilet to let my seed drain from her.

I stand outside the closed bathroom door. "Really? You still won't pee in front of me? I have licked and loved every inch of your body, but this makes you uncomfortable?"

"No, I won't. If you have a fetish for urination, don't ever tell me. That's a deal breaker for me. Now, go away!"

"I'll keep that in mind. Okay, you'd better hurry, your ride will be here in fifteen minutes."

"I would have been ready if you hadn't distracted me. Now leave me alone."

I walk through the bedroom and into the hallway. The idea of being without Rayna for two whole nights, already has me feeling lonely and she hasn't even left yet. I'll have to keep myself busy with the kids. Maybe I'll show up in Las Vegas and surprise her. Hmm, I'll have to give that some thought.

"Hey kids! If you get ready for school and don't miss the bus, we'll have pizza and beer tonight!" I yell out as I make my way toward the kitchen to see if the kids are eating their breakfast

I hear Rayna yell something about *no beer*, but the kids are talking and laughing too loud for me to hear what she said. I got their attention, and that's a good thing.

"Don't get your panties in a bunch. I'm referring to root beer! What do you take me for? Huh?" I yell back to tease her. She mumbles something else, but I'm walking into the kitchen now, so I don't even try to strain my ears. I roll my eyes dramatically and say, "Moms! Right?" They laugh even harder.

* * * * *

Rayna slips into the passenger's seat while Dr. Jessik tucks her suitcase in the trunk. He waves and I nod. Something about that guy has me not trusting him.

It's obvious to me that he has a thing for Rayna. I wonder if she has a clue. She might think he's a shy man and is awkward around everyone. Maybe it's just that I don't know him all that well, or maybe he's especially timid around me for a reason. He's not Rayna's type, at least, I don't think he is. She doesn't like men who are quiet and reserved, like this guy is. Still, I wonder what his intentions are.

The kids hop on the bus shortly after Rayna leaves with Dr. Suspicious. As I'm getting in my truck, I call Renee, not that I like talking to her.

"Hello," she answers on the first ring.

"Hey, Rayna just left."

"So, you're calling me because?" she questions.

"What would you say about watching the kids while I surprise Rayna in Vegas? I can leave after dinner tonight."

She's quiet for a moment. "Yeah, I don't think that's a good idea."

"Why not?"

She scoffs, "Why do you think? Think about it for half a second. What do you think she's going to say when you suddenly show up at her work convention?"

"Hello, is a good start."

"You're such a dumbass!" she says, irritating the hell out of me. "She's going to think you don't trust her."

"That's not it at all. I want to surprise her, in a good way. She'll be thrilled to see me."

She laughs purposefully because she knows how much I hate her smartass attitude. "She'll send you back home. Why don't you just let her be? Seriously, can your dick not manage to have one fucking night without shoving it into her? Why can't you just jerk off, like most men do?"

That's all I can handle of her shitty attitude. I hang up, thoroughly pissed off. She's such a bitch, especially with me. I have been nothing but respectful of her since she started living with my best buddy, Tim. She's been a total bitch to me ever since I turned her down when she made a pass at me, and then made light of it so Rayna wouldn't be angry at her. She's nice as pie when somebody is within earshot.

If I threw her over a table and fucked her hard, I'm sure she'd soften up to me, but that'll never happen. She irritates me so much that I'd tease the hell out of her after beating her ass red hot, and then I'd fuck her backside until she wet herself. I won't, because I respect Rayna and Tim too much. But, fuck, I want to teach that cunt some fucking respect.

My workouts today are going to be rough. I hope my clients are ready for me. I'll make sure to workout heavy so I can let off some steam before the first person shows up.

CHAPTER FOURTEEN
Rayna

My seat on the plane is next to Dr. Jessik. I wonder if he conveniently arranged for me to be beside him, crammed against the window. I cannot easily escape to the bathroom unless I slide over him with my ass inches from his face. Why we are sitting together, has me scratching my head. Wouldn't it make more sense to have Jennifer and I sitting together, leaving the doctors to talk shop? This new seating arrangement isn't typical. Jennifer gazes my way with a frown and I wonder if her seatmate will take offense. I take notice of the pout I'm wearing and do my best not to look so disappointed.

Most of my time on the flight is spent reading. Renee gave me a book about a woman having an affair with her boss. I sure hope Dr. Jessik hasn't read it. He might think I'm giving him a hint. He is busy reading too, but I've noticed that he hasn't flipped the page in about ten minutes. He must be lost in thought.

"Rayna, would you like a drink?"

"Yes, actually. White wine would be perfect."

He leaves, returning a few moments later with two drinks. After handing me a plastic cup half filled with wine, he takes his seat.

"Thank you, Dr. Jessik."

"Rayna, please call me Ray. You're always so formal with me."

"Oh, I didn't know you preferred to have me call you by your first name. It's strange that I never thought to ask you." He seems a bit put off by my comment. I should say something else. "I suppose I just respect you too much to call you anything other than Dr. Jessik."

He smiles, "Thank you, Rayna. It's nice of you to say that. I want you to think of me as a friend, not just your boss. We are friends, aren't we?" he asks with a nervous tick in his left eye.

"Yes, we are." We hardly speak for the rest of the flight, other than a few common pleasantries.

When we get to the hotel, the four of us have rooms next to or across the hall from each other. It's convenient for when we are expected to attend a function together. This way we can arrive as a group.

The first thing I do is text Coach to let him know I arrived safely and my room number. He doesn't respond, so I unpack and take a quick shower to liven myself up. The flight was torturously boring, to say the least. The book wasn't very interesting and the few short conversations between Ray and I, fell flat. I slip on my jeans and red blouse, fix my make-up and brush out my hair. After checking my phone again and not seeing a response from Coach, I make my way to Jennifer's room. She is talking to her mom on the phone, when she opens the door for me.

I flop on her bed, propping a pillow behind my back so I can sit up comfortably. She rolls her eyes and waves her hand, as if to urge her mother to finish talking. I can picture the future, when my kids are talking to me and doing the same thing, and it irks me.

She hangs up and drops her phone on her bed. "So, what's new with you?"

"Not much. I wish we could have sat together on the plane."

"No kidding! Dr. Myri is so uninteresting that I drifted off to sleep a dozen times while he was talking. Golf! Fucking golf! The man has nothing better to do in life than chase a tiny white ball around a field? Really? The man needs to find a woman, or another man, no judgement! He needs to get laid! Seriously, his life is so dull."

"He must like the monotony," I laugh, because she's right. I've been stuck talking to him and it's always about golf. Dr. Myri has never been married nor seems all too interested in being with anyone. Nobody knows his sexual orientation, but everyone has their opinion. He's a nice enough person, just dull as fuck.

"So, you left that hot, young thing alone for an entire weekend just so you can come to Vegas for a boring dental convention? What's wrong with you?" she says while I shrug. "You could have at least brought him, so I'd have something interesting to stare at while I'm here."

"He's staying with the kids," I tell her. I'm pretty sure I'm blushing.

She looks at me and then rolls her eyes. "Get a sitter! Dammit woman! This is Las Vegas, home of sin. Then again, maybe you want to sin all on your own this weekend. As the saying goes, *what happens in Vegas...*" she waves her eyebrows.

I laugh, "No, I'm not here to misbehave. I'm here to schmooze with the big-wigs of the dental community."

"Tell me honestly, is he as good in bed as I would imagine any fit, strong, sexy, younger man should be?"

I slap her arm and blush even more, "Yes, he's incredible, and that's all I'm saying about that topic. What about you? Are there any hot men in your life?"

She shrugs, "No, not anyone special. Maybe I'm just afraid to settle down with anyone in case something better comes along."

"Well, just remember, age is catching up with you. Soon you'll be my age and finding a good man gets harder as we get older. More of them are taken, the good ones anyway, and the rest want younger women. Find a man that you can love and not want to smother in his sleep. There are no such thing as real-life fairy tales. Relationships can be hard sometimes, but very rewarding too."

"Okay, enough dragging me down the depression hole for one evening. I brought this!" she announces, holding up a bottle of Tequila.

Before I can protest, she's pouring us each a shot in the disposable plastic cups stacked up by the coffee maker. She hands one to me and then taps my cup with hers. We slug it back and wince. She immediately refills them. We chug that one too. I hold my hand over the rim of the flimsy cup, refusing to allow her to pour me another shot.

By the time the doctors rap on her door, I'm already feeling a bit lightheaded. This is going to be a short night if I don't get some food in me soon.

The four of us eat at the restaurant we always eat at when we first arrive. It's only a ten-minute walk. Before returning back to the hotel, Jennifer and I decide to do a little shopping at some of the local stores, while the doctors attend a meeting meant just for dentists. Later, we meet up with some of the other convention attendees in the pub on the main floor of our hotel. The drinks start off light and go down slowly, but as the evening wears on, the drinks start to take their toll.

At eleven-thirty, I decide that I've had enough. Jennifer wants to party on, so I start to make my way down the corridor to the elevators alone. I stumble and reach for the wall, surprised when my hand doesn't touch it. Someone has their arm around my waist. I turn to see a swaying Dr. Jessik.

"Hey, Dr. J, I mean Dr. Ray. Wait, no, it's just Ray, right?" I'm giggling like a drunken fool. Who am I kidding? I am a drunk fool.

"Are you all right Rayna?"

"Oh yeah! I'm great! How are you... Ray?"

"I'm just fine. I'm going to walk you to you room."

"Don't be ridiclll... ridiclll... silly. I'm fine! Go... party on dude! Life is short. You need to get laid! We all need to get laid more often. I mean, shit! I shouldn't talk like that in front of you. You're my boss!" I start laughing, but I don't know why. I'm more intoxicated than I should be when talking about such a private topic, especially in the presence of my boss.

He escorts me into the elevator and pushes the button to our floor. I try to focus on the numbers above the doors, but they are just a bright green blur. When the elevator stops, my knees waiver but I grasp the railing to steady myself. I am so fucked up! I should know better than to try to keep up to Jennifer. She's a seasoned drinker who loves hanging out at the local bars in search of the perfect man.

I stumble down the hall while laughing and dancing, or at least, my drunken attempt to dance elegantly. I'm sure it's anything but.

"Do you want to come in?" I ask when we arrive at my room. I'm not sure why I'm inviting him in. I probably shouldn't.

"Rayna, as much as I would love nothing more, I think I should not enter your room. You are quite drunk, and therefore, might do something you'll regret in the morning."

"Okay, problem solved," I say when I push my door all the way open and flip the doorstop down to prevent the door from closing. "See, you'll be safe now."

He reluctantly follows me in and sits on the sofa chair. "Whisky, vodka, rum... what do you like?" I ask while searching through the minibar for the small bottle of white wine I had my eye on earlier.

"I'm fine, thank you."

"Nope, you have to pick one."

"Whisky," he replies.

After tossing it to him, I crack the bottle of wine and take a swig, directly from the bottle. I flop in the other sofa chair and smile at him. He's still blurry.

"Ray, are you happy?" I ask him.

He clears his throat and then opens his tiny bottle. "Not especially. I'd like to be happier, but we don't always get what we think we deserve."

"And what do you think you deserve?"

He smiles, but it fades quickly. "I like you Rayna. I wish you were mine, but I understand that you're with him and I wish you the best."

"Thank you," I reply, not entirely sure what I'm thanking him for.

"I just hope he's good to you."

I start giggling when I think about what he did to me last night. "Oh, he treats me good. I mean, it's bad sometimes, but I like it. I like him. I really like him. We're getting married... eventually. I don't know why I haven't picked a day yet. He stopped asking me about it. Maybe I'm just gun-shy about getting hitched again. I don't know. It didn't work out so well for me the first time. Why am I telling you all of this?"

"What do you mean by it's bad sometimes?"

"Well, he's... he's kind of... he's rough around the edges."

"Does he hurt you?"

"No, no, it's not like that. I mean, yeah, sometimes, but it's not what you think. Why can't I stop talking? I shouldn't be telling you this stuff. It's private between him and I."

"I don't mean to pry. I just need to know if he's hurting you."

I smile at him and lick my lips. "Listen, he hurts me in ways that I like. He would never do anything I didn't want him to do. He asks and I either condone or dismiss. I have the final say. I hold all the power in our sexual relationship. He might be the aggressor, but it's about me. It's all about me."

"I would never hurt you. Nobody should ever hurt you."

"That would get very boring. Don't you think? I'm sorry, I'm not trying to insult you. I'm not normally a bitch. I'm not, I promise."

"You're one of the most intelligent, caring, thoughtful people I have ever met. Bitch isn't a title you could carry very well." He takes a deep breath, letting it out slowly. "Rayna, don't let him hurt you."

I had better explain before he calls the cops to tell them Coach has been beating me. "Ray, he's a dominant and I'm his submissive. I hold all the power. I used to think a woman who let a man do what he wanted to her, no matter what it was, was stupid and powerless.

It's quite the opposite. I allow him to do the things he does. If I say no, it's a no. He taught me that I am incredibly strong. I will forever be grateful to him for that. You don't have to worry about me. I am going to be just fine, whether he's in my life or not. He loves me and will always protect me from harm."

"Just because he saved your life, doesn't mean you owe him anything."

"Dr. Jessik, Ray, I know that. I love him. I really do. He's good for me."

He swallows down the last sip of whiskey from the small bottle and slowly puts the cap back on. "Well, I'm always here for you. If you ever need to talk or need protection, I'll do what I can."

"Protection?" I ask.

"From him," he whispers. "Judging by what you're telling me, he's going to really hurt you one day. I just hope he doesn't hurt your kids."

"You haven't listened to me at all, have you? He loves my kids and I trust him with their safety. I trust him with my life and the lives of my children. Don't you dare, even for a minute, think he will ever hurt them."

"I'm sorry, Rayna, I just don't understand," he says as he stands and makes his way toward the open door.

"Do something for me?"

"Anything."

"Do some research on BDSM before you pass judgement on my lifestyle. You can't make an informed opinion if you aren't first informed."

"Get some sleep. We have a long day tomorrow," he says before gently kicking the doorstop to dislodge it, as he walks out. The door swings shut with a slam, locking automatically.

Why the fuck did I tell him all of that? I'm not a great secret keeper when I've been drinking. Maybe that's why my ex-husband used to get me drunk and then ask me a hundred questions; questions he knew I would never answer if I were sober.

I pick up my phone. I had forgotten to take it with me to the bar, after having tossed it on the bed with all the new clothes I bought. I squint to read the text message lighting up the screen. It's a message from Coach saying that he's sorry he didn't get my text earlier. I video call him. It rings twice before he answers.

"Hi love. What time is it?" He sounds groggy and it's dark on the screen.

"Oh shit! Sorry! It's around midnight here so that would make it about three AM there. I shouldn't have woken you. I wasn't... I didn't even think about the time." My words are very slurred, and my eyelids feel heavy.

"Rayna, are you drunk?"

"Yeah, a little bit. Are you mad at me?"

"Why would I be mad at you? Are you in your room with the door locked?"

"Yeah, Ray locked it when he left. Well, he kicked that door thingy thing and it shut, so it's locked now."

"You had a man in your room, and you're drunk?"

"Yeah, no... it's just Ray. Dr. Jessik is a nice man. He's nice. Like, he likes me so he's, you know, nice to me. He walked me back to my room to make sure I got back safely. See, he's nice!"

"But he was in your room, alone, while you're drunk," he says with an angry tone.

"Yeah, but he's a nice guy, like I just explained to you. Are you mad at me? Why?" I'm beginning to get upset.

"I don't want men in your room when you're drunk, Rayna."

"What are you, my father?"

"Rayna, don't push me."

"Don't push me," I mock him. "He was a perfect gentleman. We had a drink, chatted and he left. And now I'm calling you but you're kind of being a jealous dick and I don't like it."

"A jealous dick?" he asks. "Rayna, you need to go to bed now. This conversation isn't going in a good direction and you're about to say something that pisses me off."

"Yeah?" I say with a smirk. "Would you like to throw me over your knee and spank my ass like you did at the mansion? That fucking hurt! It was okay, I guess."

He's quiet, other than his breathing. "Yes, I want to punish you for getting drunk and bringing a man into your hotel room with you. Yes, I am jealous, but I am more concerned for your safety than my emotions. Do you not understand how badly your decision could have played out?"

"Well, I guess it worked out just fine, didn't it? I'm safe, talking to you and not in his arms. You're going to have to realize that I can take care of myself. I don't always need you to swoop in and rescue me."

"I did need to rescue you, or did you forget?"

Now I'm fucking angry. "That asshole took me and hurt me because of you, not because of anything I did. He was your friend, whom I had never even met. He never would have even known who I was if you hadn't told him. So, you can blame yourself for that, not me."

"I do, Rayna, every day." I can hear the sadness in his voice and instantly regret saying what I said.

"I'm sorry. I know you do and it's not your fault. I don't blame you. Look, I'm going to let you go because I'm drunk and I'm talking just to hear myself talk. I don't mean to be cruel or to pick a fight. I love you, and I miss you."

"I was going to hop on a plane and surprise you, but your sister suggested I don't."

I snicker, "She's a wise woman. I would have accused you of not trusting me."

"That's what she said," he replies. I'm sure he hates to admit that she was right. "All right, love, sleep it off. Call me tomorrow, okay?"

"I will. I love you!"

"I love you, too!"

After hanging up, I flop back on the bed. That's when my stomach wretches. I make it to the toilet just in time for the first wave of vomit. I spend the next few hours hanging onto the toilet seat for dear life. At one point, I contemplate my sudden death as being an easier way out of this situation. I will survive this night.

CHAPTER FIFTEEN
Rayna

The rest of the weekend was uneventful in comparison to the first night. Ray was still sociable with me, but I could feel the tension between us. He hadn't said anything else about our chat until we were getting back on the plane to come home.

As we lined up to wait for our turn to enter the plane, he whispered in my ear, "I did some research, as you suggested. I have a better understanding but it's not for me."

"I appreciate that. Thank you," I told him.

He added, "Just know that I'm here for you if you ever want to talk."

When I turned to look at him, it was the first time I had noticed just how green his eyes are. They were quite stunning. "Thank you."

"I won't tell anyone anything you told me, so you don't have to worry about that."

"I appreciate that," I replied as I stepped into the plane.

* * * * *

The flight home seemed quick, probably because I drifted off to sleep, shortly after takeoff. The drive to my house seems to drag on twice as long as it should. I need to see my kids. It sounds strange, but I miss the smell of their hair. I wonder if other mother's miss that when they're apart from their offspring. I miss Coach too, but for different, more adult reasons. I also miss his hugs and how I disappear in them. There is no place on Earth where I feel safer, than in his arms.

* * * * *

It's been three days since I returned home, and life is back to normal. Coach has ravished me every night. He even gave me oral sex this morning before we got out of bed. He feels guilty for coming down on me, while I was away, but I don't mind. I'm reaping the rewards of his ample apologies. I've had a hop in my step all day because of this morning.

We sit down at the dinner table and begin dishing food onto our plates. Kim tells us all about her day at school. I finally have to tell her to start eating because her food is getting cold and the rest of us are mostly finished. Ken doesn't say much except that he has an algebra test in the morning that he's worried about. He turned down my offer to help him because he knows I suck at algebra. Coach admits that he hated algebra and wouldn't be of much help to him, in fact, likely hindering him.

"Rayna, go on a date with me Saturday night," Coach insists more than asks.

"A date? Where would you like to go?"

"How about the same place I took you last time we had a date?"

My eyes shoot to the kids to gauge their reactions, as if they somehow know about Fallen, but they aren't paying us much attention. I look back at him and nod, raising my eyebrows excitedly. A wide smile erupts on his face that overcomes his eyes, pinching them closed almost completely.

"Say, eight o'clock?" he poses.

"That sounds great. I can ask Renee if she'll babysit."

"I can babysit Kim," Ken interrupts. So, they were listening in on our conversation after all.

"I don't know about that," I reply.

Coach adds, "Yeah, I think it might be too much."

"I'm almost fourteen!" he hisses. "None of my friends have babysitters anymore."

Coach is looking at me, waiting for me to decide. They aren't his children. He won't tell me what to do when it involves them, unless he thinks I'm making the wrong choice, and then he'll still pull me aside to say his peace.

"Fine," I finally reply, after making them wait until I can sift through all the possible things that could go wrong. "I'll make sure Aunt Renee will have her phone readily available, in case you need her. Promise me you won't hesitate to call her if you get scared or something doesn't feel right."

"We promise," they both say simultaneously, and a lot more excitedly than I would like them to be. I still have a tickly sensation at the pit of my belly. I think that's normal for parents who are about to leave their children home alone at night, for the first time.

Coach is looking at me with no expression at all. I can't read what's on his mind. I widen my eyes slightly as if to ask him what's on his mind. He quietly watches me for another full minute without so much as a facial tick, making me rather anxious.

He finally whispers, "I'll work it out."

Oh, shit! I hadn't even thought about the fact that they'll be home when we come back from a highly sexualized night of voyeurism, aroused to the point of wanting to ravish one another in a loud, moaning, screaming, growling physical attack, like two uncivilized beasts. If the kids are home, we'll need to remain very quiet, which I hate doing when we're that aroused. I can't go back on my decision now.

What does he mean he'll work it out? Is he going to gag me with the ball again, so that I can't scream? I don't like it when he covers my mouth and nose, preventing me from making any noises, because I can't breathe. I cum very powerfully when he restricts my breathing, but I still don't like the sensation of fire in my lungs.

We climb into bed after what feels like a really long day. The kids are asleep with their doors closed and we are snuggled up under the lightweight comforter, warming our cool skin against one another. My hand glides down his washboard abs in search of his cock. I want him inside me, whether that means in my mouth, pussy or ass, I don't care.

Coach grabs my wrist before I can grasp his manhood. He pulls it up to his mouth and places tender kisses on its palm.

"Love, I want us to wait for satisfaction until Saturday night."

"What?" I ask, not sure I'm hearing him correctly.

He snickers, "I want you to wait until we go to Fallen."

"Why?" I ask while pouting.

"Trust me, it'll be more fun when you're desperate for release."

"I don't like it but, fine, I'll go along with your little experiment." I snicker, knowing I can use my showerhead when he isn't around.

"No masturbation either," he announces, as if he were reading my thoughts.

I groan with disappointment, but nod anyway. "Fine, no masturbation either. Why do you want me to wait?"

"You'll see. Now get some sleep," he whispers, after kissing my forehead.

CHAPTER SIXTEEN
Coach

I plan to introduce Rayna to something new this Saturday, but I don't want to make her uncomfortable in the process. An easy introduction is what I'm hoping for. Would I love to tie her up to an iron cross, flog her after weighting her pussy lips, fuck her with my hand and make her cum in gushing waves, all while a crowd of people watch on, speaking in hushed tones? Yes, I would! But Rayna isn't ready for such an adventure, just yet. She may never be.

To help me with this, I secretly met with Gear, yesterday. We hashed out a scenario that will both entice Rayna and satisfy her, without throwing her into the deep end, so to speak. The last thing I want to do is scare her off.

It's finally Saturday afternoon and we've just finished the weekly house cleaning, laundry and grocery shopping. Now we'll relax before getting ourselves ready to attend Fallen. I've already snuck my leathers into the car, along with the outfit I bought for Rayna. She has no idea that I went shopping without her, for her. Every time I think about her wearing what I bought, my cock stiffens. Of course, not having any release for the past three days hasn't made it easy to keep my cock from springing forth when I see a hot chick bent over at the gym, with her firm, round ass jutting into the air, begging to be spanked. Needless to say, I've been hiding out in my office a lot more than usual.

I'm sitting on the sofa downstairs watching a show about racing cars, when Rayna straddles my lap. She wraps her arms around my neck and starts kissing me with a heated passion that she's avoided since I asked her not to orgasm. I slide my hands around her hips and grip her ass firmly. She starts grinding her pussy against my swelling cock, as if she's actually fucking me.

She lets out a soft moan and I can't resist her. I grab her under the arms and toss her onto her back on the cushion, quickly slamming my hips between her thighs. She lets out another moan as my mouth presses to her. I grasp her wrists and yank them over her head, joining them in my right hand, pinning them. With my free hand, I quickly reach up her shirt and yank her breasts free from her bra. I pinch her nipple with enough force that she winces and tries to wiggle away. My mouth relentlessly abuses hers, forcibly tongue raping her.

I slide my hand beneath the waistband of her yoga pants and make haste toward her pussy. I surpass her clit completely, not giving her the satisfaction of even a graze. Instead, I slide two fingers into her drenched hole and bury them deep. She softly moans, lifting her hips to allow me easier access. I fuck her while stretching my fingers apart each time I pull back. I'm straining her opening and she's becoming very aroused by it. I'm getting to know Rayna's body very well; what urges her closer to orgasm and what turns her off. I love watching her expressions and the clues that provides.

I pull my hand from her pants and shove my fingers into her mouth, forcing her to taste her own juices. She stares up at me as she sucks my digits deep into her mouth, lapping at them until all of her flavour is gone. I release her wrists and stand up without so much as another touch.

"You should call your sister to make sure she's going to answer her phone if the kids call tonight." I reach into my sweatpants and shift my throbbing cock to a less straining position. Her eyes are shifty.

"What the fuck?" she says.

"What the fuck, what?" I reply, playing dumb.

"Um, why did you stop?"

I chuckle as I'm walking away. "I asked you not to enjoy yourself until tonight, or did you forget?"

"Oh, come on! That's not fair!" she says as she chases after me.

"You started it, woman!" I laugh as I run up the stairs taking two at a time.

"You're an ass!" she laughs as she runs to keep up. She almost has me by the time we're almost at our bedroom.

Ken steps out of his room, nearly getting himself lambasted by me. Ken squeals and ducks back into his room, but it's too late. Fearful that I'm going to take him out, I leap to the side, slamming myself into the doorframe of the bathroom. I just barely avoided him. Fuck, that hurt!

Rayna runs around me to make sure Ken is all right. I'm happy to know he's fine but my face really fucking hurts. She turns to check on me and that's when Kim whips open her door with eyes wide, fearing that the house might be falling down outside of her bedroom.

I touch my face when I feel the warmth of blood running from my nose and upper lip. Yup, that's blood all right! Kim is just standing in her doorway, unsure of what's happening.

Ken keeps saying, "I'm sorry. I didn't know you were coming this way. Why were you running?"

Rayna pushes me into the bathroom and wets a washcloth with cold water and applies it to my lip. "Wow, you really hit that wall hard!"

I turn and look at Ken to reassure him. "Little man, it wasn't your fault. Let this be a lesson to you kids not to run in the house."

Kim adds, "We already know that lesson. Why were *you* running?"

Seems right to retort to her sassy comment in a childish way. I reply, "Because your mom was chasing me, of course!"

Rayna and I are laughing but the kids are too concerned over the blood to find the humour in my immaturity. Oh well, I tried to break the tension.

I look in the mirror and notice a split in my lip and a red mark on my nose, but it isn't so bad. I've had much worse than this, from fighting when I was young and stupid.

"I think you're going to be okay." Rayna has stopped examining my cut and is now pinching my nose, which has me grimacing at her. "Oh, don't be such a big baby!"

"Big baby? Is that a hit at my age or a simple coincidence?" I'm joking, of course. She simply rolls her eyes and shakes her head. "Hey, little man, you okay?"

"Yeah, I'm fine! Are you?"

"Oh sure, I'm good! If your mom gives my boo-boo a kiss it'll heal right up." When I pucker my lips, I can feel it swelling. It hurts. I don't like pain. I love giving it, but not having it myself. It's rather sadistic to say, but that's how it is.

She puts her hand on my chest and shakes her head. "Um, no! You're still bleeding. Hold that cloth to your lip. Kim, can you get the ice bag from the freezer, please?"

"The blue one?" she asks. I nod so she heads to the kitchen.

Rayna insists, "Sit on the toilet and let me get a better look at it."

I take a seat just as Kim returns with the squishy ice pack and hands it to me. "Thank you, angel."

Rayna is examining the cut on my lip and I can't help but think about how much I love her and these kids. Had I smashed into him, he would have some serious injuries; broken bones or some internal bleeding. He's getting taller but he's so thin and well, I definitely am not. I'm a tank! So, I'm relieved, so very relieved, Ken is unharmed.

"Yup, you're going to live! Of course, I can go get my needle and thread and stitch it up for you if you'd like. Maybe we should heat up a scalpel and cauterize it. Or, I could just punch you on the other side of your lip to even out the swelling." I know she's joking around. I've heard her say similar things to the kids when they are wounded.

"I think the ice will be enough but thanks." I stand up and give her a quick hug but reach out and grab Ken, pulling him into a hug. "I'm so glad you're not hurt!"

He wraps one arm around me and says, "Nah, I'm good. Sorry you got hurt. You can really move fast for a big guy. I thought for sure I was a gone-er!"

We both chuckle but it's more of a relieved reaction than anything. Rayna scoots the kids back to what they were doing but Ken doesn't head back to his room.

"I have to use the bathroom. That's why I was walking into the hallway in the first place. I can't believe I didn't pee my pants when I saw you coming at me."

"Wow! That's a strong bladder you have, little man. I'm not so sure I would have held my waters if I saw something my size coming at me." He nods and closes the door after we've left the room.

In the bedroom, Rayna sits on the bed and takes a deep sigh of relief. I sit beside her and take her hand in mine, the other still holding the ice pack to my face. We just sit here for several minutes, silently contemplating a thank you to the universe for me not being half a second faster. Had I been one step ahead, I would have crushed him, and we wouldn't be sitting here right now, grateful for his safety.

"I'm going to take a bath. Funny how quickly a mood can change, isn't it?"

I nod and reply, "Fuck me! I saw him and…" I stop to swallow the lump in my throat. "That scared the hell out of me!"

"Me too!" she says and then pats my hand before letting it go. I watch as she makes her way to the bathroom and starts the water pouring. As the door closes, I lie back and rest the ice pack on my mouth and nose and close my eyes.

"Hey big man." The sweetest voice pulls me from the silence of sleep.

For a moment, I had forgotten about the ice pack until it starts to slide off. I toss it aside and grab Rayna, yanking her towel off and tossing her to the bed. She lands on her back and I'm on her before she can resist.

I bury my mouth on her pussy and quickly begin lapping and sucking at her clit. I know she's been aching for this for a few days now. She thinks I'm going to let her cum, but I'm not going to be that kind.

She's moaning in less than a minute. Her hips are rocking against my face as I work her clit into a stiff, swollen nub. Her breathing is becoming more rapid. I make sure to pay attention. She's close, very close. Just as her breaths start to shorten, I stop.

I stand up and pull off my shirt and pants, revealing a very hard cock. Her eyebrows are furrowed and her lips are parted. She doesn't want me to stop but she's eyeing up the pipe that sprung from my pants.

When I turn to walk away, she slams her fists onto the bed and groans angrily. "That's not fair!"

I know it's not. It's downright cruel. She doesn't realize that this is a punishment for me, as well. I would love to make her cum on my mouth and then fuck her until she can't cum anymore, but I made a request and I have to stick with it. She doesn't know why I'm holding her off, but she will, soon enough.

While I'm in the shower, she slips in and flushes the toilet. The scalding water pours over my back for a split second. I wail a high-pitched screech, sounding like a little girl, to which she laughs hysterically.

"How does that saying go? Revenge is a dish best served *cold*? I disagree, don't you?"

"Yes, I absolutely disagree," I sink back under the lukewarm water, to cool my superheated flesh. "That was unfair."

"I beg to differ," she replies as matter-of-factly.

"You'll pay for that later," I assure her.

"Trust me, I've been paying for it for three days already. I owed you!" She ducks out of the bathroom before I can reply to that statement. Oh, she will definitely pay for that.

* * * * *

We pull up in front of Fallen and shut off the car. I reach into the backseat to collect the bag I hid earlier. Rayna is watching me, curious to know what I have.

"I bought something for you to wear tonight, but before I show it to you, I'd like your word that you'll wear it, no matter what it is."

"You want me to promise to wear something even if I don't know what it is. Um, that's scary! It could be anything. Besides, I am already dressed in the little black dress you bought me to replace the one you tore."

"Yes, and you do look sexy as hell in it, too. But, as you know, you can wear anything at Fallen without judgement, so why not throw caution to the wind and promise to change into what I have picked out in this bag, for you."

Rayna hesitates, but eventually agrees. I open the duffle bag and hand her the plastic bag from inside. "When I put this on, whatever is in here, will you refer to me as Kat, until I take it off?"

"If you prefer me to I will, as long as you call me Demon while we're here."

"I did last time, didn't I?" she suggests. I know she's right. I grin and shift my eyes to the bag she's holding.

She opens it and digs her hand inside and takes out a red latex skirt. She smiles and then reaches back in the bag, pulling out a latex bra, and a pair of silky black panties with lace trim. She looks back in the bag but doesn't find anything else.

"What, no shoes?" she teases.

"The heels you're already wearing are perfect."

She nods, "Is that why you asked me to wear these particular ones?"

"Yes, now let's get out of the car and change our clothes."

"What?" She looks at me, startled. "You want me to change my clothes right here in their driveway?"

"Yes, I do. Where else do you plan on changing?"

"I just thought we could change in the house, in a bathroom or somewhere more private." She's looking all around for people who might be waiting to catch a glimpse.

"Listen, nobody here cares if we're outside naked. There aren't any neighbours who are close enough to see us, not with all these trees lining the property. I'm going to be here beside you. Trust me, nobody will care either way."

I open my door and bring the duffel with me. I round the car and open her door. She's reluctant to get out.

"You can wait in the car until I come back out, but it won't be for a few hours. You choose," I challenge her.

I pull off my shirt and unbutton my pants. She's still looking around but at least she's out of the car. She slips off the panties she's wearing and steps into the new ones. Then she pulls on the skirt, lifting her dress as she does. I catch a glimpse of the lacy panties and immediately, know I made the right choice. They fit her perfectly and they look sexy as hell.

I pull on a pair of black leather pants, heavy black work boots, but no shirt. I slip on leather forearm bands that lace up like a corset starting at the wrist and end halfway up my forearm. I like these bands because they look mean, at least I think they do.

Rayna has slipped off the black dress and is preparing to remove her bra. She's looking around with the clasp in her hands, ready to take it off as long as nobody is watching her. She moves quickly, flipping off her bra and pulling the new one on in record time. She seems relieved that no one saw her.

I can't stop scanning her body. Fuck, she looks hot! I want to bend her over the hood and fill her with my cock. It was difficult to get her to strip outside, I likely won't get her relaxed to the point of letting me fuck her out here. What a pity that will be. Maybe after I'm finished with her in the house, she'll be so calm from the endorphin rushes I plan to give her, she'll let me do anything I want to her.

"Do I look okay? I feel silly," she says, pulling at her skirt and top. "I think the outfit is too small. I would never buy this for myself."

"I know. I want you out of your comfort zone. Kat," Her eyes dart up when I say that name. "you look fucking perfect."

"I do?"

"I wouldn't say you did if I thought you didn't. Now, fold your dress and leave it on your seat so it doesn't wrinkle. That'll be hard to explain to the kids when we get home, if they happen to still be awake."

"Oh, right!" she says as she folds her dress.

I stuff the duffel back in the car and place my shirt and pants on the front seat. She slips her hand in mine and smiles at me. I pull her against me and kiss her lips, smacking her on the ass at the same time.

"Don't tease me," she whispers.

"Don't tell me what to do, Kat. You speak when I tell you to. You know the rules," I reply, giving her my most devilish smirk.

"Oh, we're starting the role play already?"

"You asked me to call you Kat after you changed, so I assumed we'd be assuming our roles. And you're breaking the no talking rule," he reminds me.

"Well, I actually don't know all the rules," she replies while returning the devilish smirk.

I whisper in her ear, "Careful, little girl. I'll take away your skirt if you misbehave."

Rayna doesn't say anything else, heeding my warning. She knows I'll follow thru with my threat. I turn and lead her to the main entrance. After passing the guards, taking the elevator and walking down the corridor, we enter the main hall where the majority of house visitors are sitting while some

stand in small gatherings. All are chatting and watching others discipline their submissives. Some people are even fucking. Some are either giving or receiving oral sex. I allow Rayna time to watch the activity, so that she'll know it's okay to do these things with me, in front of people, when I ask her to.

I take her down the hallway, past old friends and acquaintances who nod at me or say a quick greeting. Just as we near the room I've arranged for us, I see *HER* coming toward me. I debate whether I should tell Rayna the history between this woman and me before she gets too close, but she's too quick in her approach.

"Sir," she says, bowing her head as a sign of respect to me.

"Sara, how have you been?" I ask her after putting my fingers under her chin to lift her face. She's so fucking cute! I enjoyed those pouty lips of hers, especially when they were wrapped around my cock. I release her chin now that she's looking up at me.

"I am doing very well, thank you for asking. How have you been, Sir?" she asks while shifting her eyes toward Rayna. She quickly focuses her attention back on me, so I don't scold her for looking away, as I used to do.

"I'm doing very well. This is Kat, my submissive partner. Kat, this is Sara. She's a past submissive of mine." Honesty is best.

Rayna looks a bit shocked, but politely smiles to greet her. She looks at me as if to ask if she can speak. I nod. She says, "It's lovely to meet you. Perhaps one day we can have a chat."

"I'd love that! Would Sir approve?" she asks me. She's knowledgeable about how the relationships between Master and Submissive can be very restrictive. I simply nod. She asks, "Master Demon, if you would be so kind as to give Kat my phone number, I'd be extremely grateful."

"I can do that," I reply with my eyes burning into hers. I'm picturing all the past pleasures we shared; the roughest and most aggressive standing out first and foremost. I would love to make her scream again. She has the softest feminine voice when speaking, but her screams had my Demon sighing happily.

"Thank you, Sir." She looks at Rayna and whispers, "You're a very lucky woman. He's a wonderful Master, but he sure was cruel when I misbehaved. I'm sure you already know that all too well."

"That'll be enough, Sara. Where is your Master?" I hiss disapprovingly.

She bows her head. "I don't have a steady Master, Demon." Her eyes look up with her head still slightly bowed in an apologetic manner. "Nobody is as good a Master as you, Sir."

"It was good to see you again, Sara. I'm happy to know you are well."

"Thank you, Sir. Very nice to meet you, Kat," she replies sweetly, but the lingering mutual stare has me a little nervous. What will they talk about, if I do indeed share her number with Rayna? Will Sara tell her everything? Will she also describe just how vicious my Demon can be?

I can't tell if she's jealous of my new submissive or if she's genuinely happy that I have one. Knowing her the way I do, I'm sure she's happy to meet Kat and is somewhat jealous, but she would never do anything to interfere with the union between my submissive and me. She knows better than to defy me.

There were times I was a bit cruel with her, but she never complained. I treated her like she was a piece of meat that I could toy with. She kept coming back for more. She and Rayna have more in common than either of them knows. I'm sure Rayna will ask her what happened to end our playing and Sara will tell her about Brett; the asshole who also hurt my Rayna.

"I'll call you," Rayna tells her as I lead her away from the woman wearing leather shorts and a black bra with army boots on her feet. She always wore those boots.

Sara was in the armed forces for several years and did a few tours overseas. She fought in many battles. Getting shot in her right heel ended her military career and forever impeded the smoothness in her steps. I used to wonder what she was like before war forever tarnished her soul; before the smell of gunpowder mixed with blood burned too deeply into her that she could never fully recover.

Wearing high-heels is out of the question for her because her ankle won't hold her balance. She was released from the army with a medal for saving two men whose injuries were much worse than hers. Not only does she have physical scars, her mental woes were so much worse. She once told me that ever since she became a submissive, she's slept better than she had in a long time. Letting herself work through that pain via physical restriction and pain/pleasure, she's overcome quite a bit. It's her way of escaping her mind, even if it doesn't always last very long.

When I enter the room near the end of the hallway, it's all set up for us, just as I had asked Gear to do for me. Rayna is looking around the room while her feet remain in one position, as if she's too nervous to continue walking.

"Do you have any questions?" I ask her.

She looks at me with wide eyes. "Why are we in this room?"

I smile and say, "You said you wanted to be bound like the woman walking in the drive way with her domme. Well, I'm going to make sure that happens today. The only issue is that I am not all that skilled at elaborate rope binding and I'd like your first time to be done by someone very skilled."

"Not you? I'd rather you do it. I don't want anyone else to see me naked." She says, eyes so wide that she looks nearly terrified, to the point of wanting to run in the opposite direction.

"You will not be naked," I assure her. She seems to take a bit of solace in that.

"Demon, my man!" Gear walks through the door and shuts it behind him. "How the hell are you?" He puts out his hand to shake it.

"I'm very well, and you?" I say, shaking his hand and patting him on the back twice after a quick hug.

His eyebrows furrow while he looks at Rayna's body, not her face. I know this isn't going to be sexual for him. He's admiring her skin so he can decide on the perfect colour of rope to use that will compliment her colouring. His arousal isn't from the bodies themselves but the way they look bound and incapacitated. To him, the person bound is just flesh and bone, soulless and without their own thoughts. They are empty vessels that are his to use for his own artistic and possible sexual satisfaction, but it's not promised. He won't be fucking Rayna, just binding her for me to toy with.

"Very well, actually. Glitter just returned from an unscheduled trip. Her sister in Vancouver had a baby boy. She visited her own while I stayed here. Babies aren't my thing." He approaches Rayna, finally acknowledging that she's a real person. "So, what are we looking to do with you today, Kat?"

CHAPTER SEVENTEEN
Rayna

He's asking me what I want him to do. How would I know? My eyes dart to Coach.

"I'm picturing her in a web," he tells the tall man.

He smiles and asks me, "Can you put your arms behind your back and cross them, grasping either forearm with the opposite hand?"

I put my arms around my back and cross my forearms over one another. It's not exactly a comfortable position but it doesn't hurt me either.

"I'm going to be touching your body while I bind you. Don't worry, it won't be sexual for me," he warns before he gently repositions my arms until they aren't pulling so tightly behind me. It's less uncomfortable. "I think black would stand out wonderfully against your pale skin. "You can relax your arms for a few moments."

I drop my arms and look over at Coach, who is now leaning against a high stool with his hands on his hips and admiring my body. Glitter is standing next to him and whispers, "She looks good in the latex, doesn't she?"

Gear cuts in, "Hell yes, she does! Good enough to throw over my knee and spank her ass through that skirt."

"Maybe one day, but not today, Gear," Coach tells him. "She isn't trained well enough just yet to be sharing her."

He tilts his head when I look at him with questioning eyes. Would he really allow another man to spank my bottom? I don't believe he would, he's way too jealous and protective of me, to allow that. I'd rather not have another man spank me.

He agrees, "Mhmm, she is rather unseasoned. If you ever change your mind, I'd love to see her grovelling at my feet."

I can't help but shudder at the thought of being on the floor at his feet and begging for whatever it is he thinks I need. At the same time as the cold shiver runs up my spine, my thoughts are pulled to the yearning that my vagina seems to have. Do I really want to grovel at this man's feet? My brain says no, but my body disagrees.

His voice is soft, and he has a smoothness about him that makes me think his touches would be tender, even if they hurt. I think he'd whisper degrading things in my ear, but his mannerisms would make his words sound sexy. I imagine he is very sexually experienced and could teach me everything I need to know to be an excellent sexual partner for Coach. Why am I even sizing up this man? There's no way in hell Coach would allow him, or any man, to touch me sexually. If someone ever hit me, I think Coach would lose his shit. He nearly killed the guy who had me kidnapped, beaten and then, nearly raped. I have to get my thoughts back on what's happening here and now. Those thoughts will only drag me down into the dark hole of depression that I fought hard to escape from.

"Take off the skirt, Kat," he orders with little concern that I won't.

I take a deep breath and let it out slowly. Coach nods, so I follow the instructions given to me. My thumbs slip under the waistband and slowly begin to push my skirt down past my hips. It falls to the floor. I stand before two men in heels, a black lacy bra and matching panties. Never, in my wildest dreams had I pictured myself in this situation.

Gear takes my hand and asks me to lift each foot as he pulls the latex material from around my ankles. He gently folds my skirt and hands it to Coach. I'm starting to feel like I'm not myself, not really. I take a breath and let myself slip into sub-mode.

"The bra as well," he insists.

I look at Coach to see him nodding at me. When I hesitate, he quickly warns me, "Take it off or I will take it off for you."

His voice is deep and threatening, but his expression has my pussy twitching. I can't believe how horny I've been these past few days. The slightest touch to my clit will likely have me humping whatever it is that touched me. Maybe that's why he wanted me to wait; he wants me desperate and needy.

He isn't giving me a choice. Do I want the other man to see my breasts? Well, they are still quite perky, given I am thirty-eight years old and having had two children. I quickly remove it and place it in the man's outstretched hand. He doesn't even glance down at my erect nipples. After handing the top to Coach, he starts wrapping the rope around my wrists, over my shoulder and around my body. He walks around me, placing knots here and there.

My pussy is getting moist and hot. I am consciously aware of my quickening breaths. This is extremely arousing for me. I love the feel of the rope pressing against my skin and holding me in place. The way his fingers graze my hypersensitive flesh when applying a knot has me whimpering.

"Beautiful," Coach says after walking around me to examine the incredible weave. "You have a spider's web design on your back that is absolutely breathtaking."

His fingers slide down my back and under the ropes by my shoulder blades, gripping them firmly. He yanks me back until his chest thuds against the knotted web that spans my back, startling me.

The other man stands in front of me, admiring his artistic work and tracing the ropes with his fingers. Every now and then he touches my super-sensitive skin with his cool digits, sending shocks straight to my pussy, igniting the fire between my folds into a raging, desperate inferno.

Coach's hands reach around my chest and pinch my nipples. I nearly come apart. My knees weaken and my breath catches in my throat, escaping only when he releases them.

When I open my eyes, the man has left us and is now sitting where Coach was while I was being decorated in the black rope. Coach walks me over to the full-length mirror and stands behind me as I see the fancy design on my chest for the first time. He said there was an intricate design on my back, but the front is quite beautiful as well. I turn to look at the back and I'm captivated by its beauty.

"Please, Demon, will you take a picture?" I know I'm speaking out of turn, but I really want to capture this image.

"Sit on this stool," he tells me.

I sit, but he rearranges me until I'm sitting sideways, and then he pushes my legs wide apart. He ties a blindfold over my eyes and tells me to hold still. I'm not too keen on being blinded, but I trust Coach. I hear the click of the photo being captured on his phone and then feel something metallic squeeze my left nipple. I yelp louder than I should have in comparison to the moderate level of discomfort. The shock of him touching me when I can't see that he's about to, has me on edge. During other play sessions, he put much tighter and heavier ones on my nipples, and I was able to bear through it just fine. After the second nipple is decorated, I hear another click from a camera.

I screech when someone, I'm assuming it's Coach, grabs the web at my shoulder blades and pulls me back until I'm leaning against his hand. I'm nervous that he's going to drop me. My abs are straining to hold myself up, just in case he does let go, not that he would hurt me on purpose.

Coach pulls up on the left nipple clamp. Just before I'm about to scream, he lets it go. His hand slaps down on my pussy lips, shocking me more so than it causes me pain. Again, he slaps, but this time it stings. My automatic reaction is to pull my legs together.

He slaps my right thigh. "Open your legs." Reluctantly, I do as he instructs. "Good girl. I'm going to slap your clit five times and I want you to count them out."

"Thank you, Demon," I whisper, not meaning what I'm saying.

His fingers slap my clit and I yelp. My body jolts up and my back arches. "Fuck!"

"Count," he whispers.

"One," I reply. A second slap to my clit, harder than the first. "Ah! Two! Fuck!"

"I'm going to increase the intensity each time. What number comes next?"

I hesitate to reply, too afraid to speak because I know he'll slap when I do. He pinches my tender clitoris between two fingers and rolls it slowly and tenderly. It's more sensitive than what I'm used to.

I moan softly, "Three."

He slaps again, and I clamp my jaw shut, sucking air from between my teeth. If I open my mouth, a wail will fill this room. His fingers stroke up and down my pussy several times coating his fingertips with my slippery wetness.

"Does that feel good, Kat?"

I moan, "Yes, Sir."

He slaps and it hurts so much, it's dizzying. My body lurches upward, stopping only because he's holding onto the ropes. The wetness increases the sting.

"Was that number three?" he asks.

"No!" I pause, "Four! That was four. Please, no more. Please?"

"I love it when you beg," he whispers as his fingers continue to massage my pussy. "I'll save the fifth one for another time, but I won't tell you when I'm going to do it. Don't forget to count it when it happens, or you'll get another."

Coach lays me back so that his thigh is holding up my lower back and my head is hanging toward the ground, my ass still planted on the stool. This feels awkward and scary, like I'm going to topple over at any second. I love it and hate it. The support his hand was giving to my upper back falls away, furthering my insecurity. A vibrator presses onto my hot, swollen clitoris.

"Yes! Thank you, Coach... Demon!" I correct myself, hoping he won't stop the pleasure because of my faux pas. Luckily, he doesn't, not yet anyway.

Two of his thick fingers slip into my drenched pussy and push deeply into me. He waves them, stopping only to fuck me with them several times before pausing to wave once again. I no longer care if I fall over as long as he doesn't stop what he's doing.

The cycle repeats, over and over. I let myself fall into it, giving myself completely to the sensations from the vibrator and focus on relaxing my pussy, so his fingers can fuck me hard without resistance. He takes that as an opportunity to penetrate me with another digit, stretching me wider and further fueling the fire in my belly.

The sheer agony of the nipple clips being released has me screaming through my moans. That's all I needed to start the whirlwind of agonizing pleasure.

A toe-curling orgasm shreds through me like a tsunami, overcoming my conscious thought. The room around me has fallen away and I'm floating off his knee, suspended only by his fingers and balanced by the vibrator.

My body stiffens. My breath holds, burning hot in my lungs. His hand is met with a flood of hot cum as my mind falls still. An involuntary jerk from my aching abs jolts my mind from the euphoric emptiness that only an orgasm can suck you into.

He sits me up and holds me in place while I catch my breath. As he's pulling off the blindfold, the brightness of the lights has me squinting, but through those slits, I see people standing against the walls. Panic sets in.

"No! How could you do this to me? I'm so embarrassed! Why?" My words are louder than I'd planned, but I'm so angry and scared and humiliated.

The room suddenly echoes with applause. My eyes dart from person to person. They all seem pleased, which eases that insecurity telling me I'm not good enough for these people.

My sights rest on Coach. He looks in my eyes and whispers, "Love, they really enjoyed you. You are the star of the evening. How excited did you get from knowing Gear was watching? How thrilling was it? You had no idea the rest of them were watching you, so you were relaxed enough to get lost in the moment. If I'd told you there was a crowd, you wouldn't have let yourself go. Do you hate me?"

Tears start to stream down my face, and I can't wipe them away to hide my emotions from the lingering onlookers. Most have started to wander out of the room. Coach stands me up and pulls me into his arms, resting my cheek against his hard-pectoral muscle, to hide my face from roaming eyes.

"Can you untie me?"

Gear walks up behind me and begins unknotting the rope, walking around me in the process while Coach stands back and watches. My legs are weak, and Gear somehow knows when to help balance me, letting me go when he believes I'm in full control.

He stops in front of me after most of the web has been removed. "You are a lovely woman and I would be honoured to bind you again. You are a pleasure to watch when you've let down your guard and you're lost in a mix of pleasure and pain. Truly, you are. Demon is a lucky man." Having said that, he finishes untying my hands.

I rub my sore wrists and roll my shoulders to ease their stiffness. "Thank you for tying such a lovely knot on me. I really enjoyed myself. I would be honoured to be your subject again soon, should Demon approve."

With that, he nods and walks away, taking the rope with him. We're alone in the room, finally. I look over at Coach who has been leaning against the wall with his arms crossed over his chest, looking like a badass. I don't say anything and neither does he, we just stare at one another.

Coach suddenly rushes toward me. His fingers weave into my hair and his other arm around my back, pulling me firmly against him. His mouth presses to mine with so much neediness. He's been waiting for three days for relief and for him, that might as well be an eternity.

His lips work mine with a fiery passion. He grabs my ass and lifts me up. I wrap my legs around his waist and lock my feet behind his back. Oh, yes! I want him to take me hard, right here, right now and I no longer care if anyone watches.

He carries me over to the wall and leans my back against the cool paint. I can feel him fussing with his zipper and then his cock rubs against my wet panties. His finger pulls them aside. In a flash, his stiff, fat prick is filling me, thrusting hard and deep with an eagerness that I thoroughly enjoy. His carnal grunts rattle my very core.

He fucks me hard, rough and with hedonistic cruelty, but I love it and want more. He leans back just enough so I can watch his bestial expressions. His nose is flared, teeth clenched, lips pulled back and his eyes seem dark, like a predatory animal. The kind man I know Coach to be, isn't this man. This fuck does not revolve around love. He's fucking me for a purpose; to own me and make me his, just his.

The second his hand wraps around my throat and squeezes, I grasp his forearm with both hands and try to pull it away. When his eyes meet mine, I don't recognize him.

"You're mine, you little bitch! I fucking own you! Tell me!" he growls and spits.

I don't know how he expects me to tell him when I can barely breathe. His eyes glare into mine with a dark hollowness that I fear. I find him to be dangerous, but also sinfully exciting!

I mouth the words, *I'm yours*, just as an orgasm seems to explode my insides, shattering me into a million pieces. His cock swells as my pussy tries to strangle it with its rippling spasms. He releases my throat to slam his palm against the wall beside my head, as if he's trying to stop it from falling over and crushing us.

His body pounds me several more times until it seizes, stiffening painfully, as his prick empties its jizz deep inside my spent cunt. He exhales with a long primal howl that echoes from wall to wall. Each breath he expels sounds more like a canine's growl than a human's groan.

With his head hanging down, his eyes shift up at me from under his brows, slowly lifting his face while his eyes remain locked on my sights. He's still breathing through a clenched jaw. He seems to be battling with his Demon.

"Put him back in his cage," I whisper.

"Don't look at me!" he hisses through clenched teeth.

I cast my eyes down, but out of the corner of my eye, I can see his are closed tightly. He hasn't moved his hands from holding up the wall. My legs are still wrapped around his waist. I reach up and place my hands on his cheeks hoping it will help him to calm down. Instead, he glares at me and grabs my hips, pulling my legs from around him. He nearly drops me onto my feet and walks away as he tucks his withering cock back in his pants. I watch him pace back and forth. Moving toward him will be a bad idea, so would talking. It didn't work well the last time. Strangely enough, I'm not afraid of him or his craziness.

He stops pacing and looks at me with an expression I recognize. "Coach, welcome back."

"Did I hurt you? I don't think I hurt you."

"No, definitely not! That was fucking hot!"

"Good," he replies, as he retrieves a few paper towels for me to wipe myself off with.

"Are you okay?"

"Yeah, I'm good. I kept him under control."

"That was under control? Christ, I hope you never completely lose control and beat me," I joke, to lighten the mood, followed by a snicker.

"It's not funny. I don't want to hurt you. You are not ready for Demon. I can be cruel and hurtful... you aren't ready."

I stroke his cheek and smile softly, "You don't scare me. I thought I'd be afraid of your Demon, but now that I've seen him behind your eyes, I'm not afraid. You have more control than you think you do."

He kisses me softly and whispers, "You aren't ready."

"Maybe you aren't ready because you love me. You didn't love those other women, so their feelings didn't matter to you. There's more to lose if I fear you, isn't there?"

He nods, "That's it exactly. I'm not ready, but neither are you." He takes the paper towel from me and hands me my skirt.

"My panties are soaked. Can I just take them off?"

"I would prefer you to be panty-free anyway. Give them to me," he says with a grin.

I slip them off and hand them to him. He doesn't toss them out, which strikes me as odd. Instead, he tucks them into his back pocket. I take his hand in mine and follow him out of the room. People in the hallway smile at me as we walk past them. I smile back while my cheeks flush red hot. Will I ever get used to this?

CHAPTER EIGHTEEN
Rayna

"Now that you've discovered your fetish, I want to show you something," he whispers to me.

"My fetish?" Since I'm still supposed to be in submissive mode, I'm careful not to let anyone hear me speak, especially when I'm not being asked to speak.

"Ropes, rope bondage," he replies.

"Oh, I thought you meant public sex," I snicker.

"I'm hoping that excites you, as well," Coach whispers with a sexy grin. He holds his finger up to his lips to inform me that I need to be very quiet now.

He takes me into a large room. My breath is taken from me by the beauty before me. Suspended in rope are three women, each is bound to the other forming a small circle. Their necks are tied to hold their mouths against the vagina of another. Each woman is seductively licking and kissing the pussy before them. Their arms are bound behind their backs, each woman's position identical to the others. Their legs are spread wide and bound. If it weren't for the ropes, they'd look as if they are floating on their sides, weightless in the air. I am in awe of their beauty.

I don't know how long we stand here while we watch each woman come to orgasm. Their moans and jerking bodies draw me, captivating my heart and mind in a fantasy-like dream. I wish I were one of them, even though I've never imagined I would desire to taste another woman's sex. Maybe one day I will.

A man much shorter than Gear approaches the woman with the light brown hair. He quickly unties a rope setting her face free from the other woman's pussy. He grasps a wad of her hair in his hand and proceeds to slap her in the face several times, hard. She gasps and cries out. He grabs her by the neck and lifts her slowly, holding her up to use her own body's weight as a means to put pressure on her throat. Her face is reddening quickly. He spits on her cheek before letting her go. She's gasping quick breaths while still reeling from the constant lapping torture on her sensitive clit by the woman still bound to her pussy.

Him and Gear begin unbinding the women one at a time, gently lowering them onto their feet and holding them until they are steady and completely unbound. Each woman gets a long hug and a kiss on their head.

The crowd of onlookers has dwindled but a few remain. I can feel Coach watching me, as I watch them. His eyes have been on me throughout most of the show.

"Beautiful, isn't it?" he asks.

"Yes, very much so. They were floating. Orgasms make me feel like I'm weightless and floating. They actually were floating, well, sort of. I wonder how incredible that must have been for them."

"Do you want to try it some time?"

"Lesbianism?" I ask with a fearful expression.

"Sure," he replies.

I shrug my shoulders. "I don't know. I've never desired another woman, I'm not sure I'd like it. If they went through the trouble of binding me like that and I hated it, that would be a pity. Besides, I don't know how to lick a pussy."

"I would imagine that you would do to them what you want done to you."

I shrug, "I don't know if I could."

"Maybe one day I will order you to do it," he teases.

"Can I refuse that order without punishment?" I tease.

"Not without punishment," he replies, kissing my forehead after he does. I wonder what that punishment would entail.

The last woman is set free. She's the one who Coach introduced me to shortly after we arrived. What was her name again? Sara! Yes, that's it. The man who struck her is holding her in his arms and rocking her lovingly. I can't hear what he's saying to her, but she's smiling and nodding. Her eyes remain closed. He continues to carry her for another minute before setting her down on her feet. He cradles her face in his hands and whispers something else. She smiles and nods before thanking him.

Gear walks up to her and takes her hand in his, kissing the back of it. He also talks to her for a moment before she thanks him and moves toward the bench where the other two women are dressing.

She slips into her black leather shorts and crop top, and then steps into her black boots. She sits and ties them up while I watch her. Coach is talking to the shorter man who was assisting Gear, while he skillfully folds the ropes into beautiful braids and tosses them into a plastic bin. The two seem to be old friends.

I let go of Coach's hand which immediately draws his attention. When he looks at me, I glance over at Sara and then back at him. He nods so I make my way toward the woman, admiring the indented red marks from where the ropes sat. I sit on the bench beside Sara while she pulls her shoelace to tighten her boot.

She looks at me and with surprise in her voice, says, "Oh, hi! Nice to see you again."

"You too. I saw you up there. That was beautiful. Can I ask you some questions?"

"Of course," she says as she sits up to give me her full attention.

"Are you bisexual?"

She smiles, "Um, not really. Well, I don't know. I suppose you could say that I am. I don't like to put a title on my sexuality. I prefer a thick, hard cock, but I'll have sex with a woman if my master asks me to. I don't hate it, by any means. It is pleasurable to watch a woman come to orgasm because of something I did. I gather you haven't had that experience?"

"No," I reply.

"Are you opposed to it?"

"Um, I don't think so. If Demon asks me to, I will. This is going to sound silly. How do you know if you're doing it right?" I can feel my cheeks flushing.

"Kat, just do what you have always hoped your oral sex partner would do to you. Women love clitoral attention, but we have very sensitive nerve endings on our labia too. If you are only manipulating the clitoris, it could easily lose sensation. Move your tongue around now and then to stimulate the surrounding area as well, and you'll make her cum. Some women are much harder than others, but stay at it and don't get frustrated."

"That's true and men don't always get it right."

"Demon is really great at oral sex, but I'd say more than half the male population don't have a clue," she says with a giggle.

"So, have you been with Demon many times?" I tried not to sound jealous, but I think I did.

"Oh!" she looks worried. "Did you not want to know that?"

"No, I understand he has a past; a rather extensive past. For some reason, I just didn't picture you and him having sex. I know you did. I just want to know…" I say as my words drift off.

She nods, understanding what I'm asking. "He fucked me and punished me, ate my pussy and had me suck his cock. It was rough to the point of being brutal, at times. I liked it very much. My favourite part of the pain is the initiation of it, when that first blast of pain riddles through my body like an electric shock. At first, I think I won't be able to adjust to it, but after a few seconds, my mind overruns it, allowing me to accept the pain for what it is; a reminder that I'm still alive. As for Demon, I enjoyed him. Trust me sweetie, there was absolutely no love connection between us. Besides, I doubt that rock on your hand is from another man who is kind enough to let you spend an occasional evening with a guy like Demon. No man is that generous unless he's involved in this lifestyle. Don't take this the wrong way, but you aren't experienced, and the only women Demon plays with are. Going by those clues, that ring came from Demon. By watching how gentle he is with you, it's brutally obvious that he is madly in love with you."

"You didn't just watch him fuck me in the other room then," I tell her, not realizing that it came out sounding resentful, which wasn't my intention.

"Did Demon hurt you? He can be cruel sometimes, but most of his subs are into that."

"He didn't hurt me, but my fiancée wasn't behind his eyes, something else was."

She nods, fully understanding what I mean. "Yes, that would be his Demon. He's an angry beast, a take it hard and rough type personality. I desire that in a Master. Nobody does that level of bad, as good as he does. He is the best without ever crossing the psychopathically sadistic line!"

"Do many women agree with you? I haven't met any of his submissives that aren't seriously disturbed. I mean, I've only met one and she was insane."

"I heard about his ex-submissive and how she tried to kill him with her car." Sara chuckles and bends down to finish tying her boot. "There are some obsessive, crazy bitches out there."

"Yeah, I don't like that woman very much. Did you know her?" I ask.

"No, she isn't from our group. I don't recognize her name."

"She's a crazy one. Anyway, thanks for answering some questions for me."

"Kat, anytime! Hey, if you'd like to be entwined in with us next time, just let your Master know. I'm sure he wouldn't mind lending you to them. It's really a great way to escape your mind if you allow yourself to feel the pain of the ropes and the weightlessness of the air beneath you."

"I might be willing to do that," I reply. "Thanks for tolerating my naivety."

"Don't be silly. Anytime you have questions, just ask me." She smiles and then continues tying the laces on her boot.

I walk back to Coach's side and take his hand in mine. He's talking to two women, one is obviously a dominatrix, the other I'm not sure of. He leads me out of the room and back down the hall. Instead of walking straight toward the exit, he turns down another hall and starts looking around, as if he's searching for someone.

He pulls me along and then stops in front of an average sized man who has another man's wrist handcuffed to his. He hands him my panties, which seems to elate the man. He looks at me and then stuffs them under his nose, taking a long sniff while his eyes stay locked with mine. I would never imagine Coach would have given the man my panties to arouse himself with. My eyes must be huge, as I watch him enjoy my scent.

"This is Kat," Coach tells the man.

"Kat with the lacy black panties. They're still damp from your excitement. Thank you, Demon," he says before taking another long snort. His handcuffed friend seems to be irritated by his master's actions. He seems disgusted that the man is adoring the scent of a woman.

"Enjoy," Coach says with a pat on the man's back.

I follow him out of the house and back to the car. Once we're outside in the cool night's air, a shiver has me holding my arms over my chest.

"Are you cold?" he asks.

"It is quite cool out here for this time of year. Don't you think?"

"It is. Let me warm you," he says just as he spins me around by my shoulders.

He bends me over the front quarter-panel of my car, holding me in place by pinning my leg with his thick thigh. He yanks up my skirt, exposing my naked backside. I can feel him fussing with his zipper and then this hand sliding along my ass cheek as he strokes his cock.

"Don't move," he instructs.

I rest my head against the hood and wait for him to penetrate me, but he doesn't. Is he just going to jack off on me? I patiently wait, hoping he'll fuck me.

"Suddenly you're not so shy to be naked outside," he says. He pulls at the eyelets holding my top together. It springs open. He yanks it out from under my chest. My tits are resting against the cold metal of the hood. My nipples are so hard they're aching. He temporarily moves his thigh so he can quickly yank down my skirt.

"Do you like being naked outside?"

"Yes, Sir," I reply even though I'm not completely sure I do. After having people watching me cum like Niagara Falls all over Coach's hand, this isn't nearly as embarrassing.

I feel his wet fingers slide between my ass cheeks to moisten my asshole. His finger slips inside and starts pulling at the opening to stretch it. I hear him spit and feel the spatter slap on my asshole. He has good aim. I'll give him that. I breathe slowly and relax my ass enough that he can slip in two and then work in a third.

"Stand up," he says while moving his leg and grabbing both my biceps. He spins me around and leans his ass against the car. He spreads his legs, backing me in between them. He releases one arm but keeps hold of the other.

"You're going to fuck my ass out here?"

"Yes, shut up," he instructs.

His prick lines up to the opening of my butt and gently enters my ass. To my surprise, he slides all the way in with little discomfort. He's so tall that he has to spread his legs wider so I can keep my balance and not have to rise up on my tip toes in my heels.

He wraps his hands around my pelvis and slowly lifts and lowers me. My asshole glides up and down his rock-hard cock, swallowing deep into me. He fucks me slowly and gradually as the odd person or two walks past. Nobody gives us much attention, which seems odd.

A beautiful, lone woman, the one who stops to watch, asks, "Can I be of assistance, Demon?"

Coach looks at her and says, "Yes."

I'm not only shocked by his reply, but when he grips my hips tightly and lifts me, I squeal like a mouse in a trap.

"Open your legs," he tells me.

"What are you doing?" I ask while complying to his request.

"No talking!"

My legs hang over his while his prick remains buried deep in my ass. The cool air chills my clit instantly. He spreads his legs and asks her, "Would you be so kind?"

She looks at me and says, "Hi, I'm Candy. What's your name?"

"I… I'm Kat," I stutter.

"It's nice to meet you."

She bends forward and starts licking my clitoris. Her lips form a seal around it as her tongue dances around my swelling nub in a well-choreographed ballet. With his cock slowly gliding in my ass and her tongue talentedly swirling my most sensitive flesh, my head tips back as a gasp of cool night air inflates my lungs. My hands reach back and grasp his huge biceps for balance. I am going to lose myself.

I look down to see her shoulder length, light brown hair and can't believe a woman has her mouth on my pussy. Holy fuck! She is really good at this! Her mouth is so soft and small, but skilled, like no other I've experienced, even Coach, who I thought was the very best at orally manipulating my pussy.

Her mouth sucks my clit like she's sucking on an ice cream cone which is driving me wild. All of a sudden, her mouth is absent. The cool air feels frigid as the wind glides along my super-heated pussy. I look down when I hear Coach moan and he stops fucking me. Her head is lower and I'm quite sure she's mouthing his balls.

He starts fucking me again when her mouth lands back on my clit. A few of her delicate fingers slip inside of my pussy with ease. I nearly cum right then but she's stopped slurping at my clit.

I open my eyes to see her standing up, leaning in toward me. Without another thought, I lean forward and take her cheeks in my hands, pulling her mouth to mine. Our lips press together as our tongues explore one another's mouths. Her lips are small but so soft. Her face is warm and smooth, like mine. I can smell my pussy on her skin and it's turning me on.

Her fingers are working my pussy, pushing into me and pulling back slowly. All of a sudden, I feel her knuckles enter me and I know her entire tiny hand is buried within me while Coach's raging hard-on pumps in and out of my asshole. I flop back against his body and cry out. The pain and pleasure are in a battle to see which will take over. Pleasure quickly wins.

She fucks me slowly while spinning her wrist. I'm so fucking full! I have a woman's hand inside of me! She's fucking me! He's fucking me! I wail through a body-rocking orgasm while she rams me with her fist, and he slides his prick in my ass. I can't believe I'm doing this! And in public!

My body is coming back down from the climax just as her lips encircle my unbelievably aroused clitoris! My hands are gripping my tits so tightly that I know I'm going to bruise, but I like it. She's sucking and rolling my clit while spinning her wrist, all while Coach's cock fills my ass.

The air feels hot and humid as I float out of my body and away from reality. I am not screaming or moaning, just silently still in what feels like the weightlessness of death. The closer I come to orgasm, my body feels like it's swelling bigger and bigger, about to explode.

In my mind, I'm begging them not to stop, pleading for mercy and yet urging this agony to continue. I want to throw myself over the edge to end the incredible yearning ache my body is suffering, but I know that once I do, the orgasm is complete, and it will all end. It's torture, sweet torture.

My body jerks hard as I'm ripped from the pleasures of ecstasy and into the painful burning that comes with post orgasmic clitoral stimulation. She rises up, but continues to fuck me with her hand.

I'm immediately whirled into another climax the instant the fingers on her free hand begin rubbing circles over the sensitive nub that is likely ten times the size it normally is.

My panting screams are floating off into the trees as if disappearing further than my body can float away to. A final wail and I collapse against his chest, barely able to breathe, never mind holding up my own bodyweight.

Her hand pulls from my pussy at the same time his cock is taken from the depths of my ass. I can feel Coach's breathing become raged and intense. His groans are loud and with purpose. It takes all the strength I have to look down to see what she's doing. She's looking down and I think she's watching her hands jerk his cock, if that's what she is indeed doing.

He growls viciously just as his torso tightens, ending with sharp jerking that has me being tossed around on his lap. If he weren't holding my arms, I would have likely slipped off of him. He's still catching his breath when he sits me up and then grips my hips to lift me off and set me on my feet.

I'm surprised to see how short and tiny this woman is. I knew she was small, but she is quite a bit shorter than me. Coach is still lying back on the hood while I hand her my skirt to wipe her hands on.

"Thank you," she says.

"Sorry, I don't know how absorbent that will be, but it's something to clean up with."

"It's great, thank you. This isn't the first time I've had pussy and cock juice on me. Thanks for letting me play with you two," she says with a wide smile.

"That's the first time she's had a woman on her pussy," Coach tells her as he's sitting up.

"Really?" she looks so happy about that fact. "I'm honoured to be your first, Kat."

I smile, sure that I'm blushing, but happy the dimness of the evening might hide it. "Thank you. Sorry, I'm not sure what to say."

She leans in and gives me a quick kiss and then curtseys for Coach. "Thank you, is perfect. Have a great night you two."

I watch her skip the rest of the way to the house like a little girl. I haven't had a sexual liaison anywhere nearly as strange as I have tonight, in my entire life.

Coach stands up and kicks off his shoes. He drops his pants, stepping out of them as he starts untying his leather wrist wraps. He's completely naked, outside, in plain view of anyone who happens to pull up and he isn't concerned about that in the slightest. After what just happened, why would he be?

"Are you all right with me having asked her to join us?"

"Oh, yes," I assure him. "That was incredible!"

"Then why are you just standing there and not getting dressed?" His smirk seems almost childlike.

"Yeah, I suppose I could do that. Why are you looking at me so strangely?"

"I was sure you would protest by saying red. You surprised me tonight, is all."

"Is that why you allowed her to join in, as a way to test me?"

"No love, it wasn't a test. This was just a lucky opportunity that you didn't skip on."

"I'm glad I didn't. Eating a pussy though, I'm not sure I'm up to that just yet."

I duck into the car to retrieve the clothes we will be going home in, the same ones we arrived wearing. As we get dressed, I catch him checking me out.

"Stop that!" I joke.

"What?"

"Looking at me. We're done for the night. There's no way I can fuck again."

"Who said anything about fucking?" he teases.

In the stereotypical dumb blonde voice, I reply, "You have exhausted me, Master Demon." I flutter my eyelashes at him.

"Keep that up and I will fuck you, again."

I shove the other clothes back into the duffel bag and then hand it to him. He walks around the car and opens his door, shoving the bag behind the driver's seat to hide it away.

He drives us home while I tell him everything I loved about tonight, and how having the ropes tied elegantly against my flesh, restricting my movements, would excite me. Sara had suggested I express to Coach how willing I am to become a piece of Gear's beautiful artwork, that way he might be more inclined to allow me to participate in the future.

Coach smirks and nods. It excites me to imagine being bound and suspended, and secretly hope he might set that up for our next visit. Would he even be willing to allow another man to put his hands on me, even if it's for a non-sexual purpose, as it would be if he decorates me in rope? I want to experience pleasure while beautifully dangling, but I don't want Gear to be the one bringing it to me. I don't even know the man.

CHAPTER NINETEEN
Coach

This week has been grueling, and incredibly stressful for me. Normally, a visit to Fallen with a pain-slut would help me work through that frustration. Rayna isn't a pain-slut. I highly doubt she would allow my Demon out of his cage, so he can play with another woman.

The tension at the gym have been high. Some much-needed construction started on Monday. It's been loud and inconvenient, bringing on plenty of complaints from some of my patrons. I've had to partition off the men's locker room with a temporary wall, which some of the dickheads hate because they have to walk further to get to the free-weights room. My reply was simply, '*Dude, you can use the cardio*'. That didn't always go over very well but fuck them and their laziness.

It's the women's locker room that's shut down for repairs. They need to share the men's locker room, without fear of ogling eyes from those horny motherfuckers, me included. A quick, but sturdy wall, solved the issue. Unfortunately, it blocked that particular entrance to the men's free-weights room. They're a bunch of big fucking babies and I'm sure they'll get the fuck over it. If they can't make slight accommodations for the lovely women who come here in spandex to work out, they can fuck off and not come back.

I want more women at the gym. To allow for that, they need more lockers, showers and toilets. When the gym first opened, there wasn't much need for a large women's change room, because the ratio was fifteen men to one woman. Yeah, they were stared at, a lot. Now the ratio is more like five to one. Needless to say, I think the men can make small, temporary sacrifices for the women. It'll only be a few weeks until the wall comes down. A few weeks of nagging, headache inducing, annoyances.

There are two construction workers that I had to ban from the premises because they wouldn't stop watching the female patrons working out. As if it wasn't bad enough that they were watching them but the comments that were being whispered were seriously offensive. Five women complained on the first day and they were only at the setting up stage. Their behaviour would only get worse and I knew it, besides, they weren't getting their work done in a timely manner and I need that room finished as soon as possible. Those fuckers tried to deny it, but I showed their supervisor the video of how they were standing around, pointing and staring. He sent them to another work site but docked their pay for that day. They called me every name in the book on their way out of the building, escorted by myself and three other very large men. I love those guys! They always have my back, and I'll always have theirs.

It's only Thursday and I already can't wait for this construction to be finished, even though it's going to be a few more weeks still. But the women's locker room was small and needed to be expanded. It was time. More women have joined the gym in the past six years since I've owned it, than I thought would; tenfold, at least. We decided that by bumping into the gymnasium, we could create a big enough locker room to comfortably hold enough lockers and space for their growing numbers. Not a lot of people were using the gym for anything other than aerobics and they almost never used that side of the court. That void space will not be missed but the new design will be appreciated by the ladies.

Rayna set up a dinner tonight with her sister and my best buddy, Tim. The two of them have been living together for a few months now. Tim wants to propose to her, but I don't think it's a good idea, just yet. Shit, they haven't been together all that long. Rayna and I have been engaged for seven months and she hasn't even brought up the conversation of actually getting married. I think she's a bit gun-shy because of the shitty asshole she married the first time. I fucking hate that bastard, not only for how he treats Rayna but because of how shitty he is, as a father.

Anyway, I haven't been able to chat time with Tim in almost a month. His shift at work changed. Now he works steady days and spends his evenings with Renee. He's so pussy whipped it makes me gag. The man has no social life that doesn't revolve around her. I used to see him at the gym during the day. I miss my friend.

I'm going to be here at the gym, until five tonight. My last appointment is at four, with a new client. Her name is Barbie. Stranger still, it's her birth name and she looks so much like an actual Barbie doll; her face, I mean. Anyway, she's a competitive bodybuilder, who's about to start hard training for a competition. Her last coach was badly injured in an awful car accident caused by a forty-year old stoned driver. You'd think someone that age would know better.

Her training with me will be temporary, just until her coach is back on his feet. I know Barbie from seeing her at other competitions. She's fucking built like an amazon bitch! I'd love to fuck her hard and make her scream. She's solid as fuck, ripped and beautiful. Rayna would never give me permission to have this woman, and I wouldn't do anything that might cause me to lose her. The thought of that makes my chest hurt.

I've had strong women, and let me tell you, there's definitely a difference in how hard I fucked them. They're solid, stronger and sometimes more sexually aggressive than an average woman. They like to fuck back, even when I'm hammering their ass with everything I've got. Like I said, strong as fuck!

Lisa, the yoga coach, slips into my doorway and says, "Your four o'clock is here." She's working the desk until her class starts in about an hour.

"Oh, four o'clock already? Dammit, I'm in the middle of something. Okay, I'll be there in a few minutes."

"She's in the changing room, so take your time," Lisa says as she walks away.

I pick up the phone and dial Gear. It rings three times before I'm asked to leave a message. I do, asking him to call me tomorrow at the gym and tell him my phone number in case he's misplaced it and doesn't have Caller ID. It has been a while since he's called me here.

I want Rayna to experience the suspension. I'd love to play with her while she's suspended. Her first time should be calm and relaxed, so she can fully appreciate the feeling of floating. That's how it has been described to me. Personally, the idea of being immobilized while hanging from ropes, makes my inner Demon twitchy and ready to pounce. It's not something I've ever wanted to experience.

I gather my papers and tuck them in my drawer. Locking the door to my office, I head toward the change room. My timing is perfect to intercept Barbie, who is just coming out of the room.

"Hi Barbie?" I ask with my hand out to welcome her.

She shakes my hand and smiles. "Yes, that's me. You're Coach. So, do people just call you Coach all the time? Do you have a real name or were your parents both psychics who could foresee your future lifestyle choice?"

We both chuckle. "My real name is Simon, but yes, people just call me Coach."

"All right, Coach it is. If you piss me off, I'm going to call you Simon, like your wife likely does when you fuck up."

I can't tell if she's joking or not. If she does call me Simon, I'm going to have a sudden vicious desire to pin her down and fuck the hell out of her, until she apologizes and calls me Master instead of Simon or Coach. I really hope she doesn't use my real name. Nobody calls me Simon anymore, not even Rayna. If Barbie wants to taunt me and play games, I'll put her in her place faster than she can beg me rip her clothes off and fuck her hard.

"Do not call me Simon," I say in a very demanding voice.

She scoffs, "Why not? What are going to do about it?"

Her taunting has my cock twitching and my inner Demon shadow boxing in his cage.

"Just don't do it," I reply with a leer that would make most men back down.

She stands right in front of me with her face a foot away from mine, as she pulls her hair up into a messy bun. Her smirk has my palms burning, wanting to spank her ass, just to wipe the challenging grin off her face. Her hands drop to her sides, and her eyes scan up and down my body.

"Fine, I won't. I will admit that I'm curious, what would you do if I did call you Simon?" Again, her gaze follows my frame to my feet and then back up to meet my eyes. "It might be fun to tussle with you. I know you're married, so I'll back off. She's a lucky woman. You look like one of those guys who's angry enough to fuck like a raging beast."

I want to grab her throat and slap that sexy mouth of hers. I'd force her onto her knees and fuck her mouth while her split lip bleeds all over my cock. My teeth clench and I swallow hard. Why am I letting this hot, mouthy woman spark me up? I'd better calm down before my cock stands up to show her that she's right.

"If you'd like, I can always find you another trainer."

"Why the fuck would you do that? I want you. You're one of the best, so I hear. I left my nice home and moved into a shady motel, so I can train with you, in this city. So, are we going to train or what?"

"Fucking right, I am the best," I said with a boastful grin. "Okay, I went over your file, all is good. Today, you're doing legs. I think your calves could use some work."

"Fuck you, my calves are awesome!" she jokes while sticking out her leg and pointing her toes. "Okay, let's get at it then!"

I watch her work through the routine her coach has set up for her. There are a few tips I give, that make her quite happy. I think we'll work out well, if I can just manage to keep my cock in my pants. She's so fucking hot, and her confrontational personality would make a great jousting partner for my Demon.

At five o'clock I leave her to handle her cardio workout on her own. The construction workers are still hard at work when I leave. They seem to be right on schedule. If I'm lucky, maybe they'll finish earlier than expected. The other trainers; Carol, Lisa and my new guy, Joe - will keep an eye on things. Carol is the shift supervisor, so she'll be here until ten-thirty when we close the doors. Lisa is leaving at seven, but Joe will stay on to help Carol clean the equipment after everyone has left. They've been giving each other sexy eyes for about a week now, so they'll likely be fucking after they lock up tonight. I don't care what they do, as long as they clean up their mess before they leave, and I do not want drama into the workplace.

I have fucked plenty of women at the gym, so telling them not to, would be hypocritical. Some of the equipment here allows for great fucking positions. I think the smell of sweat in the gym, the atmosphere, the equipment and having a hot woman, bent over a bench with her bare ass in the air is one of the most common sexual fantasies for gym rats like me.

* * * * *

After dinner, I spark up a campfire in the backyard and give the kids each a poker to roast their marshmallows. Last week I promised them they could make s'mores but there hasn't been time to make good on it. Kim has been reminding me relentlessly, every day, since I made that promise. She's cute and I love her, but she is a determined little girl. When she wants something, she won't stop until she gets it. It's a great quality to have. If I didn't know better, I'd swear she had my DNA. She's just like me, only better. Way better.

Rayna, Renee, Tim and I are drinking the wine while the kids hold marshmallows over the crackling fire. It's a great night for this; the breeze is light and cool, but not cold. Although it's very dark, the sky if painted with very bright stars.

"So, when's the big day? Have you set a date yet?" Renee asks both Rayna and I.

Rayna clears her throat and runs her fingers through her hair, tucking an errant strand behind her ear. "Um, no, not yet. There's no rush."

"I would love to make you my wife tonight if you'd just say the word. But, like I said, I'll wait until you're ready." I take her hand and kiss the back of it. "What about you two? Any plans for making it legit?"

Tim smiles while looking at Renee. He's rubbing her back while she looks at him. She says, "We've joked about it, but no, not really."

The kids are completely ignoring us while they stuff their faces and gape their full mouths to gross each other out. Siblings are great at being disgusting to one another.

"I was thinking of taking Rayna out Saturday night. Will you two be available for phone calls from these young'uns, should one come?" I ask.

"Saturday night?" Renee's phone wakes up as she clicks on her calendar to see if she's available. Thank God it's dark, so no one can see when I roll my eyes. I know she doesn't have any plans. Tim confirmed it when I called him Monday to set this up. "Yeah, I'm free. Tim?"

"Just like I said earlier this week when you asked, we have no plans," he assures and then grins like an asshole. "Where are you going?"

I clear my throat and lie for the benefit of Renee and the kids, "Just out to dinner, maybe some live theatre." I look at Tim with an expression that screams *asshole*! He already knows where I'm taking Rayna. We discussed it on the phone on Monday.

Renee doesn't know about Fallen and I'd like to keep it that way. Even though she's not into BDSM, she acts like she's the shit when it comes to sexual deviance, which really annoys me. She really knows how to get under my skin and make me itch. I'd swear she does it on purpose.

Rayna quickly changes the subject, "So, back to you two and talk of marriage."

Tim shifts in his chair, but says nothing. Renee turns to look at him, expecting him to respond. When he doesn't, she shakes her head, disappointedly. He's told me that he wants to follow tradition, to get down on one knee to ask her, but he has his concerns. He's worried that she's still in the honeymoon phase of their relationship and will eventually tire of him. I wonder about that too, but haven't told him. I know he'll ask her when he thinks the time is right.

"How is the construction going?" Tim asks me. Now he is trying to change the subject.

"The last thing I want to do right now is talk about the one main thing that's stressing me out. It's a beautiful night, the stars are bright above us, we are warming our feet by a campfire with family and friends. Talking about work will not be part of tonight's discussion."

"Understood! Cheers to a quick completion, my friend," Tim says while holding his glass toward me. We lean in and clink them together, with a nod of our heads.

Rayna adds, "It's been chaotic, but it is coming along quite well. Everything is on schedule and the workers aren't bothering the patrons anymore. It is going to look great when it's finished. The women really needed a bigger room."

"I will have to come by when it's finished to take a look," Renée says, while watching me. When I glance her way, she quickly looks back at her sister. Yet another perfect moment in life, is ruined by Renee, as I know exactly what her intentions are. She doesn't care about the construction at my gym. She's made a pass at me before, and I wouldn't doubt she would try it again.

Tim is my best buddy and if she's willing to cheat on him with me, I know damn well she already has, or soon will be, fucking someone else. I am just going to have to make sure that Rayna is at the gym when Renee visits. Then again, I would like to know what she has in mind before she accepts a marriage proposal from Tim. I want to know if she loves him enough not to cheat on him.

* * * * *

Tim and Renee left around ten o'clock. The kids were already sound asleep by then. Rayna is just getting out of the shower and I'm lying in bed. In a few minutes, when she climbs into bed, her lavender scented skin will be warm and soft. I wonder what nightie she's going to put on. She knows how much I love the blue one.

My mind flips back to before we lived together. I owned the house next door. For three years, I watched her, secretly admiring her. My favourite time was at night, when she would be standing in her kitchen making the kid's lunches. The way the light behind her would cast her silhouette against the light blue fabric. It never failed to make my cock hard. I used to jerk off while I watched her, and she had no idea I was doing it. I wanted her something fierce, but always thought she was too good for me. I still do.

I hear the unmistakable thump of the loose rack, as she hangs her towel behind the door. I could screw that thing in better, but if I do, I won't get the little flutter in my chest knowing she'll be opening that door and walking out to me, at any second. I always wonder what she'll be wearing, if anything. The light turns off as the door opens. She walks out, completely naked. This is even better than that damn blue nightie! The look on her face tells me everything I need to know. She wants me.

As she approaches the bed, she asks, "So, where are you planning on taking me?"

"You know damn well where I'm taking you," I tell her with a devilish smile.

"And, just what do you plan on doing while we're there?" Rayna slowly sways back and forth with her hands on her waist.

I lick my lips, looking up and down her impeccable body. "One thing I plan to do is fuck the hell out of you, in front of everybody. What do you think about that?"

She suddenly looks very nervous, clasping her fingers together in front of her, as if to hide her body. So many thoughts riddle my brain. Should I not have said that? Maybe I'm pushing her too far, too fast. Should I slow it down? What would be the point of slowing it down? I plan on doing that and more, with her eventually, so why sugar-coat it? She has been introduced to Fallen and didn't run away screaming. Maybe she will be fine with whatever I do to her. Maybe not.

"You want to fuck me in front of everybody? It's one thing to fuck me in front of one stranger but to do it in front of thirty of them... or more... I don't know if I'm ready for that." She's overthinking herself into a state of panic. I had better say something to ease her concern, before she outright refuses to return to Fallen.

"You have watched people getting fucked, sucked off, whipped, choked. You even watched somebody get stuck with needles. Trust me on this, nobody is going to judge you for letting me fuck you."

"It's not that I'm worried about people judging me. Being fucked is a personal thing. I was raised to believe allowing a man into your body is supposed to be a sacred thing. Forgive me if I'm having trouble letting that go. This life is all new to me, but I'm trying. I think I've been very receptive to everything you're introducing me to, so far. Even after you fucked me in front of that woman, and then invited her to play. She ate my pussy and fucked me with her whole hand. I was okay afterward. It surprised me that I was so all right with it, actually. Coach, sometimes I just need a minute to catch my breath."

"Come to bed," I say as I flip the covers making it easier for her to slide in beside me. As she's climbing in, I say, "Love, I will give you all the time you need, if you really need it. From what I have witnessed so far, you start off being afraid, but as soon as I give you no choice, like when you were bound in the web of rope, you gave yourself up to it. You have yet to use your safeword even though the option is always there. That tells me you've been enjoying everything you've been experiencing."

"I suppose you're right, but this is different. When you fucked me at Fallen, nobody was watching us. Well, that one girl outside, but it was only one person. It'll be a whole different ballgame when many people are watching. What if I do something stupid?"

"Such as?" I question with a snicker because I have a pretty good idea what she's going to say.

She shrugs, "What if I fart or something?"

I start laughing, but quickly fight to contain myself when I see the look on her face. "Love, farting is a natural act that can't be helped sometimes. When something is plunging in and out of your body, the force of that can make all kinds of weird things happen to you. Sometimes, people fart! Nobody judges anyone for that. We have all experienced it."

"Not me! It would be humiliating," she replies, rolling toward me and sliding her arm over my belly, so she can rest her head on my chest.

"Do you want to know what I think your problem is?" I feel her nod. "I don't think you're afraid. I think you are intimidated because you are inexperienced and those around you at Fallen are not. Let me just remind you that everyone there was vanilla at some point. Well, maybe not exactly vanilla when they arrived at Fallen, but we were all new to this lifestyle, at one point in time. People there are very understanding. They know you're new. They will not judge you harshly if you make a mistake. Even the most experienced sub will err sometimes. Of course, they typically do it on purpose because they want the attention of a punishment."

"They want to get punished? Why?"

"One day, you will understand the answer to that question. For now, how about I just introduce you to different scenarios, and let you decide what you favor and what you don't. We can go from there. I am going to fuck you in front of everybody on Saturday, so prepare yourself for that. If in fact you hate it and never want to do it again, so be it. But I want you to keep an open mind. Promise me you will try."

"Fine, I promise to keep an open mind. If I make a fool of myself, I will make your life miserable for weeks. Got it?"

I start laughing, "Yes, Love, you will make my life miserable for weeks."

I roll towards her, coaxing her onto her back. She instinctively opens her legs, allowing me between them. I kiss her lips lovingly, until she moans under her breath. My lips brush her neck, kissing her clavicle as I make my way down to her breasts. Her skin is still drenched with the sweet scent of lavender oil. She's soft as silk, the way only a woman can feel.

Her nipples stiffen between my thin lips when my tongue rolls over them. Her breathy moan is like music in my ears, swelling my prick. Tonight, I will make love to Rayna. I will mold my body into hers until we become one person, one entity, moving in perfect sync with the universe. How did she weave herself into my heart so easily? I need her. Goddamn, I love this woman!

Sliding down her body, I glide my hands beneath her thighs to lift and spread them wider. Her womanly scent fills my nostrils as I place a loving kiss to the most tender part of her body. My tongue gently laps at her excitement, tasting her sweet tanginess. My lips form a seal around her clit, pressing firmly against her while sucking hard and teasing her swelling nub with a viciousness that I know will push her over the edge. Should I allow her to fall so easily?

I've been patiently waiting all day to have Rayna's fingers weaved through my short hair and to feel her moans on my mouth. I've wanted to taste her, smell her, feel her heat. I won't let her cum, not yet. I want to be deep in her core when she does. I need to savour the way her muscles squeeze my cock in the most delirious of ways, as if desperate to strangle it with pulsing spasms.

I flip her onto her belly, holding her legs together tightly, with my straddling thighs. I grip her hips and lift her ass just enough that I can slide my cock into her wet pussy. While leaning forward on one elbow, I slip my other hand beneath her before using my weight to press her hips into the bed. My ring and forefinger glide on either side of her clit while the middle digit taunts and teases the nub with tender touches and light strokes.

My hips lift and lower, using purposeful thrusts to sink deeply into her. I shift my arm until it's under her chest, enabling my hand to reach her throat. I'll wait to apply pressure until she's almost there, ready to float off into the void existence she craves to escape to. Those precious few seconds are euphoric.

Her breath is forced from her body, sounding more like heavy grunts, as my hips thrust against her ass. I won't rest my full weight on her, fearing I will crush her tiny frame.

She's going to cum soon. Her clit is stiffening between my digits. I tease her by holding my fingers still for a few seconds, stroking a few times and pausing once again, only to repeat. I'm driving her wild. Her moans are desperate. Her pelvis is pressing down onto my hand. It's harder to fuck her, but her thighs squeezing around my cock, is one hell of a firm grip. I slip in and out from between her cheeks with only a portion of my prick still inside her. Fuck, she feels so goddamn tight like this!

I won't last much longer. This feels so good. I'm so fucking close! My hand grips her throat enough to make it harder for her to breathe and to get blood to her brain. I know this is heightening her pleasure.

My finger is quick to manipulate her clit, stroking and rubbing it until her body stiffens. Her pussy clamps down around my cock in the most mind-numbing way. She's coming! I let myself slip into the delirium of those few seconds where nothing in this life matters except the supreme elation that engulfs me. I've craved this all day.

My hand eases off her throat and she cries out, burying her face in the mattress. My fog clears slowly as our bodies twitch and our muscles ease. I roll off her covering my forehead and eyes with my arms. I hold each breath hoping to quickly, slow the pounding of my heart to a normal pace.

Rayna slides her body up against mine, resting her ear on my shoulder. I turn my face to look at her, as I lower my arm onto her back, snugging her panting frame against mine. My kisses to her lips are soft and effortless, perfect for the moment.

She rests her head back down and whispers, "You are an amazing lover. Sara was right."

She takes me off guard. I wasn't expecting a comment like that. "Where did that come from?"

"It just popped into my head," she replies as her finger swirls around my nipple.

"Are you jealous that I used to fuck her?"

"No, I'm not. You're mine now. I know you have a past, but," she pauses, but doesn't continue her thought.

"But?"

"Is it strange that I wish I had been a fly on that wall, just so I could see what you used to do to her? I mean, she said you can be cruel. I'm curious to know what she meant by that."

"You want to know what I used to do to her that's so different from what I do to you. Is that right?"

She debates with a long *hmmm*. "Yes, I think I do. Am I weird for wanting to know?"

"No, nothing you do is weird, other than how you look when you tweeze your eyebrows. That goofy way you contort your face, isn't normal." She laughs and pinches my nipple. I jolt and slap her hand away, rubbing the little nip while I chuckle. "Hey, stop that!"

"Seriously though, is it weird?"

"No love, it's not weird to want to know what your partner used to do with a past lover. I think it's human nature to need confirmation that you're better than they were."

"Yeah, but in this case, I know she was better than me," she comments.

I kiss her forehead and vow, "I promise that making love to you is one hundred percent more satisfying than what I used to do with her."

"If I asked to watch you do to her what you used to do, would you show me?"

I'm stunned. "You want me to play with her while you watch? Did I hear that correctly?"

"Yes. If I asked you to do that for me and she's willing, would you do it?"

"Is this one of those trust tests women give men to see if they'll cheat on them?"

She laughs, "No, you paranoid freak! I'm asking if you want to punish her how you used to?"

"Have I thought about it? Of course, I have. Do I dream about playing with her again? No, I don't. I have you in my life now and that's more important to me."

"Okay, let me put this in layman's terms so you can understand what I'm asking," she says while lifting herself up. She straddles my hips and looks down at me, forcing me to give her my full attention. "I want to watch you in action, the way you used to be, before me. I'm curious to know how you earned the nickname Demon. I want to see, but don't want to be on the receiving end of his wrath when I find out just how cruel he can be. Does that make sense?"

"Can I think about it?" I ask, still not believing that she wants me to play with Sara. "You realize that I'll likely fuck her, hard. I want you to picture that, really see it in your mind, and understand that you won't be able to forget seeing it afterward. I want you to fully understand the complications that could develop, as a result of that action."

"I have pictured it, a thousand times. At first, I was a bit jealous. Now, it really turns me on. Just now, I was imagining that I was her and you were on her, entering her, pleasuring her, making her cum. It was hot and I wish I could have watched it."

I look up at her to assess her expression. Her crooked smile with pursed lips and sexy eyes says it all. She absolutely is excited by the image in her mind.

"I was making love to you just now, mostly. With her, it's completely different and will never be soft and gentle or loving in any way. With her, it was always rough and angry, vicious sometimes. She enjoys being ruled with an iron fist. It will always be like that with her. Under no circumstances will you be allowed to interfere once I get started with her. Do you understand? Nothing; no talking, no touching."

With a hint of contained excitement in her voice, she swears, "I completely understand. I will be very quiet. You won't even know I'm there."

"If you do interrupt, I'll punish you for it. I'll be rough with you, as well. When I'm in that state of mind, it's difficult to pull myself back. I can, but why would I? If you want to be a part of it, you'll be treated just as she is."

"I understand. I like Sara. Her and I could become great friends."

"Friends?" My eyes open wide to question that. First, she wants me to fuck the woman, and then says they could become friends, afterward. "You're a strange bird, Rayna."

"Yes, I am. I think you knew that and that's why you sought me out in the first place. You somehow knew I was a freak, even before I did."

"I had an inkling. But, all this talk about watching me while I let my Demon take over another woman's body, has my cock growing hard and thick. What are you going to do about it?"

"I'm going to suck you off until you cum down my throat," she replies while gliding down my body. She's giggling like a preppy, high school cheerleader with a sexy secret and I'm not so sure I like it. I never did like girls like that, but I'll gladly take Rayna's mouth, annoying laugh or not.

I have one patient left. A set of x-rays and a cleaning, and then I'm free for the rest of the day. By three o'clock, I will be out of here. Both kids will be staying after school today. They signed up for programs that require them to stay late on Tuesdays and Fridays. I like it because I get some free time to myself and they have something to do that interests them, other than computer games.

Ken joined an archery program. He said it makes him feel like Robin Hood. Robin Hood was a thief with good intensions, so I'm torn between liking the reference, or not. Either way, he's happy, so I'm happy.

Kim joined a group that studies astronomy. She's always enjoyed looking at the stars and the moon. I bought her a telescope last year for her birthday, and she's used it quite often. Her and I had a shooting stars night, last summer. We camped out in a tent in our backyard. She used the telescope for a while, but she wasn't quick enough to catch them before they shot away, so she packed it up. We zipped ourselves into our sleeping bags and laid with our heads sticking out the flap of the tent so we could watch the streaks in the sky, the old-fashioned way – with our eyes. It was a memorable night for sure.

Before my patient arrives, I think I'll go to the stockroom for privacy, and call Sara. I'd like to see if she does want to meet up or if she was just being kind in saying that she'd like us to be friends. Coach gave me her number, but I've been too nervous to call her. After my pillow talk with Coach last night about watching him be with her, I'm more excited than nervous at this point. My hands are still shaking and my stomach feels tight.

It rings twice before her soft voice answers. "Hello?"

"Hi, Sara. This is Kat calling. Do you remember me? I was with Demon."

"Oh! Hi Kat! Of course, I remember you. How are you?"

"I'm doing well. And, you?"

"Things are great for me. So, Demon gave you my number, I gather. Hmm, I wasn't sure he would."

"Yes, on Sunday morning. He was very happy to give it to me. To be honest, he was trying not to seem too enthusiastic about me calling you. But he knows I could learn a lot from you."

"Maybe, yeah. I've been in this lifestyle for almost eleven years now, so I've experienced a lot; some good, some not so good. I'd be more than happy to answer any questions you have. I'm so glad you called! So, what's up with you today?"

"I was wondering, if you aren't busy, maybe we could meet for coffee somewhere. I'll be finished here at work in about a half hour and then I'm free for a few hours. I'm not sure what your schedule looks like."

"I'm always free, well sort of. I work at home and can do what I do at any time of the day or night. I have an idea, why don't you come to my house and I'll make coffee here. It's more private, so we can talk without interruptions or snoopy people listening in."

"Sure, that sounds much better. I can be there in about an hour." I'm trying not to sound nervous. The idea of her and I being alone together is rather worrisome, but yet exciting. I'm sure one day her and I will have sex. Today is not likely going to be that day. That'll happen when Coach – or Demon – insists upon it. I'm way too shy to come onto her. Besides, it would be my first time and definitely not hers. It's a test my confidence will likely fail.

"Would you like me to bring snacks?"

"No Kat, I'll whip something up here."

"I don't want you to go through any trouble."

"It's no trouble! I love cooking. Besides, I could use a snack or two," she giggles.

I write down her address before we end the call. I immediately text Coach to let him know I won't be home.

Me: I'm going to Sara's after work. Kids have archery and astronomy after school. Don't worry, I'll pick them up on my way home.

Coach: You're going to Sara's?

Me: Yes. Are you okay with that?

Coach: Of course. I can't help that I'll be picturing the two of you in a heated tryst.

Me: I don't think that's going to happen, but I can't stop you from imagining it.

Coach: I give you permission to play with Sara

Me: Oh, gee, thanks

Coach: What does that mean?

Me: I'm not going to have sex with her, whether you give me permission or not

Coach: If I don't give you permission first, you'd better never have sex with anyone. That's cheating.

Me: But if you give me permission, it isn't cheating? That makes no sense. I'd still be having sex with someone without you there - cheating

Coach: But if I give my permission, it's allowed.

Me: Hmm, if you say so.

Coach: If I tell you to have sex with someone when I'm not around, and I know you really do want that person, it's not cheating. It's an order that you will need to follow, unless you use your safeword, of course.

Me: Are you saying you're ordering me to have sex with Sara?

Coach: I'm saying you can, if you want to. It's allowed, but not demanded.

Me: It doesn't matter, either way. I doubt that will happen without you there. I'd be too intimidated by her.

Coach: Don't deny yourself the experience if it comes about.

Me: Okay, I have to go. I have a patient waiting.

Coach: I love you! Have fun and don't worry about the kids. I'll pick them up at five.

Me: Okay, see you later.

I slide my phone into my shirt pocket as I'm walking into the reception area.

"Hello, Mrs. Baker. Do you want to come with me?" The woman slowly stands on her well-seasoned legs and shuffles her flat, pink slip-on shoes across the tiled floor. She pushes her walker at a snail's pace. It might take longer than a half hour just to get her into the room.

"I'm sorry, dear," she says with a tender, shaky voice.

"You just take your time. I am in no hurry," I fib to her, as convincingly as I can manage.

I don't want her to rush, possibly falling and hurting herself. First of all, she'll get injured and she really is a sweet woman, so I don't want to see her in pain. Secondly, and selfishly, if she falls and does get injured, I'll be here for at least another hour. We'll need to get her shipped off in an ambulance and then I'll have to fill out a mountain of paperwork. So, no, I don't want her to rush.

* * * * *

I'm standing in the well-lit hallway on the gold and blue carpeting, unsure of whether I want to have sex with her if she asks me to, or tell her I'm on my period, or some other tale that will likely postpone that activity. I keep staring at the golden numbers - twelve-sixteen - affixed to the door, rereading them about eight times, just to make sure I have the right apartment. The building is newer than the one next to it and it's much classier.

I purposely shake my hands to ease their nervous vibration. I take a deep breath and whisper to myself, "It's okay Rayna, she's a nice woman. She isn't going to want to have sex with you today. Just lift your fist and knock on the damn door."

I rap and wait, but not for too long. She opens the door, greeting me with a huge smile. "Hi, come on in! I'm glad you came."

"Thank you. I'm happy to be here. I love your apartment!"

The brightness of the afternoon sun shining through the glass wall casts a romantic easiness about the room. The softly painted walls are decorated with beautiful pictures of the wilderness and running streams. The place seems much larger than it probably is because of the open-concept kitchen and living room. As I pass the short hallway, I can see three open doors. I can see the glass surround to a shower unit through one of those rooms making me assume that would be the bathroom.

"It's technically a condo, but thank you. I love this building much more than the place I was at before."

"Did you just move in?" I ask while breathing in the gentle scent of vanilla, realizing it's coming from a lit candle on the kitchen island. The scent adds to the calmness of the atmosphere.

"No, not really. I've been here for about two years now. It's really quiet, so I can get a lot of work done without interruptions, unlike my last place. It was way too noisy there."

"It's beautifully decorated. Did you do it yourself?" It does look professionally done.

"Yeah, I like decorating, and thank you," she says while glancing around the room, proudly admiring her efforts. "Make yourself at home. What do you take in your coffee?"

"Just a little milk, black is fine too," I tell her while sitting on a stool on the front side of the island.

A very fat, fluffy white cat comes waddling into the kitchen silently, as cats typically are. It jumps onto the counter and flops over with its tail flipping in the air. The loud purr coming from this cat has me giggling. I've never heard one this loud. I reach out and pet it. It rolls from side to side as I stroke its fine, thick coat.

"Sorry about that. Katie, off you go!" she says, shooing her away. "She thinks she owns the place."

"Cats are like that. I don't mind if she's on the counter."

"I don't like her doing that when company is over. Some people don't like cats."

"The way I see it, this home is yours and you can let your cat do whatever you want. If a guest has an issue with it, they can leave."

She looks at me and smiles. "I knew I was going to like you."

I smile as she hands me a big mug which reads, *happier with coffee*. It suits me well.

"So, now that it's just the two of us and nobody can listen in, is there anything in particular you want to talk about?" she asks while waving me to follow her to the puffy black sofa.

"Well, yes actually, but I'm not sure you'll want to talk about it."

"Try me," she suggests as she sits facing me with one leg folded beneath her. "Think of this as a safe place where you can ask anything without judgement. Whatever we talk about here is between you and I, only. Nobody will ever hear about our conversation, not even Coach."

"You know his real name?"

"Of course! He was my Master, and friend, so we would go out to dinner once in a while, or other places where referring to him as Demon, would not go over very well."

"What's your real name, if I can ask that."

"Sara. I didn't change my name and I never had a Master who chose one for me. They just called me Sara. Well, there was bitch, whore, slut, cunt, pig, et cetera. What's yours? I know Kat isn't your real name."

"I'm Rayna. Coach and I had a conversation about me being older than him and the whole cougar thing. I didn't want to be called C.A.T. because cougar is just too degrading, so I asked to be called K.A.T. Nobody is the wiser of the spelling, but I know and that's all that matters."

"I like it! Can I ask you what the age difference is between you and Coach?"

"I'm ten years older."

"Tell me about yourself."

"I have two kids with my useless ex-husband who has basically abandoned them when he recently moved across the country with the tart of the month. I'm happier now that he's not around and the kids are better off too. Coach moved in and he's been more of a dad than their biological sperm donor ever was. He's a good man."

"I know he is. He was always very good to me. He never emotionally hurt me, and he respected me... outside of the playroom, of course. He was very dominant when I needed him to be and I really liked that."

"Do you miss him?" I ask, hoping I don't sound jealous.

"Miss him?" she repeats and then sips her coffee. She is taking a moment, as if to think of what an acceptable response would be. "To be honest with you, I do. I miss him a lot. I'm not saying that I am in love with him, please believe that. I cared a lot for him, as my friend with benefits. When we split up, I didn't think I'd miss him this much, but I do."

"Would you get together with him again if given the chance?"

She sips her coffee again and then sets it on the table, folding her hands in her lap. "He's with you now."

"He is, but would you?"

Her eyebrows furrow, "Rayna, let's not beat around the bush, okay? What are you wanting to ask me?"

I look at her and set my cup down. "I've never seen Demon in action, not really. He won't let him out, with me. He says I'm not ready. I'll admit that when he says that, it intimidates me. The thing is, I don't know how bad he can get, so my imagination takes over and I picture him slapping me around and really hurting me. I just wonder if he'll be able to keep his Demon at bay for the rest of our lives or not. If he's right, and Demon is too much for me, he'll never be the man he needs to be. How miserable will he become over time?"

She nods, understanding my concerns. "So, are you asking if I'll let Demon play with me like he used to, like physically? Do you want to see how he is with me?"

I flash a smile and nod shyly. "Are you opposed to that?"

She picks up her cup and takes a large gulp, hugging her cup with both hands afterward. "I'm not opposed to it. My concern is, well, there's history between us. If he's all right with it…" She sips her coffee again, looking into her mug afterward. "Well, he already knows how I like to play, so I suppose that would benefit the situation. So, just so you are aware - watching your fiancée fuck me might put a strain on your relationship. Have you thought about that? I've seen it happen too many times. People think they can handle swapping with extra partners, but they quickly find out that the big green monster takes over and the jealousy ruins their marriage. I'm not saying it will happen to you two. I know he's good with sharing, as long as permission is granted. It's you I'm worried about. I'm guessing your ex cheated on you."

"How would you know that?"

"It's just a guess. I'm intuitive," she jokes. "Plus, you said he left with the *tart of the month*. That's a dead giveaway."

"Yeah, he fucked my sister. It happened years ago, and I guessed it had happened, but didn't really want to know for certain. It wasn't all that long ago that she confirmed it; last year, actually. I had already dealt with it years ago, therefore, it didn't affect my relationship with my sister. I think her and I are stronger now than ever, now that everything is out on the table. She hit on Coach once but that was before we were actually together, so I let that go."

"Do you trust her?"

"With Coach?" I ask, she nods. "Not in so many words. I really don't think she would, and I know Coach won't entertain her, but there's a little piece of me that has doubts about her self-control."

"I want you to close your eyes right now and picture me bound to a wooden horse while he pulls my hair and fucks me very hard."

I do what she suggests.

"Now, I want you to picture me coming hard on his cock. Remember, we'll move well together because of our history. He'll know exactly when to fuck me harder or softer, slap me or caress me. Picture him caressing me, kissing my lips, us reaching orgasm together. If he sticks his tongue in my ass, will you want to kiss him after that?"

"Right after? I don't know," I snicker.

She giggles, "Okay, maybe not right after if that's not something you're okay with."

"I honestly don't know. I haven't even been down on a woman. I'm not sure if I would be okay with him having another woman's scent on his face. I enjoy my own scent and taste on his lips, so I suppose I'd be okay with someone else's."

"But what about watching him fuck me or me pleasuring him with my mouth? What if I make him cum? Will you be okay with that?"

"Like I said, I don't know, but I want to find out. How else will I find out if I don't actually see it happen. When I imagine him fucking you and dominating you..." my words fall away, but my eyes stay locked on hers.

"It turns you on," she says, finishing my sentence for me.

"Yes," I reply, feeling ashamed.

"Have you thought about you and I having sex?"

My breath catches in my chest. My whole body seems to ignite from a flickering flame to a raging inferno. Is my face on fire? I'm sure I'm redder than a firetruck! I can feel my hands starting to shake.

"Would you like to have sex with me?"

The sudden dryness in my throat has me swallowing hard. I gulp my coffee, but it doesn't help wash down the nervousness. My stomach squeezes when a stomach full of flapping butterflies threatens to make me vomit.

In barely a whisper, I boldly reply, "Maybe, I don't know."

"Do you have his permission?" she asks.

That's a question that has me wondering its origin. "Um, strangely enough, when I told him I was coming here, he gave me his permission. Did you two plan this behind my back?"

"No! The last time I talked to him was at Fallen when you were there. I promise!" she vows with her hand in the air. "I just know he's really opposed to playing without permission. That's what split our union. I started dating someone who wasn't involved in this lifestyle. I told Coach that we were intimate, and he broke it off."

I'm relieved that he hasn't been flirting. But I wonder why I'm so concerned about it. If he starts fucking her, maybe I will be nervous. My hands are shaking again and it's not from the coffee. "I, um... I'm really nervous."

"That's okay, Rayna. I understand. We can take it very slowly."

I nod and smile at her, but have a hard time holding her gaze. "I'd appreciate that."

She takes my mug and sets it on the table. "Come with me. We can take a shower together."

She puts her hand out to me as she stands up. I take a big breath and then take her hand. What's the worse that will happen? If I don't like it, I never have to do it again. At least I won't be wondering *what if* for the rest of my life. By the end of this hour I will know if I like vagina as much as cock. This will be a learning experience, if nothing else.

She brings me into her bedroom and begins by undressing herself. I watch her while I slowly follow her lead. She stands before me completely naked. I've seen her at this level of undress, so it doesn't bother me at all. I already know she has an amazing figure.

"You are so perfect," I whisper.

"Sweetie, in no way, shape or form am I perfect."

"I don't look as good as you. I've had two children and I'm older than you." In a way, I'm confessing my insecurities.

"Rayna, I tried to have children with my ex-husband, but after four miscarriages, I decided to have some testing done. They proved I cannot carry a fetus. I left him, so he could move on and have children with someone else. Being a father to half a dozen kids was his lifelong dream. He's now remarried with eight kids--two sets of twins! It was a good thing... me leaving him. I wish I had stretchmarks and loose skin because it would be totally worth it."

"I'm so sorry," I whisper. I can see past her phony smile at how much she's hurting.

"It's in the past. If I dwelled on everything shitty that ever happened to me, I'd never get out of bed. Happiness is a choice and I choose it over sadness and regret." I'm beginning to like Sara very much.

As soon as I've removed my panties and set them on top of my shirt, bra and pants, she takes my hand and guides me into the bathroom.

After setting the water to the perfect temperature, she steps into the glass shower. I follow her in. Despite the heat of the cascading water, I'm shaking as if it were nearly freezing cold.

She begins soaping my fingers, working her way up my arms to my shoulders, neck and finally my chest. She doesn't use a loofa or a cloth, just her hands. Her tender touch feels different on my skin than a man's. Maybe the delicacy of her small hands is what makes her touch feel so faint. I don't know, but I do like it.

I take the soap and lather it up in my palms and then start at her shoulders and work my way down her arms, back up and then move down the center of her chest. I watch the bubbles lazily trail over the slopes of her breasts. I reach for the perky mounds, cupping them in my hands. I fondle them tenderly, amazed at how soft and warm they feel. Mine don't seem to feel as soft or as warm. My thumbs brush over her nipples. She takes in a quick breath and they stiffen without hesitation.

Curious to explore her, I trail my fingertips down her belly and slip my hand between her legs. It doesn't feel much different than mine. The fact that I'm touching a clitoris, but don't feel the sensations of my touch, seems odd. I'm very pleased that I'm enjoying her body. My fear has ceased, shifting more toward curiosity. I'm not even shaking anymore.

My fingers explore her labia and clitoris. My own pussy is twitching, knowing exactly how marvellous it feels to have my clit touched a certain way; a way I truly enjoy in these first stages of arousal. Is she enjoying my touch the way I imagine she is?

"Can I kiss you?" she asks.

I don't answer her, I move toward her and press my lips to hers while placing my arm around her shoulder so my hand can hold the back of her neck. Her body feels so small in comparison to Coach.

Our mouths softly kiss, our tongues dancing tenderly. Her face is so soft and tiny. Everything about her is familiar and yet a complete mystery. This is no longer an experiment, I actually want her. I want to feel her tender weight on me, or her small frame beneath me, or beside me. I just need to feel her. I can't wait to trace her sexy curves with the tips of my fingers. I yearn to taste her intimacy.

Her lips scarcely part from mine. "Let's rinse off and go to my bed."

"Yes, I want that," I whisper in response.

We quickly rinse ourselves and dry off while watching each other. Her skin has a pale creaminess about it that has me imagining her flesh donning the morning's purple bruises from a night of rope play. Her light brown hair is shoulder length and holds a soft wave even when it's damp. Her eyes are so blue that the freckles on her skin make for a huge contrast.

She takes my hand and leads me to the bed. Before we lie down, we have already started kissing. The second her body presses against mine my mind slips far away from my fears. The silkiness of her skin pressing onto mine makes our flesh mold into one. Her hair tickles my cheeks and neck.

My hands cup her face, pulling her hair from her face. She rolls onto me and straddles my hips. Her breasts are so soft that my hands want to grip them tighter than I likely should. I know how to tease her fat nipples, because I have fat nipples too. I'll just do what I want done to me.

She slowly glides down my body. She tenderly kisses my breasts, circling my nipples with her tongue. The way she does it has my pussy twitching and me moaning. She could just stay doing what she's doing, and I'd still call it a wonderful lesbian experience. But I hope she continues downward to my pussy. I want to feel that soft mouth.

I lift my head to see how it looks to have a beautiful woman eager to pleasure me. I've had dreams about this, but never imagined I'd ever go through with it. I'm pleased I allowed myself the thrill of this taboo.

Sara looks up at me just as her lips gingerly kiss the tip of my clitoral hood. Her hot breath flows down my air-chilled folds, easing a moan from my depths. I tilt my pelvis, eager for more. I want her mouth to touch me. I need it!

"Please," I beg.

Watching Sara smile just before her lips surround my swelling nub has my mind whirling from excitement. Her pouty lips form a seal and gently suck, release my clit in a steady rhythm as her tongue agilely, and with great skill, molests it.

She slips two of her fingers inside of me and immediately begins rubbing toward the front. A sudden sensation of pressure from inside of me forces outward into my clit, swelling it like a tiny balloon. It doesn't hurt, it's glorious. This internal massage is better than anything Coach has done, and he's great with his hands.

Another finger enters me, and it isn't enough. I want more. The harsh stretch doesn't hurt, it feels amazing. My pussy is full, but she's still able to fuck me at a slow and steady pace. Her whole hand pushes, hoping to enter me. I cry out when my mind swims from the sudden superb invasion. Her hand is smaller than Coaches, much smaller, and I'm able to compensate for it easily. Her hand is so much more enjoyable than his; it's less pain.

She slowly fucks me with her fingers straight, sliding in and gliding out, then pushing back in, her knuckles held out only by my tightness. Her mouth works my clit until I'm humping her hand and tongue, as she eases me closer and closer to the point of no return.

I open my eyes when I feel her hot lips on my left nipple, circling it while nipping at its tip. I reach down and cup her face with both hands, leaning up to her while she rises up to meet me. Our mouths press together with a heated passion that has me moaning for more. The familiar taste of my pussy on her unfamiliar lips is proof that her beautiful pouty lips engulfed me, tasted me.

Sara's fingers continue to fuck me while my hips hump up to meet her arm, hoping to take every inch of her inside of me. My clit burns with a need for her touch, but I'll be patient and enjoy every second she's with me.

Suddenly, a fullness has me flopping my head back onto the bed and crying out, begging her for something, anything, more maybe. I don't know; my mind is drifting further away as my body begins to float off the mattress. Her fist is spinning inside of me, pushing in, as it does. Lightly punching and spinning, punching and spinning.

Her lips suck my clit, rubbing and flipping it back and forth, up and down. Her left-hand presses down on my pelvic bone while her forefinger and thumb squeeze the lips together from either side of my clit, projecting the little button outward and into her awaiting mouth. She inhales it, taking it as a hostage between her teeth with a light nip. Her tongue continues its assault, ravishing my swollen clitoris more fantastically than I have ever felt.

My hands grip the comforter to keep from floating too far away from her. She has me so close to orgasm but has yet to take me over the top. She's holding me at the peak. My body and mind belong to her. She has me – all of me.

Her fist rotates quicker, seeming to vibrate inside of me. My clit is quivering, twitching, pulsing in her teeth. I don't exactly know what happens next because I'm lost, out of my body and gone. This all-encompassing glory has taken me away to nowhere. Nothing exists except pure, unrelenting euphoria.

My soul slowly re-enters my body, gently sinking its weight back on the bed, as it does. My lungs and throat are burning. I was screaming. I could hear myself, but I was so far away that quieting myself became an impossibility.

My eyes open to see Sara looking down at me with a sedate expression. Her lips press tenderly to mine as my breath rushes through my nostrils until I need to open my lips for more air. Our tongues dance tenderly, lovingly.

My hands explore the thighs that are spread over either side of my hips. They are so smooth and soft that my fingertips feel as rough as sandpaper in comparison.

Sara pulls away, leaning toward one of her nightstands. She opens the top drawer and pulls out a long, double-ended dildo. She lifts off me just enough so that I can open my legs, accepting one end of it inside of me. She bends it up while pushing my legs together. It's coolness rests along my hot, twitching clit. It feels so good, almost calming.

She lifts up and presses the other end inside of herself. She slowly sinks down until she rests on my pelvis. Her body has completely engulfed her half of the dildo.

I cup her breasts and tilt my pelvis. She holds my hands onto her globes. I watch as her hips sensually begin to rock up and down, forward and back. Each time she fills herself, my end presses deeper into me. As she lifts, it pulls. I squeeze my stretched pussy muscles to help hold it inside of me.

Her beauty is awe inspiring. The way the light from the window surrounds her curves, shadowing the concaves of her small muscles, as she fucks me while fucking herself.

I tilt my pelvis just a little bit more, enough so that another inch of dildo is freed for her to sink her body onto. With my hands still grasping her breast, she pulls my fingers to her nipples and pinches them so hard that my fingers ache under her grip.

Sara's head drops back as she rides harder and faster, fucking the dildo as if it were my own real cock. The friction against my sensitive clit is enough to wake it from its sedated trance. The way the dick feels inside me, rubbing on my clit while she rides it, tricks me into believing my actual cock is ramming into her. I let my mind slip into that thought, as if I am Coach and this dick is his. She is riding him, not me. It's thrilling, especially when she cums and her pussy grips and spasms, moving the dildo inside of me in unusual ways.

"Yes, cum for me," I whisper just as my own orgasm explodes through me like a tidal wave. My hips are bouncing up at her, as hers slam down. I'm fucking her. She's fucking me. We're both coming hard on the shared cock. Our bodies fight to keep moving, keep fucking, keep pleasuring the other, but it's useless. My arms and hips drop to the bed. Sara falls forward, her face buried in my neck. Both of us are panting, like dogs on a hot summer day.

She lifts herself just enough to kiss me. Our lips hold lazily together, breathing in one another's spent air. My fingers weave into her silky hair, brushing the sweaty tresses off her cheek and tucking it behind her ear.

I roll her onto her back, resting my hips between her thighs. The dildo has popped out of me, but remains inside of her, my end resting on the bed, wet and slick with my cum.

Feeling brave, I slide down her body, kissing and licking her glistening, salty skin. Between her thighs I can smell her sex. My mouth waters, something I wasn't expecting. This is the first time I've been this close to another woman's vagina. My lips press just above her clit, kissing her tenderly. I lower my mouth and press my tongue between her silky folds. I'm shocked to feel their incredible softness, as if it were pudding on my lips.

I lap at her saltiness, exploring each fold and tasting her tangy sweetness. Her scent fills my nostrils, igniting a fire between my thighs. I open my lips wide and press my mouth around her entire clitoris. Gently at first, I suck, lifting her clit against my tongue. I stroke under the hood with the tip of my tongue. Her moan is my reward.

I tenderly adore her clit and feel it swell the more I fondle it. My pussy is tingling, and I can feel the wetness of my arousal when I shift to a more comfortable position. Flat on my belly, with my hands reach under her hips, holding her thighs apart.

I try to remember what she did to me and do my best to copy. Her chest rises and falls, her breath quickening. I slip two fingers between her labia and wiggle until they are inside of her. The heat of her depth stuns me. I hadn't realized just how smoldering it is inside a woman's cavern.

My fingers wiggle and play, exploring how easily it is to push deeply into her until my knuckles press against my chin. I pull my face back so I can watch my fingers disappear into her. I add another and push.

"More," she instructs.

With her nudging, I add a forth. Her lips part and I know just how she feels. My pussy twitches, imagining my hand is inside of me, doing exactly this to my body. I do what I would want done to me. I add my thumb and gently twist, using her natural wetness to lubricate my knuckles.

Her eyes keep her mind connected to me, as I cautiously push forward. I don't want to hurt her. Sara seems to understand my hesitation and reaches down to grasp my wrist. Her hips lift off the bed as she pulls on my arm, forcing it into her. I feel her pussy let go and in a flash I'm in. What a sight this is!

My entire hand has been engulfed inside of her. The tightness that holds me in prevents me from fucking her with ease. I pull out slightly and twist, as she had done to me.

"Make a fist," she whispers through a heaving breath.

"You're so tight," I whisper in reply. "I don't know if I can."

It takes a bit of effort, but I manage to fold my fingers over my thumb and into my palm. I feel like I am in control of her body, as if I own her completely. My fist is locked inside of her, as if she were my puppet. If I pull back, she comes with me. I try again just to see if it's possible, but her outer rim is too tight. I push forward, deeper into her and slowly try to nod by wrist, like a puppet in agreeance.

Sara arches her back, releasing my wrist and reaching high above her head to clutch the rails on her headboard. Her moans ride loudly on the long, purposeful breaths that escape her. For a few moments, I'm lost in the vision of this beautiful woman skewered on my arm, writhing against it, her pleasure comes at my will. I feel powerful. I can make her cum, or not cum. It's up to me--my desire, my compassion.

I reach for the dildo as I lift onto my knees. I push it into my dripping wet cunt and start to fuck myself with the same tempo as my hand is fucking her. The only difference is my hand is waving, and the dildo unfortunately cannot. I want to feel what she feels, to know if I'm doing it right.

I lean forward and bury my mouth against her clit, sucking and flicking like a starving woman trying to drain syrup from a tree. Her thighs pull together, holding my head and deafening my ears to her pleasured cries.

My hands fuck her faster, building my own orgasm as I'm sure hers is escalating. My tongue whirls as my mouth sucks and my fist reams. The woman's strong thighs clenching over my ears are no match for her passionate wails. I can hear her song and it's revving me up. She sings for me because of what I am doing to her. If I stop, she won't cum. I am not that cruel, but it would be ultimate torture at this stage of our arousal.

Sara screams, "I'm coming! I'm coming!"

I open my eyes to watch her erupt. This is the first time I will make a woman lose her mind at my will, but it is not going to be the last. She releases the rails and grabs her breasts, squeezing them so tightly that I'm sure they'll burst. She pinches her nipples, pulling up so viciously that I'm sure she's going to tear them off. Her flesh is changing colour under her grip, darkening to a deep red.

Sara screams. Her thighs part wide as her ass tenses, lifting her crotch against my mouth. I watch her lips part as she sucks in a long, deep breath. Her cunt is twitching, pulsing around my hand making it more difficult to keep nodding it. I try to pull and push, nod and twist, to give her the most pleasure I possibly can.

Her entire body is vibrating. I own her mind, body and soul at this very moment. Everything about her belongs to me. I am giving her this gift of euphoria. Me. I am.

Her clit is swelling and stiffening, making it easier to violate it. I suck even harder while continuing to flick and stroke with earnest.

Sara's pussy grips my fist like a vice, pinning it in place. I cannot move it. The spasms are crushing my hand, but I love it. Heat surges through her cunt like a volcanic eruption. Her muscles push, giving birth to my hand. A flood of her cum washes over my hand and chin, startling me.

I don't stop lapping and sucking on her bloated clit. Maybe she'll cum again.

Her entire body is jerking each time my tongue flicks. The control I have over her is intoxicating. She weaves her fingers in my hair, holding my head in place. I watch as she continues to flinch and contort her face in a pained expression. I am familiar with this hypersensitivity after a clitoral orgasm. She seems to want it. I know she enjoys pain and punishment, but this is something I do not like.

She finally pulls my hair to lift my mouth away from her pussy. My lips cool in the air now that they're away from the fiery heat of her womanhood.

I climb up her body, leaving the dildo inside of me. Her hands tenderly glide down my ribs and around my back. Her legs wrap around my waist and hold me against her. I wish I had a cock so I could sink into her and lose myself inside her. I want to feel her heat, her passion, her lust.

Our mouths press together in a romantic embrace. Her lips separate as her tongue slips between mine. Together they dance passionately, allowing her to sample the flavour of her own orgasm. Her mouth feels rough in comparison to the softness of her pussy.

Sara whispers, "Sit on my face."

I kiss her once more and then slowly make my way up her body, noticing how much tinier her frame is than Coach's. The cock slips from my pussy, landing on her belly. I feel her jerk to grab it. My pussy hovers over her puffy lips. I hold her gaze until she lifts her head to taste me and my lids become heavy.

Her arms wrap around my thighs, pulling me down onto her face. Her tongue tickles my aroused clit, now and then dipping down along my inner labia awakening those sensitive nerves. She kisses and licks me, savouring my flesh.

I look down and watch her enjoying me. Her eyes are closed, allowing her mind to relish in the moment, without distraction. She's tender and loving at first. Her intensity gradually escalating the more aroused I become, or am I becoming more aroused from her intensity? I can't decide.

My breaths are short and quick, laced with moans. She's building me up to a harsh climax. I can feel the urgency tightening in my belly. Fuck! She's exceptional at this!

Sara is searching for the opening of my pussy with the dildo, but she can't maneuver it to get it inside me. I lean forward just slightly, and it slips into me. She immediately begins to fuck me with long, deep strokes. My thoughts are swirling, but are quick to focus solely on my impending orgasm.

I reach out and grab hold of her headboard for stability. My thighs are beginning to quiver, and I don't want to slip down onto her face. I hold tightly as if determined to bend the wrought iron bars. It's impossible, but my grip is so intense that my hands are aching.

Sara fucks me faster, continuing with the lengthy strokes, pounding my g-spot relentlessly. Her lips wrap around my clit while her tongue continues its assault.

Within seconds, my mind is slipping away, drowning in my body's pleasure. I give myself up to her, completely. I sit up taller, shifting my hips slightly. The pounding from the head of the dildo is now striking my g-spot at the perfect angle.

Oh god! That's it! Oh yes! A rippling seizure of lust releases, shredding through me. My mind is lost in the nothingness of sexual euphoria. With my eyes shut, mouth open, head tilted back, I am locked in this position by muscles that have a mind of their own.

A loud wail rips from my burning lungs as my muscles unlock and I fall forward, pressing my face against the cool metal bar. My body jerks above her mouth, refusing to accept the end of the incredible elation known to be an orgasm.

With every ounce of strength I can muster, I lift myself from my position and slowly topple to my left, coming to rest on my back, my limbs flopping carelessly.

"Oh, fuck! That was... holy shit!" is all I can whisper.

I hear her giggle and feel her soft hand slide along my belly. She presses her body against mine, resting her head on my bicep. Her fingertips lightly tickle my left nipple, but not in an arousing way. She's simply touching me, exploring the stiff, little nub.

"So, what do you think about having sex with a woman?"

I smile and whisper, "I am all for it."

"It's different than having sex with a man, isn't it?" Her fingers draw tiny circles on my breast causing my nipple to stiffen even more.

"Yeah, it is. You are soft and delicate. With Coach I can be rougher, I guess. I mean, I feel a need to be gentler with you because of your size and the softness of your skin. I didn't want to grab and squeeze you because I was afraid to bruise you. But, holy shit woman! You really know your way around a woman's body!"

She giggles, "I've been with a woman or two, in my days."

"More than that, I'm guessing. You are really good."

"Thank you," she says as she leans up on her elbow so we can talk while looking at each other. "Did you enjoy tasting me?"

I smile and nod, "I did! I was so worried I wouldn't. I feared I would attempt it and hate it the whole time, but feel committed once I got down there. It was quite the opposite. You're so soft on my lips. Your taste is sweet, but tangy and your scent is intoxicating. The more aroused you became, the more I felt in control."

"Did you feel powerful?"

I shrug, "Maybe a little. I had no desire to hurt you or punish you. In fact, I remember thinking about how cruel it would be for me to stop when you were almost there, like Coach has done to me many times. I didn't want to stop you from coming. It's kind of a power-trip, knowing I had that much control over you."

"Demon... Coach, does enjoy delayed gratification. He does it to himself as well. He will not allow himself to cum until he feels he's earned the right. Well, that's not always the case. Sometimes, if he thought I didn't deserve to orgasm, he would take his pleasure from me and leave me without. I deserved it at times, but it wasn't what I would have chosen."

"Do you miss him? Or, should I ask, did you love him?"

She looks at me and smiles while shaking her head, "Sweetie, I love him but I'm not in love with him. He is a dear friend who helped me work through many of my own demons, after I came back from my tour. I was lost, hopeless and seeking punishment."

"What happened over there to cause you to feel that way?"

"Nothing good. I don't often talk about it, but since you asked and we just did what we did, I'll tell you. We were on a routine surveillance mission. There were two cars in the convoy. I was in the first vehicle. We drove straight into an IED that tossed our vehicle, killing the driver. We took on fire from the fucking mercenaries who were waiting to ambush any Americans who passed through. We were hurting, but we managed to take them out. While making our way back to the second car, another swarm came at us. It was a nightmare scenario."

Sara's words stop. She clears her throat and swallows hard. "I lost three friends on that afternoon. I welcomed the bullet hole in my foot because it pulled me away from the pain in my heart. So, when I got back home, I needed to suffer physically to overrule the mental anguish. I tried several dominants, but none stuck. I welcomed the pain Coach seemed to be able to grant me which helped free my mind. On other days, when I felt pitiful for my own sorrows, I craved his punishment. Somehow, he seemed to know what I needed, when I needed it. Because of him, I can now function well. I sleep without having nightmares every night and I don't wallow in the memory of that day. I can appreciate the fun memories I had with the guys we lost."

Sara smiles, as if remembering something funny. She shakes her head and looks up at me with a shrug.

"I'm sorry you went through that."

"Me too. So, back to you and your first sexual experience with a female." She grins and winks. "Did you enjoy being in control of my pleasure?"

"I really did! I can better understand the benefits of being a dominant. I felt powerful and in control of you. There was a strength of mind in knowing I had that much control. It's sort of the ultimate stroke to my ego. I'm beginning to understand why dominants enjoy it."

"Most are all about their ego and I do like stroking it for them."

"Have you ever dominated anyone?"

"No, I'm a submissive with no desire to be anything different. I would never grant anyone pain, but I really love it when someone hurts me. I'm a masochist, through and through. Pain takes my mind away from reality and I will always be grateful to my Masters who've allowed it."

"I haven't dominated anyone either. This whole submissive thing is still new to me, so being the aggressor hasn't even crossed my mind. I'm not a person who likes to be in control, sexually. I mean, I have two kids and a shitty ex-husband who didn't do squat to help me support and raise them, so I've always had to be the strong one. When it comes to sex, I don't want to have to make any decisions. I'm tired, if that makes any sense."

"I totally get what you're saying."

"Can I ask you something?" She nods. "After you came, you held my head so that I would continue to lick your clit. For me, it's an intensely painful tickle that I can't stand. Why did you want me to continue?"

She grins, "Well, after an orgasm, I have a strange need to be punished for taking my pleasure. If I'm not punished for coming, it doesn't feel complete, as if I'm left with the guilt. It's weird, I know."

"Yeah, that feeling of the horrible sensitive painfulness... I hate it! Coach tortures me with that sometimes and I always beg him to stop. I haven't used the safeword to get him to, but I've come very close."

Sara sits up and runs her fingers through her hair to smooth out the knots. When the light from the window surrounds her shape, I'm reminded of how beautiful she looked when she was riding my fake cock.

"Can I ask you something else?"

She smiles and says, "Sweetie, you can ask me anything you want."

"I want to watch you with Demon."

She smiles and whispers, "That isn't really a question."

I smile and nod shyly. "Will you be with him… for me?"

"I would love to. Tomorrow night at Fallen?" She stands up and takes my hand to help me up.

"Tomorrow? I'll see if I can have my sister available for the kids. We've just started leaving them alone."

"How's that going?"

"Well, so far so good."

Sara and I get dressed and then sit back on her sofa to drink a fresh coffee. We chat about everything from family to some of the worst BDSM experiences she's been through, as well as some of her best ones.

About an hour later, I kiss and hug her before leaving. As I'm walking to my car, I feel light on my feet and thrilled that I enjoy women. This opens up a whole new world for me.

CHAPTER TWENTY-ONE
Coach

I hardly slept all night. The idea of playing with Sara has my Demon rattling the bars of his cage. It never crossed my mind that I would ever have the chance to be with her again. Tossing her aside was a huge mistake that I regretted for a long time, maybe still do in some small way. I know I wouldn't be as happy if I were with her, instead of Rayna. Rayna is the best thing that ever happened to me and I would fall apart if I couldn't have her. However, I do miss Sara's eagerness to please me and her need for harsh punishments. Actually, my Demon misses her most.

I remember how she loved to be punished and would do things to piss me off, just so I'd punish her, putting her back under my control. She wanted it, of course. But, when she went with another Master to piss me off and earn a harsh punishment, she took it too far. I remember how she smiled while she told me about it. She cheated on me, as far as I was concerned. I know we weren't dating, but she belonged to me, and she allowed someone else to touch what was mine without asking if I'd allow it. That was forbidden, and she knew.

Sara repeatedly apologized to me, telling me she did it strictly for the punishment I would inflict, for such an offense. I couldn't understand how she thought I'd be all right with the betrayal. Well, she got the ultimate punishment--banishment from my attention. She didn't see that coming.

When my alarm screams, I'm jolted from my deep thoughts. I hit the button and roll over, pulling a squirming Rayna up against my chest. Her silky nightie is the only thing separating us.

My cock is so fucking hard! I need to fuck. After licking my fingertips to moisten them, I reach under the blankets and pull up on her nightie. I slip my fingers between the fold of her pussy. I grasp her hips and pull her ass into position. I line up my stiff cock and gently push it deep into her.

"I don't want to. It's too early," Rayna groans.

"Oh, come on, Love," I beg. "My cock is rock hard."

"Can I just wake up first?" she hisses, pulling my hands from her hips and sliding out of bed.

I roll onto my back and grunt. My cock is tenting the covers and I can't help but be angry. It's not aimed at her, she's allowed to say no. My cock is not going to go down on its own, not with my mind so focussed on letting Demon out to play after such a long captivity. I wonder how far Sara wants to take it tonight.

Rayna comes out of the washroom with her housecoat on and a grimacing expression. She's in a bad mood. I wonder why. Best to not poke that bear this morning... well, poke her again, I mean.

Knowing better than to push myself on her, I jerk off in the shower. I do my best not to picture the hot image of Sara at my mercy with tears streaming down her face, but the image won't leave me. I cum so fucking hard, my knees nearly give out on me. Rayna might be grouchy, but I certainly am not. I sure hope her mood changes. If she stays miserable, she likely won't want to go to Fallen tonight. I'll keep my distance from her to give her time to work out whatever issue she's having. Women are so fucking hard to figure out.

At the breakfast table, Rayna doesn't say a lot of anything to anyone. She's pleasant to all of us, but she seems distant. I wonder what's going on in that beautiful mind of hers. I don't dare ask though. She'll likely tell me nothing is wrong. In my experience, women rarely admit to what is actually pissing them off until they are damn good and ready. Men are easy; they just say what's on their mind and get it over with.

When she came home last night, after being with Sara, she was beaming. She couldn't wait to tell me everything about her visit, and I sat quietly, listening to every word. I'll admit that I was a bit jealous, not that she was with Sara, but that I wasn't there to watch it. I did vividly imagine each position she described. In my mind, I could see every expression these women wore when they looked at each other or orgasmed. It was hot enough to have me wanting to fuck Rayna with everything I had last night.

She insisted I wait. She wants me to think of it as a reward after delaying my gratification. It's fair play because I did the same thing to her last time. She also asked me not to orgasm until later when I'm with Sara, but there's no way I could have made it through a day at the gym with a fucking rock-hard cock. I'm sure someone would have complained that they were offended at my bulge, especially if they thought they were the cause of it. A gym slut would follow me around like a lost puppy if she thought I was hard for her. I did confess to Rayna that I went against her wishes by jerking off in the shower. I could tell it frustrated her, but I couldn't simply break her rule and then lie to her about it.

After we finish eating, and the kids have gone back to their bedrooms, I start taking the dishes off the table, as is our usual morning routine. From a dead silence, she blurts, "I asked you to wait."

I stop cleaning so I can look at her. I can't read her expression to know if she's furious with me or just slightly disappointed. I sit back in my seat and lean in toward her, tucking an errant lock of hair behind her ear.

"I'm sorry if I hurt your feelings. As you know from how I woke you up, my cock was raging. I couldn't go to the gym with an erect penis."

"It would have gone away if you'd thought of something other than Sara," she hisses.

I sit back, suddenly understanding. "Wait a fucking minute! Are you jealous of our plan for Sara being with me later?"

She rolls her eyes. "No, I'm not jealous of you being with her tonight." She clears her throat and then sighs. "You dreamed of her. You kept saying her name over and over until I bumped you to get you to shut up. After that, you tossed and turned, waking me up more than once. I'm just tired. I'm not jealous. I don't like that you dreamed of her though. You sounded like you cared for her more than you say you do."

"I'm sorry I kept you up and that I was saying her name."

"It's okay. You can't control your subconscious, I know that. How could you not dream of her? Tonight, you'll be with her for the first time in quite a while, so she was likely riding on your thoughts when you fell asleep and that's the reason for the dreams."

"And because you had sex with her yesterday and told me all the lovely details. I remember how she tastes and what she looks like when she cums. Your vividly detailed description was a bold reminder."

"So, you do miss her?" she asks.

"I love you, only you. She was a play toy that I enjoyed having conversations with. She's a lovely woman, intelligent and funny."

"But, do you love her?"

What is she getting at? "I care a great deal for Sara but it's not like the love I have for you. What's with you today? Do you not want me to be with her tonight?"

"I do, wholeheartedly." She takes a deep breath and sighs heavily. "What if you enjoy being with her sexually, more than you do with me? It's a ridiculous concern and I know you're going to tell me exactly that. It's just that your Demon is going to be set free with her and you're going to realize that's what you've been missing this whole time. I don't know if you'll ever be able to be like that with me. I'm scared."

"It is a legitimate concern and I'm happy that you're bringing it to my attention. I don't know how it's going to go tonight, but you are always going to be my woman. I am capable of controlling my darkest desires, as you're well aware. My concern is that you are going to fear me, after you watch me with her."

"I could never fear you," she promises. "I might like Demon more than I like you. You don't know!" she smirks. "We won't know until I see him in action."

I kiss her forehead before continuing to tidy up the kitchen. My excitement about Sara has dwindled some, now that Rayna told me her fear. How can I truly let myself enjoy Sara when I know Rayna might be over-analyzing everything I'm doing with her? What if Rayna is so jealous to see me fucking another woman that she kicks me out? That thought will haunt me all day.

* * * * *

On my way home, I pick up the pizza and wings I ordered from the restaurant down the street from the gym.

When I get home, Rayna is in a much better mood than she was this morning. I'm taking my sweaty clothes from my gym bag and tossing them into the hamper in the laundry room, when someone sneaks up behind me. I feel a tap on my right shoulder. I turn to see who tapped me, but quickly realize it was Rayna when she hops up on the washing machine with her thighs spread. She has a glint in her eye and a deviant expression. This is the Rayna I thoroughly enjoy.

I drop my bag, immediately and rush to be between those beautiful thick thighs of hers. My mouth meets hers just as my big hands scoop her ass and pull her toward me. I kick my leg back to find the door and push it closed. Our tongues entwine, as I lift her shirt and yank her bra, bouncing her tits out the bottom of it.

I suck one nipple into my mouth and bite it while pinching the other between my fingers. Rayna squeaks like a little mouse and then bites her lips closed, as she often does to remain quiet for the sake of the kids. I bite down harder. I want to hear her cry out loud, enough to satisfy my need to hear her pain. I release it as soon as she does.

I unbutton her pants and then she lifts her ass, allowing me the freedom to yank them down her legs. I leave them clinging around her ankles and lift her legs up and over my head while I pull her knees open forcefully. I dive my mouth onto her pussy and lap at her like a dog, stroking her whole slit with my fat tongue. She pulls me in closer by using her pants as a means to hold me hostage.

I look up to see her biting her lips closed and know this is something she's been planning all day. Her arousal is proof of her anticipation.

I eat her pussy until she's panting and dripping wet but don't allow her to cum. Hey, she did say not to cum before tonight. I'm not going to break that rule twice. Yeah, I know, it's cruel.

I pull her off the machine and set her on her feet, spinning her to face away from me. I free my cock from my sweat pants and grab a wad of her hair, forcibly pressing her chest over the machine. I slide my cock into her pussy and grab her shoulder with my free hand, but don't release her hair. I start fucking her with purpose, ramming her so hard, the front of the machine is lifting off the floor and slamming back down, making quite a racket.

"Quieter!" she begs.

I release her hair and grab her hips, lifting her feet off the floor and stepping back until just her hands rest on the machine. Using her weight to benefit me, I lift and drop her on my cock, rapidly bouncing her ass on my pelvis.

"Don't cum," I whisper through my teeth.

"What?" she asks while panting with each thrust.

"No coming!"

"I can't," her words fall away.

I feel her body tightening. She's going to cum. I pull my cock from her and set her back onto her feet. With a wicked sneer, I step back and pull up my pants.

She spins around with a furious expression, hitting my chest with her little fist. It didn't even make me waver. "What the fuck?"

"You didn't want us to cum before tonight."

"But you jacked off in the shower this morning, so how fair is it that I don't get to cum once too?"

"Sucks for you," I tease, opening the door and stepping through it, leaving her flushed and angry.

She yanks up her pants, as she calls out to me, "That's not fair!"

"I never said I'd play fair." I can't help but laugh.

"You're an asshole," she says under her breath, but I heard her.

"You're just figuring that out now?" I laugh even harder.

CHAPTER TWENTY-TWO
Rayna

For some reason, walking into Fallen tonight has me feeling powerful and confident. Why the change? I've only been here twice before, and I was curious, but fearful both times. I know he's going to be with Sara and not touching me, so maybe that has me less afraid. Worrying that others are going to see me in a compromising position always makes my insides twitchy. I'm still leery about being the center of attention with onlookers ogling me.

Demon is walking down a dimly lit hallway, towing me behind him with my hand clutched tightly in his. We stop at a doorway while he peers inside the room. With a curious grunt, he turns and pulls me as he makes his way through the crowd of gawkers who are hovering outside the open door to another room. As we pass, I try to catch a glimpse of the happenings, but can't see anything beyond all the onlookers. All I hear are pleasure moans from both men and women, lots of them. Perhaps an orgy.

He pulls me into the room we've been in before. This is where he confronted that man he so obviously hates. Gear is relaxing on a beige, leather sofa. Glitter is curled into a fetal position on the floor, with her head resting on his left foot. Her eyes are closed and she appears to be asleep.

"Glad to see you back again, my friend," Gear says with a very slight smile.

Demon grunts and nods. "Always a pleasure to be here. Good to see you buddy."

Two others are sitting at the heavy wooden table, whispering while they keep their eyes focussed on Demon and myself. I feel a bit awkward. What are they saying? It's obvious they are both submissives, judging by the collars they are wearing. Both have lettering--one says slave, the other slut. They are dressed in matching red corsets, with frilly black skirts.

Demon walks over to the fridge, without acknowledging their presence. He opens the door and takes out a bottle of water. He cracks the lid and takes a long drink before handing it to me. He grasps my other hand and walks me back to the sofa where Gear and Glitter remain, unmoved.

As he sits at the other end, he shakes Gear's hand. Glitter lifts her head and smiles at me, but doesn't move to greet me. I smile and casually wave at her. She puts her head back down and closes her eyes.

When I attempt to sit beside Demon, he stops me. "I want you on the floor."

Is he serious? Should I comply or just sit beside him, refusing to be treated no better than a household dog? I shake my head and cross my arms, not following his order.

"What did I tell you?" Demon asks in a calm, stern voice.

I look at Gear and then Glitter, who remains in her position, eyes still closed. "Why do you want me on the floor?"

"Are you too good to sit on the floor?"

"No, I'm not too good to sit on the floor. I just don't really want to."

"I gave you an order. Should I punish you for not following it?" he asks, giving me the choice--do it or get punished. I'll admit, it has my pussy heating up.

I smirk and shake my head, very unlike a submissive. Gear clears his throat while cracking his knuckles by pulling each one with his thumb. I drop my arms to my sides and look back at Demon. I remain unmoved.

"Sit on the fucking floor, now!" he growls.

I look over at the two women sitting at the table. Both have wide eyes as they watch this confrontation.

"Do not disobey me, Kat," he hisses.

I decide to do as he tells me and sit cross-legged on the floor, facing him. He points to the floor beside his feet. I slide myself toward him and turn my back, resting my head on his right knee.

I'm humiliated when he begins stroking my head and whispers, "Good girl."

The two of them start talking about someone new who has joined the club, which doesn't interest me at all. What pulls my thoughts back to them is when they start talking about someone named

Valentine. Demon says he sees him often at the gym and that he's dating Kat's sister.

Valentine? Tim is a member here? Since when? Why didn't I know about this and does my sister know? Do they come here? Why the name Valentine?

Valentine was a priest who secretly wed people when it was forbidden. When jailed, awaiting his death, he fell in love with the jailer's daughter. He wrote a beautiful note to his love using violets. He was later killed by means of a club bashing. Horrible way to die, if you ask me. I wonder how he got that nickname.

"I'll tell him you asked about him. Don't expect him to come for a visit any time soon. I don't think his lady knows about this place and I doubt he'll ever tell her." Demon's hand continually strokes my head. "Kat isn't going to say anything to her sister, is she?"

I shake my head, not verbalizing my response. I am a submissive after all. Besides, I'm a bit miffed about being squatted on the floor like a damn dog. Glitter might welcome this treatment, but I certainly don't care for it.

Demon stands and puts his hand out for me. I take it and rise to my feet, glaring at him in the process. He flashes me a wicked smile before gripping my wrist and leading me out of the room. His grip is tight, and it rather hurts. My hand is going numb by the time he gets me to a dimmer section of the hallway, where nobody is within view.

He shoves me face first toward the wall, holding me against it with his hand on my upper back. I put my hands up on either side of my face as if holding up the wall. With his free hand, he yanks my skirt up to my waist, revealing my purple thong. He reaches around my waist, pushing his hand under my panties.

His finger quickly discovers my clit and begins stroking it. He presses his chest against my back, further pinning me. He grasps my hair and turns my face toward his. His breath is hot and sweet against my neck.

"When I give you an order, you are to follow it, unobjectively. You will not defy me in front of people, ever again. Do you understand?"

"Yes, Sir. I didn't want to sit on the floor," I explain.

"I don't give a shit what you want. If you're my submissive, you'll do as I ask. What you want is irrelevant. The next time you do something like that, I'll punish you in front of everyone. I know how much you hate people seeing you in the nude."

"Please don't do that," I whisper, panting from the wonderful teasing. Two of his fingers rest on either side of my clit, alternating their massage, tormenting my little nub in a glorious way. I won't cum from this, but it sure is fuck arousing.

Demon slips his fingers inside of me. Oh, yes! He starts fucking me, slowly and deeply, while rubbing the butt of his palm against my swollen clit. I try to tilt my hips, but he has me pinned. Even breathing is more difficult with his body mass holding me firmly to the wall.

"Open your mouth," he demands. I do as he says. Suddenly, he pulls his hand from my panties and up to my face, shoving three fingers into my mouth. "Suck them clean."

I lick and suck them seductively, hoping to turn him on so much that he'll want to fuck me, finally allowing me a much-needed orgasm. Unfortunately, he doesn't. I make a mental note never to insist we practice delayed-gratification again. He owes me an orgasm. I'm not worried, I know he'll satisfy me with many before the night is over. Soon though, Sara will get her pleasure.

Demon pulls away from me and yanks my skirt even higher. He slides my panties down my legs. As he lifts each foot, my panties are stripped from my ankles. He tucks them into my mouth and then takes my hand.

He steps back and whispers, "Punishment for not following my orders. Now, bend over and grab your ankles."

I do as he says, knowing he's going to spank me until my skin is a volcanic red. He does exactly that, repeatedly slapping my ass with the palm of his hand until it's gleaming and I'm on the verge of tears. It's a strange sensation - getting spanked. It hurts, but the act of being scolded, as if I'm not his equal is comforting, like he's superior to me, even though I know he's not. He will take care of me, no matter what, like a parent who scolds a child, but will always love them even if they misbehave.

When he allows me to stand, he wraps his arms around my shoulders, pulling me into a comforting hug. "You know I love you, right?"

"Yes, I do," I try to speak even though I have my panties stuffed in my mouth.

"Now, be a good girl and obey me," he instructs before pressing a tender kiss on my lips. He looks into my eyes with a friendly grin and adds, "I will never again hide you away when punishing you. The next time you disobey, without using your safeword and giving me an acceptable excuse, I will spank you in front of whomever is there. Don't push me too far, Kat."

With one final kiss, he pulls me back down the hallway to the original room he had taken me to when we first arrived. When I am led through the doorway, I notice a heavy chain hanging from the ceiling, with a metal loop at its end. Against the wall rests a high-back chair, that looks like it was handcrafted by a lumberjack in the deep forest and carried here by very strong men.

Demon walks me toward it and has me sit on the solid work of art. I hadn't noticed the wrist cuffs and ankle cuffs attached to the chair, before I sat. He proceeds to bind my wrists and ankles to the chair. He stands up and reaches over the back of it pulling two wide leather straps over my shoulders, crosses them between my breasts and hangs them down at my waist. He walks behind the chair and pulls on each strap, fastening it so that my torso is held firmly to the backrest. I am bound.

He stands in front of me. With a husky voice, he gives me his rules.

1.   Do not speak unless you are experiencing unbearable discomfort. In that case, you will use your safeword.

2.   Do not scream.

3.   Do not spit those panties out of your mouth.

4.   Do not fight to get free.

5.   Do not try to get my attention, unless you are using the safeword.

6.   Do not be afraid of me. I will not touch you.

7.   Remember that Sara enjoys this, otherwise she would use her safeword.

8.   Remember that I love you, but Demon is itching to have you in his clutches, so remain quiet.

I nod, letting him know that I will follow the rules. He smiles and then takes a deep breath, letting it out slowly. He turns away and that's when I notice Sara kneeling in the corner with her back to us. She's so quiet and looks so small.

Demon walks over to her and stands behind her. He asks, "Is there anything you don't want me to do that you didn't tell me about, yesterday?"

"No, Sir," she replies.

"On a scale of one to five, how heavy do you want me to be with you?" His voice seems deeper and more intense.

"Four, Sir," she says.

"Only four?"

"Yes, Sir. I don't want to scare Kat."

He turns to look at me. His facial expression is harsher than it was a moment ago. "Understandable. Get up and follow me."

She stands and walks behind him. Her eyes catch mine, so I wink. She winks back, her lips rising into a smile, but it's quick to fade.

Demon ties her hands into two very thick and strong looking leather mitten-style handcuffs. He lifts her up while she raises her arms above her head. He clips the hook on the loop attached to the cuffs and lets her hang. Her feet don't touch the ground.

He swings her, allowing her sundress to flow freely in the air. Her demeaner is stoical, unfazed. Demon circles her, admiring her as she swings gently, slowly spinning.

Suddenly, he rushes her, grabbing at her dress and ripping it free from her flesh, while her body jerks from the material not wanting to give way. He yanks harder and it gives, ripping down the back seam, exposing her back.

His hand spreads wide and glides its way over her exposed back, as his eyes admire her tanned skin. He grabs her ass cheek and squeezes, firmly. She remains quiet. I would have, at the very least, winced.

He cracks her ass with his palm, making her swing just slightly. I notice that her butt has a pink handprint when he walks away, giving me a chance to admire her stretched body. He takes something from a drawer and walks back to her. He has scissors in his hand that he uses to cut off the remainder of her dress, freeing her full length. Sara is only wearing thigh-high white stockings.

"White? You know I don't like white stockings," he calmly reminds her. "Did you forget?"

"No, Demon. I did not forget."

He stands before her, staring eye to eye. His lips press to hers and I gasp, nearly choking on my panties. A flutter of jealousy tickles my tummy. I wasn't expecting that. I thought I had my emotions in check. But, this… the way he's kissing her, romantically, has me on the verge of tears. His eyes quickly open and gaze over at me, as if to suggest that he's purposely trying to make me jealous. Was that a test?

He walks back to the drawer and takes out a few items before returning to her. With a quick gesture, he spins her body to face me. He stands just to the side, allowing me to witness, without interruption. He wraps elastic bands around her tits so tightly that the globes begin to change colour, almost immediately. She's remaining quiet, as she stares forward while breathing in her nose and releasing it from her mouth.

He clips a metal thing on her nipple and her face is riddled with pain. The second nipple clamp has her panting. His body reveals his excitement with a huge bulge in his leather pants.

I watch as he attaches cuffs to her ankles with an attached spreader bar to hold her legs apart. He walks back to the drawer and collects a few more things, including two thick-stranded leather floggers that he flops over his shoulders.

He fiddles with her pussy, but I can't see what he's doing. She grimaces, gritting her teeth to prevent herself from protesting. When he stands, he gives her body a shove, making her swing. I notice two identical torturous clamps to the ones that are pinching her nipples, on her pussy lips, but these have long chains with weights that dangle to her mid-calf. The weights stretch and pull at her labia each time the direction of her swing changes, as they try to catch up, making the pull even more intense.

Demon stands off to the side with his hands on his waist, watching her intently. She cries out after nearly thirty seconds of the room falling in silence. Perhaps she couldn't hold off any longer. He doesn't stop her from swinging despite her pathetic sobs. Instead, he cracks her ass with one of the floggers as she swings nearer to him. He seems to be at peace, as if he's in his happy place. She is no longer crying out, having accepted the pain for what it is, a reminder that she's alive – as she explained to me on the day we met.

He suddenly grabs her purple breasts, to stop her swing. Her whimpering is loud and has me wanting to make him stop. I can imagine how much pain that must be causing her. I likely would have screamed out my safeword. He slowly, tenderly strokes and caresses her blood-filled tits, while pulling at the clamps to contradict the loving touches. Pain and pleasure.

Demon looks at me and flashes a wink and a crooked smile. He grabs her hair and pulls her head back before planting his mouth on hers. His kiss is passionate, hard and with purpose. His other hand slaps at her left tit and then pulls at the clamp on her nipple until she screams in his mouth.

He steps back, and in a fluid motion, crosses his arms over his chest to grab the handles of the floggers, swinging them through the air, gracefully. They whip and whirl. He's precise in his movements, never letting them pause or droop. The tips of the leather strands slap at her breast – left, right, left, right – over and over until her cries fill the room. The clamps on her nipples bob and bounce, painfully. I know that pain, it's too much for me. Those particular clamps are vicious and feel like they're biting into my skin. I don't like them, so Demon rarely uses them on me.

Gear and Glitter seem to have glided into the room unnoticed and stand quietly against the closed door. How did I not see them enter? They are silently watching while he holds his submissive's hand. Are they here to observe or join in? Did Demon invite them?

The sound of the leather strands slapping at her legs and stomach is turning me on. I love the sensation a flogger grants. When only the tips make contact, it stings the flesh sharply, but the bite doesn't linger. When most of the leather strands make contact, it's more pleasurable and the ends don't seem to sting, as much. I'm becoming very aroused, watching the flogger lap at her flesh.

Sara seems to be enjoying it as well, except when it flicks the clamps on her nipples. To me, her tits look painfully sore. I wouldn't want that, I don't think. He's never wrapped my breasts before. Maybe I'll ask him to do it one day, just to see if I like it or hate it. Judging by the deep purple tone of her breasts, I don't think I'll like it.

Demon slowly walks around her, lost in thought while admiring her flesh. He swings the floggers with a rhythmic smoothness that only develops from experience. It's obvious he's used floggers many, many times. The accuracy of his aim is perfect, a well-trained movement that comes from muscle memory. I watch his eyes and the stoical expression on his face. If you couldn't see the whole picture, you would think he was decorating a cake or gracefully painting a masterpiece on a canvas, by the concentration of his motions. Her skin is flushing hot pink as he creates his work of art, perceiving her body's marks as being more precious to him than the Mona Lisa.

He stops to slap her ass cheeks with his left hand, reddening them even more. Her body jerks as he claps against her tender buttocks. She grunts but doesn't cry out. Her eyes remain closed, but her lips are parted to aide in the rapid breaths that have her body quaking.

Still standing behind her, he reaches between her legs and runs his fingers along her stretched labia. She whimpers, but it's not just from the pain of him touching her aching lips, she's enjoying the pleasure his fingers are granting her swollen clit, as they glide along it.

"You're such a whore. Your cunt is dripping wet. You want more pain, bitch?"

"Yes, Sir," she whispers.

"I didn't hear you," he utters.

Louder, she repeats, "Yes, Sir."

"That's better. Whisper again and I'll slap your face."

He shoves two fingers into her pussy forcefully. She gasps and groans as he fucks her hotness, waving and ramming deep inside of her. Her body jerks under his pounding.

"No coming until I tell you to. Do you understand?"

"Yes, Sir," she says too quietly.

His voice is deep and calm, "I said not to whisper."

He walks around the front of her, as she watches his expression with wide eyes. Demon grabs her face in his hand and squeezes her cheeks until her lips pucker, like a fish.

"Do you want me to slap you? You must because I just explained that you can't do that anymore. Did you not hear me?"

"I did, Sir," she says, louder this time.

"What's my name?"

"Demon," she replies.

"Hmm, not quite yet, but soon. Keep pushing my buttons, bitch and you'll be sorry."

He releases her face and slaps her cheek, hard. She gasps, but doesn't cry out. I think I would have freaked out and started screaming at him. I really don't know what I would have done. I know I wouldn't have whispered, that's for sure. She must be doing it on purpose, to irritate him. Maybe she's taunting his Demon.

Demon walks over to a cabinet and opens the door, choosing a white cane. As he approaches, he swings it, making it whistle through the air. He cracks her across both ass cheeks with one swing. She squeals, but doesn't protest. Her eyes are closed, mouth open with a glint of a smile at the edges of her lips. She is enjoying the pain.

He turns her, so her back is to me. I notice a red welted line across her cheeks. His fingers caress it as though he's pleased with the way it feels. He steps to the side and cracks her ass several times with the cane.

By the fourth time, she finally protests. "No! Aaaah, Fuck!" He smirks but doesn't stop, giving her three more swats.

Her once beautiful, round ass is marked in red stripes by the time he's satisfied and spins her back around. He taps the cane up between her pussy lips and side to side against her stretched flaps. Her expression is taught, while breathing through clenched teeth. The muscles in her abdomen are flexing and relaxing with each heaving breath.

He shifts his position and taps at her clit firmly, several times. Sara is jolting with each twap, yelping as she does. He slides the cane along her clit and then taps at the little nub again, harder now. Her stomach muscles flex as she fights to flee from the rod. He taps at her left tit gently, while pinching the clip on her right nipple, slowly easing it off. Now she's yelping painful cries, especially when he grabs her nipple and rolls it between his thumb and forefinger.

He repeats the process as he removes the other clamp. Again, she screams. He presses the end of the cane against her nipple, pushing it inward. Her cries stop, but her eyes pinch shut and her jaw locks, holding the pain inside. She exhales, loudly as the cane is lifted from her nipple.

Demon pulls lube out of his back pocket and dribbles it all over his right hand, putting the small bottle back in his pocket. He squats down behind her, immediately seeking her asshole with his fingers. He pushes one, maybe two fingers into her. I can't be sure how many. She moans, tilting her ass toward him as best she can. He slips them into her ass without difficulty. She must do anal often, if she's this comfortable with the invasion.

His fingers ream and stretch her hole until more fingers are inside. He reaches around her with his other hand and tenderly rubs her clit. She's moaning softly under his touch.

I look at his face which is resting against her left hip. He's lost in his own thoughts, with his eyes aimed at the floor, but likely not seeing it. He wears this exact expression often, usually while he's deep-thinking. When his face stills like this, I can rarely draw his attention, despite calling his name several times. Was he recalling situations just like this one, and so deep in the scenario that he was oblivious to his surroundings?

She wails, almost growling, waking me from my thoughts. I look at his hand and see the weighted clamp in it. He tosses it to the side, away from them. She's breathing quickly, moaning with each breath as his fingers explore her asshole. He removes the second clamp with his other hand. He tosses that one too, and then grabs at her bruised pussy lips, viciously pinching and pulling at them. Her mouth is open, but she isn't making a sound. Her chest expands and contracts, inconsistently.

He slips two of his fingers into her pussy and begins fucking her with the same tempo as he fucks her backside. His eyes are now closed, his mind pulling him even further away from reality.

"Sir, please," she begs.

He says nothing, still lost in his thoughts. His hands pound into her, filling her, pleasuring her.

"Sir," she pleads.

"Do not cum," he replies, too late. She's already coming. Her body is tense, eyes closed. Her pussy drips her pleasure from around his fingers. I watch as the clear liquid leaks down his forearm. Before she's finished coming, he pulls his hands from her body and stands.

He grabs her throat and holds her. She can't breathe. Her eyes are focused on his, but they aren't filled with fear. He slaps her cunt with his free hand, his palm landing on her clit. Judging by how she jerks her body, that must have really stung. He slaps again and again, as her eyes and lips begin to swell, as blood pools in her face. Finally, he releases her, leaving her to gasp for air as he pulls some type of apparatus behind her. It's only now that I realize it must be a fucking machine. A fat dildo protrudes from the end of a long metal arm that attaches to the box. The long cord stretches from the back of it and remains plugged into the wall, where it has been all night.

He dumps some lubricating liquid into his palm, stroking the dildo to coat it. He arranges the machine until the dildo lines up with her asshole. He twists a knob, and then inserts the dick into her butt, twisting the knob again, to lock it in place.

The room fills with the sounds of it quickly revving up. The arm pushes forward and pulls back, speeding up to a pace he seems pleased with. Sara is moaning through parted lips while her eyes remain closed. Her body shifts and jerks, as the machine fucks her.

Demon stands in front of her and reaches for her clit, grabbing and pinching it between his knuckles. He's pulling it and twisting it, painfully yanking on it. Sara protests with each loud groan. He slaps her clit and then pinches and pulls it harshly, over and over until it's swollen and fat.

He reaches in his pocket, pulling out a pair of medical scissors. He slips the edge under the elastic holding her tit hostage and begins cutting it apart, freeing her dark purple breast. She's growling, canine-like, when he frees the second dark globe. Once they're unbound, he grabs and squeezes them as she shakes her head rapidly, still growling as if a merciful screech is holding in her throat.

Demon walks back to the drawers, picking up the weighed clamps along the way. He disposes of them and the elastics in a bucket and then pulls a vibrating wand from the drawer and a leather strap with buckles on it.

He returns to her and places the vibrator on the floor while he secures the leather strap around her thigh. He affixes the wand to the strap, pressing the bulb against her swollen clitoris. Once in place, he turns it on. She immediately jolts and moans differently than she has been. Her eyes remain closed.

He slips two of his fingers back into her pussy and fucks her slowly, while the fucking machine continues its long, deep strokes, filling her ass. He adds another finger and then another. He has four inside of her and most of his palm. The muscles in his forearm flex and roll, rippling as his hand waves inside her.

She's hanging as motionless as she can manage, but her muscles are so taught that she's almost vibrating. The sounds she's making are familiar to me. I believe I make those same noises when I want to cum, but he won't allow it.

"Cum, whore! Cum, you dirty fucking slut!" he demands, while grabbing her tit and squeezing.

Every inch of her locks tight, as a long, deep moan is squeezed from her body. Clear cum pours down Demon's arm, dripping from his elbow. He continues to violate her as her suspended body jerks wildly, from the hanging chain. He slaps her tummy with an open hand, and she grunts. He places his hand just above her pelvic bone and pushes her back against the automated, fucking dick, burying it into her at a different angle and slightly deeper.

Her face jerks up and that's when I notice her eyelids are partially open, but she's staring at nothing, lost in her own existence. She cums again. He slowly lowers her, so she's hanging on her own, the dick still ramming her ass and the vibrator torturing her clit.

Demon gets up and walks to the drawer, removing a somewhat stiff leather strap that's about three inches wide and a foot long. He slaps his palm several times at different velocities, to test its level of punishment.

He slaps the inside of his forearm and then slaps her ass with the same level of harshness. She doesn't make a sound. He continues to slap at her ass and the backs of her thighs up by the crease of her ass cheek. That is a sensitive spot to begin with. He slowly rounds her until he's standing before her. He's watching her face, as he slaps at her nipples. She seems unfazed by this new pain.

He tucks the paddle under his armpit and grasps both of her nipples, pulling her forward using just them. Now I can see the artificial dick penetrating her ass, but only half of it is inside of her, as he slowly pulls her body away from it.

As he gradually lets up on her nipples, the dildo pushes deeper into her once more. She shifts her leg just slightly to move the vibrator away from her clit, and he notices her do it. He pulls at the vibrator, rearranging it so it'll press against her clit again, and this time she won't be able to move away from it.

He stops the machine to add another attachment arm to ride alongside the first one. He pushes another dildo to the end of it and then slips it into her pussy, tightening the screw to hold the arm at that length. He turns the machine back on. Now she's being fucked in both holes at once with the vibrator still torturing her burning clit.

Her body waves from the pounding, as she hangs limply. Her muscles start to tense and that's when Demon slips his hand around her throat and applies pressure.

"Open your eyes, whore," he tells her. When she doesn't, he slaps her cheek. "Open your fucking eyes."

She slowly pulls open her lids. Her blue eyes stare blankly, into his. He holds her gaze as she moves closer and closer to yet another climax. The nearer she gets, the tighter he grips her throat. Her muscles lock as her body quivers and her face reddens. I watch her face and I know exactly when she is at the peak of her pleasure. Her eyes glaze over and lose focus.

Demon releases her throat, but she's still holding her breath. Her body is taught and unmoving. Drool seeps from her bottom lips as cum floods from her depths, spurting with every thrust from the dildos. Demon watches as her face slowly drops.

He grasps her hair and lifts her face. She is totally lost in a world of euphoria. She looks horrible and yet so incredibly at peace. Now I understand why he loves taking me to the edge, like he's doing to her.

I find myself shifting in my chair. My pussy aches with a need so powerful, it has me whimpering around my panties. When I glance toward the two onlookers, I see them watching me, not the incredible scene playing out before them. I suddenly feel self-conscious about gyrating on my seat. Gear taps Glitter's shoulder and she looks at him and nods.

CHAPTER TWENTY-THREE
Coach

Sara is coming so hard on the two cocks fucking her. If only they were real men taking her body and using it for their own benefit, that would make this even hotter than it is. I get off on watching women get used up like pieces of meat, by big, strong men, especially if I'm one of those men.

My cock has been so cramped inside my pants that I can barely keep myself composed. I want to fuck this bitch! I want to cum down her fucking throat. She's hot! Fuck, I forgot how easily she drives me mad! I knew I missed playing with Sara, I just didn't realize how much. I've let Demon out of his cage, but I won't set him completely free. This is the first time Rayna has seen me with another woman and I don't want her to regret allowing it to happen. Each time I glance at her, I can't read her expression. I can't gauge whether she's enjoying this or if she's doubting her decision to ask us to play. Her thoughts are deep, so much so that they aren't showing on her face. What is happening in her mind? I wish she would smile or grimace, do something to tip the scale either way, to let me know if she is pleased, or furious.

I have to stop worrying about Rayna and do what I set out to do – show her some of my wickedness. I let go of Sara's throat, but she continues to hold her breath. I have her lost inside herself. She's checked out and lost deep in subspace. This is where Sara is happiest.

When I used to play with her regularly, she told me that when punishment and pleasure take her into subspace, she is unreachable by the nightmares of war that haunt her through her conscious thoughts and nighttime dreams alike. Her memories can't touch her right now. The ghosts of those she's killed, and those she failed to protect, can no longer haunt her. I cherish being able to give her these moments of peace and I am honoured she would allow me this opportunity.

I slap Sara's face to snap her back to reality, for just a moment. She's too close to blacking out. She needs to breathe. The shock of the slap pulls her back to me, long enough that she starts breathing, again. Her eyes are still glazed over, but at least she's taking in air.

My fucking cock is starting to throb. I have to free it. I need to be inside her, in any hole, maybe every hole. I turn off the machine and slide it back until the dildos have slipped from her body.

She's whimpering, begging for me to put them back. "More, more, more…"

"Patience, whore!" I scold. She quiets down after I turn off the vibrator, but I don't remove the wand from her leg. Instead, I unclip the spreader bar from the ankle cuffs and leave it on the floor. After standing back up, I wrap my arm around her firm ass and lift her, while detaching her wrist cuffs from the hanging loop. As her arms fall limply onto my head, the blood begins to flow back into her limbs. She moans from the painful shift of position.

With an exhausted Sara now draped over my shoulder, I carry her over to the horse. The horse is basically a bench covered in leather, but it is only about two feet long and just high enough for most Masters, and Mistresses, to be able to fuck their bound subs without straining themselves. It is adjustable for height, for those much shorter or taller. Gear had set it at the perfect height for me, before I arrived.

I lie Sara facedown onto the horse and clip her wrist cuffs to the sides while her head limply hangs off one end. I secure her ankles to the base at the other end, which leaves her pussy partially sticking off the edge. I will rearrange the vibrator so that it's pressing onto her incredibly red, swollen clitoris, before I begin to take what I've earned. I will have her body and I will use it, however I please.

I glance toward the door. This is when I notice Gear and Glitter standing on either side of my Rayna. They are looking at me for approval to touch her. I'm sure they were watching to see if she was enjoying the show. She must have been, otherwise Gear wouldn't be asking permission to touch her. If Rayna had been showing signs that she is angry or hurt, he would have noticed and would have left her to work through her emotions. He is very good at reading people, better than I am, actually.

This is when I notice Rayna shifting her ass on the seat. Yes, she's sexually wound up and needs to release her frustration. I nod at Gear and he nods back. Glitter reveals a vibrating wand she had been hiding behind her back and presses it against Rayna's clitoris. I hear her muffled moan and watch her eyelids slowly close, but they open after only a few seconds. She locks her sexy gaze on mine.

After securing Sara on the horse, I leave her, to collect the fucking machine. As quickly as I can, I remove the added bar with the second dildo. I pull off the remaining dildo, switching it for a very long, fat one. I lubricate it, not that Sara isn't wet enough to handle it. Very carefully, I work it into her cunt. She is nice and loose, able to take it quite easily. I knew she would be. I turn on the machine and let it fuck her at a medium pace using long, deep strokes. Sara is moaning with each lazy thrust. To add to her pleasure, I turn on the vibrator, also at a medium speed. I'm sure her clit is numb, yet sore, so the less intense vibration will help it to awaken.

I remove my pants and toss them aside, and then stand before Sara's mouth, throbbing cock in hand. I reach for her and fist a wad of her hair and pull up to reveal her opening mouth. She is well trained, knowing what I expect of her. I shove my fingers deep inside to explore where my cock will soon be. I want to feel it first before I sink between those puffy, red lips.

"Suck my fingers," I tell her.

She does as I ask, sucking and lapping at them, as if they were a melting popsicle. Her grunts make it even more arousing. The air is pushed from her tiny body by the massive size of the dildo which fills her. I look over at Rayna and see her blinking often. Each time she opens them, she looks at Sara's mouth, watching her lap at my fingers. I watch Rayna's chest quickly expand and contract, just as she always does when her climax nears its peak. Glitter removes the vibrator and Rayna protests by gyrating her hips and whispering what I can only assume are pleading words.

Gear is standing behind her chair. He weaves his fingers in her hair and pulls her face upward, forcing her to look at me, not the wand near her clit. As Glitter places the vibrator back in its place, Rayna sucks in a big breath. That's when I aim my cock and slowly bury it all the way down Sara's throat.

I take my eyes off Rayna because I have a fierce need to watch my cock disappear into this woman's face. I pull back to allow her a breath. I shove forward and hold her firmly, so her nose is pressing against my belly. She can't breathe anyway, not with my cock blocking her windpipe.

I look up at Rayna to see her panting with an enraged expression. I don't think she's upset with what I'm doing. Glitter simply won't let her cum. She's getting her close and then moving the vibrator, to forbid Rayna's release. She's edging her and it's arousing me even more, to see her struggle against her bindings.

Gear has his hand around her throat, holding her head to the backrest, while his fingers roll her right nipple. He's crouched down, whispering in her ear. I'm curious as to what he's saying. Whatever it is seems to be stirring something inside of her because she's suddenly pulling at her restraints. Glitter replaces the vibrator and Rayna moans, loudly. Almost immediately, Glitter removes it again.

I pinch Sara's nose with my fingers and begin fucking her with long, deep strokes, making sure I bottom out each time. The nasal pinching adds an extra level of breath control that makes the submissive feel like they're smothering. Some begin to panic, but Sara lavishes in the anxiety. She's a pro.

Glitter slips two of her long, slim fingers deep into Rayna's pussy. Rayna groans and tries to hump the woman's fingers, but her movements are quite limited by the bindings that have her secured to the chair. Glitter taps her clit with the vibrator, repeatedly, only leaving in place for a few seconds at a time. It's enough to force Rayna close to orgasm, but not enough to allow her the pleasures of a much-desired release.

I pull my cock back to let Sara take two quick breaths. Her whole body is quivering as her muscles tense, desperate to free themselves. An orgasm tears through her. When she gasps in a breath, I push forward, blocking her windpipe again. This time, I fuck her face quicker. No more Mr. Nice-guy.

Sara has never been quick to gag. I recall thoroughly enjoying that about her. I fuck her face with long and deep penetrating strokes, poking twice when I'm buried deeply, before retracting. Fuck this feels good! I fuck her mouth with a dozen fast thrusts, while she gasps and makes sloppy, spitting sounds.

I step back and make my way behind her. Fuck, that ass is fine! The dildo fucking her pussy is stretching her wide. What an amazing sight to see. As the dildo pulls out, her labia glides along it's circumference like tiny blankets being pulled along a floor. As it pushes in, the labia curls inward, dragging along the silicone shaft.

I straddle the machine's arm and position myself to enter her ass. Before I shove into her, I gaze over at the other luscious scene in the room, simultaneously stroking my cock.

Rayna's face is flushed, glistening with sweat, and she's breathing erratically. Her eyes are looking my way but I'm not sure she's actually seeing us or if she's completely lost in her own body's desperate desires. Glitter is still rhythmically tapping Rayna's clit with the vibrator, while fingering her. Gear remains behind her, holding her neck while fondling her breasts and whispering in her ear.

I close my eyes for a moment and give into my need to set him free. I can feel the sadistic temptations building throughout my body with a rushing wave of heat. I open my eyes, see Sara in front of me, still pinned down and taking the huge cock in her dripping cunt. The dildo is slick with cum, as it casually fucks her. I crank up the machine, and watch it ram her twice as fast as it was.

My cock is thick and pulsing in my hand, as I roll on the condom. I need to fuck her, now! I slide my meat deep into her ass, in one quick motion. She bellows, but it only turns me on. She can say the safeword if she wants it to stop.

Sara's body locks up and her asshole pinches my dick with a vice-like grip. It won't stop me. She's coming. Gushes of pussy juice splash onto my legs each time the dildo pulls back. My beast is beginning to rage.

My hips start slamming against her, keeping up to the tempo of the machine. My cock buries deep into her anus while getting stroked by the fake cock within her twitching cunt. I reach forward, grasp her hair and pull back, until her moans are strained. I slap her ass cheek again and again, until it's fiery hot and then switch hands to redden the other cheek.

I release her hair and reach for the back of her neck, pinning her throat against the edge of the bench. It's very difficult for her to breathe and that's my goal. I pound her with everything my Demon has to offer, while growls of pent up rage fill the room. I bury into her backside, destroying her and taking what I want, not caring if she is finding any pleasure in this. She's had her pleasure, now it's my turn. I will have her how I want and for as long as I want.

Sara is barely making a sound. She's lost in subspace and that thrills my beast even more. I reach down and crank up the vibration on her clit. Judging by the increased volume of her moans, it's as if Sara's engine is revving up again. I know it hurts her, but in a way she enjoys.

When I look over at Rayna, I'm instantly filled with rage because Gear is so close to my woman. Demon doesn't like to share his toys with other men. It enrages him, so I fuck Sara harder, slamming against her red ass violently, filling her with every inch of me as if taking my rage out on her.

Glitter holds the vibrator to Rayna's clit, no longer pulling it away. Gear is watching me while holding her throat tightly, choking her. Her face is flushing, and her stomach muscles are flexing, erratically. She's coming. Fuck! Yes! Come, bitch!

Sara's asshole grips my cock again, as another brain-numbing climax shreds through her. I'm using Sara, at this point. My focus is on my woman. She's peaking over there, but I can feel her on my cock. Gear releases her throat and she screams with her mouth wide, allowing me to see the soaking wet panties that muffle her cries.

"Cum, you fucking whore!" my Demon yells in a deep and husky voice.

Rayna jolts, her eyes springing open, locking on mine. The colour of her face is slowly returning to normal as her climax comes to an end. Glitter doesn't move the vibrator, refusing her clit the much-needed pause it craves. No, she keeps it there, forcing Rayna to cum again, and again. Each time she nears, Gear either covers her nose and mouth or grips her throat. Breath control can either heighten an orgasm or ruin it. He is experienced with this dangerous game and I trust him, otherwise, Demon would have ripped his throat out.

I pull out of Sara's ass and turn off the machine. After yanking the vibrator from beneath the leather strap, sure to leave a bruise in its place, I hurry to unbind her restraints. She hangs limply, so I slide my arm under her waist and lift her body off the bench. I carry her over to the thin mattress and toss her down, as if she were a sack of fuckable potatoes. She lands with a slight thud.

"Do you want more, slut?"

The corner of Sara's mouth lifts, just slightly, letting me know she's still willing. "Yes Demon! Thank you, Sir," she can barely form words.

I grab her legs and yank her left one straight down on the bed, straddling it while lifting the other, so that her thigh is pressing against her stomach. I hold it in place while I slide my rock-hard cock back into her ass.

Sara's mascara is smudged down her cheeks and she is exhausted, but I'm not finished taking what I've earned. I can hear Rayna, but it's only spiking my arousal to a boiling hot level of desire. I lean forward and press my hand over Sara's mouth, sinking two fingers inside.

"You're a fucking slut. Nothing but a useless whore for men like me to use, for our own pleasure. Open your fucking mouth wide and let me see where they've all dumped their cum. You're a dirty, cum-guzzling whore," I growl.

She opens wide. I form a wad of saliva in my mouth and spit it right into the gaping hole. She whimpers her protest, but doesn't fight back. I spit again and she gags.

"Thank me, whore!"

With her mouth still held open by my fingers, she manages, "Thank you, Master Demon!"

I pull my fingers from her mouth and tell her, "Leave your fucking mouth wide open." I cover her eyes with my spit slicked fingers, blocking her from looking at me. I don't need her judgemental eyes. She's a carcass; nothing more than a warm body to fuck.

Rayna is coming again, screaming wildly as the vibrator continues to torture her hypersensitive clit. I fuck, hard and fast, ramming my prick into this tiny little whore's ass. I release her eyes and grab her hair, lifting her head, so I can kiss that gaping mouth of hers. My lips press to hers, forcefully. I know it pains her already swollen lips. My tongue digs deep in her mouth, tasting her sweetness.

I push her back down and grab her throat, holding her against the mattress. Her hands grip my forearm and hang on. My other hand viciously grips her upper thigh, using it to lift her hips off the bed so my cock can get a better angle and really fuck her deep.

I only slam her a few more times, before I can't hold it back any longer. In one quick movement, I yank out of her ass and lift her face toward me using her hair as a means. I tear off the condom and toss it. My fist strokes and chokes my cock as thick globs of cum shoot, splattering all over her flushed face. Only one wad meets its target; her open mouth.

When I release her hair, she drops onto the mattress in a sweaty, panting mess. I remain on my knees admiring the used-up slut before me, as I try to calm my breathing. I wipe my forehead with my arm, preventing a salty bead of sweat from dripping into my eye.

I look over at Rayna and see that she is also fighting to regain her composure. Glitter and Gear are unfastening her, but she hasn't moved her freed limbs from their position, even though she can. Her slatted eyes follow my movements. Yes, now it's obvious that she thoroughly enjoyed herself. The smile of her face is evidence enough.

I lean forward and kiss Sara's lips tenderly, letting her know that I appreciate her, but also to show Rayna that I still respect and care for Sara, no matter how I just treated her.

When I sit up, I pull her into my arms, cradling her on my lap like a child. She has her face pressed against my chest with her arms wrapped around my torso.

Before our guests depart from us, Gear helps Rayna to her feet and walks her over, to be with us. He kisses her hand before, nodding to me and taking his leave. Rayna sits beside me, looking ragged and worn out. I lean toward her and kiss her tenderly.

"I love you, lady," I whisper.

"I love you and your Demon," she replies.

I'm thrilled that she isn't afraid of that part of me or that she doesn't hate me, for fucking another woman. It's one thing to imagine how thrilling it might be, to watch your partner be intimate with someone else, but to see it happening is where the real emotions will break through. It'll either be exciting, or dreadful. The latter is something a relationship can't often recover from.

Rayna kisses Sara tenderly, and then wipes my sticky cum from the exhausted woman's cheek by using a small hand towel Glitter had given her to clean herself up with. We spend the next half hour drinking water and talking about what we enjoyed and what we didn't. There wasn't much that we didn't. Rayna said she felt jealous but was able to use the emotion to heighten her arousal.

At this very moment, I am the luckiest man on the face of the earth.

CHAPTER TWENTY-FOUR
Rayna

Since watching Coach fuck Sara, I've been experiencing a wide range of emotions. This is something I hadn't expected to happen. I thought that I'd have sorted through all of my emotions while it was happening. I didn't think I'd be feeling like I'm on an emotional rollercoaster--happy and turned on one minute, the next I'm crashing into a world of sadness, or worse yet, anger.

Coach has been great about asking me how I'm feeling and if there's anything I want to talk about, but this is something I have to work out on my own. Worrying him with the lame and pathetic emotional pity-party I've been experiencing, isn't going to improve my mood any. He'll likely regret going through with it and then he'll feel guilty, which will make me feel worse. I don't want either of those things. So, for now I will keep saying that I'm fine. At least until I can figure out why I'm all fucked up.

When I think about how dark his eyes got when he was fucking her, it turns me on. But, when I remember how turned-on he was when he was fucking her, I cringe. What's wrong with me? I asked him to be with her. I told him I would be okay with it. So, why am I not? Am I not?

My work staff have been curious, wondering why I've been so unusually quiet today. I keep telling them that it's the Monday woes from lack of sleep. Most of them seem to be accepting that. The people who really know me, know there's something more going on. I can't talk it out with them. I can't tell anyone about this. Maybe that's one reason why I'm so out of sorts.

"Rayna, you have a phone call." Kelly pokes her head into the exam room.

"I can't take it right now. Can you take a message and tell them I'll call back?" I'm knuckle deep in a patient's mouth.

"Sure thing!" she replies, and then ducks out of the room, as silently as the wind on a prairie.

My patient, Mr. Ugavail, says with his mouth open and tools scraping a tooth, "You can take the call. It's okay with me."

I snicker, knowing he hates being here. "Mr. Ugavail, you can't get away from me that easily. You'll likely run away if I leave you here unattended. Whoever it is, can wait."

"What if it's important?" he says clearly, having had the instruments removed from his mouth. "It could be a life and death situation. What if you won a new car and this is the only chance to collect?"

"Nice try, but I'm not falling for it. Open wide, please," I say, leaning in as he reluctantly opens his jaw.

I finish the cleaning and check-up with no other interruptions, and then let the doctor know his patient is ready for him. I feel bad for this man because his teeth are in terrible condition and he needs extensive procedures. The man doesn't have a lot of money to spend on dental work, so his teeth are pretty much rotting and breaking into sharp shards. They need to be pulled and replaced with dentures, but he simply can't afford it.

When I make my way to the head desk, Kelly hands me a scrap piece of paper with '*call Coach immediately*' written on it. As I make my way to the lunchroom to make a cup of tea, I pull my phone from my pocket and dial Coach's cellphone. I'm surprised when it goes straight to voicemail. I click on my messages and listen to the first one.

It's the secretary at the kid's school. "Hello Ms. Baxter, this is Luanne from John Frame. It's essential that you give me a call back, as soon as you get this message. Thank you."

I immediately dial the school and nervously wait for an answer. After only two rings, I'm already getting frustrated from waiting, but then I hear a click. "John Frame Elementary."

"Hello Luanne. This is Rayna Baxter returning your call."

"Oh, yes, Rayna. I hate to have to tell you this, but Ken has fallen on the playground and was transported to the hospital in an ambulance. We believe his arm might be broken. Just know that he's okay and being taken care of. We don't want you rushing to get to his side and have a car accident on the way. We tried to call Mr. Baxter, but there was no answer. We were able to contact someone named Coach. Ken asked us to call him when we couldn't get hold of you. I hope that's okay. He seemed very concerned and said he would be at the hospital when Ken arrived."

"Shit! Shit, shit! Okay, umm... thank you, Luanne."

I hang up quickly and start opening my locker to retrieve my purse and sweater. My hands are starting to shake and I'm suddenly sweating. My heart is about to pound out of my chest and I'm becoming increasingly more lightheaded with each breath. I sit and put my head between my knees, forcing myself to breathe slower. I can't help him if I'm a basket-case!

As soon as I'm feeling stronger, I slam my locker and rush to find Dr. Kim. I'm supposed to do a cleaning on one of his patients in about ten minutes.

"Hi, sorry, but I have to go. My kid broke his arm," I say while he's knuckles deep in a woman's mouth.

He sits up and looks over at me. "You'd best go then. I'll manage without you. Take care of your boy. Let us know how he is."

"I will. Thank you," I say before rushing to the entrance. "Kelly, I have to go. Ken broke his arm at school."

"Oh my god! That sucks! Okay, go take care of the little imp." Even though she's smiling, her eyes show her concern.

* * * * *

"Hi honey. How are you feeling? Does it hurt?"

Ken's eyes are glossy and heavy-lidded. "Heck no! Not anymore, right Coach?" he's giggling from the painkiller the doctors pumped into him.

"Hi love," Coach says, as he rises to his feet and kisses my temple.

"Thank you for meeting him here."

"I'd do anything for Little-man," he assures me.

"Mom, honestly, I'm okay," he says with a very wide grin and slurred words. "Stop worrying. I'm not a little boy anymore. I'm, like, a man almost. I have man-hair on my body now." His laughter is masked only by the drug-induced calmness.

"What did they give him?" I ask, as I attempt to brush an errant lock of hair from the boy's forehead. He blocks it by pushing my hand away, and then he rolls his eyes so obnoxiously, I'd likely scold him for it, if he weren't high as a kite.

Coach is chuckling. "Something I wouldn't mind having a wee bit of. The nurse told me the name of it, but I can't remember what she said. You're feeling good, eh buddy?"

"I feel great!" he announces with a freakishly wide smile. "Mom, can we get some of this and take it home?"

"No, we can't." I finally take a deep breath, knowing he's not in dire need of help, but a little sad that he doesn't seem to be needing me, at all. What happened to the little boy who used to cry for his momma when he scraped some skin from his knee?

I sigh heavily, "What did the doctor say?"

Coach says, "Doc said he'll need to get it set before they can cast it. They want to keep him for a few more hours to see if it stops swelling. They won't cast it, until it does. Hopefully, they can cast it tonight, otherwise he'll have to come back tomorrow morning."

"How bad is the break?"

"Here," he replies, pointing to the x-ray the doctor left hanging against the darkened screen on the wall. We walk over to it and he flips the switch to turn the light on. "This is the break. It isn't all that bad. It's off kilter but he doesn't need surgery." Coach chuckles when he adds, "I've done worse."

My head suddenly whirls, and I want to vomit. Coach sees me waver and grabs my arm to steady me.

"Hey, you all right?"

"Yeah, I just got a bit woozy for a second. I'm okay now, I think. Thank you."

"You're pale as a ghost. Maybe you should sit."

"I'm fine, really."

Ken is staring at the clock hanging on the wall in front of him. He looks lost in thought. Those drugs are really spacing him out. Coach chuckles, as he watches the kid try to refocus his eyes by squinting between repeated blinks.

"So, how did you break it?" I ask.

His smile is all contorted. "Well, I didn't do it on purpose, that's for sure!"

"No, not likely," I say, trying to hold back my laughter.

"I was running beside Kyle because Leslie was going to kick the ball into the goalie's net. When Barbie crashed into my knee, I flipped right over her, and then the red dog licked me, and he was really stinky."

210

"What? That doesn't make any sense," I whisper to Coach, who is still laughing while shrugging. He's obviously heard this same story and couldn't make sense of it either. "What dog?"

"The big red one that lives in the blue house beside my math class," he replies, adding another level of confusion to the mystery.

"You said a Barbie doll hit your knee?"

"What?" he asks while looking at me, as if I suddenly grew another head. I'll bet he's seeing double.

"You said it was a Barbie."

He laughs hysterically. "No, not a doll. The dog's name is Barbie. She tripped me."

"Oh, I see. Barbie is the name of the big red dog. I get it now."

"No, Mom! I don't know the big red dog's name. He stinks a lot though. His breath smelled like he had been eating worms. Maybe he was. I don't know."

I cringe at the thought. "I'm still confused," I whisper to Coach.

"Yeah, I can't make figure it out either. We'll have to wait until the drugs wear off."

"Was he here by himself or did the principle come with him? I should have had the volume up on my phone. I'm an awful mother."

Coach hugs me against him to reassure me. "Love, you are the world's best momma. You're a better mother than the moms who own those coffee mugs that claim they're the best. They aren't, it's you."

"Thank you, but he shouldn't have been here alone."

"He wasn't alone. Mr. Kants was here when I arrived. He rode in the ambulance with him. He's Ken's homeroom teacher, or so he told me. He only told me what he knew and that was that he fell outside and landed on his arm wrong. I told him he didn't have to stay. Ken assured him that I was a trustworthy guardian."

"I'll add your name to the official list of safe people. I'm surprised they called you."

"Ken told them to."

I look down at Ken to ask him if he enjoyed the ambulance ride, but he's already passed out. He looks so grown up in this bed. His limbs are long and lean, but his face remains childlike, not yet gaining the characteristics of an adult male. One day soon, he will be taller than me and his voice will deepen. Will I still see him as my little boy? Mothers always claim they do, but how is that possible?

"He's asleep," I whisper.

"That's probably a good thing," Coach replies in the same hushed manner.

Standing behind me, he wraps his arms around my shoulders and pulls me into him. He softly kisses the top of my head. He hugs me against his chest while we stand silently, watching our young man breathe deeply.

Coach can be so rough and threatening, with very little effort, but right now, here, in this moment, he's the most tender, loving man I have ever met. I love that he can sit at either end of the spectrum, at will. I've never felt this safe and loved. I would give this man my soul, if he should ask for it.

Some time passes before I shift out of his arms. He groans, but I pay him no attention as I unfold a blanket and rest it on top of the thin sheet covering my son's body. Tears well up in my eyes and I try to blink them away, but it's no use. They flow down my cheeks in silent streams.

"Love, he's going to be okay. It's just a broken bone. He will heal." Coach sits me in a chair and squats in front of me. His thick fingers gently wipe away my sadness. "No more tears. You need to show him that it's not a big deal to break a bone. Odds are he'll break at least two more before he reaches twenty. Well, if he starts to copy me, that is." Coach's faint chuckle has me smiling, but the idea that my baby boy might suffer through another trauma, does nothing to ease my concern.

"It's not just the broken arm." I take a deep breath and clear my throat. I look up at Ken to ensure he is still unconscious. "The school tried to call his father and he couldn't even be bothered to pick up the phone."

"Love, maybe he was at work and couldn't get to his phone, like you were."

"Maybe you're right. I hope you're right."

"I'm sure he wasn't purposely ignoring the call." I can tell Coach doesn't fully believe the lies he's trying to convince me of.

I whisper, "I'm just having a rough time with my emotions since…"

"Since Saturday," he says with a nod. He doesn't look upset, overly concerned, nor unconcerned. I figured he'd be one of those, but he seems calm and ready to hear what I have to say.

"Yeah," I confirm with my face scrunched. Is he wondering if I'm overthinking the situation that I asked him to put before me?

"Love, you have to tell me what you're feeling. I promise, whatever your emotions are, they are completely normal. Please, just talk to me. I need to know what you're thinking, so we can talk it through."

"I know, I just have to work it out on my own."

"Why? We did it together, so why can't we talk about it?"

I want to say that I feel foolish but instead, I shrug and glance at Ken. I stand up and take Coach's hand, leading him into the hallway. We can still see him sleeping soundly, through the window.

"It's hard to explain what I'm going through. I mean, I had sex with her too, so why should it bother me if you did? That's not fair, right?"

"We aren't counting fairness here. If watching me with her bothers you, it'll never happen again. It's simple."

I shake my head and cross my arms over my chest. He doesn't understand the point I'm trying to get at. How can I explain my thoughts and feelings if I'm not exactly sure of what they are?

"No! I don't want that either. I don't know what I want. I feel like my thoughts and emotions are so scattered. Like I said, let me work it out on my own. We can talk about it when I figure out why the images keep spinning around in my head. It was fun, I really got excited by it, but…"

"You enjoyed watching me fuck her, but you didn't like how much I enjoyed fucking her. Am I getting close? Maybe my Demon scared you a little bit, even though I kept him calm."

I'm surprised how accurate his guess is. "Something like that. It was so hot watching you take control and make her cum so hard. When you fucked her, you looked at me and your eyes…" I shake my head, while looking away from him.

"You didn't like how I looked. I've heard people say my eyes change when my demeanor does." He shrugs.

"They do." I slip my hands in the front pockets of my nursing shirt and turn to watch Ken through the window, partly because I don't want to look at Coach when I try to explain. Maybe it's guilt for laying it all on him, or the idea that watching him take his needs out on another woman, instead of me has me jealous, but also, grateful to her. I really need to figure out if I loved it or hated it.

"You looked different--meaner and raging with dominance. You wanted to own her. Your expression proved your ravenous desire for her. I've never seen that look on you, even when we're playing hard, or what I've perceived to be hard. When I picture that moment now, I am jealous. I wasn't at the time. I was fine while it was happening. I even orgasmed a few times, myself. It was sexy and dangerous and... fuck, you looked hot! Your muscles were flexing, hard and bulging, like a gladiator. Your thighs were thunderously strong when you were pounding against her small frame. I'm getting aroused right now, just remembering how I felt while watching you, but I shouldn't be getting aroused by watching my man fuck another woman. Based on everything I've known up to this point, I should feel it's wrong! You are supposed to love me enough, not to want to fuck another woman. Yet, I asked you to, so I have no right to feel jealous. I just don't understand why I can't regulate my stupid fucking emotions. I'm all over the fucking place! I'm sorry, I shouldn't... I mean, I asked you to do it. It's not like you had an affair."

Coach caresses my arm, tenderly. He turns me so he can look at me. "You feel ashamed because your moral value was tested. It's okay to want to watch me with another woman. You don't have to feel guilty, for enjoying it. It's unfortunate that people are raised to believe that it's wrong to have sex with someone else while you're in a relationship, even if that person approves. They go so far as to say that I shouldn't want to be with anyone else, like you said. Rayna, we can set up our relationship however we want it to be. It's 'our relationship' and no one else's. Their beliefs are theirs and ours are ours. We set our own rules and we follow them, unwaveringly. We enjoy our lives how we choose to, not how society tells us we should."

"I know, but it still feels wrong, but yet, completely right."

"Nobody is getting hurt by what we're doing."

"That's not true," I say stoically.

He asks with concern, "Who are we hurting?"

"Well, you did make Sara scream a few times," I say, with a smirk slowly overwhelming my mouth.

"You're such a smartass!" He wraps his heavy arms around my head and holds me against his hard chest. "Love, always tell me what you're feeling, so we can work through it. Whatever you're experiencing is not abnormal. You aren't the only one to feel jealousy. I was so enraged that Gear was touching what's mine, I wanted to rip his head off. Demon doesn't like to share his toys."

"So, what kept you from decapitating him?" I ask with my face pressed against his firm chest.

He chuckles, "Gear is such a great friend that I would miss him too much. And Glitter would cry. It wouldn't be worth it. So, instead, I used that rage as a tool to fuck her harder. When you came, I nearly exploded myself. My balls were throbbing from slamming her so fucking hard. It was a hot scene--yours and mine."

I pull away from him and look down at my shifting feet. Shyly, I say, "Yeah, it really was, but…"

"But, what?"

My nose wrinkles when I tell him, "Don't ever spit in my mouth. I guarantee I will hurl if you do."

He laughs and nods, "In that case, I definitely won't do that to you."

"Thank you. It's… gross!"

"It's a way to show that person that they are worthless, to humiliate them." Even though he's explaining the reason, not that I needed him to, I'm still shaking my head. "We can talk about it more, later, if you'd like. Should we go sit with the sleeping prince?"

"Yes, we should. Any idea when the doctor is going to set the bone?"

"Soon, I hope!"

"You don't have to stay if you have clients waiting. I'm here now."

Coach looks at me and grimaces. "You don't want me here?"

"Yes, of course I do. I'm just letting you know that you don't have to be. I mean, as you said earlier, he'll be okay. You likely have a full schedule of clients waiting for you."

"I do, but I rescheduled two appointments and April is going to take over the third."

"When did you have time to reschedule?"

"On my drive here. I called from my truck."

"If your crazy ex-girlfriend hadn't smashed up that old truck of yours, you wouldn't have had the Bluetooth handsfree calling feature. So, I suppose we could claim that her jealous rage was beneficial."

He frowns, "It took weeks for that gash to heal on my leg. She's just lucky I walked away, instead of pulling her out of her window and beating the hell out of her." I can almost see his inner Demon twitching behind those eyes.

"Coach, take a breath. It's over and she served her time. She hasn't bothered us since her sentencing. Even if I pass her in a store, she always walks the other way. I think she's sad, but moving on with her life. Enough about her, she doesn't matter to us anymore."

"I'm not leaving, Rayna. Little Man needs me to poke fun at him when he wakes up. Besides, I want him to clear up that damn story about the dog tripping him. Being drugged is not conductive to storytelling."

* * * * *

The doctor set Ken's arm and wrapped it in a flexible bandage a few hours later, and then we were sent home with a time to return tomorrow morning, to have it casted. Ken explained that there were two dogs involved. One dog tripped him, and then the other licked him and he had bad breath. His story made sense, once some of the drugs wore off.

He's passed out in his bed with his arm raised up on a pillow. I will keep pumping the Ibuprofen into him every four hours as prescribed. He doesn't need to suffer. I've never broken a bone, so I can't judge his pain level from personal experience. Coach says he's broken too many bones to bother counting, especially in his teen years, when he was fighting a lot. He had a ton of misplaced rage that he eventually learned how to channel into better vices-- working out and BDSM.

CHAPTER TWENTY-FIVE
Coach

It's been nearly a week since Ken broke his arm, so life has gone back to being normal. He's enjoying all the attention he's getting at school. His cast is coated with multiple coloured ink doodles and so many signatures that they're starting to blend together. Rayna takes comfort that it doesn't seem to hurt him anymore, unless he bangs it on something. Little does he realize just how itchy and smelly it's going to get.

Rayna and I have talked about the night with Sara, Glitter and Gear enough that she's comfortable with doing it again, one day. Sara, Rayna and I have reservations for dinner at Altobelli's for tonight at seven. This will be the first time the three of us will have a chance to talk about the events that had Rayna's moral values causing her great inner turmoil.

Rayna has battled with her moral code. She's made the conscious decision to enjoy her life. She wants to live in the moment, as often as possible, and enjoy wherever that moment takes her. I made sure not to influence her decision in any way, that would only come back to bite me in the ass later, if I had.

She mentioned that she'd like Gear to bind her to Sara. Since she mentioned it, every time I think about the two of them bound together, my cock swells. Rayna and I haven't had sex since Saturday and my urges are raging. She's wanted to hold off on intimacy while she sorts out her mind, and I was happy to give her the time she needed. Well, maybe not happy about it, but I never let her think she was depriving me of anything.

It has helped that I jerked off in the shower, at least once a day. It keeps my cock from announcing to the world that my hormones are like a teenage boy. I don't know what it is about the ideas of Rayna and Sara naked, bound to one another and lost in the throes of erotic pleasure, that has my body reacting so intensely. I have had two women simultaneously. Shit, I've had four at once. That was exhausting. I don't recommend it. But, those two beauties together... fuck!

My five-thirty appointment showed up late, of course. Unfortunately for him, he isn't going to get a full workout today. I usually let the workout run over to compensate for their lack of punctuality and to ensure they get the full hour, but not today. Today, I will be joining two very hot ladies for an evening of great conversation and flirting. Little do they realize, they have the power to convince me to do anything, even submit, should that be their desire. Who knows, if it goes well, they might want to share me tonight. That's not the main objective, of course, but it would top the night off, perfectly. Most would agree.

The kids are each sleeping over at a friend's house tonight. While dropping them off, Rayna brought me a change of clothes, appropriate for tonight's dinner. My anticipation is already at a boiling point, so prolonging my arrival by first needing to head home to shower and change, could easily send me more over the edge between being the calm man I usually am, to becoming a sadistic fucker, with a desire for release.

She's going to be picking Sara up on her way to the restaurant. Their time alone together will give them the opportunity to talk about their *girlie* emotions, something I try to understand, but for obvious reasons, can't. I'm not so sure I want to go there anyway, I might lose my man-card, if I do.

Those two women mean a lot to me. You could say I love them both, but in different ways. Sara is my friend, a great one. I enjoy her body and the trust that she grants me. For that, I am under her spell. She owns my gratitude for all the times she allowed me to be the Demon that I crave to be, and for never condemning me for it. She has her own mental demons that need to be tamed and I am happy to help her scratch off the scabs. Even though she betrayed my trust, she can still cast a spell on me with a simple glance and hint of a grin.

Rayna, of course, owns my heart, mind and body. She can love and support me or choose to crush and destroy. She is the only woman I have ever known, including my mother, who could completely destroy me. I have given myself to her, whether she realizes it or not. She holds my life in her hands, and should she choose to drop me, I will shatter into a billion pieces. I love her and her kids, eternally. I swore I would never allow a woman to have so much power over me, but I want and need her to own me as her lover, friend, Master and soulmate.

Just as I'm unlocking my locker in the changing room, my phone starts vibrating. I hurry to finish spinning the dial, effectively opening to the lock and dig through my gym bag in search of my phone.

"Hello," I say while fighting to keep my towel around my waist.

"Hey man, how's it going?"

"Oh, hey Tim. Not bad. Ah, I'm in a bit of a rush though. I have to meet Rayna and Sara for dinner and I'm running late. So, what's up?"

"Rayna and Sara? Sara... the Sara? Your Sara?"

An exasperated breath leaves me when I give up my battle to preserve my dignity, letting the towel hit the floor. "Yeah, that Sara."

"No shit? I thought you two were finished."

"Rayna asked me to," I pause to look for eavesdroppers. "I was with Sara on Saturday. Well, Rayna was there too. She wanted to see my Demon in action, but I didn't completely take off his reigns. This dinner will be the first time the three of us will have a chance to get together. It'll be good to talk about it." He's silent. "Rayna needed a minute to toss her morals out the window and accept the idea of living her life how she chooses, and not to have regrets about it."

While I'm waiting for a response, I bend down and collect my towel, holding it up against my cock to keep it PG, not that anyone is even in the locker area.

"Hey, you still there?" I ask.

"Ah, yeah! I'm just wondering why those two gorgeous women would bother with an asshole like you. They should find someone more handsome and a better lay, like me, for instance."

"Fuck off, asshole!" I hiss with a hint of laughter in my voice. "But seriously, I have to let you go. Can I call you tomorrow?"

"Call me any time after eleven. Actually, you know what, maybe I can make it to the gym around four-thirty. We can hang out and talk more about this Rayna/Sara situation."

"No can do! I have a session at four and another right after. Can you come around two?"

"Nah, I'll be at work. All right, I'll let you go. I'll try calling you tomorrow. Have fun fucker!" His jealousy is radiating through the phone. I take pleasure in that, for some warped, testosterone driven reason.

"You have yourself a great night thinking about me ravishing my two beauties," I say, teasingly.

"I'm not going to picture you, just the ladies. Chow!" he says before hanging up.

I toss my phone in my bag and rush to get dressed. She packed me a pair of black denim pants, a turquoise dress shirt and a dinner jacket. She has great taste in clothing. I wonder what she's going to wear. I guarantee she'll dress sexy, but elegant, just to keep Sara and I enticed.

When I arrive, the ladies are already seated at a table near the back of the restaurant. They are leaning toward each other and talking rather secretively. I'd bet anything that their conversation, if overheard by fellow diners, would peak a keen interest. They each have a glass of burgundy wine in front of them, Sara's is mostly gone.

As I approach the table, I go to Rayna first and look her up and down. "You look beautiful, my love."

She intentionally wore a dress that would bring back a hot memory, that would ensure my cock would swell. The black spaghetti strapped dress she's wearing is one I am very fond of. The last time she wore it, I bent her over the hood of the car in the restaurant parking lot. I slid the short skirt up to bare her ass and ate her pussy and asshole until her knees were shaking. And then I fucked her dripping cunt until the car was rocking so hard the alarm started screaming. Did I mention it wasn't our car?

I give her a look as if to say I know what you're doing. She smirks smugly. She will pay for the attitude later when I spank her ass red hot. She's likely doing it on purpose, to fire me up. It's working.

Sara has a generous amount of make-up on, and she looks like a goddess. She rarely wears make-up, doesn't need to. Her skin is like silk and she's absolutely gorgeous, even without all the gunk on her face. But tonight, I appreciate the effort she put into looking even more striking than I've ever seen her look. Perhaps later, I will gag her with my cock until her eyes water leaving trails of mascara down her cheeks.

"You are stunning!" I whisper before taking her hand and kissing the back of it, my eyes never veering from hers. I hear her breath catch. Yeah, I still affect her in a way that pleases my dominant nature.

"Are your panties damp?"

"They would be if I were wearing any," she replies.

My cock twitches. I turn to look at Rayna. She shrugs to confirm that she is panty-less as well. My jeans are feeling a bit tighter in the crotch area and the girls know they got the better of me.

After taking my seat and ordering a glass of wine, I ask, "So, what were you two talking about when I arrived?"

They both look at each other and smile, giggling like high school girls. It's annoying, but hot, nonetheless. All I can picture is the two of them kissing, caressing each other's breasts and moaning into each other's mouths. I can visualize the shimmer of their skin as the soft light illuminates their perspiration. I can almost smell the sex in the air.

Sara speaks first, "We'll see how the dinner goes before we decide whether to tell you, or not."

"Mhmm, you'll have to wait," Rayna confirms.

My curiosity is spiking, and I don't like it. I find it irritating when I ask a question and expect an answer, but don't receive it. My jaw tightens. For some reason, the sexy expressions the women have are easing my need to spank the answer out of them.

"What are you two planning?" I ask, knowing I won't get an answer. They shrug. I glower at Rayna to let her know that she's going to regret teasing me.

"Don't worry, you'll like it," she confesses.

"Have you decided?" the waiter asks.

I quickly scan the menu while the ladies place their orders. By the time he asks me, I know what I want; stuffed mushrooms, baked lasagna and a salad with Balsamic Vinegar. My stomach is growling, and my mouth keeps filling with saliva. It might not be my need for food that's causing this reaction, but rather my desire to taste both women.

"I would love to bend each of you over the table and fuck you into a puddle." I'm not whispering. My voice hasn't altered in pitch from when I placed my order.

The waiter hears what I said, but doesn't react, other than clearing his throat. He quickly gathers the menus and walks away.

Rayna is covering her mouth, embarrassed that I said, what I said in earshot of the waiter. Sara's eyes haven't veered from my face. She's smirking like a cat who just nabbed the squirrel who's been taunting him for months. She's used to my crassness.

"I can't believe you said that!" Rayna hisses.

Sara says, "What's he going to do? The worst thing he can do is stare at us, with jealousy in his eyes."

"He might give us free dessert," I add, looking at Sara. I start snickering. "Do you remember that quaint little restaurant on the east side?"

She suddenly remembers, a smile lighting up her face. "That was thrilling!"

"What happened?" Rayna asks.

Sara tells the story, "It was a long time ago, but we were sitting at a table with a long table cloth. He slid closer to me and fished his hand down my pants. Needless to say, I was just starting to cum when the waiter came to the table to ask if we wanted dessert. He said, 'Oh, I see you're already enjoying dessert.'" She starts laughing too hard to finish telling the story.

I add, "He stood there calmly watching her ride out her orgasm. When she was finished, he walked away, but came back with two lava cakes. He didn't charge us for the desserts. I'd bet that guy jerked his cock for months, recalling how you locked eyes with him when you orgasmed."

I can tell Rayna feels like she's an outsider at the moment. She doesn't look upset, just not included in the memory.

Sara whispers, "If your skirt were a little shorter, I'd tickle your clit right here, right now."

Rayna shakes her head, "I don't think so. My luck, I'd run into one of my kid's teachers. That would be humiliating."

"You worry too much," I tell her. "It's a fantasy many people have, but never act upon. They would likely be envious."

"Maybe, but I can guarantee they'd tell everyone that I was a sex-craved hussy who loves public sexual encounters. I don't need that type of controversy."

"I promise," Sara tells her with a seductive undertone. "We are going to make many memories together that we can look back upon one day and thank our lucky stars for."

Rayna takes her hand and gives it a squeeze. Fuck! I want them both naked and on their knees in front of me, ready to comply to my demands. I can picture them open-mouthed, begging for me to let them pleasure me. To alternate mouths, feeling each woman swallow my cock with their individual talents. It will happen, one day.

"Okay, so, about last Saturday," I poke the elephant in the room. "Sara, what's your take on how it went?"

"I thoroughly enjoyed it. You weren't as rough as I know you can be. I was wondering if you had lost your touch, or if you were taking it even easier on me than I had requested, for Rayna's benefit."

Rayna mutters, "That was taking it easy?"

I smile at Rayna and reply, "I did take it a bit easier on her than I used to. It's been a long time since we've played, and I didn't want to jump right back into it with the same intensity. We'll have to work up to it, with Rayna's approval, of course. And, I also didn't want to shock you, Rayna. I can be very cruel to women, and have on occasion, at their request. I didn't want you to see that intensity just yet, maybe never."

Sara is pouting, "I like it when you're cruel to me. The pain takes me away. You're the only person who has taken me completely out of myself. I miss that. Maybe after Rayna is more comfortable, things will progress. If not, I'm okay with that, too. I really like you two and would be honoured to be a part of your relationship. I know I can't move in with you two, but I'd like to eventually enjoy you both, freely. Can we leave that as a possible option for the future? After I earn your trust, of course." She looks at me and gives me an apologetic grin.

She looks at Rayna while still holding her hand. Rayna nods, but looks a bit reserved at the notion. That is something Rayna and I will have to talk about when we are alone.

"Trust needs to be earned for you to become a third in our relationship. I am perfectly fine with the two of you spending as much time together as you'd like. If Rayna is nervous about me being alone with you, Sara, then that's off the table."

"I'm okay with that. Never would I do anything to disrupt your relationship. Your love for one another is beautiful. Attention to me is a bonus and never expected."

"I really like you Sara, but we'll have to take it slowly," Rayna explains. "I'm just getting to know you, so you'll have to give me time to catch up to the two of you. I'm trying not to feel like a third wheel here."

"A third wheel? Why would you feel like a third wheel?" I ask her.

Sara tells Rayna, "I'm the third wheel here. I'm the addition, not you."

"But you two already know each other, very well and have all these memories together."

With a loving kindness, Sara replies, "But you and Simon have something so much stronger than what we ever had. I really respect the love you two share. One day, I hope to have that for myself. It's not looking like I will, but you never know."

Rayna leans toward Sara and kisses her softly on the lips, stunning me. I can't believe Rayna would do something so bold in a crowded restaurant. Like she said earlier, *what if one of her kid's teachers are here*? I'm happy that she's opening up. She'll enjoy life more if she's not always so worried about what other people think.

Rayna whispers, "Let's just enjoy what we've started and see where it takes us."

The women are looking into one another's eyes, lustfully. My cock twitches, shifting my attention from their obvious flirting. What have I started? I think I've awoken the sexual deviant in Rayna. Sara has always been wild. The union of these two women is a good thing, I hope.

We've filled our bellies and swallowed down more wine. I've only had one, but the girls have each drank three glasses. They're getting to be a bit too obvious with their flirting, that could get us kicked out of this posh restaurant, by these stick-up-their-ass (not in a good way) people. I pay the bill and usher the women to Rayna's car. Compared to my truck, hers is far more comfortable for three adults.

Instead of one of them sitting in the front, they both get in the backseat, giggling and whispering, the entire time. I shut their door, making sure it's closed. By the time I'm sitting behind the wheel, the two of them are already kissing, passionately. At first, I watch them in the rear-view mirror, but that only lasts for a few minutes. I turn around when Rayna moans.

Sara's hand is between Rayna's spread thighs. She wasn't lying when she said she wasn't wearing any panties. The car quickly fills with the heavy breathing and scent of sex. My cock is squeezed in my pants, bent at a weird angle, and the erotic scene before me is making it that much worse. I lift up and shove my hand under my waistband to shift it to a more comfortable position.

Sara's legs part and the silky hem of her skirt climbs her creamy white thighs. Her left leg drapes over Rayna's right thigh. Their pussies are bare, clits swollen and their inner labia glisten with their arousal. They each have a hand between the other's legs, rubbing tiny circles over each other's clits. This is a beautiful moment. Each woman is masturbating the other and it is so fucking erotic. I would love to help them out, but being in the front seat would make for a very difficult task.

"Seatbelts are on?" I ask, hating to interrupt them.

"Yes," they moan.

I start the car and drive as cautiously as possible, while the women wind each other up. It's hard to keep my focus on the road and not on the sensuous scene playing out behind me. I can't lose myself in the seductive, rhythmic moans coming from the back seat, no matter how much I want to.

"Ladies, I hate to have to interrupt you again, but where are we going?"

Sara parts her lips from Rayna's. She replies, "Take us to Fallen."

When our eyes meet in the mirror, it's the deliberate wink following her words that tells me to drive and not to ask any more questions. It's obvious the two of them are cohorts in the planning of this night. What are their intentions?

I feel uneasy, probably because I'm the one who always plans how we spend our time at Fallen. When we arrive, I won't know what to expect and I don't care for it. Is this how my submissives have always felt, like they were walking in blindly? I had never really thought about it. They're submissive. They do what I say, without asking why. That's what is expected of them. However, I'm not submissive.

My stomach is feeling a bit tight. As much as I hate to admit it to myself, I don't want to go, if I'm not in control. It's selfish, I know, but I'm not the sort of person who follows along. I always know what comes next because I plan it. I'm an asshole, a control freak.

Besides, I didn't bring my leathers to wear, not that I need them. I like to dress the part. I'll be going into the house in jeans and a dress shirt – turquoise, not even black. I do look good, just not as intimidating as I prefer.

The scent of sex waves through my nostrils, drowning my brain in a sea of possibilities. Their moans and the sound of their breath catching in their throats has my cock desperate to penetrate something. I'd love to have them side by side on their knees with their mouths wide open for me to fuck one, then the other, and repeat.

The drive seems to take an hour, but still doesn't feel long enough. I was enjoying the two of them and hoping one or both of them, would orgasm, but neither did. Maybe they are saving their pleasure for me. That is an honour I will never take for granted.

"Ladies, we're here," I say after the car is in park and shut off, but neither seemed to notice. "Girls?"

They both look out the windshield, realizing that we're no longer moving. They smile at each other before undoing their seatbelts. I step out and open the passenger door. Sara takes my hand and steps out of the car, brushing her hand over the swollen bulge in my pants. Rayna slides across the seat, taking my hand and stepping out. She's grinning like she has a secret she wants to tell me, but is forbidden to.

She kisses me quickly and smiles. "Are you all right with being here?"

"I would have liked a little warning, so I could have planned something for you two and brought something else to wear."

Rayna tells me, "Open the trunk." When my eyebrows bridge, she repeats with a smile, "Just open the trunk."

I do as she instructed and find a black box. When I look up at the two of them, they have their arms around each other's back, and they're giddy. I flip off the lid and pull back the red tissue paper. The scent of new leather fills my nostrils.

"Sara bought you a new harness," Rayna says.

"Try it on. Try it on," Sara begs.

When I take it out of the box, the girls rush over, taking it out of my hand. Rayna starts undoing the buttons on my shirt while Sara fiddles with the buckles on the harness. I brush a stray tress of hair off Rayna's forehead and follow along her hairline until I can tuck it behind her ear. Her eyes look up into mine. She looks mischievous.

"What are you planning?"

"Trust me?" she asks. Of course, I nod. "You don't have to do anything. We brought you here so we can do something that she and I both want. I hope it'll be all right with you if we don't tell you right away. Can you be patient until we're ready for you?"

She knows she's asking a lot of me. I'm not all that patient, and I don't like the idea of being separated from her in the house. It's not that I don't trust the people there. I do. I just want to be there, to witness her expressions when she sees something new. And I prefer to ease her fears when she is afraid. Rayna isn't as fragile as she once was, and I know I don't have to worry about her, but I do.

"I will try," is all I can say with positivity.

"That's all I can ask of you," she replies.

My shirt comes off and is folded and set neatly in the trunk. The women fit me into the harness and buckle me in. This one isn't broken-in so it's stiffer than my favourite one. Time will work the leather, so it moves better with my body. All-in-all, it fits pretty damn good.

"Well, Demon, what do you think?" Sara asks.

I lean down and plant a soft kiss on her lips. "I love it. Thank you, Sara."

"You're welcome. It's my way of thanking you for reconnecting with me. Even if we never play again, after tonight, I want you to keep it. It looks good on you. You look dangerous, as always."

They each put their hands out for me to take. I am a lucky man indeed, to have these two beautiful goddesses on my arms. How did I get so lucky? I cherish them, both of them.

As soon as we step out of the elevator, Sara lets go of my hand and takes Rayna's. She says to me, "Can you wait in the kitchen until someone comes to collect you? Kat and I have some setting up to do."

I don't like it, but I promised Rayna, A.K.A. Kat, I would try. "I can do that. "Nobody fucks either one of you, but me."

Both ladies nod enthusiastically. I watch them walk away, hand in hand, in the opposite direction from where I have been asked to wait. The house isn't nearly as busy as it usually is, but that's not uncommon during NFL playoffs.

"Hey Demon! How the hell are you?"

I turn to see Sprat. "Oh, hi. How are you?"

"I'm doing well. Did you come alone? Don't tell me that gorgeous woman of yours finally wised up and left your ass."

I scoff, "Pfft, no way! That woman wouldn't dare. Now that she's used to having all of this," I point to my body, "she knows she can't live without it." Yeah, I'm talking shit, but that's what guys do.

He teases, "You ain't nothing special. So, if she isn't sick and tired of your bullshit, where is she?"

"Her and Sara have something planned that I'm not supposed to be a part of, until someone comes to get me."

His face contorts. "I thought you were the dominant and they were the submissives?"

I scratch my head and grunt. "I know, I know. But when you have two hot women moaning in the back seat of the car you're chauffeuring, you'll agree to do just about anything."

Sprat widens his eyes and nods, "Been there!"

"You want to join me for a coffee?" I ask.

"No, I offered to help Kristi with something. Trix and Liv are in there. At least, they were a few minutes ago." He pats my shoulder before wandering off in the direction I just came from. "Hey, you let me know when Kat does kick you to the curb. I'll show her what it's like to be with a real man."

I shoot him my middle finger and smile with a hint of sarcasm behind it. He just laughs and continues walking. I get along great with that guy. We met here at Fallen about five years ago. The first time I was introduced to him, we hit it off.

Trix is sitting at the table sipping on a bottle of water. Her corset is pushing her round breasts up and together, forming a great cleavage that could swallow my cock, if she were into me, or men in general. Her three-inch high, stiletto boots are resting on the small of Liv's back as if she were an ottoman.

Liv, being on her hands and knees in front of her Mistress's chair, hangs her head, but tilts her face up to catch a glimpse of me. She doesn't smile, she simply casts her eyes back at the floor, staring blankly. Her red corset doesn't cover her breasts, allowing them to hang, gravity pulling hard on the weights dangling from her nipple clamps.

"Hey Trix, how's it going?" I ask as I make my way over to shake her hand.

"Oh, you know me, always excellent! How is life treating you these days? Where's Kat? Did she get tired of your shit already? Tell me where to find her so I can comfort her in her sadness." She leans forward and pats Liv on her bare ass cheek. Liv smiles at the floor. "You can get up now."

Liv stands with the aid of Trix's hand. She continues to hold the skinny woman's hand until she's seated on her lap. She kisses her shoulder tenderly as she slowly unclamps her left nipple. Liv buries the pain deep inside of her, not crying out when Trix pinches that nipple between her thumb and forefinger. She's rolling it slowly, her attention still focused on me. Liv doesn't react to her nipple being manipulated but I'm sure it hurts like hell.

"She's with Sara." I pour myself a mug full of coffee and take it to the other side of the table. After sliding a heavy wooden chair out, I sit and pull at the front right strap that extends from the middle of my back up and over my shoulder. "I think Ra... um, Kat buckled this wrong."

"Go help him," Trix whispers to her submissive, who stands up immediately, and tends to my harness. She quickly readjusts the buckle.

"That's good. Thank you, Liv. So, Trix, what have you been up to?"

"I got the promotion I've been working tirelessly at getting for the past three years. The guy who held that job, dropped dead last week." She waves for Liv to sit back on her lap.

Trix is a lawyer with very rich, well-known clientele. She is on retainer by a politician, an actor whom we regularly see in movies, and a doctor who was acquitted of murder last year, when he performed emergency surgery after he had a dinner engagement that included drinking several glasses of wine. He was on call that night and shouldn't have been drinking in the first place. I might not approve of some of her clients, but everyone who needs a lawyer, is entitled to have one, even if they're guilty as fuck!

"I'm sorry to hear he died."

"Don't be! I think he died from boredom. Either that or he needed to get away from *Mrs. Poppins*, and death was the only way to do that. Fuck! The first time I met that women, she was so damn cheerful, I wondered if she was too stupid to realize the world sucks, or if she's a drunk. Hey, maybe she had a butt plug jammed in her ass and was riding high on the naughty little secret. Either way, he's probably better off. Even at his funeral she was smiling. She's such a fake woman. Nobody is that happy, all the time."

"Maybe she killed him," I post the thought.

"Nah, he was hit by a fully loaded cement mixer on his way home from work. In my opinion, I think he crossed that center line because he knew it would be a relief not to have to see that fucking smile of hers even one more time," she shrugs, letting out a hearty laugh.

"Some people can walk through life without a care in the world. Maybe she is one of those people."

She shrugs again and then drops her hand onto Liv's thigh and lovingly strokes it with her hand. "So, how's Kat doing with her submissiveness?"

"She's doing well. She's a stubborn woman, but who knew I'd enjoy the challenge. I can never say she's boring, that's for sure. Her and Sara have hit it off nicely."

She scratches her head, "Yeah, what's with that? I mean, with the history between you and Sara, are you sure it's such a great idea to hook up with her again? What if she's still in love with you? What's going to happen when Rayna realizes that?"

I swallow hard and then clear my throat. "Yeah, I've thought about that."

"And?" she asks.

I shake my head, "Hopefully, history doesn't repeat itself. Sara seems like she's in a good place and her mind is strong, from what I can tell. I think it'll be all right. I'm paying attention."

With concern in her voice, she asks, "Does Kat know everything?"

My eyes meet hers, but I say nothing.

"You know you have to tell her. A secret that big... You're playing with fire," Trix warns me.

She's right, I should tell Rayna the entire story, all of it. She needs to hear it from me, not someone else. I should have talked to her before she went over to Sara's place and they ended up in bed together. If she finds out, she's going to be furious that I didn't tell her. This is big and she won't like it. Maybe that's why I didn't tell her right after she met her. Fuck! I'm an asshole!

"Do you think Sara will tell her?"

"No, I don't think so," I reply with a head shake.

"Not many people know the story, so Kat might not find out, but if she means a lot to you, you might want to tell her just in case."

I nod and sip my coffee while I mull over what she suggested. She's right, I do have to tell her. Let her make an informed opinion of Sara, and whether she likes her for who she is now, or doesn't want her around because of who she was, that would be up to her. She's going to be furious that I kept it from her for this long.

"I'll tell her," I say under my breath, knowing that if I speak it, I'll have to go through with it.

"So," I change the subject. "So, tell me about this new position at work."

"Do you really want to talk shop?" she asks with a questioning quirk in her voice.

I chuckle, "No, but I'm trying to change the subject."

She laughs, but her expression quickly sours. "Ah, Ranger was here the other day. He has a new submissive. She looks young, no older than eighteen. I know Glitter checked her identification to make sure she was twenty-one, but I didn't ask how old she is. I wouldn't put it past him to date a high school girl with a fake ID."

"If he hurts her, I'll kill that motherfucker!" My mood has instantly shifted to pissed off. "I still can't believe they let that fucking asshole in here."

"Nothing was proven, no criminal charges were laid, and the women refused to file a complaint. There's nothing Gear and Glitter can do about it. They don't particularly care for the guy's style of dominance, if you want to call it that. As long as he isn't hurting anyone here at Fallen, they don't think it's right to kick him out with simple third-hand accusations and no solid proof."

I stress my point, "He is not a dominant! He is an abuser of women! A proper dominant will treasure his submissive and allow them a safeword. He does neither. That is not dominant, that is abusive. Did anyone warn the poor girl? Did they tell her what he's going to do to her?"

"Glitter suggested she find another Master, but she said she really likes Ranger. I think he hasn't actually hurt her yet, so she doesn't know what he's capable of." Trix shakes her head sadly.

"If he hurts her…" I stop talking. My mind drifts off, creating scenarios where I am wrapping an elastic around his balls, so tight that the blood supply is cut off. I'll tie him to a tree in the forest where nobody will hear him screaming, and I'll wait until his nuts rot and fall off. All the while, I'll nick tiny cuts in his flesh, not enough where he'll bleed out, but the pain will be immense. I will do so much more to that asshole. His death will be a happy release for him.

"Don't worry, by the time you hear about it, he'll have disappeared."

I ask, "Why hasn't someone done that already?"

"Because he's connected. His brother is a detective and his sister-in-law is a high-end attorney. If he disappears, he can never come back, if you know what I mean. And nobody is willing to go that far without solid evidence. Don't worry, it'll happen soon enough. He can't contain his warped desires forever."

"He's under the misguided notion that he's untouchable. Good, he won't see it coming."

A beautiful, dark-skinned redhead comes skipping into the room. She's wearing a very short plaid skirt that doesn't hide her rounded hips, a snug white t-shirt that barely covers her full breasts, and high-heeled running shoes with thigh-high white socks. She pops the cherry-red lollipop from between her bubble gum-pink lips. I'd love to throw that little hottie over my knee and have her count the spankings I give her before shoving my fingers into her tight asshole.

"Are you Demon?" She stands in the doorway swinging her hips back and forth. I nod. "They're ready for you. Do you want to follow me?" she asks with a high school girl head tilt that has her two ponytails swinging.

My inner Demon is twitching from the irritating memories her appearance brings forth. I couldn't stand those pretty little bitches that thought they were fucking perfect in high school. Those little cunts didn't turn me on at all. My friends would go on and on about how they'd love to fuck them if they ever got the chance. When I showed no interest in them, the bitches made up rumors that I was gay.

I took the head cheerleader out one night and fucked her hard on the bench seat of my truck in her parent's driveway, at her request, of course. I held her hands over her head and let her have it. Afterward, I told her that I'm not gay, I just don't like stuck-up little twats, like her. I made her get out of my truck. Her legs were still shaking when I drove away without saying another word to her. The harassment stopped after that.

"Sure, why not?" I stand up and watch the little tease bite her puffy bottom lip and scan my body, as I set my cup in the sink. I look over at Trix and say, "Maybe I'll see you two later."

"Have fun!" Trix replies.

CHAPTER TWENTY-SEVEN
Rayna

Gear and Glitter began wrapping and knotting ropes around Sara first. They finished Sara's elaborate chest and pelvic harness before beginning with mine. Our bindings closely resemble one another with only slight differences. Our breasts protrude from between twelve lines of soft black rope. The decoratively weaved pattern over our abdomens and lower backs function as a safe and strong harness to elevate our lower torsos with minimal stress to our skin, or so I'm told.

The excess of rope left hanging from the back of Sara's chest harness is fed through a seven-inch metal ring that hangs from a thick chain leading to the high ceiling. Sara is asked to step onto a wooden crate that Glitter positions below the chain. The rope is then meticulously weaved into the front waffle-like knot of her pelvic harness, back up and through the loop once more. The rope is pulled until it is taut before being tied to Sara's pelvic harness with a strong knot.

She is told to clasp her hands together behind her back. They are carefully wrapped before the rope is pulled up through the metal ring. Gear pulls it until her arms are stretched high behind her back. He then secures it back at her wrists. They wrap separate ropes around her knees, in triplicate, before pulling her legs up to her chest harness and weaving the rope through it.

Sara is suspended with her arms straight up behind her back and her thighs pulled up on either side of her chest. He gives her a swing and she begins to laugh. He stops her before putting a black leather collar on her neck.

Gear asks, "Kat, are you ready?"

I take a deep breath. "I am so very ready!" My elation is obvious by the way I nearly run to him with a smile so wide that all of my teeth might be visible.

He smiles, "You look like you're ready."

"I can't wait! Where do you want me?"

"Stand on the box," he instructs as he pushes the crate with his foot to reposition it.

I step up, so that I'm standing behind Sara, who is still giggling. My mind is whirling from excitement. How is he going to bind us? When I raise my hands, at Gear's request, my adrenaline rush has my hands shaking so much that he tenderly clasps them between his hands.

"Take a deep breath and try to calm yourself. I don't want you to burn out too quickly."

I do as he says, closing my eyes for a moment while I breathe deeply. It helps calm the shaking, but I'm still grinning like a fool. That, I can't stop.

Glitter stands behind me, ready to assist Gear. He binds my hands behind my back, but doesn't affix them to my pelvic harness. He feeds the rope dangling from the front of my chest binding alongside Sara's hips and up through the metal ring. After weaving it through my harness, he pulls the rope slowly, guiding my chest under Sara's lower torso.

Glitter puts her hands under my shoulders to give me a little more support, and a sense of security, in case I fear falling. Gear ties the black rope through my harness before tying it off.

The rope hanging from my pelvic harness is guided around Sara's shoulders, through the ring and back through my harness and tied off. My legs still dangle uncomfortably. I hope he fixes that otherwise my back is going to be sore later.

Glitter kisses my forehead before taking the rope Gear is offering her. They each bind an ankle and lift my legs up, tying the ankle bindings to one of the other ropes. When I wiggle my feet, I can feel the heat from Sara's arm so they must be very close.

A black leather collar is buckled around my neck and it's snug fitting. Sara rests her cheek against my vagina, and I fear she'll find my aroused wetness disturbing, but she hasn't lifted her head or commented so it can't be all that bad. My wrists are tied to the back of my pelvic harness, no longer left to dangle.

A rope runs around the back of my head and is pulled until my mouth is pressing firmly against Sara's hot, wet pussy. She is just as wet as I am. I'm no longer as self-conscious about my arousal.

Sara's mouth presses against my pussy and doesn't pull away. She must be tied the same as me. Her breath is hot and has me moaning. I desperately want her to lick me, just as I'm doing to her, but she isn't.

Glitter taps my cheek. "Not yet. Wait for our guest of honour's arrival." She smiles lovingly, kissing my forehead once more.

The ropes dig into my skin, but I like it. The sensation of floating outweighs the discomfort. Sara's scent fills my nostrils, exciting me further. Each time Glitter and Gear's warm hands touch my skin, my pussy tightens. I know they're only checking the bindings but it's setting my skin on fire. I'm already breathing heavily. If she flicks my clit, I might cum immediately.

Gear whispers in my ear, "Does anything pinch too much?"

All I can do is open my eyes slightly and mumble into Sara's pussy, "No, just some tingling." Everything pulls, pinches and digs in, but nothing hurts enough to complain, not yet anyway. I knew there would be discomfort, so I had no expectations of feeling like I was resting in a recliner. Quite the opposite actually. I feel less pain than I had expected.

Glitter opens the door and steps out, whispering something to someone. I strain my eyes to see who it is. I catch a glimpse of a cute woman dressed to look like a sexy high school cheerleader. I wonder if Coach would like her. He might want to smack her ass a dozen times, but I doubt he'll be sexually attracted to her. During one of our lengthy talks, he told me that high school was a difficult time for him.

Gear smiles and brushes a tickling strand of hair from my cheek, drawing my attention back to him. The way he's looking into my eyes fills me with warmth. I instantly feel loved, adored, treasured. His eyes are kind and I can see the depth of his appreciation for letting him rope my body. To him, this is his art. All I know is that it's beautiful, sensual, and so fucking arousing. I don't know how to thank him enough for allowing me to play a role in his creation.

Gear walks around us, taking multiple pictures. I must remember to ask him to email those to me. It's thrilling to be one of the subjects of his admiration, but to view his creation would really be something wonderful. The lights dim slightly, and I know that Demon is on his way.

I don't know how long we hang here, but the painful tingles in my hands and feet became almost overwhelming and nearly broke me. Now, however, they have fallen numb. Strangely enough, I am totally comfortable at this moment. Sara's calm, rhythmic breathing was the only thing that kept me together. I focussed on the expansion of her belly as it pressed into mine with every breath. And still, the light warmth of her expelled air continues to soothe my overheated sex. I am connected to Sara in more ways than just physical. We are one in the same.

The door opens slowly, and two people walk in. I can hear the scuffing of their shoes on the painted cement floor. My eyes have been closed, allowing my other senses to sharpen. A warm hand brushes down my shoulder to my elbow as someone walks lazily around us, shoes thumping with each step. I know that stride, it's Coach, or should I call him Demon, since we're at Fallen?

Sara moans softly, vibrating my clit with her voice, causing me to moan as well. She whimpers in response. I feel cool dribbles glide along my asshole. It takes me needing to swallow the wad of saliva that's formed at the back of my mouth for me to come to the realization that the drips gliding down my asshole are of Sara's saliva. It's arousing me even more, which I didn't think was possible.

"Pleasure each other," Demon instructs, his voice is deep, but spoken quietly and with firm instruction.

Sara and I begin sucking and licking each other's clitoris with great urgency. I'm on the verge of orgasm within a matter of a few seconds. Sara's clit swells in my mouth almost immediately. She cries out and stops licking just long enough that my orgasm ebbs, disappointing me. I lick and suck her mercilessly, hoping she'll return the favour and grant me an orgasm as well. Her body jerks involuntarily as she rides through her climax. I don't let up, nibbling on her sensitive clit to torture her deliciously.

She cries out again, but this time a hint of pain rides her scream. It wasn't an orgasm that caused that outcry. What is he doing to her? I wish I could see.

She sucks my clit hard, gently biting it between her teeth while her tongue whips wildly back and forth. My mind and body are swept into a mighty orgasm. I am floating--literally and figuratively. My thoughts have disappeared into a fog of nonexistence. My clitoris is the only thing I know to exist. Her tongue is my tongue, doing exactly what needs to be done to drag my climax on as long as possible.

In a snap, the intensely gratifying slurps she was granting me have flipped and are now the exact opposite – sweet torture. My body jerks, desperate to pull away from her mouth but the ropes prevent me from doing anything other than twitching, which has us both moving together.

Two thick fingers slip into my pussy until the hard knuckles are pressing against my opening. My clit twitches beneath the tip of Sara's tongue. The digits fuck me slowly at first, dipping into me and twisting, waving now and then, to add more fuel to my inner blaze.

My moans muffle into her pussy. The closer I get to orgasm, the more intensely I lap at Sara's sex. Her belly puffs with each quick lungful of air, forcing my breath from me. A finger slips into my asshole and I'm drifting away, lost in the fog again. I can hear my muffled screams, but they sound far away, as if someone else is riding through a bone-melting orgasm, and not me. But I know it's me.

His fingers slip from my sloppy wet pussy and ass, leaving me craving their return. Something cold, possibly metal, is worked into my asshole. I don't know why, but it feels like it's on the verge of popping out, but it keeps moving, as if the exposed end is swaying somehow--pulling back and forth. It remains in place, but I can feel the bulbous orb inside me pressing toward the back, as if it's touching my spine. When it moves, my clit twitches as if it were being lightly electrified.

We're given a push and we begin swinging, not much, but enough where the thing in my ass is pulling here and there, igniting my inner inferno.

Something touches my nose. My eyes open in mere slits, it's all I can manage. Two of Demon's black latex laden fat fingers are buried inside of Sara's pussy. The view is incredible. He pulls them out only to allow for a third finger to join the other two. He uses his digits to fuck Sara, effectively maintaining our swing.

I'm so intrigued with what Demon is doing to Sara that I'm able to hold back my third climax. If I cum right now, my eyes will close, and I'd rather watch him finger her. He pulls out and slips in a fourth finger with almost no difficulty. Sara is moaning like a wild animal about to ravish the carcass it just slaughtered.

He buries his fingers up to his palm inside of Sara, using it to swing us. Each time we swing toward him, his fingers bury deeper, pulling halfway out when we swing away from him. She isn't licking me anymore, only breathing quickly, and purring. She is lost in her body.

Her secretions are running over my lips and into my mouth. Her taste is tangy, but pleasant. I can't believe I'm doing what I'm doing. A year ago, I would have never dreamed of a situation such as this. *Porn does these things, not real people.* I was so naïve!

Demon folds his thumb against his palm and begins working at getting his whole hand into her. It takes a few minutes for her pussy to compensate his fist, but when it slips inside of her, she defies the ropes by curling her body. Just as quickly, she falls limp, giving in to the invasion and the rope's restrictions. He pauses before slowly twisting his hand until his inner wrist rests against my nose. He begins pushing carefully into her and pulling back, causing us to softly swing again.

Sara is screaming like a cat in heat. I know she loves fisting, loves the sensation of complete fullness. Her tongue resumes its rapid assault on my clitoris. She sucks, screams, moans and licks. Between her expert tongue and the heavy tugging by whatever is swaying in my ass, I'm so close to coming again.

I suck and lap at her clit, mirroring her mouth's actions. Both of us are breathing heavily and moaning wildly. My mind begins to slip away, but I do my best to keep working her clit. I feel light, but safely molded onto Sara, as if my featherlight weight is powerful enough to float her up to the sky with me.

Demon pinches my nostrils closed, preventing me from breathing. I try to pull my lips from her cunt, but I can't. My orgasm shreds through me, exploding the world around me. Every muscle in my body is locked in a struggle to test my strength against the ropes. My scream is imprisoned in my throat, as is Sara's. We both hold perfectly still, while our minds fade into a euphoric existence that has us wishing we could remain frozen in this moment for all of eternity.

I need to breathe. My lungs are burning. My chest is squeezing, aching to expel its last breath. I'm yanked back to the reality by a hot flood of Sara's cum pouring from her roughly fisted cunt. My nose, cheeks and lips are drenched. Streams of hot liquid soak my hair, and drip into my ears.

His fist is yanked from her throbbing pussy. It's as if it just left both of our bodies, leaving us feeling vacant and alone, together. My nose is released, and I suck in air as quickly as I can, but it takes a moment until the fresh air clears the clouds in my consciousness.

The weighted bulb is carefully extracted from my ass and then cold lube is smeared around my stretched opening. Demon's thick, hard cock slides into me, painfully spreading my asshole wider. I don't like the tension, but I do my best to relax and allow my butt to accept his size. I welcome the invasion and he knows it.

Slowly, he begins humping into my backside. My thoughts focus back on her tongue and how it's working over my clit. My pussy twitches. Sara is sucking and flicking my little button tenderly. It's so fucking good, even though the painful sensitivity of it is nearly overwhelming.

His hot, latex laden hand glides down the underside of my thigh and around to my hip, enabling him to hold us against his body. He steps into us and uses our weight as a counterbalance. He humps and we push away only to return with a thud. His muscular figure is like hitting a brick wall. He's powerful enough to prevent us from swinging in a direction he doesn't wish us to go.

Sara hasn't let up, she's licking and sucking tenderly, but intentionally focusing her attention on the underside of my clitoral hood. The sensation her gliding tongue rewards me with is purely angelic. I copy her talent as best I can, giving her the same glorious pleasure.

Demon's hand drops away from my hip. I immediately hear Sara cry out. She stops breathing for a moment, but then quickly screams. Her clit is stiffening against my tongue as if begging me to mutilate it. I bite my teeth into her, pressing my upper teeth just beneath her clit while my lower teeth press just above it. She wails until it fades into her throat, sounding more like a growling dog than a woman filled with pleasure. The vibration against my clit is sending me into another muscle clenching climax.

My tongue works her clit as our bodies clench. Our muscles pull at our bindings, adding an element of pain to go with the tenuous lack of freedom. We are coming, drifting together in a smoke-filled nothingness. We have molded into one body, one existence--it's beautiful.

I gasp in a quick breath and open my eyes. Did I pass out? Demon is looking down at my face, my hair is wadded in his fist. He's smirking. He's so strikingly handsome; his vicious looking eyes are dark and scary, but his features are sharp and perfect, like that of a magazine model.

"No sleeping!" he instructs. Maybe I did pass out.

He rolls on a condom and rams his prick deep into Sara's pussy. He fucks her hard, his balls slapping at my nose. When he holds himself inside of her, they rest on my eyes.

The ropes holding my face to Sara's pussy are released. My head is slowly allowed to hang. I'm grateful that he didn't just let it drop. I'm not sure I have the wherewithal to have stopped it from dropping hard enough to pull a muscle or tendon.

Demon pulls his thick, hard prick from Sara. His fingers reach around to the back of my neck to give it support. He pokes his prick against my lips, and I open wide. Slowly at first, he pushes his prick into my throat, nearly making me gag. He pulls out and then fucks into Sara's cunt. He leaves her and pushes into my throat. Over and over, he repeats this action, until I'm sure I'm gasping between throat penetrations.

My eyes are watering so much, I can't see anything other than blurs. Sara isn't moving anymore, but she's still lapping at my pussy, just not as intensely. She moans each time he fills her, licking my pussy as he exits.

When the light fills my eyelids, I know he's walked away. The ropes around me are being altered and my body is being manipulated by several people. It's a good thing they all have a good hold on me because I have no strength in my limbs. I'm surprised when they don't set me down. They spin me so that I am face to face with an exhausted looking Sara.

My ropes are refastened so that my legs are spread and wrapped over Sara's, my ropes bound to her ropes. My waist is cinched to hers once again and not left to droop. My chest harness is fastened to the ropes suspending her chest.

My lips find hers. They are soft and warm. She smells of my pussy and I, of hers. Together, our musk is seductive and stimulating.

The hands leave us suddenly and we are left to dangle, suspended above the floor in a sensual pose, kissing one another as if we are deeply in love. Our lust for the situation has both of us lost in a euphoric mindset brought on by relentless orgasms. Our kisses are loving and tender. Our tired tongues beg to explore one another's flavour but fail due to utter exhaustion.

His prick enters my pussy, fucking me hard. He doesn't let up even for a second. The rhythmic pounding against my cervix thrusts me into a screaming orgasm. As soon as it eases, he pulls out, shoving his prick into Sara and fucking her just as thunderously.

He repeatedly pleasures both of us until I can't remember how many times we've each cum. Sara's cheek is resting against my throat as my head hangs back. Our bodies hold still. I hear his boots on the floor, approaching our heads. My hair is wound into his grip, lifting my head until my mouth is once again, level with Sara's.

"Open your mouths!" he hisses.

Hot jizz splashes around our mouths, some finding it's mark and landing on my tongue. I hold my lips open wide, begging for more of the reward of his orgasm. He moans, groans and whimpers before it all comes to an end. He slowly backs away, huffing and puffing.

Sara and I lick Demon's cum from each other's mouths while the three of them unbind us.

I am set free first and carried by Demon and sat on a large pillow that's resting on the floor against the wall. He crouches down and smiles at me. This isn't Demon, this is Coach... Simon. My Simon.

"I love you, so much!" he whispers as his fingers brush a sweaty lock of hair from my face, tucking it behind my ear. His eyes are peaceful and affectionate, as if I am the only person in the world that means anything to him. He leans in, pressing his lips to mine and holding them there until he finishes taking a long, deep breath, and letting it out slowly.

He stands up quickly and returns to aid Gear and Glitter in unbinding a very exhausted Sara. Her hands and legs have a purple hue. When the ropes are removed, her limbs hang loosely. Coach scoops her up and carries her over to me, placing her beside me on the same big pillow. She is waving her hands and shaking out her legs awkwardly, as if they have fallen asleep. It's obvious how heavy they feel, by the effort she has to put in, to get them to move.

Our eyes meet and we burst into laughter. It's an exhausted laughter, but one I will never forget. We are joined now, closer than most women ever get to be. I care for her and want her in our lives for as long as she would care to be. I want us to become best friends and share in the good and not so good times our futures hold. Maybe I'm feeling all warm and loving after such an incredible experience. Am I looking through rose-coloured glasses, as the saying goes? I don't know, but I love how I feel.

COACHING RAYNA #2 - BOUND HEARTS

After our harnesses are painstakingly removed, we dress and then walk arm in arm behind Gear, Glitter and Demon, as we make our way to the kitchen for something to drink and a snack.

We talk about what we loved and what we didn't love while we laugh through the more serious moments. No matter what we say, it isn't frowned upon and we aren't made to feel foolish. The way we are respected, is not what I had expected. Sure, I knew they would be honoured that we allowed them to use our bodies, but my heart feels as if it's filling with love. Maybe it's not true love in the romantic sense, but I feel bonded to these people.

More than an hour later, we say our good-byes with hugs and kisses. We drive Sara home before Coach takes us back to the restaurant. He follows behind me, as we each drive our own cars home. We make love so romantically that I start to cry. My heart is so full of love that I swear I can't bear it. Please, oh please, never let this end.

We sleep, still wrapped in each other's arms. Our bond is forever secured. He is mine and I am his, first and foremost. If ever we want to stop, for whatever reason, I know we will remain happy together, as two people who can't tell where one stops and the other begins. He owns me and I own him. We are the same, yet different. I would die for him and he would for me. I trust him with my life and for that, he gives me his undying gratitude.

EPILOGUE
Rayna

Renee and Tim are still together, but haven't married yet. He finally broke down and told her about his dominant side. She was excited to learn more about it. Even though he has told her about Fallen, he hasn't brought her there and I don't know if he ever will. They have a lot of issues to work through that have nothing to do with sex.

For a dominant, he's very passive, but only to a certain point. She's a bit of a hot-head who throws a fit if she doesn't get her way. He's a sweet guy and she's going to lose him if she keeps this up. I love my sister, but I feel bad for Tim.

Ken recently started his second year of high school and he's been considering joining the football team. Coach and Tim have been teaching him how to throw the ball, and I'll admit that he has a hell of an arm. The guys think he has a chance at being a star quarterback, one day.

Kim is doing very well with the brainier aspects in life. She's a heavy reader now and loves joining the science fairs and math competitions. Her best friend is a boy named Curtis. I can tell that she has a crush on him, but she swears they are just friends. I believe her because I'm pretty sure he's not into girls, but rather boys. When Coach walked out of the bathroom wearing only a towel, his eyes nearly popped out of his head. He sat down right away and kept his hand in his lap to hide the bulge he was sporting. I don't blame him, Coach looks damn good in a towel.

As for Rick, my ex-husband, he's still living across the country, but he has been single for nearly six months. He's been going to therapy because he says he's a sex addict, but I'm not so sure. I think he's just an asshole who needs to be with young women to feel young and important. He has been calling the kids once a week, which is a huge improvement. I give credit to his therapist for convincing him to not throw his relationship with his kids away, just so he can get a piece of ass.

Coach and I got married about six months ago. So far, I don't regret it and doubt I ever will. He treasures me more than anyone ever has, and I try to take care of him as best I can. We make sure to have date night with just the two of us, at least once a month.

Aside from our sexual intimacy, Sara and I have become very close. She's like a second sister to me. One might even say she's a better sister than the one who shares my DNA. This sister hasn't gone behind my back to try to fuck my man. Then again, I allow her to, so I don't think it's a relevant comparison. It's a trust thing and I don't trust Renee like I do Sara because Sara is always open and honest with me.

She has become an acting second-aunt to my kids, as well. They both adore her and see her as being fun and bigger than life. I can see the love she holds for my kids when she's laughing with them or having a one on one conversation with them. Her eyes beam, right along with her smile, when she's with them. Of course, they don't know her true role in our lives and I hope they never do. We told them that she is Coach's friend from many years ago. They need never know anything else.

Even though I allow it any time they want, Sara and Coach still ask permission to play, every time. I tell them they don't have to, but by them asking shows me respect, and I appreciate it very much.

I love them both. Coach holds my heart, obviously, but Sara runs a close second. I love her, but I love her differently than I do Coach. It's hard to explain the difference, but I'll try.

He owns me. I own him. We rent Sara, in a way. He and I are married now. Sara doesn't live with us and likely never will. She wants her freedom to hide out in her own place when she needs time away to sort through her emotional demons. If ever it stops feeling right between the three of us, she will be asked to leave our bed and that will be that. If that happens, we hope to remain friends with her because we do love her. If she prefers to part ways, our hearts will break, but Coach and I will recover, because we have each other, always.

Coach told me the whole story about what happened between him and her. Now I know everything about why they stopped playing together. She explained that she thought going with the other dom would only earn her a harsh punishment. She didn't think he would ever cast her away because they cared for one another. Maybe they didn't say it out loud, but the feelings were there. As far as he was concerned, she cheated on him.

Sara fell into a severe depression after that. She tried to get his forgiveness, but he ignored her completely. She spiraled and ended up in the hospital after trying to take her life. Her demons got the best of her one night and without him to take her mind off of it, she lost herself. He was told by Glitter what happened, and he rushed to be by her side, but she refused to see him. She was embarrassed and ashamed, also very angry at him at that point in time. She sought counsel and found her strength. She's been doing very well, ever since.

I now know they were emotionally connected, even though there was a time when they denied that they ever felt love for one another. What happened years ago can't be changed. We learn from our mistakes and move forward, never looking back. We accept each other's flaws and don't harp on the past.

Now, nothing is hidden, and nothing held back. If something needs to be said, it is said. We immediately work through whatever comes up so that nothing lingers to fester, creating wounds that will surely scar our relationship.

Our individual lives have brought us together, in one way or another. I hate so much of what has happened to me; the shitty marriage, the awful divorce, the backstabbing sister, the kidnapping and near rape – but all of these things have made me into the strong and independent woman I am today.

I am powerful now. I claim the power I never thought I had. I own it. It's mine, and I won't let anyone take it from me. Coach taught me that. He taught me many things, but my unending power was the very best lesson I will ever learn.

To say that I am happy is an understatement. My elation each time I open my eyes in the wee hours of the morning, makes my heart flutter. My kids have me laughing every day, loving how they are growing and testing my patience, as they try to figure out what type of adult they are going to become. I am so proud of them! They are my best achievement, by far. How could I be so lucky to have everything I could ever have hoped for?

When I hear our lawnmower fire up, my heart still skips a beat.

* * * * *

The End

ABOUT PEBBLES LACASSE

Pebbles Lacasse has been writing books this genre for several years. Previously, she wrote and self-published six novels, sci-fi and mystery, under a different author name. Being that her tales kept leaning toward love stories involving some rather explicit sexual acts, she changed the path she was on and set forth on a more exciting venture—erotic, romance.

She believes that we all have different ideas of what is considered to be sexy and erotic. Each person has their own kink, whether they want to admit it or not. As long as all parties are consenting adults, they shouldn't be judged. Her only hope is that reading her books will help them to recognize that no matter how bizarre you may think your kink is, there are others who share that same turn-on. You are not alone.

Pebbles has been happily married for many years and has two adult children whom are living their own destinies. Although her heart aches to be near them, they too have paths that they must travel. So long as their journeys lead home now and then, her life is grand.

If you enjoyed this book, you might like:

My JoeSmith #1
My JoeSmith #2
Alexa & Blaire
Mistress Tarah
Coaching Rayna #1

www.ingramcontent.com/pod-product-compliance
Lightning Source LLC
Chambersburg PA
CBHW050340030726
47503CB00008B/2547